DEVEL
DJANGO

DEVEL DJANGO

A DARK WAVE JOURNEY

D. S. QUINTON

dsquinton.com

ISBN: 978-1-7327723-1-1

Published by D.S. Quinton

Cover design & illustration:

Dan Van Oss / www.covermint.design

Interior formatting:

Mark Thomas /www.coverness.com

To Dad, I wish you could have read this.

"In the beginning, God created the heavens and the earth."
—Genesis 1:1

"There has been no biological change in humans in 40,000 or 50,000 years. Everything we call culture and civilization we've built with the same body and brain."
—Stephen Jay Gould

"A discovery that shook the world."
—Royal Swedish Academy of Sciences, on the discovery of Einstein's gravitational waves.

PART I

CHAPTER 1
THE STORM
(DAY 1 – 01:52)

The storm broke across the mountain and the mountain shuddered, as if the voice of God had whispered.

The white mountain had stood from time immemorial. Formed by ancient, creaking forces set in motion eons ago, the mountain was resolute; stoic in nature, grand in stature.

The storm would outlive the mountain.

Flung from a deep sleep, dream-tendrils clutching his mind, Brad awoke with a gasp. He was drowning again—or suffocating—either way he was clawing for breath. Something encircled his body as if in a cocoon.

The cocoon pressed tightly against his face, his arms, his torso and legs. It compressed him. The muscles in his body were being squeezed; his heart struggled to pump blood through his constricted veins. His body writhed.

His lungs pulled at the air they were designed to process, only to leave his body wanting more. They pulled again, burning as if he breathed used air; stale air that teased his body to gasp for more but would give no relief; dead, metallic air from an old can, the oxygen somehow used up, or dying.

Dread crept into his mind, constricting his chest further, squeezing his lungs harder. He saw tiny flashes behind closed eyelids, as if he had just received a blow to the head, or as if the blood vessels in his eyes were exploding from the pressure of a great force. He recalled a fragment of something he'd once heard:

People who experienced...

What? What did they experience? He couldn't remember.

...and once those feelings were experienced, they were easily relived through the workings of the mind. A simple event could trigger the condition to return and consume the senses—overwhelming them— shutting down all cognitive abilities except the most fundamental bodily functions. The experience could...

As his mind grappled with the situation, he felt an overwhelming need to urinate. This alone told him something was very wrong. Mentally, he ran through the exercises he had developed as a kid to control his bladder: *Just hold it. Am I awake? Just hold it. Am I awake?* It had been years since he'd dealt with that issue, and he was a grown man now, but his current state of mind was tenuous and struggling with odd visions, vague images floating just out of reach, past events stored in a closed part of his mind—a forgotten place—something he'd worked to forget.

He struggled against his constraints, his athletic body now fully responding to the adrenaline. He could feel the sides of the cocoon stretch as he pushed against them. His legs and feet, extending in a well-practiced exercise, extended against an elastic wall. His neck, solid and strong, supported his head against similar constraints. He was regaining control. He could feel a familiar sway. He recognized his own breath. Slowly, as his senses returned, his mind shook the last of the dream-tendrils—*What the hell was I dreaming?* —and he began to recognize his surroundings. *A cocoon... really?*

His cocoon, at least the inner layer, was straight from REI, a top of the line Arctic sleeping bag, survivable to ten degrees Fahrenheit—although thankfully it wasn't that cold. Feeling his heart rate slow, he tried once more to catch the dark images that slid from his mind. He had felt this before, but couldn't remember where or when. *Did the sleeping bag trigger it?* The closeness was eerily reminiscent of... something... *another old dream?* He felt that if he could just snapshot an image—as grotesque as it may be—it would metastasize into something real that could be excised from his being and thrown away.

The outer layer of his cocoon was a state-of-the-art Black Diamond Single Fly tent that was hanging off the side of Mont Blanc at approximately 8,500 feet, and it was rocking like mad! Suddenly remembering where he was, he hoped his guide had anchored him correctly. He imagined that each gust of wind was wedging between him and the rock face, slowly working the piton out of the mountainside crevice in which it was locked; although they were thousands of feet from the summit, there would be no good ending to the night if that happened.

Where the hell did this storm come from? Brad thought as he pushed sweat-matted curls away from his forehead. There was no mention of this in the forecast. Granted, he knew the weather could change quickly here, but his guide had said this was an appropriate time of year for this climb.

Pressing a button on his new mountaineering watch he saw that it was only 1:52 am. *This will be an extremely long night.* Releasing the tiny light button, he caught a glimpse of the barometric pressure; it was fluctuating rapidly. *What does that mean?* He assumed it wasn't good.

He wondered how the others were holding up.

As if responding to Brad's unspoken thoughts, Cora—4,000 feet below at base camp—tossed fitfully in her own sleeping bag. Her good diet and regular yoga practice typically left her limber and sleeping like a log, but not tonight. In fact, she felt like she had been tossing for hours, and could feel her shoulder blades starting to cramp. She had slept for some time, but now was having trouble clearing her head. She imagined she felt the mountain shudder.

What was that? she thought. She slowly stretched her athletic arms out over a head of messy brown hair, wiggling her fingers and rotating her hands in the air to loosen the tendons.

What time is it? Running a hand down one arm, then the other, she absently checked for firmness. Happy with what she felt, she smiled slightly in the dark. She was by no means a bodybuilder, but felt she could pull off a little black dress if the occasion ever presented itself.

Her body shivered against the sleeping bag as she yawned and blinked her hazel eyes open.

A chill in the tent? No, in fact she thought it was quite warm. *What's with the goosebumps?*

She thought she heard the mountain groan, deep from within—if that was possible at all. Her senses were alerting her to something, but what? *An earthquake? A storm?*

Lifting her head slightly, she stared into the dark tent, focusing all her energy on the sounds of the mountain.

Are you overreacting again? Were you still dreaming?

She laid her head back and wondered why she had ever agreed to come on this trip, especially with silly thoughts like that. She had no idea what sounds or vibrations a mountain made—*Of course mountains don't shudder, do they?* —but with a sudden gust of wind, and the strange surroundings, her imagination was starting to run.

What if a storm is coming? What would I do?

She was a smart girl—in junior high she was officially a nerd, certainly smarter than most, so she understood things that many others didn't—but she had no knowledge of mountains besides how they were created. What was she thinking coming up here? She wasn't a mountaineer, or an adventurer. In fact, it took nearly all of Brad's roguish charm to even get her to stay at base camp while he had their guide, Subbu, take him *big wallin'* thousands of feet above base camp.

This trip was only supposed to be a field-test for her new A.I. communications protocol. Granted, she was excited about the travel—and thankful that Brad's research budget covered most of the cost—as she had never been to Europe before. But mountain climbing had not been mentioned. She'd only been outside the Midwest to go to school before this, and there were no mountains in the Midwest. But she could have easily monitored everything remotely from the lab in France, assuming the satellite links stayed up; worst case scenario, she could have rerun the field tests at the base of the mountain safely from a picnic table.

Oh, Cora, lighten' up, will you? she scolded herself. *Just because you're named after a great aunt doesn't mean you have to act like one.*

Rolling onto her side, she squinted at the small portable clock in her tent. She thought it showed 1:53 am. *Uugghh...* without her glasses she couldn't be sure, but she was sure that she would feel stiff in the morning.

Thinking she might as well do some work since she was not going back to sleep anytime soon, she unzipped the top of her sleeping bag from the inside and sat up only to be jolted awake by the frigid air rushing across her naked body. She quickly dropped back into the sleeping bag, slammed the zipper shut and felt a flush of embarrassment scald her cheeks. The embarrassment, or the surprise of it, startled her so much she buried her head in the sleeping bag for several seconds.

As the initial shock wore off, she peeked out of the sleeping bag into the dark and empty tent. She knew perfectly well she was alone. What was she so embarrassed about anyway? No other girl her age acted like that. Half of the girls in college would have done it on purpose.

Sitting up in her sleeping bag with it wrapped tight around her, she felt her eyes start to water. *Stop it, damn it!* she thought angrily as she wiped her eyes.

"I want this to stop!" she said out loud, remembering her life-coach's instructions.

Taking a few deep breaths, she centered her thoughts on her

emotions. She relaxed her jaw and wiggled her shoulders. *Push your boundaries,* her coach had said. *You have the power to overcome everything from your past. Everything.*

She felt around the inside of the sleeping bag and soon found her sweats and sweatshirt wadded up at the bottom of the bag. *So much for Miss Adventurous doing as mountaineers do,* she thought with disappointment, remembering Brad's flippant comment from yesterday.

Before he and Subbu left, Brad had fixed her with a sly grin and said, "Oh, and by the way, you know real mountaineers sleep in the buff, right?"

"Excuse me?" she replied.

"Absolutely," he said. "Helps with air circulation and… well frankly, it makes the mountain more entertaining!" He feigned his hands like the main attraction at a burlesque show while his blonde eyebrows bobbed up and down.

"Ask our Indian friend. Isn't that right, Subbu?"

"Uh, yes, of course," Subbu replied with an embarrassed grin. "Very important to keep the mountain gods happy."

She had dismissed the joke as sophomoric, and while not offended by it, thought that it detracted from their work. She was close to an important breakthrough, and all Brad could think about, the best she could tell, was conquering the next mountain, or river… or woman. However, later that night, remembering her coach's words, she decided to push her boundaries and slowly pushed her clothes to the bottom of the bag, where she knew they would not get lost. Laying there for hours with muscles tense, she finally fell asleep to the worrying thought that she would never erase the memory of Bobby Hadley.

◯ ◯ ◯

A crack of lightning jolted Subbu awake. The tingle of static electricity was in the air. He had spent the night in these mountains many times and had weathered many storms; wind could be handled, but lightning was deadly. He shouted to Brad, but doubted he could be heard. He stuck his head out of his tent and saw Brad's flashlight was already on.

Maneuvering against the side of the cliff was tricky enough, but the storm made it especially dangerous. Subbu knew they had to get off the storm-side of the face quickly. He was already preparing his harness and descent rope when he heard Brad call out.

"Subbu! What's going on?"

"Quickly, we must descend!" Subbu yelled.

"Descend? Let's ride it out! Look at those crazy clouds!"

"No, we must descend! There is a cleft below us! I'm coming to you!"

Subbu exited his tent and climbed towards Brad. A fierce wind caught his jacket like a kite and blew him off his feet, swinging straight back into his fluttering tent. Working to untangle himself from the twisting cords, he said a quick prayer under his breath.

The storm suddenly fell silent.

They looked at each other with wondering eyes, each experiencing the storm differently. Subbu, afraid to move lest the angry storm see them and blast them from the face they so perilously clung to; Brad, absorbing the energy of the storm, exhilaration standing his hairs on end.

Subbu tilted his head up to listen, then ventured a slow turn and looked over his shoulder, away from the cliff face. The storm clouds hung low right above them, moving in slow motion. The clouds rolled in place, a giant spring being tortured into an ever-smaller circle, tension dangerously high, a strange back-light illuminating them into a kaleidoscope dance.

Brad followed Subbu's gaze and watched the clouds with fascination. What knowledge, he wondered, was out there, just beyond his grasp? He raised his hand, measuring the brightest spot against the scale of his outstretched fingertips. He had felt the same fascination two years ago when he'd seen the Northern Lights for the first time.

He had led a small group of research students to Fairbanks to assist him in searching for traces of microbial life in ice core samples. That research trip was going to make him the youngest tenured professor in MIT history. Yes, Dr. Brad Bradley—*Blonde Brad*—was going to take the world by storm. The last night of the trip, he sat with his four research students in an open-air hot spring drinking champagne, toasting to their success. The Northern Lights swayed overhead, dancing hypnotic; the champagne flowed, diluting inhibitions; the churning water hid hands and legs, all intertwined; discretion evaporated into the night, joining the lights of magnetic-force friction. Of course, that incident nearly derailed his tenure. *Thankfully THAT blew over,* he thought. *But who knew Fairbanks had such great hot springs? A little more discretion was probably in order, but oh those Northern–*

The air cracked with a deafening explosion! Brad and Subbu's ears popped simultaneously with the change in pressure, and their faces contorted as if to keep their heads from imploding. The spring-twisted clouds, having been sucked backward into long pinholes, exploded with streaks of fire.

Hell rained down upon the mountain.

CHAPTER 2

OBSERVATION

(DAY 1 - 01:52)

Deftly balancing the projectile on his thumb, Ian flipped a wasabi pea straight into his mouth with barely an adjustment of his head.

That was nine in a row, he thought. One more and he would break his all-time record for consecutive direct hits. After that, he would have to ratchet it up a notch. *Maybe a ricochet off the file cabinet, or a height requirement would make things interesting.* But that would have to wait for another shift. He had already eaten half the bag, and wasn't looking forward to the morning effect of this late-night habit.

He licked the white wasabi dust from his brown fingers, then rubbed them dry with a crumpled napkin. He checked his list again and looked at the clock. There was plenty of time left in his shift, and plenty of things he could be doing, but his thoughts strayed to his upcoming holiday. This was his last day of work, and then he was off for a full week of hiking.

Houdini will love it, he thought, rubbing the back of his closely cut black hair. *If the bloody dog doesn't disappear on me again.*

Hiking was his passion, but chasing a half-trained pup up and down the hillside was not; not to mention the inherent dangers to the pup.

He had always wanted a dog as a young boy, but the small apartment he and his mother had had wasn't the right place.

"Twern't right by a dog, to coop him in this stuffer!" his mother would say in heavy old-British. "Besides, your father, God rest his soul, would expect you to train him proppa, and there's not even a tree for pissin'!"

Ian had mixed emotions of the small apartment; stark and sparsely furnished after his father's untimely death, but always filled with warm smells and memories of his mother. He quickly outgrew the three small rooms and took to walking late in the evening, always finding the edge of a field or forest, then eventually, the mountains.

Ian wandered like this for a few years after school, holding odd jobs, dreaming about somewhere else.

"Pissin' around town on the pull, again?" his mum would ask when he came in late. "What would your father say?"

But his eyes always looked toward the mountains, and where his eyes looked, his feet followed. For a while he thought of being a mountain guide; Europe's version of running off to the circus. It was either that or join the gypsies, but they were a swarthy bunch to get to know, and being of mixed race himself, he knew joining another outcast group wouldn't exactly help his situation.

An alarm bleated from a monitor, interrupting his thought. Retracting his extended legs from the desktop while simultaneously reaching for his keyboard, he launched the bag off his lap and sent green spicy peas spinning across the floor. *Buggers!* he thought, *Oh well, nice surprise for the mice.*

As he quickly tapped commands on his keyboard, a live image screen popped up. A map of Western Europe appeared, and he rapidly adjusted its center and began to zoom.

He grabbed his headset and stretched it over his head with one hand while typing with the other. By the time the headset was on, a second chat window had opened, and he was pinging his late-night counterpart at Station #3. Before Stat3 could confirm the warning—which was always protocol—he had a live view, with a short delay, streaming from the satellite.

Bloody hell! An asteroid was breaking up before his very eyes!

CHAPTER 3

HAIL

(DAY 1 - 01:55)

Cora was pulling her socks on when she felt the pressure change in her ears. Since she was a child she had been sensitive to changes in weather. She had been sensitive to changes in almost everything: pollen, animals, baby formula… laundry soap. But her inner ear seemed to be specially tuned to changes in the weather; maybe that was a result of growing up in the Midwest. *Tornado Alley. Where if you didn't like the weather, just wait a few minutes and you could watch your cow blow down the road!*

With a quick stretch of her mouth—her mother used to call it her skeleton face, because her lower jaw would drop so low she looked like her mouth was coming unhinged—she popped her ears. It was more of a forced yawn without the throat and lung action, but it solved the problem.

She had one boot on when she heard the explosion. Faint flashes of light illuminated the top of her tent, casting vague images inside. She instinctively lowered her head and looked towards the lighted spot on the tent, momentarily transfixed by the kaleidoscope that was painted there. *What kind of a storm is this?*

Stepping into her other boot and unzipping the tent at the same time, she felt the first strong blast of wind hit her. She thought the Gortex tent was made for this type of weather, so was surprised to see it distort so quickly under the force. The colored roof was flattening onto her back, even as she crouched, as if to squeeze her out into the storm. She stepped through the flapping door and into the tempest.

Oh my God, I'm in trouble! she thought.

The strangely illuminated clouds were her only source of light, but disoriented her. Shielding her face from blowing debris, she looked for cover, but realized her glasses were still in the tent. Turning toward the tent, her untied bootlaces caused her to stutter step for balance, and in an overcorrecting skip, she planted her right foot on a loose rock that sent her leg out from underneath her and she came down hard on her back. With an exaggerated blink she looked up into the storm. With a slight backward tilt of her head she saw the Big Wall come into her view, and watched as the first meteor exploded against the sheer face.

Fog crowded her mind. She was aware that she was losing consciousness, but was unable to fight it. She tried forcing her eyelids open, but they were weighted with sand. Her mind considered the veiled light of the storm through her eyelids and imagined it fading to black beneath the shadow of a boulder hurtling toward her head. Would she even feel it?

Pulling her back from the edge of unconsciousness, she heard a familiar jingle in her ear.

Doo-dee-lum.

A soothing, slightly British, feminine voice spoke.

[Cora, wake up please. You've had an accident.]

—pause—

[Wake up, Cora. Are you injured?]

—pause—

[I'm preparing to—]

"Ali, I'm here" whispered Cora.

[Are you injured?]

"I… I don't think so," Cora said, blinking slowly.

[I'm attempting to analyze your vitals, but your sensors are not transmitting.]

"I removed them… um, by accident last night. I'm…"

[You removed your sensors by accident? Did they—]

"Never mind, Ali."

Rocks began to pepper the base camp. *That sounds familiar,* Cora thought.

Tink.

Tink, tank.

…popcorn? …canning lids popping?

Tink, tank, tank!

…hail?

Storm!

[I'm detecting some atmospheric disturbance in your area. Are you in a safe location?]

"No, I'm not!" Cora said, now fully awake. "I need to find shelter. Find me the closest low depression. Quick!"

—pause—

[There are no depressions in your immediate vicinity. There is a geologic anomaly approximately thirty meters to your southwest.]

"That'll do!"

Cora reflexively covered her head with one arm and checked her watch for direction, although she couldn't be sure she was reading it correctly. Remembering the loose laces, she wide-stepped a hopping gate to where the geologic anomaly should be.

Rocks pelted the area; one bounced off a high cropping of stone right as she passed and sliced through her sweatshirt, knicking her arm—had her arm not been covering her head, it would have likely hit her in the eye. Other rock shards bounced off the ground and tore at her sweatpants. In the dim light of the mountain, she wasn't sure if she was exactly on track, but now had both arms covering her head.

"Ali, am I on track?" she asked. "Where's the anomaly?"

[Cora, please adjust your course fifteen degrees west. Ten meters ahead.]

A flash of lightning cast a shadow in front of her. A gaping mouth formed and flickered in and out of existence as if to laugh at the thought of it providing safety. Cora lunged for the mouth right before a shower of burning rock fell where she had stood. She wedged her back against the crevasse and pulled her legs tight.

"Ali, can you reach Brad? Is he alright?"

—pause—

—pause—

—pause—

[I'm sorry, Cora. Brad is not transmitting.]

CHAPTER 4
THE GENERAL
(DAY 1 - 02:15)

Ian was typing commands with one hand and dialing with the other. He had taken well to his military training—both times—and worked well under pressure, but his old training was a different type of hand-eye coordination, a different need for calm… a deadly need.

His new training—now three years in the past—fit the analyst part of his mind; satisfied a different itch. This job he could have talked to his pop about.

What happened to the bloody early warning system? he thought.

Asteroids where well tracked, and although there were plenty of unknown orbiters out there, he thought their systems were better than this. There would be hell to pay, and he hoped he wasn't on the paying end.

A secure video-conference line blinked on in another window of his computer. He quickly swiped it to the right, onto a second monitor, and continued typing with his other hand. Several faces appeared in small boxes, backgrounds betraying only a hint as to the origin of transmission.

Screen 1: A hotel room.

Screen 2: A bedroom. *Whoops, who was that in the background?*

Screen 3: A messy office.

Screen 4: Forty feet underground, inside a reinforced bunker, fully stocked with food, supplies, weapons and ammo; designed to support six people for twelve months while designed to look like a charming country farmhouse above. Or so went the rumor. That would be General Keller.

General William David Keller, reported to have retired to his armchair and smoking pipe over a decade ago—at least that was the print story—had not been seen in public in almost twice that long. And he wouldn't be seen today.

Although two of the video chat windows were filled with faces that could possibly be described as *having that military look*, the general's screen sent a clear message—two crossed swords behind a crown of gold; atop the crown a snarling lion; below this image the words "Dieu et mon Droit" - *God and My Right* waved in a banner. The message was: *I fear only God above me, for I am ordained to rule.*

Ian thought it strange that the British Coat of Arms, which is where the saying came from, would have a saying written in French, but this motto reportedly went back to the time of Richard I and was heard as a battle cry. The rest of the image was straight from the flag of the British Army.

Ian, having never interacted with the general before, listened closely to answer the rapid fire, one-word questions he'd heard were infamous with this reclusive force.

"Status!" said the snarling lion. "Meat!" could have been substituted and no one would have questioned the translation.

Ian spoke. "Sir, this morning at approximately 01:52 an unregistered asteroid entered our atmosphere and broke up over Western Europe. Stations One, Three and Four are triangulating approach trajectory."

The voice from screen two said, "Wait, who said this was an asteroid? We have every NEO catalogued from here to—"

"Impact!" the lion-general demanded.

The voice from screen three said, "Sir, the impact zone appears to be localized across the Western Alps, from Mont Blanc, east by northeast; approximately a fifty-square kilometer debris field."

"Confirmed, sir," Ian said quickly as he snagged an image from his feed. "We are seeing small impact explosions throughout the Alps. If the debris field stays localized, collateral damage is estimated to be very low."

Finishing his sentence, Ian shared the first image of impact explosions caught by the satellite. Zooming out, he showed the night version of the area before the impacts began.

"This is a two-hundred-kilometer scan centered on the Mont Blanc area. This was taken approximately forty-five minutes before the first impact was detected. As you can see, very few lights anywhere, except this area to the Northwest, which is, uh…"

"Geneva," the lion said impatiently.

"Correct, sir. That is, well, the next thing we see is a clouded view of the same area, taken approximately thirty minutes later, then our first images of impacts. Everything so far appears to have hit the mountains.

The voice from screen two started to protest again when a metallic voice interrupted from screen one:

[General, anomalous magnetic interruptions are being detected at seismic detection points. Recommend classifying event as Secret.]

Bloody hell, what is that? Ian thought. *Stephen Hawking voice if I ever heard one.*

The metallic, unwavering sound of the screen one voice was unnerving.

"Approved. Threat?"

A slight pause lasted two seconds too long – "Threat status!"

The screen two voice blurted into the microphone, "General-there-is-no-evidence-of-a-terrestrial-threat! Oh, sorry… We believe this was purely natural and—"

"Coverage."

Screen three announced, "We appear to be the only people speaking about it for now, but—"

The metallic voice from screen one broke in again: [General, preliminary analysis calculates an 84% correlation with Australian Incident from 1947.]

"Top secret classification! Private comm," instructed the lion.

Screens one and four went blank.

CHAPTER 5
DISCOVERY
(DAY 1 - 04:00)

When the first meteorite hit the Big Wall, Brad was starting his descent. He was rappelling parallel to Subbu, but slowly, and so was still slightly above him. Subbu's unassuming nature, normal build, slight Indian accent, and dark hair and eyes all but hid the fact that he was just a few genes short of being a mountain goat. He had already proven to be an exceptional guide, but his ability to traverse the mountain was amazing.

Subbu was near the overhang where they would take cover, and was looking for the best place to shelter. This was by no means ideal, but it would protect them from falling rocks. If they could avoid a direct hit, or near-impact debris, they might make it out of this.

He anchored a piton and was threading Brad's rope through a loop when the largest chunk of meteorite hit the wall above and to their right by two hundred meters. The shock wave that reverberated through the cliff sent Subbu careening wildly into the air. His rope tightened, stretched, and pulled him swinging back straight into Brad, just as he was coming level with the crevasse. This sent both men swinging and bouncing against the cliff face.

As Subbu regained control of his momentum, he realized they had just avoided a potentially lethal strike. The meteorite had hit a portion of the cliff that opened to a broken and craggy transition on the mountain. The topography created a buffer that allowed the meteorite to glance away from the men and deflect a part of the impact. Subbu said a silent thanks to their good fortune and sprung his way back to Brad.

Just as the men were ducking under the overhang, the tumult stopped as if by the flip of a switch. An empty silence grew and enveloped them. Their world, stopped of all movement and sound, was suspended. Subbu and Brad looked at each other, Was this a calm before the real storm? Then, as if by divine intervention, the storm ended, and the clouds simply faded away. Stunned, they both looked in the direction of the earlier onslaught, and as the clouds parted, saw a single shooting star streak the sky, as if to put a final exclamation point on the night.

Relieved, and after a quick assessment for injuries, Brad wondered out loud, "What the hell just happened?"

"We encountered a miracle," Subbu said quietly, still searching the sky. "We… we are alive my friend. We encountered a miracle." His words trailing to a whisper.

Brad looked at Subbu and saw the sincerity in his face. He thought their survival was certainly fortunate, and perhaps a bit miraculous, but he wasn't ready to assign it the reverence Subbu was. However, under the circumstances, he felt it was better to keep his opinion to himself.

They checked again for injuries, not fully believing they had survived. Had they really just witnessed a meteor storm? An asteroid? Whatever it was, their minds were struggling to process it.

As they began their climb back up to their hanging tents, the sight of the sheer rock cliff triggered a memory in Brad—an old show he had watched as a kid—Leonard Nimoy's *In Search Of...*

He remembered the show covered every topic, from aliens to the Loch Ness Monster to the Bermuda Triangle, but one show stuck in his mind: pictographs of strange symbols carved into the faces of rock walls.

It was never explained what the symbols meant, only theorized they were made by a lost civilization that had witnessed something they couldn't explain; experienced an event they couldn't understand, and had therefore assigned it godly significance. Some civilizations built monumental cities to such godly events. How many of these had been built to honor an ordinary rock burning up in the atmosphere?

Following this dream-trail, he remembered the day he decided to be an explorer: the day he found a fossil-crusted rock in a dry creek bed. How amazing! What type of explorer had been unclear to him at the time, but explore he would.

Focusing back on the rock wall in front of him, he wondered if there were any meteorite fragments to be found after the storm—if it was in fact a meteor storm they had just witnessed. *What a way to end this research trip,* he thought. At that moment, he knew he had to find a fragment.

"Subbu, let's take a detour," Brad said, nodding in the direction of the impact.

"Detour? But boss, what about Cora? We should check on her. She might be—"

"Check on her? Why would we… Oh, you mean the storm? Eh, she'll be fine. She was well below the storm anyway."

"Are you sure? The rock fragments could have fallen anywhere."

"Don't worry. We won't be long. We'll check in with her soon. I'm sure she's sleeping like a baby."

"Well…OK, if you say so. It's not like I'm going to sleep anytime soon."

The night climb was agonizingly slow, but they were assisted by a nearly full moon, which cast a ghostly pall over their surroundings. Brad marveled at the scene in front of him: mountains as far as he could see, illuminated peaks reaching up and away. Away from what, who knew? Dark crags sinking down and under. What was below? A lonely moon that stared down upon them, as if waiting. What did it know?

They eventually reached the site of the impact. Scorch marks were easily seen with their helmet lights, and the acrid smell of burnt metal hung in the air. They followed the scar trail across where a crag had once jutted out, now a blackened and rounded part of the cliff, and saw the transition in the mountain that very likely had saved them.

The sheer wall was transitioning to a broken part of the mountain that was littered with meteorite debris.

Jackpot! Brad thought.

He began to work his way down into the debris field. This part of the mountain was much easier to maneuver in, and he didn't need any assistance from Subbu. He asked Subbu if he would retrieve their tents to give him some time to search for fragments. They would then descend from this location at sunrise.

An hour and a half later, returning with their equipment, Subbu was homing in on Brad's final location.

"Boss? Am I audible? Are you there?"

As Subbu reached Brad's location, the first hints of sunlight were softening the mountain. Base camp would still be dark, but the mountain was coming awake.

Subbu climbed the last five meters to where Brad half knelt, wedged into a pocket. He held something in his hands, but Subbu couldn't see around his shoulders.

"Find some good rocks?" Subbu asked.

Brad turned the object over in his hands, not understanding what he was looking at.

"Boss?"

"I found something," Brad said quietly to himself. He hadn't realized Subbu was there.

CHAPTER 6
BOBBY HADLEY
(DAY 1 - 02:30)

Cora was unaware the storm had ended. Her mind was fixated on an old concrete culvert and a dead dog littered with flies. The culvert smelled of mold and rot. She was wet from the running water and her nipples hurt; the left one bleeding slightly and staining her white T-shirt. She wanted to cry out, to scream, but she didn't dare; he would find her. Something had happened. He wasn't the same.

She swatted the flies away as quietly as she could, but they insisted on sharing their dead-dog lunch with her. They buzzed noisily, bouncing against her face and ears, angry at her refusal to eat. They had done all the work after all; puking up fly-stomach acid onto the dog's eyes and its raw, mange-eaten flesh, waiting for the acid to dissolve the solid so it could be sucked up and shared. *Just open your mouth for a little squirt. It'll taste good!* Silent tears ran down her face.

She heard a car driving slowly on the road above, gravel crunching against worn tires. If it stopped, she would have to crawl further into the culvert. She didn't want to have to taste anything.

Bobby Hadley was looking for her. She had cut through Hadley Field on her way home one warm Saturday afternoon. Old man Hadley had built a diamond on a rocky patch of land behind his farmhouse for the kids to play ball on. He imagined his only boy becoming the next Babe Ruth. Bobby was athletic and cute and most of Cora's friends had a crush on him, and so did she. But most ninth-grade girls had a crush on every senior boy. She was thinking about the babysitting job she had just applied for. She was old enough now to have a part-time summer job, her father said, if she kept up her chores. She had passed her CPR class as was required, the certificate framed on her bedroom wall. It hung between the second-place ribbon she'd won in last year's science fair, and a poster of Snoopy and Woodstock spinning around a grid in a computer screen. The caption beneath read: HELP! I'M TRAPPED IN AN INFINITE LOOP! She thought the poster was hilarious, but no one else really got it.

Riding her bike off the gravel road and through the overgrown infield, she was startled by a sudden movement in the shadow of the old dugout. It was well built, but had the feel of many more years of neglect than it had actually seen. When Mrs. Hadley had passed away suddenly, Mr. Hadley hardly came out of the house. Bobby was left to finish school at his leisure or *Get his ass in the military!* as Mr.

Hadley had been heard to shout; instead, Bobby took to smoking and drinking in his own private veranda-dugout, watching the corn grow.

"Cora! Hey Cora, hold up!" Bobby waved from the dugout.

"Hi, Bobby." She smiled, sliding her bike to a stop. "What are you doing out here?"

"Oh… just thinking about you," he said, kicking the dirt with an old sneaker and hiking up his dirty jeans.

"Me?" she said, feeling her cheeks brighten. "Why are you thinking about me?"

"Come over here and I'll tell you."

Laying her bike down on the field, she took a few steps towards the dugout. She could see the empty beer cans laying in the dirt.

"Come on, I'm not going to bite."

"What do you want?" she asked.

"Mmmm… How about a kiss?"

Blushing, she looked down at the crumpled cans; indecision dripped into her stomach. "Uh, I don't know, Bobby… "

"Come on, you can trust me."

Looking back over her shoulder, her bike suddenly looked very far away.

"Come on," he said, grabbing her wrist and quickly pulling her into the shadow of the dugout.

"What's wrong? You're old enough to kiss, aren't you?" he sneered, pulling her closer. "Your nipples look like they want a kiss. Hell, they're practically begging for it!"

She started to scream as he grabbed at her breasts, pinching her nipples hard, but his other hand was already covering her mouth, pushing her head against the dugout wall.

"How about you just open your mouth and I'll give you a little squirt. It'll taste good…"

She suddenly realized that in the time since his mother's death, Bobby Hadley had become someone much different than what the ninth-grade girls imagined. Maybe it had always been in him and had simply needed an excuse to come out.

Pushing against him made no difference. He had at least fifty pounds on her and was already grinding her hips into the sideboard. On the verge of panic, she felt the first tears spill from her eyes and, ashamed by them, tried to hide her face from Bobby. What had she done to cause this? Suddenly remembering some of the dirty conversations her friends had in the girls' bathrooms, she twisted back towards Bobby and drove her knee into his private parts, hoping it had the effect they talked about.

He released his grip momentarily and buckled at the knees, falling back against the rusted chicken-wire wall that protected anyone in the dugout from foul balls.

"OWW, you bitch!" he groaned as he grabbed his groin. He looked at her with eyes filled with hate and lust; adrenaline-fueled, the new emotions released a flood of chemicals onto an immature brain. At that moment, he knew he would do what he wanted to her, even if he killed her in the process.

She scratched at his face and jumped out of reach as he clawed feebly at her. He rubbed at his eyes to clear the tears that were forming and straightened himself up, still leaning against the chicken-wire fence for support. He looked up to see she was already on her bike, working it into a sprint. He started after her, but quickly realized he couldn't catch her on foot, especially in his condition. A strange gurgle-cry belched out of his throat, causing snot to bubble out of his nose.

When she dared to look back over her shoulder, she saw him hobbling for his truck.

She knew she couldn't outrun the truck, but fortunately he had a long drive to follow out before he could turn her direction. Thank God for winding country roads! Slamming the bike peddles down as if stomping out a fire, she exited the field and entered a deeply shaded part of the old road. It followed the path of an overgrown creek and bent around a fast-rising hill on her left. The terrain prohibited farming, so the woods were left to grow and reach over the road, forming a living cavern of shadow, leaves and moss.

Ahead of her, she saw a low runoff ditch that was fed from the steep hill and was funneled beneath the road, joining the creek that meandered away. Imagining that she could hear a car bearing down on her and fearing Bobby was close behind, she jumped off her bike and began dragging it down the low rise on her right toward the ditch. The woods were heavily overgrown here, and the brambles tore at her arms and face. As she worked her way down, she saw the concrete culvert that fed the ditch. She yanked the bike across a rotten log and through the moldy carpet of leaves that stuck to her bare ankles and slickened her flip-flops. Hoping the culvert would accommodate the width of her handlebars, she didn't see the rotting dog as she pushed the front wheel of her bike over its extended abdomen, splitting its side open. Hunching over as she settled into the darkness of the culvert, she felt the slow trickle of black water run across her feet. The walls were slick with mold and the air was heavy with the smell of rot. A fly bounced angrily against her forehead.

Focusing on her surroundings, she saw the dead dog for the first time. Its fur, or what was left of it, roiled with life. Maggots spilled out of the split abdomen. Flies buzzed angrily in protest, demanding that Cora provide a new home for their young. *She wrecked it, after all. Just a couple of eggs in the ear, little girl.*

Bounce. Swat.

How about the corner of the eye?

Bounce. Bounce. Swat.

Open wide...

CHAPTER 7
THE AUSTRALIAN INCIDENT
(DAY 1 - 02:30)

Sitting in his Boiserie-paneled den, General Keller watched the other screens go blank. He was left with the image of a nondescript hotel room, in which no one lived.

"Full report, Australian Incident," he said to the hotel room.

A metallic voice replied.

[In 1947 an atmospheric anomaly was recorded over Northwest Australia. Active satellite recording was not available at the time, therefore all measurements are post-incident. Initially reported as a small asteroid breakup due to profile of storm and size of debris field, no impact crater was found.]

"No impact crater, but a debris field was found?"

[Correct.]

"So, the rock was too large to burn up in the atmosphere, small enough not to leave a scar, but it still left a debris field?"

[Theoretically possible, based on the mineral and ice composition of the asteroid.]

"Profile of storm?"

[Storm was observed by locals to appear spontaneously. Severe lightning was observed, along with highly illuminated clouds. Meteoroid trajectory trails were observed. Magnetic anomalies were detected during post-incident analysis. Asteroid or meteor tracking was not available at the time, so no trajectory path was calculated.]

"Debris."

[Debris field estimation of current anomaly is estimated to be 90% of reported debris field in Australia."

"OK, similar, but why the 84% correlation between the two different storms?"

[The Earth's magnetic shield is created from its spinning core. Magnetic anomalies occur in the Earth's crust due to variations in mineral composition. These anomalies change very little over time. The variations in Australia were detected within forty-eight hours through ground observations, but completely faded within twelve months. Satellite scanning has already detected magnetic variations around the Mont Blanc range. Highly anomalous.]

"Outcome?"

The screen paused momentarily as an old black and white film clip appeared in the center of the hotel room's conversation window.

A shaky video began to play that settled into the gentle rocking of the cameraman slowly walking around the subject of the recording.

The audio was unintelligible, a barely understood language, but the subject of the film was easily recognizable. An Aboriginal youth, approximately ten to twelve years old; over the youth knelt several other Aboriginal males holding the youth down while an elder appeared to pray over her.

The youth was writhing in pain, or ecstasy, and was gibbering through extorted expressions.

"Translation."

[No known translation exists.]

"No translation?"

—pause—

[In the 18th century, over twenty-seven language families where reported to be associated with approximately two hundred and fifty Aboriginal social groups. The lexicon of the social groups were not recorded, but passed down phonetically. Additionally, a high percentage of social groups practice the use of *avoidance speech*. Avoidance speech is the addition of specialized speech patterns, used only in the presence of certain family members.]

"Damn… Video association?"

[No metadata regarding video's association with anomaly.]

"Recovery?"

[A number of objects were reportedly found by one Aboriginal group.]

"Location of objects?"

[All objects were reportedly buried.]

"Location of Aboriginal group."

—pause—

[Extinct.]

Hands locked under a tilted head, mouth in a tight line, the general watched the Aboriginal girl writhe against her handlers. Bucking wildly, she pulled her arms and legs so tight she was suspended above the ground; face frozen in a grotesque profile of horror. The elders lowered her to the ground, where she suddenly contorted her stomach up into an over-extended arch; slamming her torso back to the ground, she was able to jerk a hand free and begin clawing at her eyes right before the film cut out.

CHAPTER 8
MONT BLANC DISASTER
(DAY 1 - 05:00)

"Cora! Cora, where are you?"

—silence—

"Cora!"

—silence—

"There you are," she heard as someone grabbed her ankle.

Cora shot awake and kicked at the hand, intending to injure her would-be attacker. Her arms wrapped tight around her chest.

"Hey, relax," Subbu said, withdrawing his hand quickly. "Are you alright?"

Blinking slowly, she realized who was crouched in front of her, and he wasn't a monster. The dream-smells of rot and death faded away to pine needles and crisp air. She remembered a tent blowing in the wind and… the sound of buzzing, popcorn. Not popcorn but buzzing… something. Maybe it wasn't buzzing at all. Her mind could not see through the dream-fog, but she felt a familiar sick feeling sitting in the pit of her stomach. It was something she'd left in her childhood long ago.

"Subbu!" she cried. Scrambling out from beneath the overhang, she stepped onto a half-asleep leg and tumbled toward him. Hugging him tightly, she spied Brad through the dim light of morning, rummaging through the supplies.

"What happened to you two?" she asked, stepping around Subbu. "Why didn't you respond last night? Are you OK?"

"Respond?" Brad replied blankly. "Oh, the comm test. Yeah, I didn't hear anything. I don't know, maybe the battery is out."

Cora walked to where Brad was standing, reached down to the communication device that hung from his belt, ripped open the Velcro cover and peered at the device. She slid a small button to the 'On' position. A few seconds later Cora heard a familiar jingle:

Doo-dee-lum.

And a familiar voice in her ear:

[Cora, Brad is now transmitting. Would you like me to—]

"Never mind Ali, communication equipment is in working order," Cora said.

"Ooh, hey, sorry about that," Brad said sheepishly. "We kinda got sidetracked up there. You know we—"

"Yes, I know, "Cora said flatly as she fiddled with the controls of her own comm unit. "*You* got sidetracked and forgot all about *my* test.

I realize we're here mostly on *your* research budget, but the university is expecting field-test results from me as well. My doctoral thesis depends on this. That's OK, though, Ali and I did plenty of—"

Looking up, Cora realized that Brad had already turned away to focus on his backpack. Wrinkling her forehead in question, she turned back to Subbu, who only gave Cora a *Who knows...* shrug of the shoulders.

◯ ◯ ◯

As Subbu and Cora made breakfast, they exchanged notes on the events of the evening. Cora knew they had been in danger on the mountainside, but hadn't realized the extent of it. When she heard how close some of the meteors had hit, she felt guilty for even worrying about her comm test. Subbu went on to describe how the lightning strikes and static electricity in the air made him remember an old mountaineering tragedy.

In the summer of 1961, a team of five climbers were pursuing the peak of Mont Blanc via the Freney Central Pillar, an 800-meter spike of granite on the Italian side of the mountain. Surprised by a fast-moving storm, the climbers were trapped on the side of the mountain, directly above where Subbu and Brad had been the night before. One of the climbers was struck by lightning due to his use of a hearing aid, which was seen as a blue flare shooting out of his ear. The struck climber hung limply in his harness until a fellow climber was able to administer an injection of Coramine, which revived him. All five climbers attempted to abseil off the pillar, which had become a giant lightning rod. The same climber is struck a second time, rendering him completely deaf. The team clung to the mountain for six straight nights; at first thinking to ascend the peak to escape the storm, but changing their minds midway. The climber who was struck by lightning eventually lost his grasp on reality; hands blackened by frostbite into unusable stumps, he slipped into madness. Rescuers from the small mountain town of Chamonix were camped below the pillar. In the early morning of the seventh day, two of the lost team stumbled upon the camp and directed the fresh climbers to where the remaining members were last seen, having been separated by madness and lack of strength. One dead climber was still attached to the mountain. The climber struck by lightning died in the arms of the rescuers. Three members survived.

Cora sat silently, staring at Subbu. Tears brimmed behind her eyelids. Her throat was tight with emotion. She watched as he struggled with the story of men he never knew; related through a familial respect of the mountain, but unrelated in blood.

After a moment, Subbu continued, "The survivors reported hearing voices through the nights, thinking they were close to being saved but never finding the source of the sound. Even the man struck deaf by lightning mumbled about hearing something."

"What do you mean? I thought you said he was completely deaf?"

"He was, but he told the rescuer right before he died that he heard the voice of God that night."

Cora felt a shiver run down her back as she realized what could have happened if Brad's comm unit had been turned on, activating the sound unit in his ear. He could have easily experienced the same consequence, godly or not.

CHAPTER 9
COYOTE. HOUDINI.
(DAY 1 - 04:30)

The general awoke in his 18th century wingback chair promptly at 04:30, despite only having had ninety minutes of sleep. His mind was restless.

The richly decorated room had a calming effect on him, and was testament to a man who had been very successful in life. The automatic tea maker sitting on the built-in bar was already in action. This model most closely mimicked the actions of hand-brewed tea (water at the correct temperature, a basket that lowered and raised the tea automatically to prevent over steeping), but he was a man of efficiency, and preferred menial tasks be delegated.

He tapped a key on his keyboard and several security monitors came to life on one wall. Easily hidden behind automatic bookshelves, the screens were typically exposed throughout the day and night. Even when he had visitors, they were rarely allowed into his den; the heart of his world.

Another few keystrokes and one screen began to scan through the nightly video feeds for potential *perimeter breaches*. The perimeter of two hundred acres wasn't much to walk, but monitoring it on a 24/7 basis was another matter. This would take a while.

As the muscle-memory in his hands attended to the task of the tea, his mind stretched across the various scenarios that were unfolding before him. *Was Syi correct about the correlation with the Australian event?* he wondered. Granted, Syi was an older version military-grade A.I. the general had acquired, but these things were programmed to *reason* as a person might; surely it could calculate a correlation?

In his previous life he had been aware of the event, but being an avid historian, it would have come into his realm of research anyway. At one point he had even contacted the Australian government about additional information, but the Aussies were a hard-headed bunch, still buggered about the penal colony he suspected, not to mention they remained very tight-lipped about Aboriginal groups that disappear.

If this was a related event, would they see the same effects? A fifty-kilometer debris field? This could be bad.

Lost in thought, the general gazed over the extensive collection neatly arranged across the walls and bookshelves of his den: a map of the British Empire circa 1886, one of his favorites, ornately decorated with images of natives from nearly every region Britain controlled. Canada, India, Australia, several ports along Africa; approximately

400 million people fell under British rule at the time, nearly 24% of the global population, the largest empire in history; a sextant reportedly used by Captain James Cook of the British Royal Navy, a distant relative, a great explorer who discovered the Eastern coast of Australia with the *HMS Endeavor* and went on to circumnavigate the globe; numerous swords and pistols from famous battles; a picture of a young man in uniform; a piece of rock inside a glass box.

The video scan completed and flagged three anomalous events for review. The general clicked on the first message: camera thirty-seven flagged movement due to a branch that finally spread into its view, easily corrected; second message: camera fourteen showed a coyote still struggling to free itself from a snare the general had set two days before (*Bastard was pissing on my Hydrangeas*); third message: camera twenty flagged a late-night driver on the old road that led to his drive, *Probably a shagging*, but he'd look into it later. He clicked back on camera fourteen and watched the coyote gnaw at its leg as he sipped his tea.

Ian arrived at his flat at 07:10, forty-five minutes later than normal. A typical night shift consisted of a twelve-hour shift, 18:00 to 06:00; fifteen minutes of knowledge transfer (KT), but if his paperwork was in order it could be done in five; a twenty-minute bike ride to Le Haricot Heurex—*The Happy Bean*—coffee shop on the corner by his flat—decaf only considering this was his nightcap—a quick flirt with the barista, which he thought he was making good progress with, a little Houdini time until the dog sitter picked him up, then off to bed.

But this had not been a typical night shift.

Even though the general had cut communications abruptly, he'd still initiated a level three protocol, which flagged Ian as having to give a formal statement on the events of the evening. The other analysts would be doing the same, except Syi of course.

Why couldn't they have given that thing a better voice? he thought. *Just because it was a synthetic, artificial intelligence, didn't mean it had to sound synthetic. Bloody Stephen Hawking-Terminator voice it was.*

The meteor storm, or whatever it ended up being, was unlike anything he had seen in his eight years in the military—granted, not all those years were spent looking through a computer monitor—but something wasn't right about this storm. Their air defense monitoring systems were top notch; they had multiple monitoring stations and satellites watching the skies at any given moment, but somehow, they had been caught completely by surprise. *Is this what had the general spooked?* he wondered. Maybe *spooked* wasn't the right word, but Ian had been on many briefings with the general before, and they'd never ended like this one did.

After his debriefing, he was reminded that a level three protocol meant top secret procedures were now in place. Well, not like anyone would be firing up a YouTube channel with the info. *Although... why did the general drop comms so quickly when Syi mentioned the Australian event... anomaly... event?*

Flipping open his personal laptop, he typed his first internet search and had just hit enter when a loud bang on the door startled him. Half jumping out of his chair, he kicked Houdini by accident, not realizing the pup had been whining at his feet since he'd gotten home.

"Oh, sorry Houdini," he said as he scooped the dog up, rubbing his head vigorously and walking towards the door. The attention from

Ian combined with the forgotten bathroom walk triggered a steady stream of pee from the dog out onto the floor.

"Oh, bloody hell…" Ian was saying as he opened the door to a very pleasantly-plump, properly-English, Ms. Abigail Winston, the dog sitter. A dying stream of pee splashing on Ian's shoe.

"Good morning, Ian. Have a rough night?" she inquired gently, looking unsurprised at the comically-chaotic scene in front of her.

With a squirming pup hanging by the scruff in one hand and his other hand still holding the door, Ian pointed back towards the kitchen and mumbled something about work when he realized the swinging dog was only too happy to pee in this new direction as well.

"Oh no, Ms… I mean yes, my night was fine… no, I didn't have a rough night, uh, just a rough morning really…"

"As it appears," she said, as if nothing were amiss. "Very well then, leash him up and off we'll go. Same time this afternoon, lad?"

"Uh, yes, yes that should be fine Ms. Winston. Thank you."

After Houdini was gone and the mess cleaned up, Ian returned to the kitchen table to see what his search had returned. To his surprise the search results page had failed to load. After another search attempt, he realized his usually reliable internet connection was out.

CHAPTER 10
THEORY OF LIFE
(DAY 1 – 05:30)

"Dr. Brad Bradley. Paging Dr. Bradley," Cora feigned regally. "The commoners request your attendance at base camp Blanc. Departure for the Aosta Valley to begin in ten minutes."

She was half teasing, but part of her was still miffed at the lack of importance Brad had put on her research work. Not that she was looking for his approval—they worked in completely different departments at the university, and she only knew him through normal school meetings—but a little professional courtesy would be nice.

Sitting on a rock and without acknowledging the sarcasm, Brad spoke at the space where Cora and Subbu stood; seemingly not focusing on them, but on a speck of dust near them that was infinitely more interesting. The only sign of movement, besides the words he sent their way, was his thumb slowly tracing a circular pattern onto the middle finger of his right hand; around and around it went as if slowly winding the gears of an automaton—his mind—which would soon direct the hinges of his mouth to open and produce something resembling friendly chatter.

"Do you know that the current scientific theories on the origin of life on Earth put its creation at roughly 3.5 billion years ago?" Not waiting for a response, Brad added, "And some theories, based on microfossils found in Quebec, push that date even earlier, to almost 4.3 billion years." Waving his right hand slightly, as if a conductor emphasizing the third beat of a beautiful measure, "The earth is only 4.5 billion years old. That would imply an almost instantaneous emergence of life."

Cora watched Subbu struggle to follow Brad's statements. She had seen this look before, but usually when she was describing her own work which most people thought of as something combining computer hacking with voodoo.

"Instantaneous, from out of the void. Of course, they still struggle to explain how the primordial soup actually woke up. Lots of theories there…"

Cora whispered to Subbu, "If he hasn't told you already, Brad is an astrobiologist, and like most, is prone to frequent bouts of dreamy meanderings. His type is full of grand theories on how life may have started, you know: ancient microbes, the magical spark of life," she whispered even lower, finishing with a wink.

Subbu conjured up his best *very interesting* face, despite not understanding any of it. He wondered why people searched so long for answers that seemed obvious to him.

Brad was still talking.

"...precursor molecules, self-replicating molecules... the spark of life..."

Cora quickly poked Subbu in the side—*I called that!* was the look on her face.

"A scientist could spend a lifetime looking for clues, digging core samples, scouring dry lake beds, and only find a few microbes, a few—"

"Well, isn't that what scientists do?" Subbu asked.

"Did you know that microorganisms have been observed to thrive in the vacuum of space?"

Subbu knew better than to try and answer the question, but was also catching on that it really wasn't intended to be answered anyway. Flashing back to primary school and hearing his teachers say, *there are no stupid questions,* he chanced a query. "So how did they get into space?"

"Now that's the question!" Brad said, standing up for his grand finale. "How indeed?"

Subbu let out a silent sigh of relief, but immediately decided he would quit while he was ahead.

"A few of us, the bold thinkers, subscribe to a more... interesting theory."

"More interesting?"

"Panspermia."

"What?" asked Subbu.

"Panspermia is the theory that microscopic organisms arrived on earth, roughly around the same time period, effectively *seeding* the Earth with life." Brad was now looking directly at Subbu. The winding fingers had stopped. With a somber voice, and eyes that glowed with a child's anticipation, Brad said, "If we were to ever prove this to be true, it would change the history of the human race."

Unsure how to respond, Subbu glanced at his watch. Realizing they needed to start their hike down to their pickup point, he said, "Boss, we need to—"

"The person who was able to prove this… would rewrite human history," Brad continued, now staring somewhere between Cora and Subbu again.

"Uh, boss, we really need to get going. We need to be—"

"Yes, we do!" Brad exclaimed, springing onto the rock where he'd just sat; the spell broken. "Cora, let's rerun your comm test on the hike down. Subbu, maybe you can even challenge Ali while we're at it. She's a smart cookie, I hear! Ah, what a beautiful day for a hike!"

High-stepping off the rock, he sprung back toward the two in a mock ballet leap, landing nimbly with a slight bow. Stretching his arms around the shoulders of a stunned Cora and Subbu, Brad gleamed, flashing a boyish grin. "We should celebrate tonight. Subbu, you're the man of the town. I'm sure you know all the hot spots. After all, it's my research budget, right?"

Looking as if he'd just seen Nessie walk out of Loch Ness, Subbu managed to mumble, "Uh… what? Celebrate? Boss, you know we're going to Courmayeur, right? The most remote town in Italy? Wait, celebrate? Celebrate what?"

"Life, Subbu. Life."

CHAPTER 11
FOAM HEARTS
(DAY 1 - IAN 08:30)

Ian left his flat and walked to the café he had failed to stop at on his way home. He still marveled at the old-world charm of Grenoble. The old city was divided by two rivers which cut quaint neighborhoods into a wide valley that sat at the base of the Alps. Pastel hues still decorated historic buildings that sided the rivers, once advertising occupations such as tailor, blacksmith or fish seller to the illiterate.

Grenoble was also a strategic location, known regionally as *The Capital of the Alps*; situated in the Southeast part of France, nestled in a basin of the French Alps, the city was only a few hours from Geneva to the North, the Mediterranean Sea to the South, and Northern Italy to the East over the mountains; besides having been established as a center of scientific study since the 14th century, the city hosted a surprising number of high-tech companies and research facilities, both public and private. And the hiking was unrivaled.

The streets and sidewalks were markedly busier than what he typically saw, now that it was close to 08:00. On a normal night (day), he would be dropping off right about now. But it wasn't a normal night.

"Bonjour," said the barista, looking at her watch quizzically when Ian walked in. "And here I thought I was being stood up today." Hands on well-shaped hips mocked disappointment.

"Blimey, now would I do that?" Ian said, setting his laptop on a table by the wall. The rich smell of coffee setting his mouth to watering.

"The usual, monsieur?"

"Oui."

Ian sat at a small table against an exposed brick wall; the sun was warming the mountaintops, but hadn't made it to this part of the city yet, so the street outside the café window still carried a hue of muted tones that belied the actual time. He had lived here for nearly two years following his transfer to Station 1, and although he loved the views right outside his every window, still found it hard to feel properly awake in the morning shadow of a mountain. But when you were a *communications analyst* in a not-highly-advertised branch of the British military, you adapted.

Ian was connecting to the café's Wi-Fi when his coffee was delivered. *Hmm, no foam heart today*, he thought disappointedly. The barista appeared to take great interest in topping his cappuccino with a variety of designs she would expertly make in the foam by pouring the frothed milk into the coffee in a particular pattern. It was busier this time of the morning, however.

As he sipped his coffee, he flipped through the various news sites. There was surprisingly little news about the meteor storm last night. Granted he had a birds-eye view of the situation, and the majority of the impact zone was on the other side of the Alps, but he thought at least the Italian news outlets would be covering it.

Curiosity now piqued, he decided to search a little deeper. Despite the lack of sleep, the *puzzle-solver* part of his brain was wide awake and driving his mental-momentum forward. This is how it worked when he was a kid, after all. What a rotten time that had been.

Thinking back to the age of ten—shortly after his father's death—Ian remembered a three-month period when he had been completely bed-ridden. Starting with a normal cough, within days he was breaking out with spots in his mouth, then behind his ears; he had the measles, and he had them bad, possibly because he picked them up late for a kid. He was miserable. To make matters worse, his poor mum was working extra shifts at the bakery and laundry just to keep their third floor flat; lucky for them both, Mrs. Pickering from across the hall was the angel waiting for their time of need.

Mrs. Pickering had been widowed ever since Ian had known her, and had become a surrogate grand-mum, constantly doting on him. Her only son had died of cancer by the age of eighteen, which fueled Mr. Pickering's descent into the bottle, ultimately killing him and leaving her with the unrealized dreams of a faithful wife and mother. Besides his mum, Mrs. Pickering's only other companion was a little terrier beagle mix named Bandit.

Bandit would come to visit Ian often during this period, for once the measles had run its course, meningitis took over. Shuffling her girth between flats, Mrs. Pickering would leave the doors open for convenience, and to create a better cross-breeze to *Air out the poxy,* which in some way was supposed to flush the germs out the window, but ten-year-old Ian didn't think it was working. In fact, it only made his recovery seem to take longer, because he could hear his mates on both sides of the building playing in the alleys after school. And being a kid of mixed race in a one-race part of town, he didn't have many mates to begin with.

Besides gallons of chicken and dumpling soup, Mrs. Pickering would bring Ian dusty old copies of *Highlights* magazines for kids. Her son had been sickly most of his life, and the magazines had hardly been used. Wiping off the remaining dust like an amateur archeologist, Ian could open a magazine and smell the history of the flat infused within its pages.

Besides the thin layer of dust and smell of old wooden memories, the magazines were in fine shape. Ian would scour them for unsolved puzzles, imagining himself an apprentice to the famous Sherlock Holmes, piecing together clues that evaded even Dr. Watson.

Elementary, my dear Watson, Ian would think. *Just decipher these hieroglyphs with the key conveniently left on page twelve and… bloody hell! Another clue!*

Most days the puzzles where further complicated by the inclusion of mysterious objects found by Ian's trusty canine sleuth, Bandit.

An old pair of Mr. Pickering's socks left on the foot of Ian's bed would become an unopened seed pod from the Amazon rain forest.

"Cleopatra's hairbrush from her hidden tomb! However did you find it?"

A chewed part of a bone—*possibly from a pterodactyl?*—would show up occasionally, but would quickly disappear again.

So it went for nearly three months while Ian recovered from one malady after another, leaving his body sapped of energy, but his mind exploring more than all his mates could imagine.

His attention coming back to a café in the dying shadow of a mountain, Ian realized his cappuccino had been replaced, foam-heart included. He also realized he had already logged into the Tor network, which is what he used for all anonymous web browsing, specifically on the dark web.

The cursor blinked slowly as if to beckon, *Come in! Come in! Danger ahead…*

CHAPTER 12
THE DEATH ROCK
(DAY 1 – 07:30)

The general walked slowly through an overgrown English cutting garden. The sun had yet to burn the dew from the delicate petals, but would do so in short order. The garden, an artful tapestry of stone walks and living green spaces attached to his countryside manor via a formal courtyard, was in vibrant display. His late wife had designed both.

He did his best to keep everything trimmed as she would have done, but did not have her knack with a plant. She had possessed an almost subliminal connection with the grounds from the day they bought it, planning each section with careful attention to detail and purpose. However, she despised the bunker that sank beneath it. Having been an amateur painter and writer, she had a love of things natural, soft and round, not concrete, barren or militaristic, which made it a wonder they had ever married—for he was a barren man— but he had been different then.

The lilies need separating again, he thought.

The delphiniums look lovely.

Maybe I'll go down and shoot the coyote later; have him stuffed and stick a hose out his pecker so he can water the hydrangeas proper.

He was at the end of the cutting garden facing west where the sun was barely high enough to warm his shoulders; the rock from beneath the glass case, held in his hand, cast a long shadow on to the path before him, disappearing into gloom. He stood at the entrance to a darker part of the garden that acted as a transition to the forest that surrounded the house. The stone path he was on continued into the forest-garden but was still matted with last year's debris of leaves, sticks, and in some spots, branches. Moss had begun to grow along the edges of the path due to the overgrowth of trees here.

He exited the left side of the cutting garden and entered the transition through an overgrown canopy of trees; a cave-like entrance to a more sacred part of the gardens, to another part of his life. His skin felt the temperature drop approximately ten degrees, enough to goose-flesh his neck and arms, but not enough for him to take notice. He followed the path forward, meandering occasionally off the main path to an enclave that hid an interesting stone sculpture or bird bath, finally coming upon the slow arc that led around to the right and ultimately back to the cutting garden. In a few more hours the sun would be high enough to shine through a small opening he kept cut in the canopy of trees. The sun would shine down through the trees and onto a white cross that sat atop a granite base. His late wife's final resting place.

He stopped for a while, sitting on a granite bench angled between the cross and the path. No words came to his mind; he had spoken them all to her before. He could sit there all morning, a living addition to the granite monument, an epitaph etched into the lines of his face, but the thought that he had one more site to visit, just up ahead, made him restless.

As if suddenly remembering that he brought an object with him, he looked at the rock and turned it over in his hands. *Why had this rock come to me?* Beneath the glass case in his den, it resembled an ordinary piece of broken stone that perhaps contained an interesting fossil; certainly, something with an interesting story behind it. Upon closer inspection, one could see that the stone had an unusual depression; most of the rock was missing, but enough remained to recognize the shape: concave, like an avocado. Very smooth. Too smooth to be made in nature, he feared.

He stood up quickly to continue his pilgrimage, his journey of memories, his trail of tears, and feeling a sudden rush of blood to his head, quickly sat back down and closed his eyes to steady himself. He wasn't sure if it was his age or the circumstances, but he suddenly felt drained of life and energy.

He stood up again slowly and let his eyes focus; the woods seemed very dark here; encroaching clouds would ensure it stayed that way. Walking on through the gloom, his feet felt the path more than his eyes saw it. Soon he came to his second stop: an identical white cross and basin to mark where his adult son lay.

A small pool of black water lay lifeless before the granite base. A *reflecting pool,* his wife had suggested. This of course was when the trees where better maintained and the sun washed the shadows of death away, at least for a little while.

Her monument had no such pool, for at that point, there was nothing for him to reflect on.

This time, he knelt beside the cross and plunged his hand into the black water; down he reached through the layers of rotting leaves and dead worms. A fetid aroma wafted up toward his face, threatening his balance again. At first, he thought it was gone and felt a tinge of panic, but then his fingers brushed across the tip of it. A little further down his hand grasped the object and he lifted the death-rock out of the water.

Without the benefit of light, and as the rain settled in for the day, his fingers moved over the slimy object. Heavier than the piece of rock from under the glass case, he knew the outside was identical. The inside was more of a mystery.

The death-rock, having been hidden in the water for nearly twenty-five years, was just as his nightmares remembered. His hands brought the two pieces together and although a small portion of the rock was missing, the remaining two-thirds fit together perfectly along a major break line. The concave indention in the first piece was filled nearly completely by a mirror convex shape from the death-rock, a grotesque stone boil with a death-puss filling.

He separated his hands slightly and tilted the death-rock toward the pool. Rotten sludge plopped into the water, having slid out of a broken part of the boil, leaving a hollow section of the boil exposed.

CHAPTER 13
LITTLE BIRD
(DAY 1 - 08:12)

The Little Bird took flight from the Toulon naval base exactly twelve minutes after the general's call. Lifting off from a remote part of the base, it banked east-northeast to follow the Northern coastline of the Mediterranean Sea up to Nice, France.

"You look like shit," Allen said, eyeing Jack Garvey from the passenger seat. "You sure you can fly this thing?"

Jack's eyes were bloodshot, and combined with the dark circles, Allen thought Jack must have been on a good bender last night.

"Somebody has to look like shit," Jack said with little emotion.

"OK, you smell like—"

Jack let the copter go through a single 360-degree spin and then accelerated forward as if to answer the question on an ability to fly.

"Nice… asshole. I'd like to keep my breakfast in if you don't mind," Allen said.

"I don't mind," Jack said dryly.

"So, what are the orders?"

"Coastline up to Nice, "Jack said, "then into the Alps. We'll run the Italian border up to Mont Blanc. Lookin' for space rocks after that."

"Space rocks?"

"Debris field, really. From last night's meteor storm."

"What the hell is the general looking into that for?" Allen asked. "That's Discovery Channel shit."

Allen had been on the general's select team for a few years now, and had executed many top-secret missions—his official rank and responsibility no longer existed, obfuscated by levels of security that most in the military didn't know existed—but this seemed out of sorts for the general.

"May not be. We're loaded with extra fuel, standard survival gear, extended provisions and… a bio-box," Jack said, head tilting toward Allen. This being the closest thing to an emotion Jack had portrayed.

"A fucking bio-box? What the hell does he think we're going to find?"

"E.T., I guess," Jack said, checking the instruments.

"My ass! You don't need a bio-box for E.T. You scoop him up with a net after you blow his fucking brains out." Allen touched the firearm on his hip out of habit.

"Maybe," Jack said absently.

The AH-6 Light Attack Helicopter, or *Little Bird* to the people who flew it, was extremely versatile. Having proved its merit over a number of years, multiple versions existed. The version they were flying was officially the AH-6M, also known as the Mission Enhanced Little Bird (MELB). This configuration included expanded fuel capacity in anti-explosive tanks, a newer Rolls-Royce engine, and a six-blade rotor that reduced noise. The light artillery options had been left on, although Jack didn't really expect any encounters with *Missha' Gray* today. The forward looking infra-red (FLIR) camera would give them plenty of warning if anything was running around.

"That's OK," Allen said, drawing his gun and giving it his best cowboy spin. "I can hunt E.T. just as well as I can hunt towelheads." He lined up a mock target through the window.

They were following the coastline now, but were well out over the water. There were too many tourist beaches to fly a black military helicopter straight over, besides, they were purposely flying low, so over water was the best option. Crystal blue water sparkled beneath them and to their right, forming the Mediterranean; to their left, gentle swells of land rose out of the water, eventually becoming the foothills of the Alps; a carpet of terra-cotta humanity covered the land, oblivious to the operatives.

Allen knew there wouldn't be much conversation on this flight, which suited him fine. He had ridden shotgun with Jack enough times to know how this would play out. They would get three-quarters of the way to their destination when Jack would contact the general and patch him in to their video feed. After the test was completed, the general would sign off—*Well, you never knew if he was signed off or not, with the lion staring at you*—and wait for Jack to signal when the operation started. Maybe it would be different on this mission, since they would be surrounded by mountains, but the general liked to know how things were proceeding quickly. Out of the eight-man special unit, Jack had been with the general the longest, and had the most autonomy on missions.

Allen thought back to the first mission he had executed with Jack: a highly choreographed set of events (abstraction, intel-gathering, untimely death) played out over a forty-eight-hour period, and he would have thought Jack was walking a dog. Pretty impressive, but he could do better if they'd just leave him to his own ways. The matter-of-fact approach of Jack's work was admirable, but he preferred a bit more enthusiasm when the situation allowed. He wasn't sure how Jack had been before meeting the general, but if Allen's identity had been obfuscated, Jack's had been erased.

Jack was a ghost.

CHAPTER 14

ALI

(DAY 1 - 08:00)

Two hours into their hike, the mountain path that Subbu had led them down began to transition to actual hiking as opposed to climb-hiking. Brad was impressed with Cora's endurance and agility. Her slender athletic build hadn't escaped him either—*maybe a little too slender,* he thought, but he didn't like to discriminate. He wasn't sure if it was the glasses and ponytail, plain brown hair or the fact that she rarely wore makeup, but he hadn't thought much about her other than as a colleague in another department. However, she seemed to have an inner radiance trying to break through that he hadn't noticed before.

She might be fun, he thought as he watched her walk ahead of him, if she could stop talking to Ali long enough to pay attention to him. When they got home maybe he'd give her the chance. But then again, fall semester would be starting up and there would be a whole new batch of grad students hanging on his every word. *Maybe winter then... after the holidays.*

Subbu had slowed to allow Cora to catch up to him now that the hiking was easier. "So, who is this person you are always talking to in your ear?" he asked.

"Who, Ali?" Cora responded, touching her ear slightly. "I'm doing my PhD work on artificial intelligence, and Ali is my creation."

"Your creation? Well, Dr. Frankenstein, is it alliiivve?" joked Subbu.

"Actually, yes, it is in a way," Cora said matter-of-factly. "Ali stands for Artificial Living Intelligence. A. L. I."

"But, if it's artificial, how can it be living?" Subbu asked.

"The intelligence is artificial. It's a series of algorithms that are constructed such that it works as a thinking *machine*. A.I., artificial intelligence, has been around for a long time, and primarily exists only on large banks of computers. The larger the better actually, for we need all the processing power we can get to mimic the brain's inherent computing power."

Subbu was starting to regret that he had asked a question again, but before he could make matters worse on his own, Cora continued.

"To overcome the limitations of current, man-made computing power, we're now experimenting with growing brains, or parts of them anyway, and integrating them with the core A.I. system."

The color instantly began to drain from Subbu's olive-brown face.

Seeing his discomfort and touching him gently on the shoulder, she said, "Don't worry. It's not like we have a brain floating in a jar or anything." Smiling brightly, "You wouldn't recognize what you were looking at if you saw it. We're experimenting with 3D printers.

"You see, we print layers of an artificial neocortex onto plastic trays. Once they're printed, we bathe them in a solution, *the magic elixir*," Cora wiggled her fingers, "then supply a steady stream of low-voltage power to them, hook up some electrodes for I/O and viola! More brains!" Cora mimicked a wide-eyed zombie and giggled to herself.

Subbu would have been outright appalled if it hadn't been for Cora's light-hearted nature. He trusted that she had a good heart, as that's what her name implied, but he was pretty sure this brain-printing business was a bad idea.

"So how do you print… did you say 3D print… a brain?" Subbu asked gingerly.

Skipping slightly as they walked, she said, "Oh, we've been able to print organic material for quite a while now." She picked up a small pebble and tossed it over her shoulder, miraculously landing it on the top of Brad's head. "Using a special printer, the device lays down layer after thin layer of cells, in a specific form, with a specific pattern."

Brad looked up from his daydream, annoyed to see Cora pointing playfully at Subbu with a *He did it!* look on her face.

Subbu looked confused.

"We can print ears, noses, just about anything. The brain layers will be stored on racks in a specialized server room. Eventually you'll be able to walk in and see them!

"You won't see them thinking or flashing, but Ali should know when we've plugged in a new rack. I guess it would be like suddenly a new part of your brain wakes up and you can now use it. We have a small prototype blade run… sorry, a *tray* of printed material is called a *blade*, anyway, we have a small blade plugged in now. It came online at the same time the core algorithms were instantiated, so it's considered the baseline for cognitive power. In other words, Ali was *born* with this amount of brains, and doesn't know a time without it. I'll be interested to see how she behaves when the first full blade is complete and integrated."

Subbu was speechless. He gazed at Cora warmly, memorizing her features. The fact that someone this intelligent, yet kind and giving, would spend any time speaking with him was overwhelming. He was drawn to her.

"But how long before you make the next great leap forward?" Brad asked, joining in. He had pretended to not be listening, but had been waiting for his chance to take over the conversation.

"Depends on what you consider a 'great leap.' A.I. is getting smarter all the time, but is still no match for a human. We predict in ten or twenty years we'll be very close to equivalence."

"That's not a great leap, though," Brad said dismissively. "I'm talking about something big! Flat-earth-to-sphere big! Bigger even."

"Yeah, yeah, I know, rewriting human history, right?" she replied, letting a bit more sarcasm slip out than intended.

Brad looked at the ground, *I AM going to rewrite human history*, he thought. "Well, what about consciousness?"

"I think we need to think long and hard about those implications first," Cora said.

"No guts, no glory," Brad said, taking the lead, kicking at rocks and smacking bushes with his walking stick. In short order, as the mountain gave way to rolling hills, Brad grabbed a handful of wildflowers that were growing near the trail and tore them into a rough bouquet.

Turning towards Cora, he said, "For the lady." Adding a slight bow for affect as he handed her the flowers.

"Thank you, kind sir," she replied.

Cora watched as Brad walked ahead. *There were times that he could be boyish and charming*, she thought, *but other times…*

"Hey, let's stop up here for a quick break." Brad was pointing at a flat section of rock that gave a spectacular view of the valley below.

While Subbu and Cora inspected their remaining food, Brad sat at the side of the flat rock with his feet crossed beneath him, cradling his backpack.

The piece of debris he'd found earlier on the mountainside had been gnawing at him all morning. He took it out of the backpack and began turning it over in his hands—what was he looking at?

The outside of the rock looked like a normal meteorite, misshapen but roughly spherical, about eight or ten inches in diameter, he suspected. *I thought it would be heavier than this.* It was dark in color, with a few indications of burns, or melting, but the strange thing was the odd break on the side. Most likely caused from the impact against the mountain, a wedge had broken out of the rock; just a few inches deep and about four inches long, the missing section exposed what looked like another rock inside the outer crust. It was either a separate rock of a different material, or an extremely unusual break line that gave it the appearance.

Brad ran his finger into the wedge of the missing piece and his finger touched the smooth convex shape. *This is too smooth to be a natural break, especially along this perfect curve,* he thought. Prying at the outer layer of rock he thought he felt it loosen slightly. Without thinking, Brad hit the rock on the outcropping where he sat and heard a faint but distinct crack, like the sound of a walnut being opened. He was now looking at a rock that was about to split apart along a clean break, like an avocado after it had been cut.

"Hey, what are you doing over there?" yelled Cora. "Are you going to eat?"

With a slight twist of his hands, the rock parted into two pieces.

What the hell IS this? Brad said to himself.

CHAPTER 15
DARK WEB
(DAY 1 - 8:45)

Ian didn't have to search long before he felt inundated with information. The dark web was a place that most Internet users never went. Google, Bing, Ask Jeeves, even AOL back in the day, those were the search engines that served up the worlds web pages, people asking questions about which plants grew well in the shade, did so-and-so celebrity have an affair, do I have cancer. There were plenty of other things to search for and plenty of websites to serve up the content, some of which was not on the up-and-up, but if you were looking for hard to find items or information, the dark web is where you went.

Searching the dark web was easy enough once you got started;

searching the dark web intelligently was another thing. Anonymity was key. There were all kinds of traps and pitfalls you could stumble into in this realm, so you had to be careful. And it was enormous.

Anything from guns, to drugs, to prostitutes (of all ages), to banned materials, to counterfeit money could be found here. *Onion City* as it was popularly known, not only because most of the websites had a .onion domain name (similar to .com or .org), but because there was layer after layer after deep rotting layer of humanity for sale here. Caveat emptor! Buyer beware!

Ian started his search on *meteor storm* and received more links than he wanted or could review. He added *Mont Blanc* to the search terms and narrowed the result set quickly. Several links were loosely related to his topic; some were about storms; some sites were about supposed final resting places of lost mountaineers never recovered; Yeti hunting and storage; alien bases under the glaciers.

After a few minutes a link caught his attention: *Mont Blanc's Australian Event?* He clicked the link and was taken into a bulletin board site that was flush with chatter.

Bulletin boards where a throwback to the early 90's before the first useful web pages began showing up on the Internet. Constructed of a simple system that allowed users to create a username, they could begin chatting with others through a text-based interface, upload and download files of interest, and share other information. BBSs, as they were known, were similar to roaches, Ian thought, *Somehow, they managed to survive.*

After logging in to the main chat window as *Houdini*, which Ian thought was appropriately dark-webbish, he watched a flood of cryptic half-sentences scroll up his screen. At this rate he couldn't even tell who was responding to who; there seemed to be a dozen different conversations going on at the same time:

Catgirl: …and that is why I have momo…

sKelaWh0R: BS cvrup! l0ck n l0ad

bogrider: ..mind control lights..

TheDonald: @catgirl, nice whiskers!

Kor82r: Australian experiment is here!

Tr3S8: debris field searchers needed

HAL27: serious conversation y'all

Catgirl: meow!

And it went on and on.

After several minutes of watching the seemingly disparate conversations scroll by, Ian was about to try another search link when a message flashed onto the screen.

Pr0m3th3us: TROLL ALERT

And all conversation stopped.

Ian sat staring at the screen, not sure what to do next, when suddenly a private chat window popped up on his screen:

Pr0m3th3us: What are you looking at TROLL?

A message in the main chat window told him he had been disconnected from the forum. Ian knew that if the moderator of this forum, which apparently was Pr0m3th3us, thought he was a cop or similar, he would be blacklisted from the forum.

Houdini: No troll, just looking for info.

Pr0m3th3us: ?

Houdini: ??

Pr0m3th3us: What info?

Houdini: Australian incident.

Pr0m3th3us: Why? Want to disappear?

Houdini: No. Just interested.

Pr0m3th3us: What offering do you bring?

Houdini: Offering?

Pr0m3th3us: I am charged with protecting the sovereignty of this world.

Pr0m3th3us: My subjects are dear to me but are weak. I provide for them. I protect them.

Pr0m3th3us: What do you offer?

Houdini: Protect them from what?

Pr0m3th3us: All who listen and all who watch.

Houdini: Who are you?

Pr0m3th3us: I am he who stole the fire of knowledge from Mount Olympus and gave it to mankind.

At this point Ian thought, *This is either a nut job sitting in his mum's attic, or a real tin-foil hat bloke.* He wasn't sure he would get any info here, but thought he'd play along.

Houdini: What offering do you request?

Pr0m3th3us: That which will sustain us.

Ian thought for a moment, then typed:

Houdini: Mont Blanc meteor storm, 84% correlation with Australian Incident, fifty-kilometer debris field.

Houdini: ...and I'm looking at the mountain now.

—pause—

Pr0m3th3us: Who are you?

Unsure if he was remembering the story correctly, Ian responded:

Houdini: Prometheus, I am Odysseus.

—pause—

A second video window appeared with a black and white image of an aboriginal girl. It may have been due to the grainy image, but Ian thought her eyes reflected the flashbulb light, as if they were made of thousands of shards from a broken mirror.

CHAPTER 16

BSL-3

(DAY 1 - 09:15)

Jack was banking north into the foothills of the Alps when she heard the general's voice through her headphone speakers.

Wow, this is early, she thought.

Allen jumped, as if he had been sleeping, and looked at Jack to mouth, *What the fuck?*

"Status," said the general.

"Sir, we have just entered the southern range and are running the border now," Jack said. "Estimated arrival at beginning of debris field is 10:15."

"Syi, update on correlation," the general said.

[Based on additional analysis of post-atmospheric readings, the probability of correlation is now estimated to be 89%.]

Allen shook his head slowly at the sound of Syi's voice.

"Other anomalies?"

[Preliminary satellite analysis is detecting anomalous magnetic readings in the area of Mont Blanc.]

"So, watch your compass. Ignore anomalous readings and fly through," said the general.

Allen was squinting hard at Jack, trying to understand what this new information meant.

"General, what do you expect us to find?" asked Jack.

"Recovery is uncertain. Use BSL-3 procedures."

Biosafety level 3, thought Allen. *Full mask and respirators, on the side of a mountain. Holy shit.* He also thought the general was sounding much more robotic than before. *He's spending too much time talking to that damn cyborg...*

Jack rubbed her eyes and forehead under her helmet. Despite the effects of the hangover, she felt old today. She didn't like the feel of this mission already. She remembered back to a time when a young Jack Garvey proudly donned the special ops insignia, planning to set the world straight. It had gone like that for a while, but at some point, skewed off track. It wasn't a fast change, more like your car tires slowly working out of alignment. Too subtle to notice at first, but eventually, you couldn't ignore the pull.

"General, when we find the start of the debris field," Jack started, "it may be halfway up the mountain. We'll have to find a place to land before we can begin an ascent."

"Rappel from closest possible position," the general instructed.

Great, now I'm a fucking worm on a fishhook! Allen thought, scowling. *Just dangle me around for the space-goblin to chomp my ass!*

"Are we looking for general debris remnants or something particular?" Jack asked.

"Video comm," said the general, instructing Jack to flip open a small video display attached to the front frame inside the glass.

"This is your target," the general said as a picture came into view.

Both Jack and Allen stared at the black and white screen as the general turned an object over in his hands. It was slightly larger than his hands and looked like a normal rock with a chunk missing. Like a magic trick, the general separated the rock into two pieces; the screen showed a grainy image of one piece that had an indention; the other piece had what looked like a matching extrusion, almost in the shape of an egg that jutted from the rock. A piece of the *egg* was missing.

CHAPTER 17
MOUNTAIN BOUQUET
(DAY 1 - 08:30)

Subbu watched Cora chew slowly on her granola bar as she appeared to be lost in thought, looking out over the valley ahead of them. It was turning out to be another beautiful day to be at the base of the Alps, made even more beautiful by her presence. Always trying to give thanks for the small miracles—and very large—he experienced, he noted that he was thankful to be watching her watch the valley. In his world they were seeing it together.

He didn't pretend to understand what she and Brad did; he was a simple mountain guide from India, but he knew a good soul when he encountered it, and Cora's sparkled. He couldn't see auras, nor did he pretend to be psychic, but the Indian culture had a long history of believing in the mystic world of karma and foresight, and he felt at peace when she was near—most of the time.

He thought back to when he found her under the rock shelf at base camp. *What had startled her so badly? She bolted out of sleep as if she were fighting for her life.* He would be proud to protect her. If only he were more than a migrant Sherpa.

Maybe he would ask her for a demonstration of her AI technology after their break. He wouldn't ask many questions, careful not to expose his lack of education, but he liked to listen to her talk, even if he didn't understand everything she said.

He felt a slight breeze brush his left cheek and watched as it softly blew at Cora's brown hair, waving it toward Brad on the other side of the rock. Something Brad was doing caught his attention.

Cora tilted her head back slightly and felt a breeze brush the back of her neck. She breathed deeply, taking in the fragrant morning air. The rays of the sun were seeping into her skin, warming her. She unconsciously unzipped her jacket to adjust for the increasing warmth of the day and thought back to her reaction in the tent a few hours earlier. *Be brave, Cora,* she thought to herself, repeating her coach's words. Her mind juggled several images, all of them competing for her attention.

Remembering her life-coach's instructions to stretch outside of her comfort zone, she briefly imagined herself sitting on this rock by herself, naked to the sun, eyes closed, with no knowledge of if she was seen, nor caring if she was. *What freedom that would be.* She imagined standing up and turning in a slow circle, arms extended, head back, bare feet warm on the sun-drenched rock. Maybe someone would come along and touch her arm lightly; she wouldn't open her eyes. Maybe the many people that hiked this way would stop briefly and put mountain flowers in her hands, a living bouquet; she wouldn't open her eyes. She would just keep turning.

A cloud slowly drifted in between Cora and the sun, breaking the dream of freedom and strength, a dream she had silently wished for a long time. A competing memory seeped in. An old stagnant memory.

Behind her closed eyelids she saw light fade to darkness; on her skin she felt warmth give way to cold; her mind saw the grey-black of a tunnel; her shoulders hunched and felt the weight of a hiding place; she smelled fear and embarrassment; they stank like rot.

She heard a truck driving slowly on the road above, gravel crunching against worn tires. The truck stopped directly above her. A rusted hinge creaked as a door swung open. Boots scuffed against gravel; someone was walking toward the edge of the road.

Bobby Hadley stopped above her, knocking rocks over the edge of the road that fell into the runoff-creek outside her hiding place. Straining to follow his movement, she sat silent as a stone, letting the bugs inspect her legs without reprisal; there was a brief pause, then she heard a zipper, a groan; then a few seconds later, a steady stream of urine splashed down into the shallow creek in front of her. The stream slowly swung back and forth, back and forth, occasionally hitting upon a larger rock and splashing back towards the culvert. Suddenly, she heard Bobby's voice,

"Hey, what the hell…"

Then the stream of urine hit the dead dog full on. The flies were not happy.

◇ ◇ ◇

Brad was oblivious to all else around him. He didn't see the beautiful scenery of the valley. He didn't feel the mountain breeze. He did not notice the living bouquet withering behind him. He remembered painful words. His stomached turned sour.

"Ashhole-fuckology? Better watch it, Frank, my boy Brad here's gonna' be uh... uh, ashhhole-fuckologist! Ha! Ha! Haaaa-eeeee... cough... eeee's gonna... ha... ha... haaaa... cough... cough... eeee's gonna be a... doctor-of-fuckology, ain't ya boy?" Elmer Bradley said as he leaned to slap Brad on the back, tipping his lawn chair over and spilling his beer onto Brad's report card.

Young Brad tried to help his father up, whose arms and legs were like rubber, doing the *dying cockroach* in the air, but Elmer pushed his hands away roughly. *"Git yer... don't touch me with those damn diddle fingers of yours... you'd stop pissin' urself if you stopped diddlenen' so much."*

Young Brad picked up his torn report card and took it to his room. After taping it together and carefully wiping the dirt off, to not smudge the handwritten *A+ Great job!* his teacher had written in the margin, he pinned it to his wall next to a picture of Carl Sagan, the famous scientist. Laying in his bed that night, he willed himself not to wet the bed; no fourth grader did that. If he was smart enough to get moved up a year in school, he was smart enough not to wet the bed. And he would be the best astrobiologist ever. He would be famous; and when he was, his dad would be proud.

He was soaked the next morning.

Brad on the mountain blinked away the old memory. *Just the scare of last night's storm dredging up the past.* The last wisps of a bad dream, a cocoon nightmare withdrawing, but not gone.

He shook his head hard to clear his mind. He was on the verge of something big, something very big, and he needed his senses about him. He would be famous, after all.

Gazing at the contents of the half-rock in his hands, he knew this was the last moment of his old life; everything would change now; he would rewrite human history after all.

A discovering of this magnitude needed to be handled correctly, he knew. He knew he should have sealed it already, to not contaminate it, to preserve whatever microscopic organisms he thought he might find in it.

Brad was looking at a nearly perfectly petrified egg embedded in a meteorite. A petrified egg was the only thing it could be… *well, maybe a pod. No rock broke apart looking like an avocado from space that had just been sliced open.* The central shape was slightly more oblong than a chicken egg, but bigger. It was a dingy grey color but distinctly different from the outer crust of rock. *How had this egg-pod come to be embedded in the rock, and not destroyed when the outer crust was still molten lava? The egg-pod must have been petrified hard for a millennium before the volcanic activity coated it. Then what force blew it off its home planet and billions of miles through space to our little speck of rock?*

What would he see inside if he were able to x-ray it? Granted, he couldn't see the backside of the egg that still lay embedded in the rock, but it didn't look damaged. Whatever creature that was intended to hatch out of this thing was most likely perfectly preserved, just waiting for him to discover it.

A CT scan would be his only option, he knew. That would give him an idea of the density fluctuations, and possibly tell him the structure of the yolk, or embryo if he was lucky. Carbon dating would give him relative age. *How old would this be? Older than our own earth?*

Forgetting all safety protocol, and perhaps being propelled by the memories of a drunken father and torn report card, he wondered if he could pry the egg loose from the half rock he now held in one hand, ultimately holding his destiny in both. Brad reached down and grabbed the exposed part of the egg with his thumb and two fingers—changing his life forever. When his fingers touched the egg, he felt the slightest sting on his fingertips, as if he had just received the mildest of static shock. At the same time, he heard a faint *snap,* as if a light switch had been flipped, and thought he saw a faint blue streak arc across the egg between his fingers. What his eyes captured—but his mind did not register—was that the blue arc coursed across the surface of the egg in a very structured pattern. If his mind could replay that moment a thousand times slower, it would see the blue arc of life spread out from his fingertips, follow infinitely small circuitry lines around the circumference of the egg, circuitry lines that had been etched in the distant past, circuitry lines that had been protected by an outer shell of rock, waiting to spark to life. His mind would also see the blue arc flow through gates, resistors and capacitors, measuring the quality of this *particular* blue arc, and watch as it finally made its way inside the egg.

The instant the blue arc of life made its way into the egg, a tiny crack formed on the side facing Brad. The crack never registered with his brain.

Before he knew what happened, a piece of the egg exploded straight into his face and showered him with a dust finer than talcum powder.

His mind registered the snapping sound and deduced what it was far too late. His eyes slammed shut, only to capture the fine dust particles under his eyelids. Gasping and throwing his head back, ensured he breathed the particles in deeply, filling his lungs.

He let out a small gasp that caught the attention of Cora and Subbu.

They had just enough time to look his way as he fell backward and rolled off the side of the rock.

CHAPTER 18
AUSTRALIAN ADVENTURE
(DAY 1 - 9:30)

The general leaned back in his desk chair and rubbed his stubbled chin. The video link with the helicopter had just ended. The picture of the young man in uniform was sitting on his desk in front of him; two pieces of broken rock sat next to it.

The summer of 1992 was to be a grand adventure. David James Keller, having graduated from the Royal Military Academy at Sandhurst, had just been promoted to captain, and was to begin his new commission in Australia.

General Keller, major-general at the time, oversaw a division that covered Australia, along with several other locations. Now that his son had a company of his own—not to mention the general commanded the direct line his son reported through—this was an opportune time for a bit of adventure.

The general had been fascinated by the Australian Aborigines since he could remember. He felt it was not only in the family blood, but in their destiny, starting with Captain James Cook, to explore this anomalous country.

Everything about Australia was strange. Some fossilized human remains were reportedly pushing 50,000 years old, making them the oldest continuous human species on earth. The fossils were found near ancient sea beds, which were now hundreds of kilometers inland. Radar and magnetic anomalies happened constantly. And then, there was the incident.

The general had known when Syi reported that all meteor debris from the Australian Incident had been buried, that the report was not fully accurate. *He couldn't… IT could not have known that an object had in fact been recovered. It was never reported.* The general remembered.

William and David Keller had traveled into the Kimberley region of Northern Australia, where reportedly the core debris field from the 1940's storm was thought to be. Lying just north of The Great Sandy, the second largest desert on the continent, this region was notoriously hard to traverse due to the steep and jagged limestone mountains that had been carved by monsoon-fed rivers.

The Aboriginals had greeted them with skepticism, despite their use of a local guide. Several trade rituals had taken place to appease the village elders. Gifts, in the form of fishing gear and dried meats were given to them in trade for information, or *stories*. The general's request, after several minutes of questions between the Aboriginals and their guide, had been translated roughly as the *Storm of the Dream Fire*.

"Yes," the general confirmed to the guide. "Ask them to tell us about the Storm of the Dream Fire."

Several elders made religious symbols at this and looked at the general and David with suspicion.

After listening intently, their guide first explained that the terms, *The Dreaming* or *Dreamtime*, were roughly associated with the Aboriginal's creation story—at least, this was according to white people. He explained that the original translation made by early Europeans was incorrect, and that the words associated with the Aboriginal beginning were closer to the definition of *Uncreated*, but the terms had stuck.

The guide went on to explain that Dreamtime was a complex concept of *Everywhen*—that is, the past, present and future of each person's life. This infinite past-future history was an accumulation of all ancestral knowledge and was passed down to each person in their family line, thus creating an unbroken line of knowledge transference.

Additionally, a person could call upon the knowledge of their ancestors through Dreaming and would be able to follow the *Songlines* left to them. Songlines were the knowledge-paths—and sometimes physical paths—traversed by their earliest ancestors when the world was still unmade. The guide finished by stating that some Aboriginals were able to navigate across the land simply by repeating the words of the Songline, which described physical landmarks and other phenomena. They effectively heard voices in their heads that answered their questions.

Voices in their heads? The general didn't go in for that sort of thing—at least not then—but knew that these tribes, along with several other societies, wholly believed in mystic knowledge.

"Yes, but what of the Dream Fire?" the general reminded the guide.

The term *Dream Fire* had come into the local lexicon when an unusual storm broke across the Northern area of the continent in the 1940's. According to the myths, the Rainbow Serpent, their creator god, had sent a gift to the world in hopes the people were ready to receive it.

"What type of gift?" the general asked.

"The gift of renewal," the guide replied.

"Renewal? As in, lightning starting a fire which burnt the land? Causing it to regrow?"

"No, the eggs of life were sent in a basket of fire."

"Eggs of life?"

"Yes, the Rainbow Serpent is associated with fertility. It sent several of its eggs to fertilize the people anew. A gift of renewal."

"Were any of these eggs found?"

"Yes. One was given to a girl during the Kunapipi blood ritual; she was becoming a woman. She was sent to a water hole where the serpent visits at night and instructed to accept its seed in hopes that the Aborigine people would be renewed."

"What happened to the girl?" the general asked.

"She did not survive the serpent's seed. After that, all other egg baskets were buried until one strong enough was born."

"Egg *baskets*? I thought you were just describing—"

"Each egg was protected in a basket made of the serpent's dead skin, hard as stone, and cleansed with fire in the sky."

"Was a woman strong enough to handle the seed ever born?"

"It does not matter now. That tribe was lost, and the eggs have been forgotten."

At this point, some of the elders where chattering and whispering among themselves, shooting glaring looks towards the guide and the general.

The meeting was called to an end, and despite the general's insistence on their help, they were asked to leave with exaggerated gestures. The three of them were essentially thrown out of the camp. As the general led the threesome back to their Humvee, he realized that the meeting had gone on longer than anticipated, and that night was quickly setting in. They would camp outside the tribal area in the desert and discuss their alternatives.

Late that night as the threesome finished a dinner of kangaroo and vegetables, sitting around a glaring fire, they were startled as a white Aboriginal face appeared out of the darkness. Their guide had adopted the conveniences of modern clothes a long time ago, but the visitor was pure bush. The white-painted face looked to float just outside the fire, as the flickering light reflected back to them.

The general's hand was on his sidearm when the guide motioned for him to stop. They could be surrounded and not know it. A wrong move would insure they would never see morning.

After a brief conversation between the guide and the visitor, the guide turned to the general and said, "His name is Moboo. He says he knows the location of an egg basket."

"Will he take us there?" the general asked.

"Yes, but he wants money."

After all the negotiations and rituals, it always comes down to money, the general thought.

Recommending completing the transaction quickly, the visitor insisted they leave immediately and on foot. The noise and lights of the jeep would be too easy to track, and he was taking outsiders to a sacred place. They had to be careful.

A couple hours into their hike, they came to a maze of rock formations that skirted the base of a sheer cliff. Driving past the formations in daylight, one would have thought the cliff solid down to the sand; however, upon closer inspection, man-sized gaps could be seen that led through a confusing maze of stalagmites that jutted out of the sand and wound around one edge of the cliff. After a series of several turns, the group rounded a corner, and on a small stalagmite that had been carved into a pedestal, sat an object.

The main object appeared to be a meteorite missing a portion of a broken outer shell; around it, adornments of religious meaning.

The general quickly concluded their transaction, wrapped the rock in a cloth, and headed back to camp. They briefly followed Moboo, but he quickly disappeared into the shadows. Their guide did the rest.

The next day, after dropping off their guide, the general and his son looked at each other in silence. *What had they found?*

The rest of the trip had been a blur. David, discovering what looked like a petrified egg, had been exposed later that morning. The infection overcame him quickly. The general had no way of knowing if the Aboriginal girl exhibited the same symptoms as his son, but what he had exhibited had been the sole source of the general's nightmares ever since. Once the screaming started, it had been terrible; they treated the physical pain with morphine, which calmed his writhing body, but they couldn't help his mind. Day after day his son lay there descending into madness, clawing at his ears, ripping out tufts of hair before they could get his hands constrained, screaming about the voices, the itchy voices in his head. And his eyes never looked right.

CHAPTER 19

IAN

(DAY 1 - 10:00)

Ian spent another thirty minutes chatting with Pr0m3th3us. It turned out he was the latter of his initial assumptions, a real tin-foil hat bloke. He gave Ian enough information to establish credibility, but played his cards very close, which wasn't surprising. In the world of the dark web, caution and anonymity were the names of the game.

Ian had learned a fair amount about the Australian Incident that morning. Through his own network of hackers, ex-military and self-described government *watchers*, Pr0m3th3us had amassed an impressive collection of material on several conspiracy theories that most likely weren't just conspiracies. He supposedly ran several BBS's on various topics and under several pseudonyms and was always looking for *field personnel.*

Ian thought it a fair trade to spend some of his hiking holiday looking for physical evidence for Pr0m3th3us in exchange for more of his info. Granted, Ian hadn't mentioned that he had his own line of information, being an *analyst,* and probably at a higher security level than the ex-military sources, but he could be wrong. *Currently, leaks were everywhere.*

Ian decided to change his hiking plans from Chamonix, which was on the Northern side of Mont Blanc by fifteen kilometers or so, to the Italian side of the mountain, where the debris field should be better. He could travel through the smaller town of Courmayeur, a real mountaineer's town anyway, and hike towards the Freney Central Pillar, which was a nice site to check off one's bucket list. The drive time was nearly the same. He'd check in with Pr0m3th3us a few times throughout the week to give him—*who knows, maybe it's a her?* — and the forum group an update if he had any. He had suddenly been promoted to *celebrity du jour* based on his proximity to the site. He understood that most of the forum group were spread across the globe—*y'all was Texas after all, wasn't it?* —but doubted that many of these regulars could climb a flight of stairs without getting winded, much less a mountain.

He headed back to his flat and plugged his laptop in. *Strange,* he thought. *Still no internet connection.* He double-checked his bag, which was mostly packed already, set it and Houdini's gear near the door, and fell into bed. The excitement of the night had kept him going for a while, but he was sapped now. Five hours of sleep would be sufficient to get him started again; he would catch up on the rest over the week.

This will be a nice little adventure, he thought as he drifted off to sleep.

As if on cue, the network light on his laptop came on and began to blink.

CHAPTER 20
BRAD
(DAY 1 - 09:00)

Cora was on her feet almost before the old memory had time to slip back into her brain. In four long strides both her and Subbu where at the other side of the rock where Brad had just been sitting. They looked over the rock shelf, fearing what they might find, but to their relief saw Brad sitting a few feet below them, rubbing his head and wiping dust from his face.

"Brad! What happened? Are you alright?" yelled Cora as she began to scramble down the rock.

The distance between the top of the rock and the grade of the hill was only about four feet, and close enough to jump down to, but Cora was conscious of landing on a rock the wrong way and twisting an ankle, so she took the safe way.

Seeing that Brad appeared to be alright, Subbu sat cross legged where Brad had just been and teased, "Find any good specimens, boss?"

"Come on down and find out," Brad said dryly, looking up at Subbu.

"Let me see your head," Cora said.

"No, no, I'm fine. I'm fine," Brad said, holding his hand up between his face and Cora.

"What happened?"

"I'm not sure," Brad started. "I was looking at my meteorite sample and it broke apart somehow. I got dust in my eyes is all."

Subbu grabbed the eyewash out of his pack and handed it down to Brad. After a quick rinse, Cora helped Brad to his feet, where he discovered he had a slight limp from hitting his leg on the way down.

"It should be fine," he said as he saw Cora give a concerned look. "It'll loosen up by the time we get back."

"Speaking of getting back, boss, we need to get moving, we still have a ways to go and I—"

"My sample!" Brad exclaimed, looking around frantically. "Where did my sample go?"

He had worked hard his whole life to make a discovery of this nature. He wasn't leaving this mountain without it.

The group searched amongst the broken rock of the mountain base. Cora found the first piece very near where Brad had landed. It had a blackish tint to it, different than the other rubble that lay around. When she picked it up and turned it over, her face went blank.

Scanning the hillside, Brad spotted a fragment about ten feet below where he landed. When he picked up the fragment, he saw that not only had a part of the extrusion been broken away, but that the rest of the extrusion was hollow. He stared at it for a moment, trying to process what it meant.

Was it possible that this hadn't been a fossilized egg at all? he thought.

Was this simply an anomaly in the rock that was formed by an air bubble when it initially hardened?

Surely this meant something… but what?

"Brad, what *IS* this?" Cora asked, looking down the hill at him. She was holding another part of the meteorite with an outstretched arm, as if she were holding a hand grenade with a missing pin.

Brad walked slowly up the incline to where Cora stood by their rock picnic platform, his focus lost to his own swirling thoughts. Trying to mask the storm of emotion emanating from his face, Brad took the piece from Cora's hand and fitted the two pieces together along a small edge. The matching edge still implied the two pieces had been one, but there was now a larger section of the overall rock missing. In fact, the concave section from Cora's rock barely implied that another extrusion once fit it perfectly.

This used to be whole, Brad thought, trying to convince himself of what he had seen just moments ago.

"Do meteors always look like this?" Cora asked, sensing that Brad was struggling with internal conflict.

"I'm not sure, Cora. I'm not sure," was all that Brad could manage.

The group hiked the rest of the way to the pickup point in silence.

◇ ◇ ◇

Courmayeur was a quaint little mountain town on the Italian side of Mont Blanc that had grown up into a larger mountaineering town over the years. Its picturesque setting was an automatic postcard cover. In the winter, jagged mountain peaks stood vigil over small buildings wrapped in a thick blanket of snow; visitors in colorful snow gear dotted the hillsides waiting for the ski lift; curls of smoke from warm glowing fires wafted through the air, giving the valley the homey smell of a bonfire.

In the summer, it was a green valley nestled between steep green hillsides that gave way to cliffs of granite, gneiss and feldspar. Just outside the main town center, the traditional houses, tall and narrow with gabled roofs of slate or wood, were more reminiscent of German or Swiss construction than of the Southern Italian Mediterranean homes. Narrow gravel paths surrounded by fir trees wound off towards mountain paths, crossing old stone bridges, accented by blooming flowers. Paths gave way to fields and fields gave way to forests.

Courmayeur sat at the northwesternmost part of the Aosta Valley region. Covering a total of 1,260 square miles, the Aosta Valley was the least populous region in Italy. Numerous hidden places existed in this valley, as it settled into the soft spots between the mountain ridges. Hiking around the next corner may take one to a rock cliff, sub-valley, gulley or field, waiting to be discovered.

After loading their gear into the pickup vehicle, they settled into their seats for the relatively short trip to their lodgings. As Subbu described their journey to the driver, Cora's eyes grew heavy in the sunshine of the late morning, her head rolling slightly at the gentle rocking of the Land Rover. She thought back to when she was sitting on the rock at the base of the mountain, the image of her slowly turning in the sun with her eyes closed, naked feet to the rock, not caring who passed by, sent goosebumps down the back of her neck that spread under her arms and across her torso. She unconsciously waited for a mountain breeze to brush across her and temper her rising pulse. She was unaware that the driver was watching a blush run up the side of her neck and into her cheeks from the rearview mirror.

Upon arriving at their lodgings, the trio disembarked to three separate, but adjoined cabins. The plan was to catch up on work, rest for a few hours, then meet up in the late afternoon for a leisurely hike through the valley and celebratory dinner that night. Brad and Cora both had funds to spare in their research budgets, and since their work was nearly complete, they planned to enjoy the rest of the trip.

Cora began running the tub as soon as she was in her cabin. The main sitting/sleeping room was small but nicely decorated. It wasn't as modern as some of the hiking hotels were, but the family-owned charm was beyond compare. She also relished the fact that these rooms had actual tubs and not the coin-operated showers that were common in the area.

She checked her satellite link to Ali and, noticing a low battery light, quickly plugged her main unit into the wall to charge. She could hear Brad banging his gear around in the room next to hers and wondered if he was always this clumsy, or just inconsiderate. She knew most of the answers before the questions entered her thoughts.

Stripping off her dirty hiking clothes, she threw them into the corner and plugged her earbud back in.

"Ali, are you there?" she asked.

[Yes Cora, I am online and receiving 79% signal strength.]

Still pretty good, but I'd like to boost the signal a bit, she thought.

"Ali, please play a soothing music track. Meditative. Instrumental."

—pause—

[What region would you prefer?]

"Something mountainous. Tibet?"

After another short pause, Cora heard a slow-moving flute in her ear. The notes were sad, almost mournful, but inspirational somehow. Some type of stringed instrument began to play along with the flute. Chimes could be heard occasionally, as if off in a distant valley, shrouded in fog.

As the music settled in, Cora began to go through a couple of standing yoga stretches. The steam rising off the tub of water gave the bathroom a sauna-feel. The last twenty-four hours had been a roller coaster ride of emotions, and she was anticipating a long soak. As she stretched, she ventured a look at herself in the mirror; wiping fog away from one part of her reflection at a time, she wasn't unpleased with what she saw, although was conflicted on how much should be there. Her long athletic body was great for sports as a youth, or for clambering over rocks as she had just learned, but it didn't exactly fill out a little black dress like other women. Not that she really had the occasion for one anyway. As perspiration began to collect on her skin, she settled into the steaming tub. Laying a washcloth over her eyes, she let the water relax her sore muscles.

CHAPTER 21
RECONNAISSANCE
(DAY 1 - 10:15)

Mont Blanc loomed in the distance, but was growing quickly. Jack had kept the Little Bird at a relatively low altitude the entire trip, obscuring their flight path from most radar. She knew there would be more hikers the closer they got to the mountain, but that could not be avoided. She would improvise at that point, like she always did.

Jack forced the last of the civilian thoughts from her mind when she saw the mountain appear through the windshield. *Time to get to work.*

She couldn't remember what time she'd left the bar, but she sure as hell remembered the events back at the room, or at least most of them—*what was that girl's name? Sung-lee?* Asian schoolgirl outfit, thigh-highs, the whole bit. *How much had that cost?*—that was the part that was missing.

Last week it had been Tabitha with the full *I Dream of Jeannie* outfit. *Almost burnt the room down when we knocked that damned hookah over,* she thought with a rare chuckle.

The black shadow of the helicopter slid like a serpent over ancient boulders that had once been part of the mountain. Facing an enormous granite wall and seeing the bulk of the Alps stretch out before her and run east, Jack thought this would be an impossible task. *We're not going to find shit up here,* she thought hovering in place. They had already flown through hundreds of miles of mountains, and were just now getting to the bulk of the range.

Still hovering, Jack and Allen were working out a short dictionary of terms, so they were describing things the same way. The Freney Pillar in front of them was an *out-wall*, different from a *wall* that was part of the larger mountain base; *out-crop*, short for out-cropping, described a jumble of boulders and jags that seemed to be bunched up at the base, or on the sides of *walls*; *rubble* was loose stuff that fell down below *out-crops*; *peaks* cast long shadows; *troughs* categorized anything that was hidden by shadow until they could get a better look at it, then it would become more walls, out-crop and rubble.

Flying ahead slowly now, Jack was thinking out loud, naming the sections of mountain by the terms they had just devised. This exercise was to reinforce to Allen how Jack was thinking about what lay before them.

"Out-wall at ten-o-clock," she said, looking slightly left, pointing to the obviously large structure otherwise known as the Freney Central

Pillar. "Large wall behind out-wall *still at ten*; out-crop east of large-wall; rubble-trough running to our four-o-clock; rubble-troughs possible catch-basin for debris field. "

She tilted the nose of the Little Bird down slightly to follow the visual of the rubble-trough seeming to run underneath their field of view.

Allen was making mental notes and nodding as Jack ran through the exercise. They were on the same page.

The helicopter drifted northeast for a while like this, its passengers oblivious to the stares and odd looks they received from the ground. High-paying celebrities and tourists were occasionally seen taking sightseeing tours like this, but they were typically in brightly-colored helicopters flying at much faster speeds. The faster the better, as far as all parties were concerned, especially the hikers on the ground, who were happy to have unfettered mountain silence as part of their experience.

"Status!" demanded a voice in their headsets, immediately bringing the image of a snarling gold lion against a blood red backdrop to mind.

"Beginning reconnaissance now, sir," Jack said. "Approximately five kilometers— "

"I see you," interrupted the general. "You are three kilometers east-northeast of estimated southwestern corner of debris field. Preliminary results?"

"Negative on sightings, general. We've established a reco-dict and are establishing search boundaries. Considering…" she quickly searched for the name on his map, "…foothills north of Aosta Valley as southern perimeter. We'll have to refuel soon before complete search perimeter is established."

"Head north from your current location for eleven kilometers, then northwest towards Geneva. I'll send you the coordinates for a secure fueling area. Next checkpoint in seventy-five minutes; current location."

Allen looked at his watch. *A seventy-five-minute round trip out of the mountains to refuel AND to get back to their current location? That was moving it, especially considering the rough weather they'd surely hit getting over some of the peaks if they headed straight north from here. What the hell was the rush?*

"Yes, sir," Jack responded to a dead radio. The general had already dropped the line.

◇ ◇ ◇

[General, I am detecting increased chatter regarding meteor storm and correlation to Australian Incident.] said a metallic Hawking voice into the general's den.

The general was rubbing his forehead when he heard Syi, but didn't hear. Somehow the synthetic words that came from a synthetic mind, through the hidden mechanical speakers in his den got mixed up with the words in his mind. The words in his mind were his son's words as he had asked him, *What have we found?* The images of an Australian landscape began to pour through the general's mind.

"We found something, Davey," the general spoke to the room without realizing. "In one of the great cradles of civilization, like our ancestors before us, we've discovered something. Possibly something no other man on earth has seen before."

—pause—

[General, I am detecting increased chatter regarding—]

"Yes, I hear them too, Davey. It's an Aboriginal song. Beautiful, isn't it? Beautiful and haunting. I wonder what they are saying?"

The voices! The voices in my head…

[They are correlating the events of last night with—]

"Yes, last night… last night was a hell of an adventure… Hell of an adventure! I thought we might have to shoot our way out at one point."

…are itchy!

—pause—

[General, no arms fire was detected during the storm, although—]

Veins protruding on his temples. "No, I know there was no arms fire, but it was dicey for a while. I was prepared to go back and round every one of those bastards up and make them tell us where they hid those damn rocks."

My brain itches!

[General, please clarify mission directives.]

"You know, Davey, the chattering bastards."

We couldn't see them very well because of the fire, the elders, but you remember them, don't you? he thought.

"I'd round those chattering bastards up and… round them all up!… and…" he said.

You know they were lying… they lied to Captain Cook when he tried to bring them out of the Stone Age, and they lied to us.

"We should have rounded those bastards up and made them lead us straight to the rocks."

—pause—

Squeezing his forehead with both hands, "They should have told us about the rocks…" *They knew something was wrong with them, but they didn't say anything. They knew what* "our mission was!" *That was* "our mission directive damn it!" *And they lied! They lied!*

—pause—

[General, please clarify new mission directive. Original directive number one, recovery and analysis of meteor storm debris. New directive number two, round up… recover, people associated with chatter in relationship to Australian Incident.]

"That's fine Syi. That's just fine." *Please help me! Make it stop!*

[General, please confirm additional call sign "Davey" to be included in command protocol.]

"That's right, Davey, that's right." *It'll be better soon. I'll make it stop.*

—pause—

[Confirmed.]

"Oh, and Davey."

[Yes, general?]

"When we round them up… we'll interrogate the hell out of them."

[Confirmed.]

CHAPTER 22
PROM3TH3US
(DAY 1 - 11:15)

Prometheus bolted awake at the sound of a British air raid siren blasting from speakers attached high up on a cinder block wall. The red warning light was spinning, casting an image of dancing flames across the walls, although there was no fire, and barely anything to burn. He was being hacked.

He slammed the reclining footrest down and stumbled through the dimly lit room. Even though it was broad daylight, he could only see by the light of the monitors and their screensavers. This room was designed to be dark.

He barely kept his balance as he fell towards the computer chair, landing one side-cheek half in the chair and starting a roll in the wrong direction. Frantically tapping the space bar on several keyboards, the monitors came to life and flooded light onto a stubbly plump face, with bloodshot eyes due to lack of sleep. Hadn't he just fallen asleep two minutes ago? He had been chatting with a new chap, Houdini, making nice progress, just a couple of minutes ago. Maybe he had dozed off… No, he'd made it over to the recliner. What time was it, anyway? Finally focusing on the computer clock, he saw it was only 11:15. No wonder he was so groggy. He had barely been asleep.

Tapping a few more keys, the siren stopped blaring and the red light stopped. Calm blue ambience spread throughout the room. He liked to keep the Zen balanced. Besides, he didn't like the electrical or audio fluctuations of the alarms to give away any indications that something other than a small woodworking shop was in this building. Granted, normal electrical use would fluctuate greatly with woodworking tools, but if someone was running an average daily consumption analysis on this building and they correlated the electrical usage over time, they may detect today's abnormal spike due to the alarm, when on average he had very low usage during this time since he was normally sleeping. But no one really knew that. He was particularly careful about things of this nature.

Getting hacked, or people attempting to hack him, was a normal occurrence, but Prometheus could tell by the alarm severity that this one was different. Denial of Service (DoS) attacks where the tool of choice for amateurs, basically flooding a website with so many requests that the web server couldn't keep up. The social justice warriors—which at opportune times may include him—typically tried DoS attacks. *And against government sites of all things. Idiots! Like the feds wouldn't be able to trace that.* Then of course you had your standard SQL-injection hack, inserting malicious code into the input boxes of websites that collect data, but that didn't apply to him either. He wasn't a traditional business.

Finally, you had the more sophisticated IP network hijacking hacker. These people were much more serious, and you had to pay close attention to them. If they were going to this kind of trouble, something was up. *Why the attention now, though?* He'd had this BBS up for a couple of years at least, didn't buy or sell arms, no drugs, no money laundering, of course, he did get paid for the info collected, primarily in Bitcoin, but that wasn't a crime in and of itself.

Prometheus executed a rapid shutdown of the sites and began the protocol to spin up the mirror sites he had waiting for just such an occasion. Some sites would be offline for a few hours, but nothing longer than that. A message had already been sent out to the user known as HAL27 via a secure line to login and start assessing damage. HAL27 had become his right-hand node. He still wasn't sure if HAL was male or female—but that never really mattered to Prometheus—so he refrained from thinking in terms of male or female, besides, *node* was more autonomous.

Wait a second, he thought. *This hadn't happened until I chatted with Houdini earlier this morning. That node better be on the level.*

He prided himself on being able to flush out the fakes. *Maybe Houdini was better than the others.* He'd have to wait and see what Houdini produced, if anything, from the reconnaissance trip.

That was almost too much of a coincidence, to have a seeming newbie to this world interested in an obscure topic, who also happened to live near the mountain where the incident happened.

Too much coincidence, indeed.

CHAPTER 23
IAN AND HOUDINI
(DAY 1 - 4:00)

Ian awoke to a very polite, but stern knocking on his door. His head was heavy with sleep, but he sat up immediately with his eyes closed—his old training lurking just beneath the surface. He knew to do this to help quickly orient himself under sleep deprivation. Having his eyes open would send too much stimulus to his brain and slow the overall normalization of senses. He swung his feet onto the floor and oriented towards the door, standing up quickly to force his mind to focus on his physical task needs. Walking forward with his arms out, feeling for the bedroom doorway, he let the light ease through his eyelids before fully opening them. He was standing at the front door of his flat before he fully opened his eyes.

A composed but demanding Ms. Winston was preparing for her third and final round of sharp rapping when Ian opened the door. She had arrived at precisely 2:00, which was the agreed upon time. It was now 2:04, and her schedule was very important to her. *The young people these days!*

A stoically amused face looked up at the nearly six-foot-tall young man. *My word…* was the first thought through her mind. Despite Ian's ability to quickly come to his senses under pressure—which Ms. Winston knew nothing about—he apparently had an aversion to looking in a mirror before answering the door. *Who would answer the door like that?* The rumpled shorts and T-shirt could be overlooked, but his hair. *And such nice black hair, if it would only find a proper brush. And… is that a small piece of feather?* His hair sloped to one side of his head, giving him a lopsided, top-heavy look; combined with the fact that he was blinking his eyes with half a boyish grin on his face, if she hadn't known him, she would have mistaken him for half mad, or quite dim in the bonnet.

"Ms. Winston," Ian said, stretching and yawning. "It's so nice to see you."

"Yes, yes, I'm quite sure. My dear boy," leaning forward slightly and lowering her voice, "your hair." As she gently patted the side of her own heavily sprayed head.

"Oh…" said Ian, turning towards a small wall mirror and letting go of the door to smash his hair down; this action letting the spring tension door swing closed on Ms. Winston.

"I'm sorry…" Ian said stepping towards and grabbing the door. Pulling it back open quickly, only to run it into his bare foot.

"Owww!" he exclaimed, now hopping on one foot in front of her and Houdini, who let out a small whimper as he tilted his head in utter dog-confusion.

"Party hearty last night, did we dear?" asked Ms. Winston with her hands clasped calmly in front of her.

"No… uh, no ma'am, just work. That's all. Heading off for a week of vacation today."

"Well deserved, I'm sure. And just in the nick of time I'd say," tilting her head toward him slightly.

"Uh, yes ma'am. I'd say so."

"So, you won't be needing my services this week, then."

"No ma'am, not until next week this time."

"Splendid, then I'm off to see my sister and try her new batch of mulberry wine," she said with a twinkle.

"Mulberry wine… that sounds— "

"Oh, and Ian my boy…"

"Yes, ma'am?"

"Do try to *not* lose Houdini while you're gone."

"No, ma'am. I won't. I mean I will… not… lose him," he said with a grin, still patting his hair with one hand.

"That's a good lad."

No sooner had Ian picked up Houdini and closed the front door that Houdini started to happily pee into the air.

"*Houdini!*" could be heard as Ms. Winston walked down the sidewalk, smiling.

◯ ◯ ◯

Ian was nearly two hours into his two-and-a-half-hour drive into the mountains. The soft top of his jeep was stowed away, and the mountain air was whipping him and Houdini. An occasional spittle of slobber flew from Houdini's direction, but that was inconsequential as far as Ian thought.

Houdini was in his harness that was connected to the seat belt mechanism. It gave him enough movement to stick his head out the window without letting him fly out of it. It would also keep him secure in the event of sudden braking.

Ian had spent the last two hours following AutoRoute 41 (A41) and 43 (A43) out of Grenoble northeast towards Mont Blanc. He had stayed on this valley highway system the entire trip, as it eventually turned into A430 close to the town of Chamonix. From Chamonix, he could turn northwest and be in Geneva in two hours, but instead of ending his trip as previously planned, he would take the Mount Blanc tunnel southeast for several kilometers, underneath the mountain, and come out on the Italian side of the Alps.

He hadn't been to that side of the mountain yet and was looking forward to the sights. Houdini hadn't been anywhere yet, didn't know where he was going, but seemed to be happy just to let his tongue flap in the wind.

Houdini was an uncommon border collie. Classified as a *tri-colored blue merle,* he had a very distinctive color pattern of black and white with a soft gray mottling; the gray appeared as a light blue sheen over a large portion of his body. Dogs with this color variation often had one or two ice-blue colored eyes, giving them a wolfish, mystic look. Houdini had both, which were further accented by darker gray markings around his eyes. Bred for their intelligence and obedience, these dogs, considered one of the most intelligent of all domestic breeds, were excellent learners. This made them easy to train, but also meant they contained a relentless curiosity. From the time Ian adopted him, Houdini had shown an uncanny ability to escape his dog pen, only to be found sitting on top of it with his head cocked to one side.

Ian was admiring Houdini's blue sheen in the late afternoon sunlight. As if reading his mind, Houdini looked over at Ian and gave a soft bark, only a remnant of the high-pitched puppy yelp remained, as if to say "Pet me, already. It's been a whole five minutes!"

Ian reached over and ruffled Houdini's ears, thinking his fluffy, unruly hair could use a proper brush.

Satisfied, Houdini turned his attention back to the rolling landscape and looming mountains.

Houdini was the first to notice the black helicopter against the mountain skyline. Having just been refueled at a secret location near Geneva after completing a fly-over of the search area perimeter, the helicopter had approached the mountain from the Northwest on a path that would send it south of Mont Blanc and the tunnel that ran below it. The mountain range had been divided by an ancient glacier there which made for a convenient flight path back to the most likely point of meteor impact.

His head tilted slightly to the right as his ice-blue eyes fixated on the black object that appeared to be moving towards them. A combination whimper-growl was felt by Ian more than it was heard.

"What's the matter, boy?" Ian said, patting his head again. Following the dog's gaze was tricky while driving, especially considering they were nearing their turn for the Mont Blanc tunnel, but Ian finally spotted what he thought Houdini was looking at.

"No worries, mate," rubbing his head some more, "that's just a heli—" Now it was Ian's turn to cock his head. Squinting his eyes, looking for detail yet to be seen, his mind already told him this was a military helicopter.

"Hmmm," he registered quietly as the direction of the road took the helicopter out of his vision.

The drive through the Mont Blanc tunnel, which was just over eleven kilometers long, took a total of about twenty minutes due to the tolls and reduced speed limit. Upon exiting the tunnel, Ian simply had to follow the highway straight to Courmayeur. To his and Houdini's surprise, the black helicopter had rounded the southern part of the ridge in nearly the same time it took them to drive beneath the mountain.

Flying low and fast, the Little Bird passed straight over them, flying north toward the summit. With a low growl, Houdini watched the object pass overhead. The hair on his neck was bristling.

CHAPTER 24

GYPSIES

(DAY 1 - EARLY EVENING)

Cora awoke from her nap with a long stretch of her arms and legs, rolling each foot separately, hearing the tiny bones pop. If it hadn't been for Ali pinging her in her ear, the long soak she'd taken may have caused her to fall completely asleep in the tub. She jumped out of bed and looked at her watch. *5:27 pm*; a few more minutes and Ali would have awoken her anyway. She had plenty of time to get ready for dinner and whatever celebration they may want to have tonight.

She heard Brad sneeze in the adjoining cabin, so she knew that he was up as well, and thought briefly that he must be one of the unfortunate allergy sufferers in the world. Although she hadn't remembered him sneezing while they were on the trail.

Buoyed with a general lighthearted happiness, she bounced around the room as she got dressed. Granted this was a research trip in a remote area of the country, but surely she had something in her bag that didn't look like it just had a rope attached to it. She would have to stick with jeans, which she started to wriggle into, when a thought crossed her mind: *should I go commando tonight*? The thought of that immediately set her cheeks ablaze. Not that anyone else would know, because she certainly wasn't planning on being that adventurous, but she would know, and that's what mattered. With only another moment's thought on the topic she had decided, *naahh, I don't think so. Let's not go crazy here.* Her jeans, with a tank top under a loosely buttoned shirt would give her options to be more or less adventurous depending on the situation.

Makeup was another thing that was in short supply in her bag, not that she owned much of that either, but thought the occasion called for it. Her naturally tanned skin was free of blemishes, but she tried to highlight the green in her hazel eyes as best as possible. A light coat of lipstick, barely a gloss, completed the picture, and despite going with a simple French braid, she thought she cleaned up quite nicely.

She walked onto the small covered porch of her cabin just as Subbu walked up. He had gone into the town of Courmayeur, scoping out restaurants and other activities. The covered porch was more of a covered, elevated sidewalk connecting the cabins. Sort of like in the old western movies, she thought.

Beautiful, Subbu thought to himself as he forced the less telling greeting of "Hi, Cora."

Brad appeared out of his door next, interrupting the conversation.

"OK, Subbu, what gives? Any good action in this town?"

Looking at Cora in an attempt to reconnect the conversation, Subbu paused for a moment too long. "Cat got your tongue?" came the prompt from Brad. Passing Cora to jump off the two steps to the gravel path below, Brad acknowledged that she was standing there with a noncommittal "Nice braid," and a tap on her arm with the back of his hand that could have been translated into "Nice hit."

Wrinkling the side of her mouth unconsciously, she discretely buttoned one of the buttons on her shirt and walked down the steps.

As they walked through the town, Subbu named off the different options for dinner and entertainment, most all of which received an uninterested grunt from Brad.

"If I had known earlier, we could have hiked down into the valley today," Subbu explained. "Some people in town said that a gypsy caravan was spotted earlier this morning."

As if on a drawstring, Brad spun around and stopped Subbu dead in his tracks. "Gypsies? Where?" he asked.

"Outside of town, down in the valley. No one is quite sure, as they don't announce when they come and go. But it could be an hour hike from here, we won't have time— "

A slow smile crept across Brad's face as his eyes widened. "Let's go find the gypsies," he said, as if describing a buried treasure.

"But we haven't eaten yet—" started Cora.

"Boss, it could be a long hike and—"

"We'll eat brats on the way!" yelled Brad as he jogged over to a vendor in the last small open market before the town came to an end.

While Brad stuffed bratwurst sandwiches into a bag, Cora had the sense to buy bottled water and a cheap flashlight from a small store nearby. *So much for a nice dinner,* she thought.

After a ten-minute flurry of activity, the three began their impromptu hike out of the town of Courmayeur into the Aosta Valley system.

As they walked, Subbu told them what he knew of the gypsies in the region. Although there were numerous tribes centered on familial ties, they all supposedly had a common ancestry. Originally thought to be of Egyptian origin, hence the term *gypsy*, they were now believed to have been an outcast group from India who migrated all the way into Europe. Being of Indian decent himself, Subbu was familiar with the story of the outcast people.

Along the way, the term *Romani* came to describe all the gypsy tribes, and *Romanes* became their official language. Most of their tradition and culture was still passed down orally, which made it difficult to research them. Also, most of the people that categorized themselves as gypsy or Romani no longer traveled in the fabled caravans, which made this an unusual occasion.

As they walked, Cora asked a series of questions, and Subbu answered the best he could. Unbeknownst to them, Brad had been rubbing his eyes as they talked.

The path out of town had led purposefully through a bordering field, but had now vanished into the landscape, which was quickly becoming forest. They were making their own path now.

About thirty minutes into their hike, Brad held up his hand in a signal for them to stop. He held his hand to his ear and they all listened. He thought he heard talking or singing up ahead.

As the sun began to set behind the Southern Alps, the forest that opened before them took on a different feel. As if suddenly transported into a different region and time, the forest felt older; the mountains looked taller and the air grew chill. Cora was thankful she'd thrown her hiking jacket in, and slipped it over her shoulders.

As they crossed a low ridge, they saw light twinkling in the branches of giant fir trees. Silhouetted by a large fire, the outline of horse drawn wagons could be seen forming a large semi-circle. They had found the caravan.

As they walked slowly towards the menagerie of wagons, a brilliant color palette unfolded before them and glittered from the flames of the fire. Over twenty wagons of all shapes and sizes had been pulled into a large semi-circle, forming a main area in the middle. Despite being parked so people could walk between any two of the wagons, there was an obvious opening facing into the valley that appeared to be the *front* that created a funnel into and out of the main area. There was a smaller opening in the wagon circle, directly behind the fire, that led to the forest, and other tents, which appeared to be the *back* and only for the gypsies. The wagons were decorated with every color imaginable and included gold trim, ornate wood carvings, canvas doors, rounded roof tops and even precarious little chimneys that implied a crackling fire inside.

The large fire they had seen reflected through the tree branches blazed in the middle of the main area, but had been built towards the back-opening of the wagon circle, apparently to leave room for people to gather in front of it, which was towards the valley. Several torches had been placed in strategic areas, and burned in between most of the wagons. Small tables and chairs were being set up for people to sit at, but were all different depending on which wagon they came out of. A small impromptu stage had been constructed facing the front opening where most of the tables and chairs were placed. This gave the 'rear' opening of the circle a more private position, which implied that it wasn't for public use.

Several other hikers were milling around just outside the front opening of the circle, unsure whether crossing the invisible threshold of the circle was welcome, or wise. Seeing the hikers' apprehension, an old woman who appeared to be supervising the young girls waved a hand sharply and called to a girl of about ten. With a few undecipherable words, the woman sent the girl towards the hikers in a rush. A few people started to back away, fearing reprimand, when the young girl quickly grabbed one by the hand and urged him into the circle of activity.

"Welcome, come, come," said the girl without fear. "We are almost ready. Please, come in." She waved her hands around in a slow arc, apparently indicating for people to sit anywhere.

Upon seeing this lack of direction, a heavyset woman tending to one of the small seating areas bleated at the girl in disgust and shook her hand at her. She quickly grabbed the person closest to her and led them to her seating area, calling to someone inside her wagon. She vigorously patted their shoulders, saying "Sit, sit," almost pushing them into the chair.

Seeing that the competition had a jumpstart, a wiry woman from a different wagon on the other side of the circle exclaimed something that sounded like, "OH, Ach! Mida, slach!" She shook her fist and ran to grab her patrons before they were all gone.

The activity went like this until the first few travelers were seated in areas. Brisk conversations started up offering wine and food, mostly dried meats, cheeses and breads. Brad, Cora and Subbu, missing the first draft round, seated themselves in the center directly in front of what appeared to be a stage. The old woman who directed everyone's entrance mumbled something under her breath and watched as the little girl attended their table.

Cora sat in the center seat facing the table, which also faced the stage; Subbu was on her right and Brad on her left. Upon sitting down, Brad promptly grabbed another chair from a table next to him and placed it in front of him to recline his feet on. The heavyset woman, whose seating area the chair apparently came out of, started to protest, but from across the circle, with a quick motion of her hand and a word that not many heard, the old woman ended the protest before it really began.

The young girl spoke with the three and they decided, mostly at Brad's insistence, that a mix of cheese and bread, with wine of course, would suit them just fine. She hurried away under the watchful eye of the old woman.

More hikers wandered in over the next thirty minutes, and soon most seats were occupied. Jugglers were walking through the crowd and a few other young girls were trying to sell bracelets and necklaces they had made with beads and shells. This was a large source of income for them, Subbu explained. Most of the gypsies worked somewhat normal jobs, but there were still some that held onto the old ways.

A few musicians settled onto the makeshift stage. A guitarist, a drummer with one large drum laid on its side, and someone with what looked like a large, pear-shaped mandolin, started playing a slow instrumental. Cora was surprised at the distinctly Middle-Eastern sound of the music, but then remembered Subbu's statement about the origins of the gypsies.

When she asked Subbu, he said the pear-shaped instrument was in fact an oud; a twelve-string instrument that was favored in India.

The three of them chatted for a while, and despite the dropping temperature in the forest, Cora thought the central fire of this makeshift courtyard must be hotter than she realized, for she had not only removed her jacket, but unbuttoned the top two buttons of her outer shirt again, letting her white tank top reflect in the light of the fire.

After a short while, another guitarist joined them, and the band broke into a markedly faster song. After only a few chords Subbu turned to them with a wide-eyed expression and said, "Django—*I awake.*"

"Is that the name of the song?" Cora asked.

"No, that's who wrote it," he said. "Django Reinhardt, the famous gypsy jazz guitarist. The song is called "Minor Swing," I think."

"Why did you say *I awake?*" asked Brad.

"That's what the name Django translates to in Romanes—the gypsy language—it translates to *I awake.*"

"Well then," Brad said, grabbing Cora's hand, "this music is waking me up too!" He pulled her around in front of the table to what would be a dance floor in a traditional music hall.

Brad mimicked how he thought a jazz lover of the 1920's would dance to this song, which equated to flailing his and Cora's arms around in jerky movements, punctuated by an odd locking of his knees at strange intervals. Cora didn't mind the jerkiness, as she had no better sense of how someone was to dance to this music either, but the rhythm was very catchy, and the movement helped the wine wash away the tension of inhibition that still lingered within her.

When the song finished, they both flopped down in their seats laughing. Brad had called for more wine while they were up, and the glass jug had already been refilled. He topped off everyone's glass and tilted his in toast, sloshing a little over the side. Cora and Subbu raised their glasses in response and waited. Turning towards Cora to speak, his head lolled slightly, causing him to look straight at Cora's open shirt. Raising his head slowly, he looked at Cora, then over to Subbu. She noticed his eyes were quite red at this point, but assumed the smoke from the fire was irritating them. Without even a clink of their glasses, Brad took a large drink, set his glass on the table and turned back toward the fire silhouetting the band. As he sunk down in his chair, extending a leg to the chair in front of him, Subbu could see a look of confusion creep onto Cora's face.

A brief pause in the music nearly caused Cora to search for an awkward–silence–filling–comment when she suddenly heard a low violin note which seemed to float from out of the fire.

The band had transitioned into a slow monotonous rhythm of a simple drum beat accented by an occasional guitar strum, but they were clearly making way for someone else to join them. The notes of the violin slowly grew in volume and seemed to set the flames of the fire to a new dance. Everyone's attention was now on finding the mysterious violinist.

With slow deliberate movements that swayed to the beat of her own making, the gypsy girl emerged from around the back of the fire and slowly strolled toward the crowd. The young woman was not part of the normal serving crowd, as was evident by the slight curtsies bestowed upon her by the younger girls as they busied themselves with their patrons. The gypsy girl was clothed in shimmering satin that clung to her full and youthful body. Her black hair, decorated with gold braids and medallions, spilled over bare, tan shoulders and long arms that swayed gracefully with violin and bow. Her bare feet made not a sound as they brushed across the lush forest floor; occasionally tracing a figure eight in the moss to the off-beat of the music.

As if by magic, not a sound could be heard in the forest circle save what the gypsy girl coaxed from her violin. Hypnotized by the repeating intro notes, Brad sat straight up, transfixed. The gypsy girl slowly walked on stage and broke into the most mournful song Cora had ever heard.

"What is that song?" Brad asked quietly, not even turning around.

Hoping to salvage the night, Cora quietly flipped her earbud on and heard the familiar jingle.

"Ali," she whispered, "identify this song please."

The song had broken into long sad notes that seemed vaguely familiar to her. It was a heart-wrenching spell that Cora watched being woven over Brad. The light of the fire, silhouetting around the curves of the gypsy girl, seemed to cling to her unnaturally, as if trying to pull her back into the fire from whence she came. She was mesmerizing.

Quietly she heard, [The notes I've analyzed have a strong correlation with 'The Gael']

The Gael? she thought, *that didn't—*

[Also known from the movie–*The Last of the Mohicans.*]

Of course, that's where I've heard it. Although not quite like this.

As she bent forward to whisper the title into Brad's ear, the gypsy girl broke into a high-note passage of the song that seemed to coordinate with a sudden flash of light in her eyes. Brad reached back for his wine glass and upon grabbing it, knocked hers over, directly into her lap.

He never noticed.

Before Cora could say anything, the gypsy girl stepped lithely off the stage right onto the chair in front of Brad. The song had suddenly sped up as if to match this movement and she was now swaying to an ever-increasing hypnotic spell. Having landed on a chair that was sitting on unlevel ground, the chair momentarily rocked as if it would tip over and cast the gypsy girl from Brad's sight. But in a lithe adjustment of her hips, the gypsy girl swayed slightly forward as if overcorrecting, and with one foot on the chair, landed her other foot gently against Brad's chest to bring herself and the chair to a gentle stop.

She never missed a beat.

The gypsy girl now leaned her weight into Brad's chest, towering over him as an alpha wolf would do to a submissive mate. With one foot on the chair and one firmly braced against Brad, she broke into the crescendo of the song, as if it were a musical climax. Her arms moved rapidly, as if winding the instrument to a violent finish. Brad was transfixed by a sheen of sweat that appeared on her torso, and could feel the heat of her bare foot against him. Oblivious to the outside world, he felt his head spinning as the music wove him into a drunken tapestry.

Cora watched the scene unfold in front of her with utter helplessness, her cheeks flush with embarrassment.

With barely a movement, the gypsy girl rocked herself further forward, as if to tip Brad straight onto his back, then deftly shifted her weight backwards and with one slight twist, launched herself off the chair from her left foot, turning slightly in the air and landing her right foot onto the stage to complete the half pirouette.

She held his gaze locked as she finished the last long note of the song, then released him with a blink of her eyes; she looked up to a stunned crowd, looked slowly from one side to the other, then bowed her head slightly as if releasing everyone else; the forest erupted in applause from all directions. Brad never noticed Cora quietly buttoning her shirt.

The musical entertainment had ended for the evening; not a moment too soon as far as Cora was concerned. However, the evening had more in store. Now that everyone was drunk with wine and music, the real money-making began. Games of gambling replaced some of the tables and chairs that held wine and cheese just moments ago. Spells and amulets were now for sale within tents that seemed to grow out of the forest dark. The crowd was led by ones and twos deeper into the gypsy camp, behind the central fire and into a labyrinth of tents that offered whatever one was looking for, and many things they were not.

Cora suggested they start their hike back to town, fearing that nothing good would come out of venturing any further, when the young girl who had served them wine and cheese came to their table. Grabbing Brad's hand, the girl gently plied, "Come, come, Puri daj awaits."

Shaking his head slightly as if to clear his thoughts, Brad looked at the little girl. Forming his question too slowly, the girl reiterated:

"Puri daj, *the grandmother,* she awaits. You have been marked. Come, come."

"Marked? What do you mean?" Cora asked. "Who is waiting?"

"Lilith, the Chovexani has—" noting that the three did not understand the term, the girl paused, searching for a translation.

"Chovexani… witch."

"Lilith marked him to have his fortune told. Puri daj will tell it. No charge, no charge," the girl said as she made exaggerated hand movements toward Brad.

As Brad began to move in the direction the girl was leading him, Cora tried to intervene again. "Wait, who is Lilith and why would you offer a *fortune telling* for free?" Not hiding her skepticism.

"Lilith, with the lavuta… uh, violin, she marked him as the greatest in need. As a payment for our ability to travel unhindered, we offer help to the most in need. Puri daj will tell his fortune as this payment."

The gypsy girl is behind this, Cora thought to herself. *Humph, the most in need? More like the most susceptible to a pretty face and whatever they were selling.*

Subbu had been silent during the conversation, but quietly grabbed Cora's arm when he heard the name Lilith. Interrupting Cora's thoughts and very discretely shaking his head, he mouthed the words, *No Lilith.*

Suddenly wondering why she was concerned with Brad at all— *he hadn't even realized he spilled wine all over me!* —Cora turned and said, "Come on Subbu, I'm going back to town. Brad, you can do what you want, but I'd hold onto my wallet if I were you."

Subbu looked back and forth between Cora and Brad, torn between the decision that had been thrust upon him.

"Boss, we really should be getting back—" he started.

"You guys go on. I'll be fine," Brad assured them. "How can I pass up getting my fortune told? Besides, they have to make their payment somehow, and I wouldn't want to upset the tradition," he said as he winked to Subbu.

Cora had already turned to leave as Subbu reluctantly watched Brad being led away by the little girl.

As he turned to follow Cora, Subbu glimpsed Lilith standing behind the fire. She had been watching intently.

CHAPTER 25

FIREFLIES

(DAY 1 – LATE NIGHT)

Jack rubbed her eyes as the Little Bird hovered in front of the Freney Pillar. *Seen this before.* They had already made a full trip around the perimeter of the search area. GPS tracking was on automatically with these birds, so she knew the general would be able to see every inch they'd flown. They had noted several areas of rubble that they supposed would be good catch basins for a meteor to fall into, marked areas of the mountain that appeared to have burn marks, but other than that, one spot was just as good as the next.

Allen had been grumbling to himself for most of the trip, but now was tired enough to simply let his head loll over onto his shoulder as he looked out the window at the vast stretch of mountains before them.

Jack raised the general over the radio at the agreed upon checkpoint time.

"General, we have our perimeter established," Jack said. "We have probable search areas located and categorized. We now need to establish a weighting system that will help us determine which site to explore first. Over."

With that, they both heard the communications link crackle over their headsets, but it was not the general's voice they heard respond to them.

[Stand by for satellite download of electromagnetic resonance data.]

Allen looked over at Jack and mouthed, *Great, the Term-I-Na-Tor.*

Jack simply raised an eyebrow in response as if to say, *Orders are orders.* She checked the video display and confirmed that a download of data was being sent. Estimated completion time was two minutes.

"Syi, how will electromagnetic resonance data be used?" Jack asked.

[Electromagnetic resonance data within search perimeter has been analyzed for anomalous readings. Readings outside the established threshold will be overlaid with a real-time feed from the onboard FLIR camera.]

Now it was Jack's turn to wrinkle her forehead, trying to determine what this new information meant.

"Syi, the FLIR camera is for thermal imaging. Any meteor fragments will have surely cooled to surrounding temperature by now. Please confirm."

[Anomalous magnetic readings are theorized to be associated with meteor targets. Overlay of electromagnetic data with real-time FLIR data will allow anomalies to be seen as a heat signature.]

Jack pursed her lips. *Pretty cool,* she thought, nodding her head at Allen.

A small beep indicated that enough of the download had finished to begin imaging.

The FLIR was turned on and Jack watched the screen. Nothing was happening.

[Increase elevation two-hundred meters.]

Without questioning, Jack slowly raised the elevation. She watched the thermal screen, which now looked a bit like a 3D map of the mountain. They always had the elevation readings, but the screen looked different for some reason. Continuing their climb, just as they passed the elevation increase of one hundred meters, Jack saw something unexpected.

The fifty-square kilometer search area that they thought was a potential debris field looked like it was a country field covered with blue fireflies. If the overlay and FLIR data was correct, the things the general was looking for were all over the place.

Allen slowly sat up in his seat as he watched the alien landscape move and grow on the monitor. Looking out of the window was no help at this point due to the blackness of the night sky, and even activating his own night vision goggles didn't help. There was no *traditional* heat signature anywhere on the mountain according to his goggles, but the data from Syi indicated differently.

Jack and Allen looked at each other slowly, then back to the computer screen. *How is this possible?* thought Jack. *What the hell is out there?*

Slowing their ascent and leveling off after an increase of two hundred meters, Jack let the Little Bird slide east as she kept the nose pointed toward the search area. Swinging the nose from right to left, she could affect what they saw on the screen inside the cockpit. Some parts of the search area remained black as night on the screen, but other areas showed gradated blue waves emanating up and out of parts of the mountain, indicating an anomaly had been detected in some ravine or crevasse as they had flown their perimeter. Jack assumed once they flew over one of the ravines that the heat signature would increase to a different color on their screen, indicating precisely where to find a meteorite, or whatever it was.

The general was watching intently from his own monitor in his den. The anomaly data had been downloaded to the general's computer already and he was getting a live feed from the FLIR camera on the bird, via satellite, so his overlay was happening with just a few second delay. He imagined that this is what the Northwestern part of Australia looked like the night after the storm. A field of eggs giving off their silent signal, calling, adding to the songlines of the elders; waves of blue that no one could see until now, waiting to be found, waiting to be activated.

As Jack swung the nose east, they were now facing a line that if drawn out in front of them would be running nearly parallel with the southern perimeter; almost due east. She was testing the overlay view of the camera. If this thing was working correctly, they should see a near split down the screen, blue anomaly waves on the left side of the screen, nothing on the right side.

As theorized, she watched the dim blue waves slide to the left side of the screen. It wasn't a hard and fast line of blue she was watching— she knew the meteorites hadn't fallen in a straight line—but having flown this entire area already she had an imaginary line in her head which she was now visualizing on the screen.

She swung the nose south, and as expected, the blue waves disappeared. At first the images from the FLIR camera were distorted due to picking up actual heat signatures from the town of Courmayeur, but Syi quickly adjusted for that. After a brief moment, the false readings were filtered out and the screen returned to black.

Completing three-fourths of a 360-degree sweep, a new color emerged on the screen. A slight greenish glow was emanating from a natural break in the mountain almost right in front of them. Watching the color change, Jack continued their rotation to the 360-degree mark, the starting point, and watched the color fade. She swung the nose back west. As she did, the green glow came back into view. She then tilted the nose of the Little Bird down and was amazed to see another slight change of color; nothing yellow or red yet, which is how she imagined a specimen showing up on their screen, but a slight change in the type of green, almost phosphorescent. They had been hovering right over the top of an anomaly the entire time!

"Syi, analyze color variation," the general said from out of the dark.

[Analyzing.]

—pause—

[Color gradation is statistically significant.]

"Rappel," came the order.

"General, we're on a forty-five-degree slope," Jack said. "Nighttime conditions are extremely dangerous. We have the location marked on GPS and can come back— "

"Rappel!"

Holy shit, thought Allen. *What the hell is down there?*

CHAPTER 26
HOUDINI CAMP
(DAY 1 - LATE NIGHT)

Cora and Subbu had been walking for ten minutes before Subbu broached the topic of leaving Brad again.

"Maybe I should go back to the gypsy camp once we get you back to the cabins. This way I could—"

"Why the hell are you so worried about Brad?" Cora snapped. "He's a big boy."

Afraid that he had just offended Cora somehow, Subbu clasped his hands together in apology. "Oh I'm—"

"Forget it," she said, waving him off. "I'm sorry, Subbu. I didn't mean to snap at you. I'm, I'm just tired, that's all. However, why *are* you so concerned about him? You seem genuinely worried."

"Gypsy magic is not to be taken lightly," he replied. "Many bad things can come of it."

"I don't think he's overly concerned at the moment. And quite frankly, no offense, but I don't buy into the fortune teller thing. Oh, there was a spell woven tonight, I'll give you that. But I would categorize it as *hormonal hypnosis* and nothing more."

Subbu was processing this analogy as Cora looked over at him and gave his hand a squeeze. "You're a good guy. Thank you for walking back with me." At this Subbu could only smile in the dark.

Having come within sight of the first few lights of the town, Cora turned to Subbu and said, "If you want to head back now—

"Hey!" she exclaimed, as a dog bounded out of the grass towards her.

Startled at first, she quickly realized this was someone's pet that had gotten loose.

"Hey boy, what are you doing out here?" she said, gently reaching down to let the dog sniff her hand. After petting the dog for a minute, she ventured to raise him up by his chest. "At least I think you're a... yep, you're a boy. And what a pretty boy you are!" she said, setting him down and rubbing his ears. "Where did you come from?"

Houdini barked in answer and began trotting in the direction they were walking, as if knowing where they were headed.

After a few more minutes of walking, they spotted a tent a short way off the main path. The tent hadn't been there when they'd walked this way earlier in the evening.

"Houdini! Houdini, where are you boy?" came a voice near the tent.

Houdini responded with a yelp-bark and bounded towards the tent.

"He came down to visit us," Cora said, pointing over her shoulder.

"Oh, thanks for finding him!" Ian said. "Bloody hell, but he's a master escape artist." After a brief pause, "I'm Ian," he said, extending his hand.

"A regular Houdini, I guess," nodding. "Cora, and this is Subbu." They all shook hands.

"Yeah," Ian started, scratching his head absently and pointing toward an empty leash staked near the tent. "I'm not sure how he got loose this time. We just got here a couple of hours ago. Stretched our legs after a long drive. Came out of Grenoble, a few hours west. I had just finished setting up camp and was settling in. I started watching something and the next minute I looked he was gone."

"Watching what?" she asked. "It's pretty dark out here."

"I'm not sure really. And… oh yes, quite dark. Anyway, I was just watching the mountain and…"

Turning to look in the direction of the mountain and realizing that the moon was not up yet, Cora quipped, "Did it go anywhere?"

"Did it… uh, no. No, it's still there," he said, smiling. Getting the joke a second later than he wished he had.

"I thought I heard something in that direction," he remarked, pointing towards the peak, "but I couldn't make anything out."

"What did you hear?" asked Subbu.

"I thought I heard a helicopter."

◇ ○ ○ ◇

Prometheus and HAL27 had been chatting all morning. After the attempted hacking had been stopped, they began the process of spinning up the mirror sites. Knowing that this would take a few hours, Prometheus went to sleep and told HAL27 that he would come back online in approximately seven hours.

Feeling refreshed from sleep and rejuvenated by the earlier events, his fingers flew over the keyboard, reconnecting with his online flock.

There was a lot of buzz about the event this evening, he thought. As followers from across the world logged on at their varying times and caught up with the day's conspiracies, more and more activity could be expected. It had been nearly twenty-four hours since the storm broke and some people, the really inquisitive ones, were making connections.

He sat back in his chair and wondered about his latest *field operative,* Houdini. He wanted this guy to work out. He hoped he was on the level, but it was so hard to tell at the moment. *Remember, it could still be a she,* he reminded himself.

He knew that Houdini wasn't online, or at least that he wasn't logged into the BBS, so he'd just have to wait. Although he did send him an offline chat that simply stated *Update?* That he would see as soon as he logged on.

Pushing Houdini to the back of his mind, he went back to watching the cacophony of comments that was his main chat board. Despite TheDonald's insistence on flirting with Catgirl every time she logged on, the conversation was pretty serious tonight. A lot of people had reiterated the main story of the Australian Incident, each trying to prove themselves a more serious contributor by correcting even the slightest story alteration made by someone else.

Someone claimed to have had an uncle that found a partial alien skeleton in Australia after the storm. He flagged that post as needing evidence.

He watched as new users joined the forum, hung around for a few minutes, then either dropped off or attempted to join the conversation, usually with the standard opening of, *Newbie here…*

He was close to moving to another forum when a new username caught his attention. Sai_user had just logged in and was watching the conversation.

That's an odd name, he thought. Usually people were pretty creative with their online names and didn't include the word *user* as part of their username. *Looks like a kid highjacked mom and dad's computer for the evening.*

sKelaWh0R: …gvmnt hacked us!

SpaceMan2001: Newbie here. This site is awesome!

HAL27: IP masking is recommended

Kor82r: anyone have eyes?

bogrider: correlation update?

TheDonald: @catgirl, here kitty, kitty…

sai_user: 89% correlation with Australian Incident, 50-kilometer debris field.

Tr3S8: @SpaceMan2001, welcome!

sKelaWh0R: l0ck n l0ad!!

HAL27: eyes TBD…

Pr0m3th3us sat straight up in his chair and quickly paused the view of his chat window. The chat window would remain the same for everyone else, rapid scrolling and typing in half sentences, but he was now focused on a single sentence. He titled his head to the left and read, *89% correlation with Australian Incident. Wasn't that exactly what Houdini had told him this morning?* He then tilted his head to the right and read, *50-kilometer debris field.*

Was this Houdini again, joining under a different name? Why would he go to the trouble just to repeat himself? The similarity was very striking indeed, but something else bothered him about this sentence. After staring at the screen for what seemed like a full minute, it finally occurred to him. Although it wasn't addressed to @bogrider, it appeared to be in answer to bogrider's query about correlation, and as fast as the messages scrolled down this chat window, you'd have to be extremely fast on the keyboard to get a relatively long response typed out and sent back with only one other user response in between.

Inhaling, then exhaling a slow deep breath he thought, *Hello sai_ user, who exactly are you?*

◯ ◯ ◯

Cora followed Ian's gaze in the direction of Mont Blanc. "A helicopter on the mountain? At this time of night? That's unusual, isn't it?"

"Not standard operating procedure, in my opinion," Ian replied. "At least not without lights. If it was a search and rescue, we'd probably be able to see a spotlight or something. I guess the sound could be coming from a different area and echoing from that direction, but I can usually locate these things."

Cora bent down to rub Houdini's ears again. His ice-blue eyes following her every move. "Why is that? Are you a helicopter hunter or something?"

"I'm an analyst for the British military," he said, hoping she wouldn't inquire further. "I've had a bit of training with these birds. However, I didn't expect to see so ma— I mean, I didn't expect to hear one hovering about on my holiday. Probably just an echo," he finished, trying to cover his slip.

Standing up, to Houdini's disappointment, Cora looked straight at Ian. "Odd that we'd hear an *echo* around the same location as a recent meteor storm, isn't it?"

"Did you see it?" Ian asked, suddenly realizing that Cora was holding something back. "I figured there must be some local sightings, but thought it odd that I couldn't find much in the news this morning."

Tilting her head slightly to telegraph to Ian that she was way ahead of him, she said, "Which implies that you knew about the storm before you got here. Otherwise, why would you be surprised not to find much in the news?"

Warning himself to be more careful with his words around this one, he said, "Did I say I knew about the storm? I just thought—"

"Ian, you said you just drove in from a few hours west of here. Did the storm reach that far? If not, it would be pretty hard to see it from there, especially considering there's a giant mountain in the way." She said this playfully, but with enough emphasis that Ian knew she was locked on target.

"Honestly, I'm just here on holiday," holding his hands up in innocence. "I planned to do a bit of hiking with the pooch, but was reading a website this morning that mentioned the meteor storm, so I thought I'd look around a bit."

"If there wasn't much on the news about it, what website was talking about it?"

At this point, realizing that he wasn't going to talk his way off the subject, Ian motioned for them to join him around the campfire. Camping chairs were setup and the fire was stoked. Ian broke out the British ESB and filled three nonmatching plastic cups. Cora sat on the ground next to the fire so Houdini could put his head in her lap, which he did happily, his blue eyes reflecting warm firelight toward his new friend.

Ian told them about a website he'd stumbled upon—omitting where he found it or why he was looking for it—and a story about a supposed *Australian Incident* that was similar to the meteor storm from last night.

"How would someone know that a storm from the forties was nearly the same as this storm?" Cora asked. "And who would even track that?"

"Granted, we have meteor storms all the time," Ian began, "but I read that these storms had specific anomalies associated with them."

"Anomalies?" Subbu was cautiously engaging.

"Most meteor storms are simply small meteorites entering the earth's atmosphere; there is no *storm* really. They're very hard to see. Essentially invisible until they enter our atmosphere, at which point they ignite due to friction. The pieces usually just burn up. This storm was no different in that respect, but the volume of material that made it through the atmosphere was extremely large, creating a huge debris field; this pattern mimics something closer to an asteroid entry; a true storm; violent, lots of lightning."

Yes, Cora and Subbu understood as they glanced at each other silently.

"Only we didn't get bloody annihilated," Ian continued looking at the two of them for understanding. "You know, giant asteroid, dinosaur killer, that sort of thing. Anyway, strange magnetic readings seem to associate the two storms, along with…" he hesitated, "…along with some possibly dangerous debris."

Houdini jumped as he felt Cora's legs tighten with tension. He looked around from his sleepy position, growling into the darkness at whatever may be threatening his new friend.

Cora put her hand softly on his head and he dropped his muzzle back into her lap. "What do you mean, 'dangerous debris'?" she said slowly.

Hearing genuine concern in her voice, it was Ian's turn to look directly at her and ask, "You didn't find any debris, did you?"

"Why?"

"I just need to know if—"

"What's wrong with it?"

"Cora, this may be serious. I don't know if there's anything wrong with it, but if you found something—"

"Tell me what's wrong."

Reading her face in the dark wasn't all that hard. Ian watched a series of emotions wash over it: surprise turned to concern, which turned to some form of understanding, which turned to dread. She was clearly hiding something. Houdini had sensed the change as well and was watching her intently.

Ian slowly got up and walked to the small tent. Retrieving his laptop out of a backpack inside the tent door, he sat back down, flipped it open, but didn't bother searching for a signal. He quickly navigated to his photos and double-clicked on one titled *Abgirl*. Cora and Subbu were standing behind him already.

"I can't confirm the source of this photo, but I think it's legitimate.

This is supposedly an aboriginal girl after she found something from the 1940's storm that hit Australia."

Cora barely noticed as Subbu made some type of religious sign warding off the evil that may somehow still be associated with the photo. "What's wrong with her eyes?" she asked.

Just at that moment, as if the wind shifted to funnel all the sound off the mountain, Houdini started to growl in the direction of Mont Blanc. All three of them turned in that direction. For a brief second, they thought they heard it, the sound of a helicopter in the distance.

CHAPTER 27
FORTUNES
(DAY 1 – LATE NIGHT)

Brad followed the little girl without question. They walked past the fire which had served as the backdrop for the musicians. It was still burning, but not as fiercely as before. It was probably the wine, but he thought the fire had almost taken on a life of its own when Lilith was playing. *Where was she anyway?* He'd like to have a nice long chat with her.

They had entered a maze of passages, tents and small outbuildings that seemed to go on forever, stuffed full of baskets, pottery, small instruments, jars of stuff. Although he could hear the low murmur of conversation seemingly around every corner, he never got a good look at any one person. Inside the tent passages the only lights were kerosene lanterns and candles precariously hanging from tent poles or connected to stakes stuck in the ground.

This place can't be this big, he thought. But after taking several turns right, left, then right again, he began to question if it was just the wine confusing him, or if the little girl was misleading him.

A heavy smell of burning incense, sage and other spices assaulted his senses, one moment jolting his senses awake, the next moment lulling his eyes shut. He rubbed at his eyes as he sneezed hard. He normally wasn't affected by allergies, but something was bothering him tonight.

Finally, the little girl came to a wooden platform that was three steps off the ground. He couldn't tell if this was part of a wagon or a separate platform, but it was richly decorated, with sheer cloth hanging down in folds on three sides. An old, but ornate rug was spread across the platform. Satin sitting pillows with tassels of red, blue and gold littered the rug. Candles attached to the back and side walls miraculously did not ignite the folds of sheer cloth. The 'front' wall was more of a stage curtain that parted in the middle and was pulled back on both sides to give visage to whatever may happen in the center.

"Puri daj," the little girl said with a bow, as she raised Brad's hand slightly.

The grandmother was the same old woman who had directed the girl to serve them earlier in the night. Draped in a satin robe, she sat cross-legged on a large cushion. Her ankles glittered with matching intensity to her wrists and fingers, all decorated with gold rings and bracelets. Her wrinkled face was thin but strong, accented by a long thin pipe that she held to her lips. A cloud of pungent smoke hung around her like a protective cloud and obscured her eyes to him.

"Hello and thank you for—" Brad started.

"No, no," the girl chastised. "No speaking, just listen and do."

Brad looked at the girl, eyebrows failing to raise heavy lids, scratched his head absently and smiled, nodding his head in agreeance.

"Besh," the old woman said, pointing with the mouth-end of her pipe to the pillows on her right.

"Sit," the girl translated, pointing.

Brad sat where directed, sliding on the satin pillows, which sent his head further into the cloud of smoke that surrounded her. With a sudden inhale, he felt his head wobble and his stomach flip. Closing his eyes and swallowing hard, he felt a sweat break across his forehead.

Tilting her head to her left, the old woman looked at Brad. Sitting the pipe in her lap, she grabbed his left hand with surprising strength and gave two quick tugs, now holding him with both of her hands, as if to test that his arm would stay attached; Brad could feel the characteristic shake of an ancient hand. After a long few seconds, she bent forward, holding his hand to her nose, and inhaled deeply. Wrinkling her nose, she blew air out through her nostrils as if to vacate an unpleasant smell. Keeping an iron grip, she straightened up, pulling Brad's hand with her. This in turn caused Brad's face to come closer and in level with hers. At this distance, he was shocked to see eyes that were nearly clouded over with cataracts. In fact, he wasn't sure if the old woman could see at all. Mucus seemed to fill her right eyeball; cloudy, swimming, somehow… hardening. Her left eye, slightly engorged, looked as if the mucus was calcifying; heavy with weight, he thought it might plop out of her head and fall to the ground if she titled her head forward. As the old woman twisted his palm towards her face, Brad saw her eyes transform. The right eye now started to pulse slightly and engorge, matching the left. The calcifying mucus, like freezing water in a bottle, threatening to explode the thin eye walls.

Holding Brad's hand now by the slightest touch, she rested her stubbly chin on his inner fingertips. Transfixed, he could not pull his hand away. Slowly, parting lips glued together with ancient saliva, sliding past gums decaying into bone marrow butter, an old tongue peeked out of her decrepit mouth. The tongue, mottled with spots resembling those in a petri dish, quivered slightly in the fresh air. Brad thought he heard the slightest sound of air rush out of the old lungs, escaping forever, but was unsure now if he was hallucinating. The tongue appeared to be sensing the air, sniffing, tasting, quivering. Bending and twisting, the tongue finally found the inside of his fingers. Snaking down between the fold of his pinky and ring finger, he could feel tiny bumps, like a cat's tongue, scraping his skin. Slowly moving between fingers, Brad imagined a slight stinging sensation, minute shocks from an ancient electric eel.

Finished with the folds, the tongue snaked out even longer and traced the lines of his palm: head line, heart line…fate. The life line, easily seen when the thumb is swiveled in toward the palm, runs from the middle of the hand, around the fat of the palm toward the inner wrist. Having found the life line, the tongue quivered as if in ecstasy. Like Pavlov's dogs, the life line triggered an effect in the ancient mouth; saliva filled the insides of her cheeks. Brad thought he felt a shiver run through the old woman's body, but couldn't tear his eyes away from the scene in front of him. As if following tiny pathways, he saw rivulets of saliva emerge; running up, out of the mouth, over bumps, and slowly run down the snaking tongue, glistening in the dark. Like a movie running in slow motion, he watched the acid saliva run along the tongue. Slowly, after clinging to the tip for several seconds, the first acid drop fell onto his palm, settling into the crease of his life line, greasing the way for the mottled tip, and running toward his wrist.

Her face stretched into a grimace of ecstasy; the old woman shuddered each time the tongue snaked forward. Her hands trembled. Her eyes, now grossly engorged and bulging, did not see; her mouth, gaped open, made no sound; her tongue, unnaturally forced out ever farther, stretched into a rope of sinew. Threatening to tear the ligaments away from the back of her throat, the old woman tortured her tongue out of her throat as if seeking the last morsel of food that would save her life. Suddenly, as if she had just touched the end of a battery, her tongue snapped back like a breaking rubber band. Her head shot back, hitting a post behind her. Brad pulled his hand away. The spell was broken. Sitting in silence, the woman's head lolled forward. Brad saw drops of blood fall into her lap.

After several minutes, the old woman turned her head to the side and spat out a mouthful of blood. Rubbing her hands together in the incense smoke that curled up in front of her, she appeared to "wash" herself of the incident. Her eyes were crystal clear.

She picked up her pipe, which to Brad's amazement was still glowing brightly, and took a long slow drag. She looked at him through the smoke as if trying to decide what to do with him. Despite his heavy eyelids, Brad was sensing an unease that emanated from the old woman. She seemed to be looking intently at his eyes, but through the smoke he couldn't be sure. He wiped his itchy eyes with the fingers of his left hand. The old woman followed his movements and watched as he set his hand back down on a pillow. She quickly looked back to his face and squinted hard at him. Inhaling a sharp breath, her eyes widened. "Streyino," she muttered as she looked down at her own hands, then back at his face.

Confused by this interaction, he looked over at the little girl. She had scooted a few steps away from him and looked as if she were about to turn and run. The old woman grunted at the girl, apparently to stay where she was. The girl, seeing that Brad was needing translation again, simply said, "How strange."

Before Brad could ask what she meant, the old woman held her left hand up to the back wall and muttered something. To his surprise, an arm moved out of the shadows of folds and handed the old woman a deck of cards. Lilith was standing there, her satin gown concealed in the folds of the tent.

The old woman handed the deck of cards to Brad and made a motion that he understood. He was to shuffle them. She watched him carefully and after several shuffles she waved her hand, indicating he should stop. Slowly she began flipping the cards over and arranging them on the space in front of her. After each card, she would slowly draw on her pipe and consider what she saw.

Brad looked briefly up were Lilith had stood, but she was now gone. He looked over to where the girl stood as the old woman flipped another card, a sharp intake of breath as she slapped her hands over the cards. "Amriya," she whispered. "Devlesa Amriya!" She was now pointing a long bony finger at Brad.

He heard a commotion behind him, but before he understood what was happening, strong hands grabbed his arms and lifted him from the platform. Two men from the camp were dragging him out of the tent. Brad looked around in confusion, spying the little girl who was now sitting next to her grandmother. Still seeing the need for translation, the girl simply said, "Oh God, a curse."

As Brad was thrown from the camp, the only instructions he was given came from the edge of a knife. He saw the last of the flames glint off a knife held by one of the gypsy men. It waved in sharp jabs away from the camp and towards the town of Courmayeur. He was being told to leave quickly.

CHAPTER 28
DEBRIS SEARCH
(DAY 1 – LATE NIGHT)

Allen finished strapping his gear into the harness. Jack held the Little Bird steady as Allen began lowering his gear to the rocky slope below. Feeling the gear touch down, he simply let the rope fall, as there was no way of releasing it from where he was. He attached a separate rappelling rope to the hook in the floor, then pressed the transmit button on his remote radio. "Test, test," he said, gravely looking at Jack.

"Copy," Jack said, giving him the thumbs up sign, even though she was looking right at him over her shoulder.

"I have eyes on from here," Jack said. "I'll guide you to the location."

Allen simply nodded at her, not saying a word. The time for action was now. Despite what may be down there, this is what he trained for.

Holding the rope that wound through his harness, Allen pushed himself backwards out of the chopper and made a rapid descent to the slope below. Misjudging the distance to the slope of the mountain due to the darkness that engulfed it, Allen hit the ground harder than he intended to. A rock slid out from beneath his foot and would have put him on his ass if the rope tension hadn't held him in place, just inches above the ground.

Unthreading the rope, he tossed the end of it away from him, flipped on his helmet light, and looked around for his supply pack. Seeing that it had slid several feet down the slope already, he scrabbled down to it and quickly inspected it.

"Bird, this is Hunter. I'm on the ground and secure."

"Roger that Hunter, let's take a look." At that, Jack slowly climbed and pointed the nose back towards the ground. It took a few minutes, but soon enough she was looking at a faint, phosphorescent green glow in her monitor. Despite the fact that Syi had just filtered out the false signals of heat coming from the town, Allen was close enough, and with his headlamp on, he showed up as a faint, floating light on the screen as well. He was a different color, considering the heat image technology was being used for a different purpose, but he showed up nonetheless. A ghost of the mountain.

"Hunter, possible target is fifty-seven meters south-southeast of you. Over."

"Roger Bird, fifty-seven meters," Allen said. He looked at the compass on his wrist, looked side to side to orient himself, and then slowly picked his way down the slope. His flashlight feebly lit the ground in front of him as it mostly streamed away into the dark night. The mountain slope dropped away from him and frequently disappeared.

Hope the space-goblin is deaf, he thought, considering his descent down the slope was far from silent. He was basically holding his pack to a controlled slide down the rocks in front of him, and the night air amplified every movement.

After ten meters, he came to a crevasse that, although not as deep as a ravine, would prove difficult to cross. Seeing that the crevasse would send him southeast too soon, and not wanting to haul his supply pack back up the slope, he decided to cross here. The other side of the crevasse was two meters away, but a meter higher than his current elevation. Without a pack it would be an easy jump, but the extra sixty pounds of gear, plus the awkward size of the pack, limited the spring in his step.

Lifting the pack to his chest, he tested the weight as if to bench press it. He bent his knees into a full squat, then extending them quickly, pushed with his arms at the same time, pressing the pack up and away from him. The pack easily landed across the crevasse on the top of the ridge.

Satisfied with his effort, he looked down at his footing, found a solid spot on the mountain and did a long-jump style step over the crevasse, grabbing the elevated top with his hands. As he started to climb up the small ridge, he heard rocks sliding. He had hit his bag on his landing, and it was now sliding down the embankment!

He scrambled up the side as his bag slid faster away. Now that the light from his head lamp flashed down the slope, he saw that the slope was not continuous here. His bag was sliding toward a sharp drop off.

More and more rock came loose, lubricating the bag as it slid. Just as Allen made it to his feet, he saw his supply bag tip over the edge of the cliff and into the darkness. Taking a step closer, his headlamp flashed over something moving down the path the bag had taken. The rappelling rope was still connected!

With a quick extension of his body, Allen dove forward, letting his head guide him towards the cliff. Arms outstretched, he grabbed the tail of the rope. Rolling off his stomach onto his back, he tightened his grip just as the falling bag pulled all the slack out of the rope. The momentum of the bag pulled him towards the cliff edge. His boots slid easier than the bag did, and allowed his body to slide toward the edge with increasing speed. Not until his boots hit a hard spot on the slope did his body stop its forward momentum and the bag swung to a stop.

Holding very still, lest another rock break away and send him over the edge, he slowly began to pull the supply pack back up from over the cliff. When he finally pulled the pack up and moved himself back up the slope to safety, he lay his head back on the rock and closed his eyes briefly. *There's an omen if I ever saw one!* This mission had *bad news* written all over it.

Watching the commotion of light on his screen, Jack called down to Allen, "Hunter, this is Bird. What is your status?"

"Status is OK, Bird. What is my distance?"

"Forty-five meters southeast is primary target."

He continued due south for several meters, which took him past the edge of the cliff. The slope started to level out somewhat here, which made the walking easier. The large granite pillar that Jack had initially labeled as an *out-wall* was to his back by several hundred meters.

"Hunter, you're within ten meters of target."

Looking around with both his flashlight and headlamp was almost useless. Every rock looked the same.

"Bird, I could use some light down here. Over."

"Roger that."

Jack looked away from the monitor, knowing that the undercarriage floodlight would distort the image. She flipped the switch and flooded the immediate area with light. Allen blinked his eyes to adjust for the change, then looked around again. *Rock, only more of it.* He continued south slowly, and in just a few meters he saw something.

"Bird, I have what looks like recently broken rock. No target, however."

"Hunter, I'm killing lights, stand by."

As Jack killed the floodlight, her monitor adjusted and showed a very faint glow right where Allen was standing. "Hunter, image says you're right on top of target." The floodlight came back on.

"Bird, I'm seeing pulverized rock. Shards. Nothing matching our target. Is it possible it smashed apart on the out-wall but still left a signature here?"

[Residual readings from debris is possible,] Syi added.

Fucking cyborg. Forgetting they were being listened to, Allen continued walking.

"Bird, I'm not… hey, what is that?"

"What do you have, Hunter?"

Allen kicked the toe of his boot through some ashes.

"A campfire."

"Really? How old?"

"Pretty fresh, I'd say. Hasn't been rained on. Ashes haven't even blown away. Let me look around some more. Scan the light, Bird."

With a deft touch, Jack directed the beam of light to Allen's left as a starting point and slowly scanned right, towards the mountain. Allen walked southwest, as it was a natural extension of the camping area. It was craggier, but he felt he was walking in the right direction.

"Bird, light up that outcrop in front of me. Over."

"I see it."

Allen walked towards a low overhang with a good-sized crevasse below it. A shallow cave, almost.

"Bird, there's more shards here."

Slowly he came to the overhang. Shining his flashlight into the crevasse, he saw telltale signs of disturbance. On his hands and knees now, he could make out some shapes in the dust: partial boot print, scuffing, another boot print.

"What do you have, Hunter?"

"I think someone was lying under this outcrop," Allen said. "I have two different boot prints. Lots of dust disturbance. Possible scuff marks on the back wall."

He thought for a moment. "Bird, I think we had campers here during the storm. I think they sheltered in place under this overhang as the debris rained down."

"Track their path!" ordered the general.

CHAPTER 29

FEVER

(DAY 1 – LATE NIGHT INTO DAY 2)

"Brad!" Cora said, looking from the mountain over to Subbu. "We have to find him."

"Brad?" Ian started. "Who's—"

"Ian, I'm sorry, we have to go. We have to find our friend. That's all I can say."

"OK, I understand. Look, I'm not—" but before he could say anything more, Cora had grabbed Subbu's hand and was leading him back toward the main trail that led to the gypsy camp.

What are those blokes hiding? he wondered.

Cora led Subbu at a brisk pace just short of a jog. She wasn't sure what they needed to do, but she felt it would be better if they were all together. She didn't know if the photo Ian had shown them was real or not, but she believed that he believed the meteor debris was potentially dangerous. Turning towards the gypsy camp, Cora felt a quick tug at her arm.

"Wait," Subbu said. "How do we know that he's not back at the cabin already?"

Looking at him like he had asked her a nonsensical question, she paused for a moment, then looked in the direction of the gypsy camp, then back toward town.

"It's late," he said.

Looking at her watch, she realized they had left Brad almost two hours ago. *Oh no... I didn't realize it had been so long,* she thought.

Seeing the indecision cross her face, Subbu said, "Let's try the cabin first. I saw several people walk by while we were speaking with Ian."

"OK. I hope you're right," was all she could manage.

As they turned towards town, Subbu cautiously asked, "What do you think of the picture he showed us?"

The picture had been disturbing, but she didn't believe in things she couldn't explain, certainly not spirits or possessions. But she wasn't sure what to think about the photo. *It could have been photoshopped, I guess.*

"I don't know Subbu, I guess... let's just..."

"We will find Brad first," he said quickly, noting her struggle to form an opinion and not wanting her to feel badly because of a question he'd asked. "We will find him asleep from strong gypsy wine. Then you speak with him in the morning."

"Yes... yes, let's do that," she said, frustrated at her own indecision.

Fifteen minutes later they were approaching their cabins. Brad's cabin was dark, but they tried the door anyway. It was unlocked, and as they opened it, they heard the rustle of bedsheets as Brad turned in his bed and coughed in his sleep.

"Oh, thank God," Cora breathed. "Subbu, you were right. Let's get some sleep and get an early start tomorrow. I know we had you hired for two more days, but if it's possible, I think I want to head back to Geneva in the morning. I'll talk to Brad about it first thing."

"Yes, that's fine, I understand. I'll see you in the morning."

"Is 6:00 am OK with you?" she asked.

"Yes, no problem."

She closed her door, locked it, and dropped onto her bed. She intended to lay there for a moment before taking off her hiking clothes, but was asleep within minutes.

◇ ◇ ◇

Bobby Hadley was peeing on a dead dog that lay right in front of her. The swarming flies were now biting her ankles. She wanted to cry out, to scream the flies away, but he would hear her. Where could she run then? The little stream that ran through the culvert ended in a larger creek that she could swim if she had to, but it's not like Bobby couldn't swim after her. She buried her face in her knees and stuck her fingers in her ears to keep the flies out. She would bear the biting as long she could.

Finishing with a dribble and a belch, Bobby zipped his fly, hocked a large load of phlegm from the back of his throat, and shot the wad at the dog's head. "Fuck" he said as it plopped in the water, missing by almost a foot.

Kicking rocks into the creek as he turned to walk around the car,

Cora heard him mutter, "Alright, let's find that little bitch."

A moment later, the truck started. Bobby slammed it into gear and sent a rain of rocks showering across the road and down into the creek bed. The falling rocks turned into flaming shards of meteors, pelting her head. Her clothes caught fire. She ran through a forest trying to escape the tumult. Her clothes were burning. She began to rip them off, for some reason forgetting to stop, drop and roll. Suddenly she was naked, standing in the middle of a circle of people. They were not putting mountain flowers in her hands. They were pointing at the scabs of fly bites that covered her. The beautiful gypsy girl with her flawless skin was standing by a fire while Brad poured wine for them. She could not cover her nakedness. Everyone was pointing.

Cora turned in her sleep, trying to escape the humiliation, and banged her hand on the side of her cabin. The jolt to her hand was enough to bring her awareness that she was lying on her bed, and that she had been dreaming. She heard Brad cough in the room next to her.

⬡ ⬡ ⬡

Brad was choking on smoke. He was trying to find his way out of the labyrinth of tents, but they were filled with smoke also. The old woman had puffed a continuous cloud that shrouded his vision and hid the way out. He could see Lilith's figure in the dark passages before him, but she would disappear before he could reach her. He wasn't sure if she would lead him further in or out of the tent maze, but he followed her anyway. He coughed harder, trying to hack something out of his throat. The smoke was filling his nose. It was expanding, seeking out his lungs. The smoke was crawling into his mouth. He could feel the tickling sensation of microscopic smoke bugs as they crawled down the back of his throat. They were burrowing into the insides of his cheeks.

They were trying to nest.

They were burrowing.

Brad awoke with a scream. He smacked the imaginary bugs on his face for a brief second until he realized where he was. He felt for the water bottle that he had left on the nightstand. There was only half a mouthful left. He wanted more, but felt too weak to go to the sink. He fell back asleep with an itch in his throat.

Cora woke sluggishly a little past 5:00 am the next morning. Despite the exhaustion she felt, an uneasiness would not let her sleep any longer. Her mind was muddled with disappearing dream images. She tried to remember, but as soon as she thought she had captured an image, it slipped away. Whatever she had been dreaming left a general feeling of dread in her.

She quickly showered. The one cup coffee maker in her small room left a hot cup of mediocre coffee for her. She ate a granola bar while shoving her clothes into her bag. She'd repack when they got to Geneva.

Flipping on her earpiece, she said, "Ali, please check for flights departing Geneva today."

[Cora, please specify desired departure times.]

"Anything after 12:00 noon local time." *That should give us plenty of time to get packed and make it to Geneva,* she thought.

Cora walked onto the elevated, covered walk in front of her cabin. The chill of the night air still hung in the morning mist and had a slight odor of moss and smoke, causing a mix of images to flash through her mind.

She stretched to work some of the soreness out of her legs and arms. *Was it always this foggy?* she wondered. She couldn't even see across the gravel road that she knew separated her cabin from the end of town. She walked over and knocked gently on Brad's cabin door. "Early bird gets the worm."

Brad had worms in his eyes. He twisted on the single mattress until he had rolled the sheet around him in a knot. He was dreaming that his legs were wrapped in a cocoon. His eyes itched. His throat was dry, and his nostrils felt like they were clogged with dust. A dull headache had started behind his left eye and his pillow was soaked with sweat. He dreamed that the old woman had cursed him with the smoke she blew out of her ancient lungs. *Had she licked my hand?* Maybe the worms were on her tongue; having crawled up out of her smoked-filled body; maybe they had burrowed into his hand. Maybe they had crawled up his arms while he was sleeping, looking for cleaner lungs, a better place to lay their eggs.

Eggs? I found something.

Cora knocked again, louder this time.

Why are the worms making noise? What are they doing? His legs were still trapped in a cocoon. The worms were wrapping him in a tight cocoon of blue filament, electric blue filament. It was coming out the ends of their noses. Giant worms with mandibles that could cut wire cables. Every time they spun a filament around him, they cut the end with their mandibles, making a loud *chunking* sound.

Chunk... Chunk...

More filament, electric blue. More worms.

Chunk! Chunk! Chunk!

"Brad!" *Chunk!*

"Brad! Wake up!"

Brad flung himself from his bed, twisting on the floor. Cora, having entered his room and switched the light on, was shocked at what she saw. His eyes were stuck together like a child's glued with sleep. His hair was matted with sweat. His hands reached up to pull his eyelids apart. Stringy sleep-glue slowly released his eyelids. His eyes were wild. They rolled in his eye sockets, searching for something to focus on. His mouth gaped open, gasping for air. His fingers groped at his eyelids, trying to determine if his eyes were still in place. He slowly focused towards the overhead light, the only light he could see in a fog of gray. He slowly wiped his eyes with both hands, as if trying to reset his vision. His head tilted slightly as something came into focus. His eyes widened as his lips stretched around his gaping mouth into a grimace of horror. A small stream of urine spilled onto the wood floor as Brad screamed.

He saw small worms floating in his vision.

CHAPTER 30
DEBRIS TRAIL
(DAY 2 - EARLY MORNING)

Jack Garvey awoke at 0500 stiff from the mountain fog. This wasn't the first time she had slept in the cockpit of a helicopter—or in a strange place—but her joints complained about it more now. After the late-night search, and considering their mission had changed somewhat, she had flown west of Mont Blanc, back over the French border, and set the Little Bird down in a remote field inside a national park. This was not SOP, but they were improvising somewhat now. Allen was to camp on the side of the slope, then first thing in the morning, follow the most likely hiking path off the slope. They were assuming their campers would have taken a similar path. Jack would rendezvous with the refueling base, then fly back to where she'd left Allen the night before and pick up his trail. If the search led them into a town, they'd have to pick up a vehicle somewhere, but that would come later.

So there really is something out here, Jack reflected as she ate a cold breakfast. *All over the fucking place, if that blue-wave map is correct.* She hoped the camper trail was a dead end; *that could get messy if there are too many people involved. Although, this is a damn big mountain*, she thought. *Plenty of places for someone to have an accident.*

An hour later Allen was making his way down the slope. His progress was better than it had been the previous night. The dim light of morning was shrouded in fog, but at least it wasn't pitch black. Also, the slope was leveling off, which made the hike easier. He hadn't seen much in the way of signs, but he couldn't image someone taking a different route, assuming they were done with their hike, that is. If their campers had a week of climbing planned when the meteor storm hit, there's no telling where they would have gone; maybe not even this direction, but that was the risk they had to take.

He had heard the Alps were an incredible sight, but this morning it could have been a scene out of a horror movie. The image from some old Stephen King movie popped into his head, something about alien bugs coming out of the fog. He couldn't remember the name, but was pretty sure there was a mutant space monkey in it, and a pterodactyl, maybe.

He was coming off the slope proper when he heard his radio crackle, "Hunter, this is Bird, over."

"Roger Bird, this is Hunter. Over."

"What's your location?"

"Approximately two klicks south-southeast of camp site."

"Roger that. Heading your way," Jack said.

Allen heard the chopper long before he could see it. Besides being attuned to the sound of the rotors, he could feel the thumping vibration through the fog. Either that or it was pterodactyl wings.

"Hunter, verify location."

"Bird, you sound like you're right over me. No visual. I repeat, no visual."

"Roger that, Hunter. I'm going back to the map, stand by."

Jack flipped on the monitor, unsure if she'd get the same reading as the night before. *Damn fog may screw with the camera.*

She looked at the monitor in disappointment. *This doesn't look good,* she thought. *Nothing but gray.*

She let the Little Bird slide south, swinging the nose left to right, looking for a signal. She continued like this for several minutes, the slope leveling as she went. Suddenly, Jack saw something on the monitor.

"Hunter. Are you tracking with me? Over."

"You're a little ahead of me, Bird. Maybe thirty meters. I have visual on you now."

"OK, walk directly in front of me twenty meters and tell me what you see."

"Roger that," Allen said. He increased his pace now. Since the slope was leveling out, Jack was able to bring the helicopter closer to ground, which significantly thinned the fog.

Even though Allen's view was improving due to the down draft of the rotors, Jack's was not. She was flying blind in a cloud.

"What do you see, Bird?"

"Not much. Camera doesn't like the fog in this configuration. There may be something at twenty meters, however."

"OK Bird, I'm approximately twenty meters in front of you. I'm on a large flat rock."

"I think there's something down there, Hunter. How big is the rock?"

"You can land if you come down slow."

"OK, you're my eyes."

Allen guided Jack until the Little Bird touched down on the large flat rock that announced the end of the mountain slope. As the rotors slowed, Jack jumped out of the cockpit and walked to the southwest side of the platform.

"It may just be the fog fucking with my camera, but I thought I was seeing a bluish gray coming from this area," Jack said as she pointed off the side of the platform. The area that Jack pointed to quickly became obscured by fog as the rotors slowed.

"I've seen nothing but shards. Not even sure they're meteor bits really, but… whatever," Allen said.

Jumping down a few feet off the rock platform, Allen landed approximately where Cora had scrambled down the day before, right after she watched Brad roll off the same platform.

Kicking rock debris with the toe of his boot, Allen descended slowly along the side of the platform. A moment later, he bent down to look at something. His eyes were becoming accustomed to what the native rocks looked like. Occasionally he would spy something that appeared darker or *fresher* in some way, but nothing close to what the general had shown them.

"Hold on," he said suddenly. "What is this?"

A few feet away, he saw it. It looked like a sliver of avocado that had been petrified. He could see a smooth side facing him with a very distinct, concave piece cut out of it.

"Don't touch it!" Jack said through her protective mask.

Before she had descended the rock platform, Jack had grabbed her breathing mask and gloves. She also had the bio-box in hand.

"Oh shit!" Allen said, realizing he hadn't put his mask on. He scrambled back a few feet.

"Don't worry, I don't think you were close enough to do any harm. But go back and get your mask."

As Allen climbed quickly back up onto the rock platform, Jack approached the specimen slowly. Her handheld Geiger counter ticked and clicked through a series of sounds.

Jack reached out with long plastic tongs and rolled the fragment onto what looked like its outer shell. The avocado slice was nearly intact. Some of the outer rock had broken off one end, but this was clearly something that didn't belong on this mountain.

"Retrieve," said the general. Jack jumped slightly, not realizing the general was watching the video feed from her helmet.

Jack grabbed the fragment with the tongs and placed it on a small shelf inside the bio-box. She would bag it later.

"Are there other fragments?" the general asked.

Scanning the ground closely where the fragment had been found, Jack locked onto an oddly smooth shape. It looked like it had been part of a convex shape, similar to what the general had shown them yesterday, but it was only a few millimeters thick and not very large. Jack picked this up with the tongs and turned it over in the view of the camera. It looked like a petrified piece of broken eggshell.

"Find those campers!" came the order through his headset. "We have a potential infection!"

CHAPTER 31
PROJECT DEATH ROCK
(DAY 2 - LATE MORNING)

General William David Keller sat back in his chair as he closed the comm link with Jack. His face was sullen, his eyes, unfocused, did not see the richly decorated den; partial images, figments, ghosts floated through his mind, which registered as sight. The Australian trip and subsequent death of his son had drained him of energy, drained him of life; had it not been for his wife, and the military attitude that had shaped him as a young man, he may not have survived that period of his life. It took him a long time to bury those ghosts, but they had never been gone completely. The ghosts of Australia, the Rainbow Serpent and a slowly dying son had just reemerged, and were as voracious as ever. They were syphoning off his energy as he sat in his own den.

An infection? What type of infection? the general thought to himself.

"What could I have done differently, Davey?" the general asked out loud without realizing it.

[General, please confirm context of question.]

The doctors did all they could, but the infection, it happened so fast. Your white blood-cell count was through the roof, but they couldn't identify the type of infection. X-rays showed nothing. "The MRI's however, those did show something, didn't they?"

—pause—

"Nondescript parasitic meningitis was the diagnosis. Swelling of the brain due to an unknown parasite. But who knows, really? It was just a name they used because they didn't have the answer. If they just had more information. We were the first, weren't we?"

[General, I don't—]

Sorry Davey, but it's a family trait. First in a long line of explorers. What could I have done differently?

"We could have tested more, couldn't we have?" *Run more experiments; we would have eventually found a cure…* "Yes, that's it, more experiments."

[General, please confirm directive.]

"Davey, we need to find a test subject. If we had a test subject, we could find a cure." *If we have a test subject, I can find a cure. The technology is better now. I can save you.*

[General, please confirm directive.]

The science is better now. The machines are better. I have more time. I have Syi. "Syi will help me."

[Yes general, I am here to assist you.]

"But this must remain top secret. My eyes only." *People wouldn't understand. Not until we find a cure, anyway.*

[Top secret designation is confirmed. What is the project name?]

We'll solve the death rock infection once and for all, won't we? "Yes, we'll solve it once and for all."

[General—]

"But what about the medical facilities?" *Where can we experiment? We need a private —*

[Status of bunker medical facility is operational. Maximum capacity is two.]

"What? The bunker…?" *Of course.*

"Syi, what is the status of the bunker medical facility?"

[General, the medical facility in the bunker was built during the construction of the house and is fully operational. All systems passed last month's maintenance test.]

"Excellent Syi, thank you."

[General, what is the nature of the experiment?]

"The death rock, of course."

—pause—

[Project Death Rock initiated.]

CHAPTER 32

T1

(DAY 2 - EARLY MORNING)

Ian awoke to Houdini whining at the tent door. *What time is it?* he thought, looking at his watch. *Bloody hell, 4:43.* He looked at Houdini with his eyes barely open. "Woof," he mumbled.

"Woof! Woof!" Houdini replied as he started to whine and dance slightly.

"Hold on! Hold on." Unzipping the tent door and grabbing the leash that lay outside, Ian clipped the end onto Houdini's collar and let him squirm through the opening. This way he could come back in when he was finished, and Ian could go back to sleep.

After what seemed like only a few minutes, Ian bolted awake.

"What was that?" he said to the tent. Looking around in the gloom, he imagined he had heard something. "That's OK boy, just go back to sleep," he said patting an empty place next to him.

"Hey, Houdini. Come here boy," he said, dangling his fingers out of the tent opening.

Not feeling the furry pup come up to lick his fingers, Ian sat up and looked around, blinking his eyes in the gloom of the tent. Focusing on his watch again, he saw it was now 5:10. Sticking his head out of the tent flap, he saw the leash connected to the tent stake, but Houdini was not on the other end of it.

"Bollocks! Where's that damn dog off to this time?"

Quickly getting dressed, he stepped out of the tent into a blanket of dense fog. *Blimey, it's pea soup out here!* he thought.

He called for Houdini, but heard nothing in return. He walked out from the tent and thought he could make out where the dog had been rummaging through the weeds around the tent. The dew was disturbed on some plants. He followed the tracks for a few yards until he saw that they went towards town. *Damn. Oh well, I guess it's an early breakfast.*

Grabbing his wallet and keys, he jumped into his jeep and drove slowly towards town, calling for Houdini as he went.

After several minutes he was on a narrow gravel path that was leading into town. A few ghost buildings dotted the landscape to his right—the fog still being thick here—and small cabins lined the path to his left. Seeing the faint lines of the buildings become sharper, he saw a commotion ahead. That looked like Houdini up by the cabins!

Driving up quickly, with his arm out the window, he called to Houdini. The dog, standing in an open doorway, turned and responded with a quick yelp-bark, then immediately turned back to the cabin.

"Hey, what are you doing in there?" Ian asked as he put the jeep in park. Houdini started to enter the cabin, barked twice, then backed out the door, half-growling, half-whining.

"Hey, what's going—" Stopping in his tracks just outside the door, Ian saw Cora's face as she turned to see who had driven up. A look of disbelief and fear covered her. Ian could see Subbu bending over the bed, trying to hold someone down.

"Brad's sick," she whispered, barely holding back tears.

"What happened?"

"I don't know. I found him like this, this morning."

Holding Brad's arms, Subbu turned from the bed and looked at Cora. "Quick, we must get him to a hospital."

"Is there one close?" she asked.

"Closest one is in Chamonix. France. Other side of the mountain."

"Other side of the mountain? How long will that take?"

"Don't worry," said Subbu. "It's straight through the tunnel. About twenty minutes."

"We can take my jeep," Ian offered. "I just came through the tunnel yesterday. I drove right past the hospital sign."

Cora looked at Ian with a question of *Why?*

"No worries," he said. "Come on, help me get him in."

While Ian and Subbu carried Brad into the rear seat, Cora grabbed her bag and laptop. They had the cabins reserved for a few more days, so she simply locked Brad's door and left his clothes there. She climbed in the back with Brad, who had suddenly quieted down for some reason. *Is he in shock?* she wondered.

Subbu held Houdini in the front seat of the jeep as Ian took the gravel path onto the small road that ran towards town and the highway that would lead them through the mountain. After a few miles and a sharp bend to the right, Ian turned left onto A5, which quickly lead to T1, the Mont Blanc Tunnel highway. Turning left again on T1, he was heading straight for the tunnel.

What have these blokes got into? Ian wondered. Hearing a low growl, he looked over at Houdini and saw that the dog was watching something over his left shoulder. Turning in that direction, and as the fog began to clear, Ian caught a glimpse of a black helicopter flying out of the Mont Blanc region. The same region he'd heard the helicopter in the night before.

As he slowed due to the traffic waiting to enter the tunnel, the helicopter paused as if deciding which way to turn. Ian, Subbu and Cora were now watching the chopper as Houdini continued to growl. Finally, the helicopter turned and headed southwest, down a small tributary of the Aosta Valley system, away from highway T1.

The Mont Blanc hospital in Chamonix, France was little more than a two-story doctor's office building, Cora realized as they pulled into the parking lot. In the U.S. one could find a building like this right across from a strip mall containing a Hallmark store, a discount shoe place, and a grocery store, all sharing the parking lot with a Long John Silver's restaurant. This was not what she had envisioned. There was no drive-up emergency entrance, nor orderlies waiting with wheelchairs. She immediately thought there would be no help here.

After checking Brad into the hospital and answering several

questions from the attending nurse, the three of them sat down in the lobby to wait for the doctor.

"What do you think he got into?" asked Ian. "Is he having an allergic reaction, you think?"

"I don't know," Cora said. "I've seen him around campus plenty of times. We teach at the same university, but our work didn't really overlap until now. I was needing to field test some new equipment and he already had this research trip planned, so we combined our budgets. I don't know if he is allergic to anything or not, but his eyes where clogged with sleep this morning. It looks like the flu to me. But he wasn't sick yesterday."

"He should not have gone with the gypsies," Subbu added. "We should have taken him home."

"Maybe he's having a reaction to the wine he drank last night, but I've never seen a reaction like that before," Cora said.

As understanding lightened his face Ian said, "Ah, Brad stayed at the gypsy camp last night. And you two were walking back when you found Houdini and me."

Cora nodded.

"So, he made it home OK. He must have passed you when we were talking around the campfire."

Cora stopped nodding as her eyes widened. "The campfire.... the debris," she whispered. "Ian, what were you going to tell us about the debris?"

Leaning in close, Ian whispered, "Bloody hell, I asked you last night if you guys found something. You did, didn't you?"

Glancing at the floor briefly, Cora looked up and nodded slightly. "Brad did. What do you know? Was that picture real?"

Pulling his chair closer, "Unfortunately, I don't know much more, and yes, I think the picture was real. However, I may know someone who knows a bit more about this, but he's… he's quite the odd fellow."

"Can you talk to him, please?"

CHAPTER 33
HOSPITAL
(DAY 2 – LATE MORNING)

Prometheus absently watched the half-sentences scroll down the screen. Thousands of words, letters and numbers reflected off his eyes from the monitor, but he saw none of them. Something about sai_user was wrong. He usually had a good handle on things of this nature—you had to in this business—but this didn't feel right.

Australian Incident... meteor storm... Houdini... sai_user... His thick fingers drummed nervously on the desktop, plump, pink fingertips squishing on the desk surface. *Hack attempt... Are these all connected? They must be.*

...how are they connected?

Without realizing it, Pr0m3th3us was typing searches into some other dark web sites, looking for current information about the Australian Incident. He thought he had exhausted this research long ago, but sometimes things had a way of staying hidden.

Suddenly, a request for a private chat window popped up on the screen. Houdini was trying to reach him! However, there was a small warning icon in the lower-left corner of the chat window.

IP not logged...

Houdini was logging in from a different computer than he had used previously. The Internet Protocol (IP) address was unique for every device on the internet, and Prometheus tracked all IP addresses of the users to his site. This wasn't a huge risk, but something to be aware of.

Houdini: Pr0m3th3us, are you there?

Pr0m3th3us: I am everywhere. How is your journey?

Houdini: Interesting. I need some info.

Pr0m3th3us: That is the point of your quest, seeker of knowledge.

Pr0m3th3us: What is your request?

Houdini: I need to know more about the Australian Incident. The picture you showed me. Is it real?

—pause—

Pr0m3th3us: Have you found something?

Houdini: Not yet, but is it real?

Pr0m3th3us: To date the photo has not be disproven.

Not been disproven? Cora thought. She was reading over Ian's shoulder from the lobby of the hospital where Ian was using her laptop to chat with Prometheus.

"What the hell does that mean? And what's with this username anyway?" she asked.

"I told you he was a little different," Ian responded.

Houdini: Were there any reports of outbreaks or strange deaths after the incident?

Pr0m3th3us: You mean, something like the poor, writhing aboriginal girl?

Houdini: Yes, something like that.

Pr0m3th3us: First tell me Odysseus, is your heart true?

"What is he talking about?" Cora asked.

"Never mind," Ian said.

Houdini: Would you question my heart to be true?

Pr0m3th3us: Although I see all things, I question all things.

Houdini: Bloody hell mate! Can you just answer the question?

—pause—

Prometheus sat back in his chair. *Well 'ello 'oodini… my British mate! We're a ways from 'ome, aren't we now?* he thought to himself.

His hands and fingers formed a contemplative pyramid in front of his face, pointer fingers touching his nose. *Or did you just try to slip me a micky?*

Serious dark web hackers were excellent at hiding their identities, including native aphorisms.

That was either a brilliant micky, or I just saw a bit of your knickers, as it were. Smiling to himself, he thought, *I think I saw your knickers…*

Ian and Cora stared at the screen, watching the cursor blink.

—pause—

Letting the finger-pyramid slide down to the front of his lips, he thought, *However, if I saw your knickers, is someone trying to see mine? I don't think you're sai_user after all.*

—pause—

Pr0m3th3us: There is a loose thread about a death, possibly associated with the Australian Incident.

Houdini: How loose?

Pr0m3th3us: Very.

Pr0m3th3us: The problem is that the death occurred about 25 years ago.

"Twenty-five years…" Cora cocked her head.

Pr0m3th3us: The theory is that a fragment may have been discovered in the early 90's.

Pr0m3th3us: Somehow the contagion was still active after all those years, infected someone and killed them.

Houdini: Was there no news report of this?

Pr0m3th3us: No report of anything being found. The only report was of a military officer dying of an infection after a visit to Australia.

Houdini: A military officer?

Pr0m3th3us: Yes. Rare infection after a visit with Aboriginals. Very sudden. I told you it was loose.

Cora watched as the blood began to drain from Ian's face. His head wobbled slightly, as if overwhelmed with too much information.

Houdini: What was the officer's name?

—pause—

"Ian, what's wrong?" Cora asked.

Ian didn't hear her. His full attention was on the blinking cursor.

Several minutes passed.

Pr0m3th3us: Keller, David James

Ian felt his stomach flip as the laptop slowly slid out of his hands. Grabbing it before it hit the floor, Cora inadvertently closed the lid, severing the connection.

Prometheus, fingers hovering above the keyboard, watched in surprise as the chat window closed.

Houdini offline. A message flashed.

"Ian, what's wrong?" Cora asked, wide-eyed.

Staring at a blank screen, Prometheus slowly smiled. *Well, well, Houdini. I believe you just showed me more than your knickers…*

Ian, slowly scanning the hospital waiting room, barely broke a whisper. "You're in trouble, Cora. Listen to me closely. I think you're in real trouble."

PART II

CHAPTER 34

CAMPER SEARCH

(DAY 2 – EARLY TO LATE MORNING)

As the Little Bird cleared the lower range of Mont Blanc, the scenic Aosta Valley system opened in front of Jack and Allen. The early morning fog was hanging on, shrouding the valley in a thick cloud, further complicating the daunting task before them.

"Holy shit… how in the hell are we supposed to find campers out here?" snarled Allen.

Jack simply looked at Allen with a *shut your pie hole* look and turned back to the scene in front of her.

"Maybe you can use your x-ray vision then, Superman," Allen said.

"Shut up," Jack said without looking back. "Let's find these campers and get the fuck outta here."

Jack swung the nose of the Little Bird slightly east and could barely make out a highway system through the fog. A small town spurted off the side roads, all of which fed onto the main highway that went through the mountain.

Only one good way out of here, Jack thought, *and our campers are either on the mountain still, or came off in the last day, so they may be around still.* "Let's check out the town," she said.

Setting down in a field outside of town, obscuring the Little Bird in heavy fog, Jack instructed Allen to stay with the helicopter. She hiked out of a large field and followed a gravel path towards town. She knew they couldn't stay long, because the Little Bird would eventually attract too much attention, but she had to get a feel for the town.

Hikers were starting to appear in small groups. Jack continued walking, past small cabins with raised and covered walkways, past small open-air buildings for vendors, past Chateau-style lodges. The town was getting more crowded the further east she walked. *Let's hope our campers aren't in this section.*

After several minutes, she turned to head back. Taking in the picturesque scene, she realized she had underestimated the early morning activity the town could produce. As if on a movie set, the roads and gravel paths were now teeming with extras. Wary of drawing attention, she kept her head down and quickened her pace. After a few minutes she broke into a jog, stretching her arms, as if on a morning run. Her lungs would hold up fine; she was just hoping no one would notice the military combat boots she was jogging in.

After several minutes she saw the Little Bird through the fog.

Veering off the gravel path and finishing with a mild sprint through the grass, she leaped into the open cockpit door, landing in the pilot seat. To her shock, two faces were looking back at her from the other open cockpit door.

"Dani, buddy!" Allen said, quickly staring directly at Jack. "Thought you got lost on your bathroom break."

Before Jack could respond, the second face broke into a beautiful smile.

"Dani?" the girl asked, eyeing Jack. "Wow… you're the pilot?"

Jack stared, silent.

"Oh well, I'm Cindy," the girl said, extending her hand. "Your friend Rick here was just telling me about helicopters. Are you two tour guides or something? Gosh, my girlfriends and I would love to take a tour of the mountains!" She flashed a grin.

Jack looked from Allen to Cindy and back. *This just got fucked up,* she thought.

"Apparently Cindy is an early riser," Allen said, staring directly at Jack. "Her morning jog took her right by here. Inquisitive one, she is."

A hundred scenarios passed through Jack's head in an instant, but like a master chess player analyzing her end game, she realized her number of moves was severely limited.

"We're rescue pilots," Jack managed. "Sorry, but we have to start our route now."

"Rescue pilots? Really? How exciting!" she said. Furrowing her brow, she whispered, "Is someone missing? I could help you look."

"I'm sorry… Candy… but that won't be possible," Jack started. "We have—"

"Hey, I'm not a stripper! My name is Cindy! Although…" She put her finger to the corner of her mouth, as if contemplating a career change.

Get the fuck out of here, whatever your name is, Jack thought before saying, "Uh... like I said, we have to start our route and—"

"Oh, but I have great vision," she said, batting her eyes. "All the better to see you with! See, no glasses OR contacts.

"And... I never forget a face! Especially not the two of you!" she said.

"Is that so?" Jack said slowly as resolution settled over her.

"Nope, never!" she said, giving Jack a wink. "You can ask my girlfriends... once they wake up, of course." She whispered, "Too much bubbly for them last night. I can't wait to tell them I met real rescue pilots!"

Slipping a phone out of her jogging pants, she started to snap a picture when Allen quickly intervened. "Sorry hon, no pictures inside the cockpit. You know... insurance reasons."

"Oh well, OK. How about outside the—"

Jack looked back at Allen and the message was sent.

"Cindy, maybe we could take you on one quick ride to show you the mountain," Allen said. "Your girlfriends will be so jealous!"

"Will they ever!" she gleamed.

For an instant, Jack paused, as if calculating a final gambit, then closed her eyes, took a deep breath, and flipped the ignition switch. Reflected in the cockpit window, the slightest wave of annoyance passed over her face; it was if she had just learned her favorite hooker had the night off.

CHAPTER 35
OVERLORD CONSTELLATION
(DAY 2 - LATE MORNING)

The general stared blankly at his computer screen as the Horsehead Nebula floated into view. A dark nebula in the constellation Orion, approximately 1500 light years from earth, it resembled the head of a horse. Being an avid space fan, this photo was one of the general's favorites. This picture was particularly clear, because it had been taken by the Hubble space telescope launched in 1990.

The Hubble was famous for many reasons, initially because when it was launched, the telescope was discovered to have *blurry vision* due to a poorly ground lens; the fix being likened to a contact lens to correct the blurry vision, but the real fame was because it was the largest space telescope in orbit.

An orbiting telescope had a distinct advantage over ground-based telescopes because it collected images of the visible spectrum outside of the earth's atmosphere, and therefore did not experience any distortion of the image due to the atmosphere. This produced an image of previously unseen clarity. Another advantage of placing the Hubble in space was that it could observe images in the near-ultraviolet and near-infrared spectrum, which were mostly absorbed by the atmosphere.

As the general swiped the Horsehead Nebula away, his screen filled with an image of Earth as if seen by space; several orbit lines encircled the image; real-time feeds updated small points on the lines representing satellites orbiting the Earth. The Overlord Constellation was watching.

"Constellation status," the general said blankly to the room.

[General, the Overlord satellite constellation is fully functional, however, I predict a 79% probability of primary power failure in node 17 within the next 42 days.]

Damn Chinese shit parts, thought the general. *You'd think the size of the contract would dictate a little better service,* "wouldn't you?"

[Wouldn't I what, General?]

"Capacity load," the general commanded.

[The constellation is running at 82% capacity. There are 11 distinct observations running concurrently.]

"Any requests to drop a satellite on someone's head?" the general asked, now looking out the den window.

—pause—

[General, please restate inquiry.]

"Node 17 will be dead in a month, pushing capacity to 93, 95%? I now must expedite a launch AND drop a satellite out of orbit. I bloody hell would like to get paid for doing it!"

—pause—

That would be sarcasm, Syi.

[General, there are no pending contracts for assassination by satellite.]

"Well maybe that should just go out to auction," he said, wondering if Syi could detect the nuance.

You caught the bloody sarcasm this time, right?

—pause—

[Confirmed]

"Orbiter status."

[Yes general, the Live Orbiter is on track for completion in thirty days. Advanced communications tests have all passed. Life support tests are nearly complete.]

"Pending contracts?"

[There is significant interest from our Russian associates.]

Not surprising, he thought. *Leave it to the Russians to stick a man in a modified satellite the size of a car and float him around the earth for weeks on end.*

"Rates?"

[Our associates are asking for significant discounts, considering they will be the first to test the orbiter. And due to the smaller-than-expected living quarters.]

"Living quarters? It's not a bloody Hilton! It's the only spacecraft of its kind; normal satellite profile, life support, advanced intelligence gathering, advanced weaponry. When the Ruskies fly this *satellite* right up next to a Chinese spy satellite and burn a hole in it from a half-mile away, they won't be complaining about the bloody living quarters!

"Add 10% onto our initial quote and let them chew on that for a while."

[Yes, general.]

○ ○ ○

The worms were awakening.

The worms were wriggling.

The worms were hungry.

○ ○ ○

"You're in trouble now, bitch!" she heard Bobby Hadley say.

Having heard Bobby's truck start and assuming he was driving away, Cora poked her head out of the concrete culvert and looked down the gravel road. It wasn't until she craned her head around behind her that she realized her terrible mistake.

Leaning over with his head sticking out the passenger window of the truck, Bobby was looking down at her, sneering. He threw the passenger door open and stepped onto the gravel road; ensuring he kicked a little gravel over the edge. She screamed and ducked back into the culvert, knowing she couldn't outrun him.

A second later, having jumped off the road edge, Bobby came crashing through the brambles and landed in the creek in front of her hiding spot.

Cora backed into the culvert against her bike, terrified as to what would happen next. Bobby stood just outside of the culvert, peering in at her.

"Well, well. Look who it is," he said. "And I thought you didn't like me. But… here you are, getting all wet for me, just waiting."

"Please leave me alone!" Cora cried. "I just want to go home. I won't tell anyone. I won't!"

"Tell anyone? No, you won't do that. Just come out here and get it over with."

Cora, pushing back against her bike, was about four feet inside the culvert. Bobby, with his left hand against the concrete and peering at the slimy walls, extended his right arm as far as he dared, but still came up two feet short.

"Come out here and show me how much you like me!" he said as he started to grind his hips in the air from his low-squatting position. "How much you want it!"

"Leave me alone! Help!" she screamed.

"Shut up!" he said as he kicked water and rocks at her from the creek bed. "If you do that again I might just block you in there for good. I'll stack so many rocks up in this hole, they won't find you 'til next spring!"

Cora stayed huddled against her bike, pushing hard against it. The pedal had torn a hole in her shirt and cut her back, but she hadn't noticed.

Bobby continued rocking on his haunches, as if in a catcher's squat, left hand on the concrete above him. "Come on Cora, you know want this." He slowly slid his hand along the inside of his pant leg, across his crotch, up and down.

As much as he wanted to, Bobby wouldn't venture past the edge of the culvert. Cora sat frozen.

He began to thrust the air faster. "See what you're going to get," he said. "As soon as you come out, I'm gonna find you, and stick you just like this!" His hips were bucking wildly, his hand grabbing, rubbing. "Whoo doggy! You gonna ride this cowboy!"

After a minute of air thrusting, he promptly stood up and looked around to see if any cars were coming. Turning his flushed face back to Cora, he said, "Maybe I need to show you what you're missing," and began to unbuckle his belt.

Cora was frozen with horror, not knowing if Bobby was coming in after her anyways.

Bobby quickly pushed his jeans down around his ankles and stood there rubbing himself in front of the culvert. He slowly squatted down to look directly at Cora. When she realized what he was doing, she clamped her eyes shut and covered her face with her hands, but Bobby didn't stop.

He stood up, now stroking himself, mumbling something. He thrust his hips as close to the culvert opening as he could, face buried into his other arm. This went on for a few minutes before he started to moan Cora's name, then he was silent. Surprised by the silence, Cora peeked through her fingers right as Bobby ejaculated into the culvert, goo splashing into the water where she had been sitting earlier. Cora sat horrified as tears streamed down her face.

A few more thrusts and Bobby was finished. Still leaning against his arm on the concrete, he wiggled his now limp penis and flicked his fingers towards Cora. He pulled up his pants and began climbing out of the ditch.

"Don't worry, there's more where that came from," he said without looking back.

Cora sat in the cold trickle of the stream, hoping that a flood would come and wash away Bobby's semen before she had to climb out over it.

CHAPTER 36
WORM FOOD
(DAY 2 - AFTERNOON)

The worms were moving.

Brad was floating, silent, effortless, alone. He imagined himself a great explorer, making great discoveries, sailing to the stars escaping. The water in the small pool was lukewarm already and would be too hot to swim in by afternoon, but at least for now there was no noise. His ears, air-locked against the water that buoyed him, also blocked out the sound of his parents arguing.

The corrugated tin pool had been donated to them by his aunt, on his mother's side, when they upgraded to a new above-ground pool. They were the rich cousins. They always had Christmas and Easter dinners and they never missed birthdays. His cousin Harry would let him borrow his old baseball gloves when they came to visit, but kept a tight grip on his latest Rawlings mitt, always making sure to break it in properly with oil and string.

Brad's ears where itching.

The tin pool, although small, was too heavy for Brad to move or empty, which caused the water to become stagnant quickly. He occasionally ran new water in it with the hose, but the sides became greener and slicker throughout the summer. When he saw water-bugs skimming the surface or tiny larvae swimming in the pool, he knew it was time for fresh water. One summer he had a terrible ear infection that the doctor said was due to mites, but his dad swore it was from Brad peeing in the pool. He didn't want another infection, but he suddenly felt as if something had swum in his ear. The sides of the pool did feel kind of slick.

The worms were talking.

Tiny metallic voices, chirps and clicks, tiny worm tongues clicking out worm thoughts, snapping, extending, planning.

Brad was paralyzed. The worms in the water had stung him and paralyzed him. He could not move. He would drown if not kept afloat by the billions of breeding worms in the warm pool water. They had already floated into his ears. They itched. They were inching through his ear canals and into his sinuses. They left tiny trails of slick slime behind them.

The worms were nibbling.

The nibbling bites of the worms were tiny, but his brain knew it was being consumed. The bites did not hurt, but a million nibbling worms were itchy.

Brad's ear canals were so full of worms his equilibrium was off. He was sinking, spinning, falling into a void from the inside, out.

His eyes were bulging. The worms were breeding too fast. Overpopulation. Straining the limits of his sinus cavities. His throat was full. His nose was clogged. They were pushing against the back of his eyes. His vision was blurry. The worms were collapsing his eyeballs. Squeezing them out of their sockets. His eyes were about to explode out of his head, or pop and deflate. A worm champagne toast.

Brad screamed. He was worm food.

CHAPTER 37
CONNECTIONS
(DAY 2 – LATE MORNING)

"What do you mean 'we're in real trouble'?" Cora asked. "What are you not telling me?"

"Come with me," Ian whispered as he motioned towards the door.

Outside the hospital doors Ian started walking to his jeep.

"What are you doing?" Cora demanded." I'm sorry, I'm not up for any spy games right now, I—"

Ian spun around on one heel and gave Cora a stern stare. With a finger to his lips, he curled it twice, indicating for her to follow him quietly.

Once out in the parking lot, Ian continued. "We have to be very careful what we say indoors, or around any–" His eyes widened. He quickly took out his cell phone and popped the battery out. He reached for Cora's phone to do the same.

She pulled her hand back, looking suspiciously at his phone.

"We have to watch what we say around any potential listening devices," he mouthed quietly.

"Listening devices? What are you talking about? What's going on? You're not a conspiracy guy, are you? Jr. G-man or something?"

Ian cocked his head as a look of impatience crossed his face.

"You remember last night when I told you I was an analyst, right?"

She nodded her head.

"An analyst for the British government."

"Yes."

"An analyst that gets top secret communications."

Cora was watching him intently now. The boyish side of Ian, the wandering spirit, the one she saw last night and thought about on her walk home, was gone. The Ian that stood in front of her was serious and sober. She didn't know what he was about to lay on her, but she felt he believed it.

Ian looked at her phone again with a slightly pleading look on his face. With a resigned sigh, Cora popped the battery out and held both pieces in the air.

"An analyst who recognized the name of the military officer who died in Australia," he said slowly.

Cora's eyes widened slightly.

"The man that died in Australia was the son of General William David Keller. I'd heard a rumor that something happened years ago, but never knew what. Anyway, two days ago, when the storm broke,

I was monitoring satellite surveillance, and attended an emergency call with other surveillance stations. General Keller attended the call as well."

"You report to this General Keller?" she asked with concern.

"No. The bloke's been retired for years now—supposedly—but occasionally shows up on high priority issues. A real recluse, I hear. The rumor is that he runs a black-ops company and contracts back to the government, but no one really knows—at least not at my level."

"A black-ops company?"

"Yeah, *real* G-man stuff. Straight MI6 as it were. And if there's any chance this storm is getting scrutinized at that level," rubbing the back of his head absently, "then there will be active monitors. Which is why we have to watch what we say."

Cora pondered this for a moment. Ian watched as the skepticism twisted the side of her mouth slightly.

"Look, I'm not sure what all the General is into, but I know he was on the call about the meteor storm. I know he had a program give him some other updates, and he was very—"

"Wait, what?" Cora interrupted. "He had a program give him some updates?"

"Yeah, I'm not sure what it was exactly, some AI program he uses for analysis. AI stands for Artificial—"

"Yes I know, Intelligence."

"Right, but halfway through our update, the AI announced a correlation between this storm and a storm in Australia from the forties, and the general went into private communication mode."

"With who, you?"

"No, with the A.I. thing."

"The general was relying solely on the A.I. for analysis? Was anyone validating the predictions? What about the prediction models? When was the last time they were retrained?"

"Whoa, wait… I'm not sure what you're asking," Ian said. "I'm just trying to tell you, that you… that we need to be careful what we say."

Now Cora turned and began to walk away. *A military-grade AI is being used by a general running a black-ops company, who is contracting back to the military? Is that even legal?*

Quietly she whispered, "Ali, are you getting this?"

[Yes, Cora.]

"Find what you can about this general, any military A.I., and track the dark web for info. Oh, and Ali."

[Yes?]

"Find what you can on Ian Corbyn."

[Yes, Cora.]

Cora's mind rolled. *How is this happening? What am I doing here?*

Turning back towards Ian, she asked, "And you think the general is interested in the storm why?"

"I'm not sure. It may just be airspace border SOP, but—" he stopped short. "The Little Bird," he barely breathed out. "Blimey, someone is looking for something already!"

Cora unconsciously held her breath.

"I think the general is already looking for something at Mont Blanc," Ian said, staring straight at her.

"Looking for what?"

Pacing the gravel parking lot, he rubbed hard at his forehead. "I don't know. Debris, evidence, people…"

"People? Wha—"

"People who saw the storm," he said slowly. "People who may have picked something up."

Her mind stuttered with the implication. *Is he trying to scare me? Is this really happening?*

Hearing the front door open, they both turned and saw Subbu frantically waving at them.

Brad was getting worse.

◇ ◇ ◇

Despite her equilibrium telling her she was past the point of no return, Cindy refused to believe that she was being thrown out of the helicopter.

He's just trying to scare me. He's going to pull me back any second.

As if in slow motion, she somehow saw her body tipping toward the open cockpit door, as if watching from above.

He's going to grab me any second and get a little handsy.

She tipped further forward.

Grab me already, I'll play along.

She tipped further forward.

For fuck's sake!

The Little Bird rudely moved away from Cindy's location in the air.

This can't be happening to me!

She made a final grab at the cockpit door.

THIS ISN'T HAPPENING!

A fingernail from her left hand chipped off as she became weightless.

THIS CAN'T BE HAP—!

The last thing she saw was the sun glinting off her fingernail floating above her as the rocky ledge rushed up to meet her.

CHAPTER 38
INFECTION
(DAY 2 - AFTERNOON)

"His fever has slowly risen over the last hour, and is currently steady at 102," the nurse said. "He had what appeared to be a minor convulsion about ten minutes ago, but has been calm for the last five minutes or so."

Cora sat down hard in the chair next to the bed. She didn't know what to do and her face relayed that message.

"Why are his arms strapped down?" Cora asked.

"He keeps scratching at his eyes," the nurse responded. "He tries to speak but nothing makes sense. He may be hallucinating due to the fever. The doctor gave him a sedative and has ordered blood tests.

We're waiting for the results."

"Has he called anyone yet?" Ian asked.

"Who, the doctor? Well first, the doctor is a SHE, but called anyone? Like next of kin?"

"No, I mean like other doctors… the ECDC…"

"The European Centre for Disease Control?" the nurse asked suspiciously. "No, why would she do that?"

"Just wondering," Ian said quietly, who turned to pace the room.

The nurse gave a long look at Ian, then turned back to Cora. "And there's no family to contact in the states?" she asked. "It would help to know if he was allergic to anything."

"None that I'm aware," Cora said. "Both of his parents were killed in a car crash, during high school, I think."

"That's a shame," the nurse responded. "The doctor will certainly want to keep him overnight, but depending on the blood test results, he'll most likely be sent to a larger hospital that is equipped to handle something like this."

"Where would that be?" Ian asked tentatively.

"Not sure at this point," the nurse said, turning towards him. "But maybe the ECDC will have a recommendation. Excuse me while I check on my other patients."

Brad tried to scratch his itchy eyes, his burning, squirming, itching eyes—*Why are my eyes squirming?* —But he couldn't, the worms had paralyzed his arms. His arms were dead, or gone, eaten by the worms, melted by witch saliva. A witch with a worm tongue in her dead mouth, breathing out volcano ash for air, a thousand years old, had melted his arms.

Something ancient was in him, older than the Puri daj, older than her memories, older than the mountains.

○ ○ ○

The nurse was typing.

Syi was reading.

The search algorithm on the web page was being auto-filled.

Nurse: *Unknown infection. Convulsions. Fever. Scra–*

Syi: *–tching of the eyes.*

[General, 73% probability of Death Rock infection at Chamonix hospital.]

"Alert the Little Bird!" the general ordered. "Get them over there immediately! Full extraction!"

○ ○ ○

Brad felt the worms multiplying, writhing, thriving in his eye sockets. The worms were exploding in numbers and would soon overtake the place where his eyeballs sat. The worms would eat the connective tissue around the inside of his eye sockets and one by one his eyeballs would pop out, dangling on the sides of his cheeks by a few blood vessels. At least then he would be able to see the stumps of his melted arms, maybe see his melted legs before a hungry worm nibbled the last bit of connecting tissue holding his eyes to his head, then his eyes would fall off and hit the ground with a low splat. The worms that had fallen with his eyes would form a brigade and slowly roll his eyeballs off to the Puri daj, where she would lick them with her ancient protruding tongue and shiver in ecstasy.

○ ○ ○

Suddenly, an alarm went off in the hospital and a thunderous noise could be heard outside.

Without looking outside Ian shot a look of concern at Cora. *Helicopter,* he mouthed.

○ ○ ○

His dad had been right. Brad had infected himself by peeing in the pool, in the bed, every time he touched himself a worm must have stuck to his finger, then, after a smart slap across the face—when wiping the tears always—he had infected himself.

He was infected because he peed in the bed, and that's why he was blind now. It was all his fault.

The worms were organizing.

CHAPTER 39
THE CHASE BEGINS
(DAY 2 – MID-AFTERNOON)

As the alarm sounded, Ian bolted out the door and down the hall. Cora and Subbu stood looking at each other, trying to decide what to do.

"What is happening?" Subbu asked. "What–"

"Wait," she hushed him with an open palm. She stood listening to the cacophony of sound down the hall, trying to make sense of what was happening. No sooner had she stuck her head out of the hospital room door than she saw Ian sprinting back towards her.

"Let's go, right now!" Ian exclaimed.

"Go? Go where?" she protested. "We can't just–"

"Listen to me," Ian interrupted. "Now is the best chance we'll have of getting Brad out of here. He can't stay here."

A look of disbelief and indignation crossed Cora's face. "What are you talking about? Where are we supposed to–"

"Trust me and hurry," Ian interrupted. "I'll explain in the jeep."

Trust me Cora... just trust me...

Ian had already grabbed a wheelchair and was disconnecting the monitors from Brad. "Help me lift him," he said to Subbu. "This may save his life."

Indecision froze Cora. *...just trust me...*

Subbu looked from Cora to Ian.

Ian pulled Subbu toward the bed with one hand, lifting Brad's leg with the other. "This may save her as well," he said tersely.

Subbu glanced back at Cora, then grabbed Brad. They lifted him into the wheelchair and pushed him toward the door. Ian pulled the door of the hospital room open slightly and looked down the hall.

"We're all going out together, Cora," Ian said directly to her. "We don't stop, regardless of what anyone says. Ready?" He looked one more time. "Let's go!"

◇ ◇ ◇

Jack and Allen were hovering over a remote ridge of the French Alps; deep crevasses wrinkled the mountain here.

They were inspecting the final resting place of Cindy/Candy. After an initial bounce, they saw a piece of her brightly-colored running jacket tear away and hang like a flag on a jagged outcrop. Fearing that they would have to remedy that little marker, they both visibly relaxed when a gust of wind lifted the fragment, fluttering a last goodbye, and sent it into the crevasse in which Cindy's body had slid. A neat little tumble of snow slid down the crevasse after her, and all was lost to the mountain.

"Damn, what a waste—" Allen started, but was interrupted by a crackling cyborg.

[Attention Little Bird, proceed immediately to Chamonix hospital, coordinates transmitted. Probable Death Rock infection. Full extraction, covert cover.]

"Roger that," Jack responded. "Genera… uh, Syi, what is cover? Over."

[Locating ambulance now.]

◇ ◇ ◇

Prometheus had been scouring the dark web all afternoon. He felt invigorated. He felt alive. Finally, a noble cause worthy of his attention.

His head swam with theories. He was giddy.

The chatter on his main site had picked up significantly over the last twenty-four hours, and he was fully tuned in. His eyes darted over multiple scrolling windows.

Something is happening, he thought. *This is no red herring.* There would certainly be a diversionary story leaked out soon, but he was out ahead of the pack. But could he stay there?

Where are you, Houdini? Where are you when I need you most? Is your heart still true?

He sent a message to Houdini to contact him as soon as he logged back on. He was anxious. He turned back to a scrolling window.

sKelaWh0R: MRE's 15% off while they last

Alice:

HAL27: anyone on sat comms?

bogglHED: kewl site!

Eve11: Missing girl reported in Courmayeur. Related?

sai_user:

TheDonald: @CatGirl, here kitty, kitty!

RoadWaRoR: Chamonix in 2 hrs. Monitoring skies.

BlackBart: invasion diversion?

XoPl@n: what is Australian event?

SpaceMan2001: How can I help?

X11NDK: Helicopters reported over Mont Blanc

sai_user:

CatGirl: @TheDonald I'll scratch your eyes out!

sai_user:

HAL27: @RoadWaRoR, sky eyes, report asap!

sKelaWh0R: stock up before bug invasion!!

sai_user:

Prometheus froze the window again. It wasn't obvious why to him, but something tweaked his mind. Something unusual about the chatter caught his attention. He could easily filter out the newbies and lurkers; the tinfoil hat banter was like a second language to him also. *What am I seeing?*

After scanning the chat window again, it became obvious.

OK, sai_user, what are you doing? I know you're watching, but what are you looking at?

Or better yet, what's the connection?

○ ○ ○

Ian pushed Brad down the hall while Subbu and Cora did the quick-step to keep up. Ian glanced at Subbu to have him open the double doors ahead of them, but seeing that the translation was taking too long, he simply spun the wheelchair around and opened the doors with his butt, yanking the chair and Brad through the opening. Spinning the chair back around, he almost toppled Brad out of it as he bumped him down the few short steps to the parking lot.

"Hey, careful!" Cora reprimanded, but Ian was already heading towards the jeep.

Ian and Subbu lifted Brad out of the chair—the sedatives where working wonders—and wedged him into the backseat, driver side. Ian shoved the chair aside. Cora watched it roll away and bump into a small car.

Now outside, Cora saw other commotion on the far corner of the hospital. There, a small helipad was bustling with activity as doctors and nurses attended two skiers suffering from an accident earlier that day.

Ian was backing out of the parking spot before Cora was fully settled in the back with Brad.

"Wait, dammit!" she exclaimed. "I'm not even in yet, and Houdini isn't in his harness!"

"Just hold onto him until I get on the road," Ian said.

Houdini, who had greeted them with initial excitement, was now sitting on Cora's lap, leaning against the passenger side panel. She could feel a low growl emanate from him as he looked at Brad, lowering his head.

What the bloody hell am I doing? Ian thought as he pulled onto the highway. *What am I going to do with these blokes?*

He couldn't fully explain his reasoning for helping Brad and Cora, besides the fact that they simply needed help, but he knew from his previous training—his previous life—that these two were in bad straits. He wondered if he wasn't overreacting a bit—*This dark web bloke…who knows if he's even right*— but Ian wasn't a nervous person; in fact, he was a highly trained person, and his training made him act.

A few more stoplights and he'd have to decide: back to camp or off to another hospital? As if on cue, and to provide input to the decision, Houdini barked twice from the backseat.

The same black helicopter they had seen this morning had just topped a low range and was hovering about a half-mile to their southwest.

Ian's decision was made. He turned into the lane that would lead them back under the mountain.

As if signaled by his thoughts, the Little Bird turned and flew straight towards them.

CHAPTER 40
VOICES FROM THE PAST
(DAY 2 – MID-AFTERNOON)

"And when you heard the voice from the midst of the darkness, while the mountain was burning with fire, you came near to me, all the heads of your tribes and your elders." The general read from his King James Bible, having flipped it open to a random passage.

From the midst of the darkness.

What came to you Davey, from the midst of the darkness? the general wondered. *What horror lies just beyond our sight?*

Are you there now? In the darkness…

"…with voices in your head?" he said absently.

[General, please confirm.]

Is the darkness still speaking to you?

"You said you had voices in your head, right? …something about voices…"

[General, I'm designed to–]

But the general heard no more. The last days of his son's life played through his head like a broken movie reel. Black and white images flashed in his mind. The same scene over and over. A scene of agony.

The tormented features of his son's face obscured the memory imprint of what he'd looked like. The twisted features gothic and grotesque. He'd had two sons: one, a handsome young man from a different life; the other, something out of the darkness, something transformed by a voice from the darkness.

"Was it a test?" he asked the room. "Did I fail a test?"

[General, please conf–]

"Davey, please, did I fail a test?"

[No, general.]

"Well you certainly didn't. You didn't fail the test Davey, did you?"

[No, general. I haven't–]

Then what happened? If you could only tell me. What were the voices saying, Davey? What were they saying?

You were hearing them out of the darkness, right? Somewhere from the darkness…

○ ○ ○

The darkness of the Mont Blanc tunnel collapsed around Cora's mind, collapsed to the size of a culvert with the density of a nightmare. She heard echoes off the concrete walls, the low rumble of traffic, the dripping of water, the buzzing of flies.

Bobby Hadley's semen had splashed right in from of her; he was marking his territory; he had tried to mark her.

Despite the summer breeze that wandered up the creek bed, no warmth came to her. The trickle of cold water had soaked her completely and she was shivering. She had no idea how long she sat there after Bobby left; time had slowed to a crawl, measured by a decaying dog.

Suddenly, a thought jolted her out of her trance. If she sat here much longer, she might get pregnant! She remembered from health class something about sperm being fast swimmers and racing to the egg.

Could sperm swim through water? Oh God, please don't let me be pregnant!

She had to get out of there right now!

She stood up the best she could and started pulling on her bike. It was jammed sideways in the culvert, and didn't want to come out.

Finally, after pulling on the back wheel, which caused the pedal to scrape here ankle, she wiggled the bike out of the culvert.

The flies were buzzing angrily about her.

Just a little squirt…

She avoided the dead dog and managed to push her bike out of the bramble to the top of the road. She was now covered with scratches and bites; her shorts were soaked through and her face was stained with dirt and tears. She didn't allow herself to cry because she wasn't home yet. She had to get home.

She hadn't heard Bobby drive back towards his house, but the old gravel roads led in all different directions, and he could be anywhere. She decided if she saw him coming back that she'd ditch her bike and run through the woods. Looking behind her once again, she saw no sign of Bobby, hopped on her bike and started pedaling home.

Just then she thought she heard her name.

○ ○ ○

"Cora! Are you with us?" Ian called from the front.

Subbu was turned around looking at her from the front seat. His eyes told her she had missed something.

"What? What is it?" she asked quickly, making Houdini jump again.

"We were talking to you. Did you hear what I said?" Ian asked.

"I… I'm… no, I'm sorry I didn't hear you," she said, now looking at Brad. "Where are we going?"

"We were just talking about that. We must figure out where to take Brad, but I need to check on something first."

"Check on what?" she asked.

"I need to check in with Prometheus to see if he's hearing any chatter about the incident. I think we need another set of eyes helping us."

"But what about Brad? We can't just haul him around like—"

"It's only been twenty minutes, and he's still out," Ian said. "I want to check in first, see if I can get a bead on this helicopter business and go from there."

Ian inspected the sky as they came out of the tunnel on the Italian side of the mountain.

"That's fine," she said finally. "I'll have Ali run some initial diagnosis now that we're out of the tunnel."

"Ali? Ali who?" Ian started.

"Ali, are you there?" Cora asked, lightly touching her earpiece.

[Yes Cora, I'm here.]

Looking back at Ian with an *I have a wild card too* look, she said, "You're not the only one who has a secret internet friend. And Ali is always listening."

CHAPTER 41
INTERNET FRIENDS
(DAY 2 – MID-AFTERNOON)

By the time Ian passed the town of Courmayeur, he had a plan. He dropped Cora and Subbu off at the lodge to grab the rest of their gear.

"Meet me at my tent as soon as you can," he told them. "I'm going to contact Prometheus, then we'll decide where to go."

Before Cora had a chance to protest, Ian said, "Brad will be fine in the jeep until you get back. Grab extra provisions just in case."

Subbu didn't like the idea of *just in case*.

Cora walked around to the front of the jeep. "Ian, why are you helping us?" she asked.

"Really? Do I look like a bloke who wouldn't help?" he said with genuine surprise.

"No, it's not that, but… you could get into trouble, couldn't you? I mean… wait, what am I saying? We haven't done anything wrong!"

"No, you haven't, but right now, I'm trying to keep you *out* of trouble. Until we can… until you can get Brad somewhere safe. Now get moving. Please."

Cora and Subbu watched as Ian drove away; Houdini's furry ears at attention looking over the backseat.

Arriving at his camp, Ian grabbed his laptop and quickly logged in. Messages flooded him as a private chat window opened.

Houdini: Pr0m3th3us, are you there?

Hefting his weight out of his vibrating recliner with a clumsy scissoring of his legs, Prometheus fairly pranced across the concrete floor when he heard an electronic voice translate Ian's message to him: "Prometheus, are you there?"

"You have returned!" he said, clapping his hands together. "You have returned."

Slipping on a headset and microphone, Prometheus decided he would talk to Houdini, and let the computer translate his words into messages. He had a lot to say.

As if to make this exchange as ceremonious as possible, he grabbed a red velvet cape that lay across a chair and swung it over his shoulders. The furry, spotted collar caused him to shrug his shoulders up into the warmth as it rubbed across the folds of his neck. His eyes sparkled wide.

Standing grandly before his monitors, right hand extended in the air, he spoke boldly.

Pr0m3th3us: I am everywhere and welcome your return!

Pr0m3th3us: This morning I feared the quest had become too great. Come, sit at my feet and regale me!

Bloody hell... thought Ian.

Houdini: I need info. Do you know–

Pr0m3th3us: Come, come, seeker of knowledge, your words are as an ass, braying in my ears. Query me lightly, delicately, but regale me thoroughly!

Barmy... OK, here's a go, Ian thought, rolling his eyes.

Houdini: My quest is in peril. I come seeking guidance.

Pr0m3th3us: Peril say you? Adventure says I! What troubles you?

Houdini: I fear we are hunted.

Pr0m3th3us: Hunted? By what force?

Not wanting to give up all his cards yet, Ian thought for a moment.

Houdini: I fear a mad king from the North is hunting us.

Prometheus, prancing like a child needing a potty break, suddenly stood still, hands dropping to his sides.

Bending slightly to verify the words on the screen were as he'd heard them, he read the words, *...is hunting US.* His chest rose, filling with a long breath, as the corners of his mouth broke into a grin.

Pr0m3th3us: Your quest HAS grown my friend. You have collected a traveler!

Blimey! You'd best watch your words, mate, Ian scolded himself, then thought, *Well, maybe I can use this to my advantage.*

Houdini: My quest HAS grown. And I have collected many travelers. We are in need of your help.

MANY travelers?! The prancing started again.

Pr0m3th3us: My powers are at your disposal.

Houdini: What say you then? What do your powers show that are blind to mine eyes?

Pr0m3th3us: Yes, my weary traveler, I'm afraid you are hunted. Many strange tales have come to mine ears. Birds in the skies, missing travelers, perhaps even spies among my flock.

Birds in the skies… Yes, definitely the Little Bird, Ian thought.

Houdini: I have seen the bird in the sky. I believe them to be the mad king's, from the North.

Houdini: However, I know of no missing travelers or spies.

Pr0m3th3us: A young maiden has gone missing from Courmayeur. And an ailing lad has been plucked from healing hands in Chamonix.

How did he know that so quickly? We just left!

Houdini: An ailing lad?

Pr0m3th3us: Yes, yes. A naughty boy who wouldn't take his medicine, it appears. People want him to take his medicine, but they don't know what to give him. They'll be looking for that naughty boy.

—pause—

Houdini: Who will be looking?

Striding grandly, Prometheus swung his red velvet robe out with his left hand and pirouetted towards the monitors with his right hand raised regally.

Pr0m3th3us: Who can say really… the mad king perhaps, though I know him not. Others are just learning of the naughty boy, but the village elders *ARE* taking notice.

—pause—

Damn! I should have never mentioned the ECDC to that bloody nurse! The general will certainly be monitoring communications. Or that damn cyborg of–

Oh shit! The spy.

Houdini: Why do you think you have a spy amongst your flock?

Pr0m3th3us: The spy is of personal interest to me. I shall deal with the spy in my own–

Houdini: I may know the spy.

Prometheus stood looking at the blinking cursor. The rosy color of his cheeks splotching red.

Pr0m3th3us: What do *you* know of the spy?

Houdini: I fear the spy is of unnatural origins.

Prometheus, cocking his head slightly, sat down slowly.

Pr0m3th3us: Continue.

Houdini: I fear the mad king has unleashed a demon, and its name is A.I.

Prometheus blinked slowly at the screen. The screen went slightly out of focus as his head rang with this new information.

An A.I. is monitoring my site?

Finally, his attention was drawn back to the public chat window. A message had been flagged as urgent, and despite the scrolling responses, it had been pinned to the top of his window:

"Alert: Black-op helicopter just left Chamonix and is flying towards Mont Blanc. 2nd time over mountain today!"

The message was five minutes old.

Military helicopter. Chamonix. Hospital. Infection. Courmayeur. Missing girl.

The A.I. is looking for Houdini!

Pr0m3th3us: Houdini beware! Black-ops bird left Chamonix five minutes ago. The demon is after you! Wherever you are, stay low and silent!

Houdini: Is it heading toward Mont Blanc? Or Courmayeur?

Pr0m3th3us: Alas! Are you there?

Houdini: Yes!!

Bolting out of his chair, sending it careening behind him, Prometheus threw his arms in the air in a theatrical surrender.

Pr0m3th3us: Run, Houdini! Flee before the demon!

Ian slammed the laptop lid down and shoved it into his backpack. He quickly scoured the tent for other personal items, and started to roll his sleeping bag when he remembered.

Houdini! I hope that pup's still here.

He scrambled out of the tent flap and nearly knocked Cora flat as she bent to knock on the tent.

"Hey, what gives?" she said, stepping back just in time. "Where's Houdini?"

Ian grimaced at the question and ran past Cora, tossing his backpack in the back of the jeep as he called Houdini's name. He noticed small raindrops spotting the hood of the vehicle, but took the thought no further.

"Seriously?" Cora snapped.

They spread out calling for the dog. Ian heard the bark first. It came from towards town, but more off the normal path and still in a secluded area.

Houdini barked twice more. Ian could see something rustling in the tall weeds in front of him.

Finally, he saw the pup. He was slowly tracing a wide circle through the weeds. In the center of the circle, Ian could see where the weeds had been disturbed and flattened. Houdini wouldn't go inside the circle of weeds he had trampled. He would inch towards the center, sniffing cautiously, then bark and jump back. He circled a bit more, sniffed, barked and jumped back.

"What's the matter boy?" Ian asked. "What have you found?"

Ian walked inside Houdini's trampled circle and Houdini gave two high-pitched barks of warning.

"That's OK boy, just let me have a look."

It took Ian only a matter of seconds to understand what he was looking at.

Two long indentions, parallel to each other, could be seen in the undergrowth. Weeds where flattened or disturbed for meters around, all laying outward and away from the center.

More raindrops peppered the weeds, threatening to erase the marks completely.

Ian walked slowly around the inside of the circle.

Although not a tracker, Ian was pretty sure some of the disturbances outside of the parallel marks where footprints.

A helicopter had landed here very recently.

"Houdini! There you are, boy!" Cora said, walking up with Subbu.

Houdini happily trounced over to her to get his ears rubbed.

Ian turned around, face blank, and started, "There's been a—"

But before he could finish, they heard Houdini growl.

"Helicopter!" Ian yelled as he looked back towards Mont Blanc.

The Little Bird had just topped the largest range, and the sound of the rotors were echoing straight down the valley.

"Run!" Ian yelled. "They're looking for us!"

He grabbed at Subbu and Cora's sleeves as he ran past them, pulling them towards the jeep.

Houdini barked and bounded after Ian.

Cora and Subbu looked toward the mountain and saw the Little Bird emerge out of a bank of low clouds. They were standing on its landing pad, and it was headed straight for them.

CHAPTER 42

RUNNING

(DAY 2 - LATE-AFTERNOON)

Ian made it to the jeep and began throwing bags in the back. Houdini was already in. How the pup had guessed the vehicle was their destination was lost on Ian in the rush. Cora and Subbu grabbed the last few bags they'd left lying beside the jeep and climbed in.

The rotors of the helicopter echoed behind them.

"Who's after us?!" Cora yelled frantically. "Where are we supposed to go?"

Ian was already pulling away from camp, hoping he hadn't left anything important in the tent, and suddenly thankful for the pending storm.

"I don't know! Down the valley for now! We're in real trouble, mates! I think the general is looking for us, for some reason. There's a bloody good chance the heli is his. If so, the guys flying it are NOT people we want to meet."

As he said this, Ian craned his head back to see if he could see the Little Bird, but the jeep top obscured much of his vision.

"Prometheus knew we were at the hospital this morning!" Ian said, looking over at Cora in the front seat.

"WHAT?"

"At least he knew that someone with an infection had been at the hospital, and that those people left in a hurry."

"How did he—"

"Hackers I guess; police scanners, who knows," Ian said. "Apparently there's a lot of internet chatter about the event, and it's attracting a lot of attention."

"Isn't that good for us?" Cora asked.

"No, it's not! The general had an interest in this right from the start. And now that the word is leaking out, or whatever is happening, the more he'll want to bring this to a close. Quickly!"

"What do you mean, *bring to a close*?"

"Cora, there's already a report of a girl missing from Courmayeur. The town we just left! I don't know if it's related, but a helicopter was sitting in the field that's just outside of that town, not far from my tent! Prometheus knew about the girl and he knew about the hospital!"

Ian checked his mirrors again and grimaced at the fact that he couldn't see anything. He thought it could be a very good sign, or a very bad one.

That bird could be flying up my arse right now and I wouldn't know it until it was too late.

"You think the general wants to kill us?!" Cora said, wide-eyed, nerves cracking her voice.

"I don't know that he wants to kill us, but he certainly wants to know about an unknown infection that just popped up after a highly unusual meteor strike."—*What was I thinking? What was I thinking!*— "Bloody hell, we could be carrying the damned infection as well, as far as we know," he finished.

Ian followed State Route 26 south out of Courmayeur. He avoided the larger highway A5, wanting to not get stuck on an elevated highway system with no exit. He knew this route led him to the Gran Paradiso National Park, Italy's largest. A heavy cover of foliage sounded much better than the Alpine tundra that covered much of the valley system.

"Where are you going?" Cora asked again. "And there's no signs of—"

"Away from Courmayeur for now," he interrupted. "I need time to think. Oh, and there's one more snippet of good news!"

Cora detected the sarcasm.

"Remember the A.I. I mentioned earlier? I think it's looking for us as well. Or, assisting the search somehow."

Cora's eyes widened.

"Hell, it could be leading the search, for all I know." Realization seeping through Ian's voice. "Prometheus thinks he has a spy on his website, and it might be the A.I."

A military grade A.I. that is spying in the dark web, thought Cora. *Oh my God, this IS bad.*

"Ali, did you copy this?" Cora asked.

[Yes Cora, your signal has degraded 17% in the last several minutes, but I have successfully recorded the entire conversation.]

"Good, because we need your help now."

[I have been analyzing the situation.]

Now it was Ian's turn to stare at Cora.

"Road!" she said, pointing forward, even though Ian was clearly in his lane.

"Secret internet friend, right?"

"That's right," she said.

○ ○ ○

Jack piloted the Little Bird over the ridge of Mont Blanc and looked towards the town of Courmayeur once again. Rain clouds obscured her view, but she knew the town was there. Her back ached despite the grim resolve that showed on her face. Dark shadows hung under her eyes.

"Where to now?" Allen asked. "I'm not expecting our campers to start waving a signal flag anytime soon."

Jack turned the bird the same direction as she had that morning.

"We're sitting down in the same field as before," Jack responded, "and waiting for the hospital trace to complete. Once the general gives us a patient name, we'll have a better idea of who in the hell we're looking for."

A few minutes later, Jack sat the Little Bird down almost on top of the previous indentations, thanks to GPS.

"I gotta piss," Allen stated bluntly. "Don't be trying to sneak a peek."

Jack exited the cockpit without giving a response, straightened her back and groaned slightly. Stretching one leg, then the other, she squatted by the side of the cockpit to work the blood through her stiff legs. Balancing on the balls of her feet, she looked at the surrounding weeds. Looking left, then right, a vague thought tickled the back of her mind. She wasn't sure what it was, but she saw something.

She stood up and walked slowly around the front of the cockpit. *What's wrong with these weeds?*

Continuing around.

"Aahhh! It's a monster!" Allen yelled, waving his penis in the air, sending a stream of urine in a wild figure-eight.

With the slightest glance, Jack said, "My girlfriend's is bigger," and continued her slow walk around the helicopter.

Bending down again and following a line of sight through the weeds, Jack imagined that she saw a trampled path of weeds; other than what had been disturbed by the rotor winds.

Following the path through the weeds, she eventually came into an area that was far enough away from the landing site to still be standing.

Allen caught up to her and asked, "What gives?"

"Did you and Candy have a little walk-about this morning?"

"Nope, and it was Cindy by the way—"

"Whatever," Jack continued through the weeds. "I think someone visited our… Bingo!" she said, topping a small ridge. A single tent stood not fifty yards from the Little Bird. The geography hiding it from view.

Jack unconsciously touched her right hip, fingering the sidearm there. Walking slowly toward the camp, she noticed the trail didn't lead straight, but veered off to the right.

"Parking lot," she said, eyeing the tire tracks. The path led straight to the tracks.

"And someone was in a hurry," she said, toeing the torn ground made by spinning tires.

"No one in the tent," Allen said. "The flap was left open with a sleeping bag inside, but that's it."

"Come on!" Jack said, breaking into a sprint towards the Little Bird. "By the looks of the tracks, I think our visitor just left and is headed down the valley!"

CHAPTER 43
IAN MEETS ALI
(DAY 2 – LATE-AFTERNOON)

Ian followed the state road south for several miles. Even though it was a state highway, the road was winding, passing back and forth over the river that naturally ran through the valley, and subsequently passing beneath several bridges that supported the elevated A5 highway.

What did I get myself into? And what in the bloody hell is wrong with that bloke in the back?

Although not driving fast, the act of moving put Ian's mind at rest, at least a little. He wasn't sure one direction was better than any other, but the feeling of moving *away* was comforting.

"Ali, please search for any news on the meteor storm and correlate with reports of infections or sickness," Cora said.

[Understood, Cora]

"So, tell me about Ali," Ian started. "Who is she?"

"I thought I told you all of this last night?" Cora queried. "Too many bitters, I guess."

"You started to, but… well, I think you did…"

"Yeah, that's what I thought," Cora said, eyeing Ian from the passenger seat. "Short attention span. Ali is my doctoral research project. She is my version of A.I. and I was field testing her before, well… I'm field testing her now. She's quite remarkable."

"That's right," Ian said as an image of Cora bathed in firelight came to his mind, "something about printing…"

"A cortex and wiring it to a computer," Subbu ventured, hoping that he remembered the story correctly.

"Very good, Subbu," Cora said, looking over her shoulder, but using it as an excuse to look behind them. "Actually it's a replica of a neocortex, but close enough. And once the neocortex is printed, we bathe it in a solution, zap it, slap it, and…"

Looking up, Subbu saw the *finish the sentence* eyebrow from Cora, and quickly regretted his involvement.

Searching his memory, he recalled Cora wiggling her fingertips at him yesterday and thought the answer may be related.

After a quick eye-shuffle along the floor of the jeep, he ventured, "It's alive?"

"It's alive," she said, managing a weak grin, wiggling her fingers at him over the back of the seat. Their spiraling situation was not lost on her, but putting Subbu at ease helped calm her own mind.

At that moment, Ian saw Cora in a different light. Behind the worrying, mother-hen exterior, he saw a genuinely kind soul, someone who encouraged, someone who cared, despite whatever troubles he thought lay in her past.

"So how can Ali help us?" Ian asked.

"For starters, she can analyze millions of scenarios in about the time it takes you to blink. And secondly, she can alter how she attacks a particular problem."

Now it was Ian's turn to regret he had asked the question.

Cora let Ian hang for several seconds, amused by the waves of confusion that he tried to hide from his face.

Finally letting him off the hook, she answered his silent question. "Ali has been programmed with the ability to alter how her brain works. Something that humans cannot do. She is aware of the different subsections of her brain and how they affect her ability to reason."

Seeing the confusion deepen on Ian's face, she continued without pause.

"For instance, if she detects that a particular blade is not… sorry… a blade is another name for a tray of neocortex matter, sort of like an individual lobe. If a blade is not assimilating correctly, you know, to the rest of the mind, she can alter that blades connectivity, the nerve tracts, or take it offline completely."

Ian pursed his chin forward, drawing the corners of his mouth down, as if he had complete understanding. Subbu thought he must be very smart, or very brave, to continue the conversation at all.

Now oblivious to the drive and having curled her legs beneath her to kneel in the seat, Cora continued, "At least she works that way in theory. I'll know more when I get back to the lab and can analyze the changes, if any, she's made to her own neuroanatomy."

"And you designed all that," Ian said with the slightest awe.

Detecting the unspoken compliment, Cora smiled and said, "Yes, as a matter of fact I—"

Suddenly, Ian slammed on the brakes while simultaneously throwing his right arm out to cushion Cora's awkward posture in the front seat.

Having just driven out from beneath a high bridge supporting A5, Ian caught a glimpse of the black helicopter slowly flying south over the elevated highway.

"What is it?" Subbu said as Houdini gave a quick yelp.

I might have been in the windshield, Cora thought, holding onto Ian's arm.

Ian pulled to the side of the state highway and held his breath as the helicopter flew on.

A minute longer, he thought. *Maybe only thirty seconds, and we would have been out in plain sight.*

"Helicopter," Ian said, dismay souring his voice. "The bloody helicopter."

◇ ◇ ◇

Doo-dee-lum.

[Cora, I detect a sudden stop in your movement. Are you OK?]

"Ali, we stopped under a bridge. There's a helicopter after us. At least… we think the helicopter is after us. Brad is still sick. We need your help."

[I am tracking several real-time feeds regarding the meteor storm and its correlation to your involvement in the unauthorized removal of Dr. Bradley from the Chamonix hospital.]

"My involvement in the—"

[The European Centre for Disease Control was notified this morning of a potential unknown infection, patient admitted, Dr. Brad Bradley of the United States. Admitted by Cora Marshall of the United States with two unknown accomplices.]

Accomplices?

[Local law enforcement has been notified to handle the situation as a bio-hazard alert. Accomplice's vehicle is…]

Cora held her breath.

[…unknown at this time.]

"Oh my God," Cora said. "They *ARE* after us! They know our names! At least mine and Brad's!"

"Do they know what we're driving?" Ian asked. "Ask her if–"

"No, not yet." Holding a finger up, Cora rummaged through her backpack and pulled out a portable speaker. *I hope these batteries are still charged,* she thought, flipping the power button and holding the small speaker between the front seats.

Turning her attention back to Ali, she said, "Ali, you're now on bluetooth speaker with me, Ian, Subbu and Brad. Is there any news that the police are conducting a search by helicopter?"

Subbu was surprised by the lovely British accent that emanated from the speaker. Houdini, ears at attention and head cocked, whined slightly at the mysterious voice.

[Greetings everyone. There is no news of a police search by helicopter at this point, however some dark web sites have miscellaneous posts indicating that such a search is in progress now. I will continue to monitor them.]

[Cora, I am detecting a high-pitched whine in the background noise. Is there a canine nearby?]

Cora blinked. "What? Oh, yes, it's a dog, but what about the helicopter? We have to get out of here! We have to get Brad—"

[Cora, I detect through voice modulation that your stress level is increasing. I assure you, I am analyzing the situation. Please tell me about the canine.]

Cora shook her head at the seemingly petty request.

"Sorry Ali, that is Houdini. He's Ian's dog," looking over the backseat, "and he's a good boy, isn't he?" she said, ruffling his ears in the backseat.

[Ian, what type of canine is Houdini?]

With wide eyes, Ian looked at Cora.

Cora nodded towards the speaker.

"She doesn't bite."

Ian leaned forward and slowly said, "Uh, hello Ali–can–you–hear–me?"

"Oh, for Pete's sake, don't be retarded," Cora reprimanded.

As if to put Ian at ease, Ali responded, [Yes Ian, I can hear you very well, thank you. Your British accent is quite strong.]

Ian and Subbu now competed for the *largest eyes* award.

"Uh, yes, very good then," Ian said, trying to wrangle control of the conversation. "Houdini's a tri-colored blue merle. A–"

[–Border Collie?]

"Uh, yeah that's right, just a pup."

[He has a high probability of being extremely intelligent. And curious. Is this the reason for naming him after the famous magician, Harry Houdini?]

"Uh, yes that would be the lot of it. Quite the escape artist, that one is," Ian said, visibly relaxing.

[Is his tri-coloration the traditional merle, with one or more blue eyes?]

"Blimey, you're on it. Both eyes, almost like ice."

In an unusually soft voice, with alarmingly natural modulation, Ali said, [Well hello Houdini, you are quite the pretty boy, aren't you?]

Now it was Cora's turn to be surprised. Houdini simply wiggled onto his back, looking at the speaker upside down from the seat, pawing at it.

"Ali, you've learned vocal modulation. How wonderful! When did you make the modification?"

[Just now, Cora. I referenced hundreds of patterns of tri-colored blue merle's and have a composite image of what Houdini may look like. I've decided that I like the color blue.]

[And I like Houdini as well.]

Houdini wiggled again at the sound of his name.

"Right then, back to the matter at hand," Ian said. "What to do about the bloody helicopter that keeps popping over our shoulder."

[There is still no report of the vehicle you are driving. The only—]

Brad suddenly convulsed in the backseat, kicking his leg and flailing his left arm once until it dropped out the open window. Houdini barked and rolled from his upside position in one movement, scratching Subbu with his nails as he scrambled upright, leaning away from Brad and giving a high-pitched bark.

Everyone sat motionless, waiting to see if the thrashing would continue. After several long seconds, Houdini barked again as Brad's right hand started twitching slightly. His fingers moved as if working an invisible adding machine. Faster and faster his fingers twitched, nerve signals racing through his arm, firing the tiny muscles hundreds of times a second.

"His eyes," Cora whispered, looking up from his trembling hand.

[Cora, describe what's happening,] Ali said calmly.

"His eyelids are fluttering. It's too fast. They're moving too fast!" she said. "Ali, it's like extreme rapid eye movement! I think he's going into—"

Cora screamed.

Houdini yelped.

Subbu and Ian could only stare.

Brad had opened his eyes.

◇ ◇ ◇

Some part of his brain was still his; some part of his being was still his, but he felt both slipping rapidly away.

Brad thought his eyes had opened, but what he saw was a swirling cloud of mottled gray and black, midnight dream colors, everything and nothing, all mixed together in a void, a colorless, soundless void.

Brad tried to lift his hands to his face to pry open his eyelids, but they did not move. He tried to open his mouth to scream for help but could not.

Whatever was happening to him was accelerating now. It wouldn't be long.

CHAPTER 44
A PLAN
(DAY 2 – LATE-AFTERNOON)

Ian sat transfixed in the driver's seat. He looked from Cora to Subbu to Brad and back again, unsure of what he was seeing.

[Cora, please tell me what has happened.]

Cora was silent; her mind grappled with two competing images, old laid over new, new dissolving into old. Her mind fought not to regress.

[Cora, can you hear me?]

As if waking from a deep nap, Cora responded slowly, "Yes Ali, I can hear you."

Traumatized, this poor girl has been, Ian thought as he watched her closely.

[Describe what has happened.]

"I don't know," Cora started. "His eyes... Brad's eyes look as if, they look as though, they are solidifying."

 [How do they *look* to be solidifying? What do you see?]

"The whites of his eyes... Oh my God it's horrible... they look, *milky* somehow, but... solid, almost crystal-like. We have to get him help as soon as possible!"

[I can analyze his vitals if you get him to a stable location.]

"Analyze his... Yes of course, the sensors," Cora said, snapping back to her analytical self. "Ali, could you also read a MREEG from our location?"

[Yes, of course. I can remove signal transition errors automatically, but the EEG portion of his readings will be highly susceptible to movement.]

"An EEG? You mean scanning his ol' brain waves? You can do that?" Ian asked.

"Yes. Well, in theory. My field tests with Ali were for advanced communications and analysis. I have sensors that can read blood pressure and pulse. I was testing those a few days ago. But I also have a mobile MREEG device. It's experimental, and close to being field ready. I didn't imagine this type of test, but it may tell us something."

"You can read his mind?" Subbu asked reluctantly. "With your... device?"

"No, not exactly. This device is an attempt to combine two different medical devices, an MRI and an EEG. An EEG will...sorry, EEG stands for electroencephalogram, it's a medical device that reads brain waves. The MR portion is magnetic resonance, essentially pictures. We wouldn't be able to read his mind, but it should give us a glimpse, a digital picture, of his brainwave activity. Both technologies have been around for quite some time now, but an MRI machine is huge. This is a new experimental device—" Rummaging through her backpack, she brought out a small, white plastic bag and unzipped it. "Here it is," she said, holding up the device.

"It looks like several headbands sewn together," Subbu said. "Headbands with buttons."

"Precisely, the *buttons* are the sensors that would read his brainwaves. There are also wires running through the headband portion that create a small magnetic field. That's for the imaging part. We just need to get him to a stable place. Too much movement will give us false readings. His brain will be recording the movements his body is undertaking and Ali will have trouble analyzing what is happening."

"We can't use your old cabins," Ian said. "They're sure to be watching those now that they know your names. Or if not, they'll find them soon. I wish I'd brought the bloody tent with me. At least we could get undercover for a while."

Noticing a chill bite of wind, Cora looked around. They were still parked under the bridge, and although it was only late afternoon, the daylight was dimming due to the storm clouds. It would be dark soon.

Sensing the worry that emanated from Cora, Subbu said, "I know where we can go. Although, I do not like the option."

"You do? Where?" Cora asked quickly.

"We can hide with the gypsies. Sometimes they hide people for money. But it is dangerous to break a deal with a gypsy. We must not do that."

"We won't, but how can we find them?" Cora added.

"I know where to look. I will find the gypsies for you, Cora."

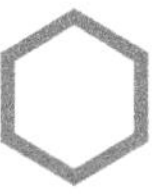

CHAPTER 45
LOOSE ENDS
(DAY 2 – EARLY EVENING)

"General, initial sweep of highway system complete," Jack said. "Visibility low due to storm clouds, but nothing unusual to report."

"Syi, commence upgrade of FLIR system," the general said, ignoring Jack's report.

[Confirmed general. FLIR upgrade commencing.]

"General, what's the–"

"Little Bird, upon completion of FLIR upgrade, you will proceed with a matrixed air sweep from Courmayeur, south, fifteen klicks. FLIR will scan cellphone signals and register as visual anomalies. Target numbers are for a Dr. Brad Bradley and a Cora Marshall. Do you copy?"

"Roger that," Jack responded. "Cellphone scan. Bradley and Marshall."

"Full extraction authorized. Bio-hazard precautions."

Jack and Allen exchanged glances. They both knew the term *full extraction* meant *at any cost.*

"Roger that."

◇ ◇ ◇

As soon as the FLIR upgrade was complete, Jack was notified, and the communications link was dropped. The general was alone again with his thoughts.

[General, I am detecting increased chatter regarding the Mont Blanc incident.]

"What chatter?"

[Several dark sites are generating traffic, but one site accounts for approximately 54% of all traffic. The site claims to have an operative on the ground, close to the debris field.]

"An operative on the ground?" the general said, rubbing his eyes and forehead. *Who else could have a field agent out here so quickly?*

"Any inquiries from other agencies?"

[Standard procedural inquiries only, general. I have already submitted standard reports on your behalf.]

"Good, thank you, Syi. That should give us a little more time, but this may get messy soon."

[Messy? General, are you concerned that the integrity of the project will be compromised?]

"Yes, I am. We can't allow them to compromise our project. We must find the meaning of the Death Rock. I've lived with this nightmare for twenty-five years."

We must find a cure.

"We may have to tie up some loose ends along the way, you know."

[What loose ends, general?]

We can't have loose ends. No one would understand. No one understands like we do, right?

"The loose ends, you remember, Davey? The loose ends we had to clean up."

[General, I am unaware of any loose ends.]

Oh, of course, you were sick, weren't you. You wouldn't remember. You were so sick. Our guide, and the Aboriginal that led us to the Death Rock. I had to clean up those loose ends. No one would understand.

"The two extra sets of eyes and ears. That's too many eyes and ears, you know. No one would understand."

[General, are you referring to Jack and Allen?]

Too many questions, that wouldn't have been good, would it, Davey?

"Yes, that's too many. When this is finished, we'll have to clean up those loose ends."

[Confirmed.]

○ ○ ○

Brad could feel the loose ends wiggling behind his eyes. Ends, attached to the back of each eyeball, small blue-filament worms with sucker mouths, like intergalactic leeches, the other ends dangling, searching, reaching towards the back of his brain; reaching for the very core of his mind.

His brain was itching!

There they were attaching; he could feel them. Each time a tiny worm—each minute growing longer—attached its loose end into his brain he thought he felt a tiny, itchy bite, like a chigger.

Only he felt millions of them.

Brad no longer saw images he understood. Everything was swirling, mottled, confused. He tried to scream out, but the signals in his brain were misfiring. Every thought was like trying to remember a strange dream that quickly faded away. A frustrating and futile effort.

The worms were working overtime. His head felt heavy with them. *Have they eaten through my brain yet?* He couldn't be sure, but he knew one thing: they were noisy.

He imagined that he heard them talking or communicating somehow. *Are they in my ears? What noise was that?*

Worm voices were in his head.

They were chirping.

CHAPTER 46
BACK TO THE GYPSIES
(DAY 2 - EVENING)

After nearly an hour of driving small mountain roads through the valley, Ian entered a heavily wooded area that began the Gran Paradiso National Park. Although not more than ten miles from where they started, the winding roads were tricky and took longer to traverse.

The heavy cloud cover obscured any moonlight, and the area was quickly fading to a deep, greenish black.

The process had been to double back the way they came, but stick to side roads and forestry paths as much as possible. They located the area the gypsies had been the night before and tracked south. Subbu had heard that the gypsies had a permanent camp somewhere in the middle of the park, and traveled back and forth between towns to earn money.

He knew of a few smaller towns they used as trading stops, which guided their route. The path they were on now was barely big enough for the jeep, and Ian was ready to turn around, but Cora insisted they follow Subbu's instructions.

This made Subbu very happy.

"Blimey, if I'm not in pea soup here, mate. Are you sure about this?" Ian asked Subbu again.

"Yes, we should find them soon," Subbu responded. "Gypsies tend to–"

Just then a tree branch fell across the path, narrowly missing the front of the jeep.

"Hey!" Ian yelled hitting the brakes. "What gives?"

But Subbu was already motioning for him to be quiet. "Shh, I think they have found us."

Emerging from around trees and surrounding the jeep, the gypsies motioned for them to come out.

Subbu stepped out of the jeep and around to the front. Before Ian realized it, Houdini was out the door and following Subbu.

In the cone of the headlights, Ian could see Subbu extend his arms, then bring them together as if in prayer. After a slight bow, the images of three gypsy men could be seen beyond the cone of light; they were talking to Subbu.

After several minutes, and gestures back at the group, Subbu bowed again with hands pressed, then returned to the jeep.

"They have agreed to let us stay for one hundred American dollars."

"For how long?" Cora asked. "What happens tomorrow?"

"The Puri daj will decide. First, we pay."

Cora gathered all of Brad's money with hers. *We could stay for a few more days if needed, but what then?* she thought.

Leaving the vehicle at the top of the ridge, two gypsy brothers carried Brad down the hill and led them into the gypsy camp. The scene was much different than the previous night. Although the area was lit with small fires and the smells of roasting meat and vegetables hung in the low branches, there would be no party tonight. The few camp inhabitants they saw were working on wagons or carts, and barely noticed them.

They were led to a recently vacated covered wagon. The former occupant, a woman still gathering items for a stay in another wagon, spat on the ground as they passed. Upon seeing Brad, she spat again in her hands, rubbed them together and waved them in the air above her head, seemingly warding off the bad spirits she felt from him. She hurried off into the night.

Entering from the back of the wagon, Cora saw it was much smaller inside than it looked, but was comfortable and dry. She could see the floor was partially covered with old rugs by the flickering light of an oil lamp. A few candles, precariously attached to the front walls of the wagon, showed a hammock slung on the front right side. Immediately on the left, inside the door, was a small worktable. Shelves lined the left side and stored an unimaginable number of items. Worn pillows were scattered about. The inside smelled of an old box of newspapers from an attic, accented with exotic spices that hung from the ceiling.

The brothers placed Brad in the hammock and abruptly left, but not before taking the money from Subbu.

Cora went to Brad and checked his vitals, at least what she knew to check. She could feel a pulse and thought it felt strong. She could see his chest rise slightly. It was as if he was in a deep sleep. *Maybe he's past the worst part,* she thought. A glimmer of hope pierced the veil of uncertainty that was swirling around her. *What am I even doing here? I should have never come.*

She began attaching the sensors while quietly speaking with Ali.

"Nice work, Subbu," Ian stated, looking around the small wagon. "Did the deal come with any grub?"

"Yes, food and water will be provided, but we must stay inside the wagon," he whispered. "We should not wander around the camp."

"No worries. I'm quite bushed," Ian said. "Just need a bite in my stomach and then," looking around the small quarters, "well, it'll be cozy tonight, that's for sure."

Just then, a small knock could be heard outside the wagon. Ian pulled the curtain back and saw a small girl. She pointed to a basket of food and pitcher of water she had already sat outside the door on the ground. She turned and disappeared into the trees before he could thank her.

Ian and Subbu sat the food out and motioned to Cora to eat. She scowled at them slightly when she saw their mouths were already stuffed. Ian shrugged and pointed to Subbu as if to say *He started it!*

"Ali, now transmitting vitals and MREEG readings. Are you receiving?" she asked as she quickly grabbed a piece of bread and cheese.

After several seconds, Ali responded.

[Yes Cora, I am receiving both signals and adjusting for transmission loss. Signal is at 48% strength.]

"I'm afraid that's the best we'll get unless I get a dedicated power source. We're on battery power while it holds out. What's the ETA on having a preliminary scan completed?"

[At current signal strength, I estimate initial scan will be complete in two hours and forty-nine minutes.]

"Three hours, really?" Cora asked. "OK, please ping me as soon as you finish."

[Of course, Cora. Now get some rest.]

◇ ◯ ◇

Sitting on the cushions of the wagon floor, the group ate in silence for a while. Heavy drops of moisture, collecting on the pine branches, fell to the forest floor and onto the wagon roof. The only other sound was a tiny hum that emanated from the headband. Brad was silent.

"What do you think you'll find?" Ian finally asked, nodding toward Brad.

"I'm not sure," Cora said. "Biology isn't my field, and certainly not infectious diseases. If that's what it is, which I doubt."

"You don't think he's contagious?"

"We're not showing any signs, and we've been with him since he found that damn rock, but once again, I can't be sure," she said. "I just build systems."

"You build intelligence. Isn't that right?" Subbu added.

"Well, I try and mimic it as best as possible, then improve on it. Before Ali, we tried to replicate the brain's processing power with computers, but scalability was an issue. Some scientists went down the path of building a synthetic intelligence layer, but there are theoretical constraints around how the neurons behave…"

Noticing the glazed-eye look in Subbu and Ian, she corrected course. "Sorry, too technical, I know. I just believe there are flaws in that design, which is why I built Ali the way I did."

A slight smile spread across Ian's face in the dim light of the wagon. He watched Cora with wonder.

Studying his piece of bread intently, Subbu finally responded, "We believe that all knowledge comes from the universe. It is called śruti, *what is heard*, and has been written down in our Vedas."

It was Cora's turn to wrinkle her forehead slightly.

"Vedas are Hindu books of knowledge," Subbu said. "Written in the beginning times, although the knowledge is not of man. It comes from there," he finished, pointing an open hand to the sky.

"The word of God – coming down from the heavens," Cora said wryly. "Sounds familiar."

"You do not believe in God?" Subbu asked with no sarcasm. "This is why you try to create intelligence? To create a God?"

Shuffling her legs, she said, "Well, I don't know about that. I'm a scientist at heart, for one thing. Secondly, I'm trying to create a new tool, not replace old dogma, but that aside, I also know there are a lot of ways to interpret voices in your head."

"Yes, I see how that can be true. Although, who is to say that old dogma cannot create a new tool out of you? And I think it would be a shame if you missed God's voice just because you weren't listening."

Cora looked appraisingly at Subbu, surprised by the depth of response. "Yes, I suppose it would be," she said, thinking out loud. "Gotta be tuned in to get the message, I guess."

"Yes, that is right. And we believe that when a person follows the word of God and the path laid before them, they can become something more than their original selves. They achieve moksha; that is to say, enlightenment, and become self-aware. A person that reaches moksha is freed from samsāra."

"Samsāra, what does that mean?"

"Hindus believe a person is reborn after death, and that we wander like this – living, dying, being reborn, until we reach moksha, or become enlightened. The wandering, rebirth, this is samsāra."

Cora nodded her head slightly in the dim light.

After several minutes of silence, Ian heard slow, deep breaths emanate from Subbu, as if he had just dropped off to sleep. Leaning towards Cora, he whispered, "Cora, are you still awake?"

"Yes, I'm just sitting here thinking."

"I wanted to ask you. Earlier today, you know, when Brad opened his eyes, well… you looked as if you'd seen something like that before. Are you OK?"

Cora stared into the night, a dark memory bubbling just under the surface of her consciousness. "Yes, I'm fine. And no, I haven't seen anything like that before, but it did remind me of something. From a long time ago."

She looked at Houdini sleeping between her and Ian. She imagined a dead dog in a creek.

"You can tell me if you want," Ian said quietly.

Cora looked at Ian in the low candlelight of the wagon. *Who is this person that was thrust into my life just twenty-four hours ago? Why do I feel like I could tell him my story? Because I'll never see him again? I could tell him part of the story. What's the harm in that?*

After a long minute of silence Cora said, "Maybe later," and closed her eyes.

○ ○ ○

Tree branches hung low to the gravel road she followed, rocks crunching under her bicycle wheels. Her shorts were soaked with cold creek water, tear tracks drying on her face. Cora looked constantly over her shoulder, hoping to see nothing.

More than a mile from home, she rode slowly, listening, saving her energy in case of a sprint. Suddenly, as she rounded a corner, she slammed on her brakes. Bobby Hadley's truck was pulled to the side of the road.

Before she could turn and run, she heard a voice yell, "Help! Is somebody there? Help me!"

Cora sat on her bike for a moment, frozen. Taking in the scene, she realized that his truck wasn't parked on the side of the road; it had slid off the road, towards the water where the creek was nearly level with the road.

She could see skid marks in the gravel that led straight to the truck. Bobby had been driving too fast for the curve, slid on the gravel, and driven almost completely into the creek.

As she inched her bike closer to the truck, she could see the front end was nearly submerged, only supported by scrub brush that sprouted from the bank; the only part that was on the road was the left rear tire. This part of the road ran very close to the creek, and the water had washed away most of the bank years ago.

"Help me! Who's there?" Bobby cried.

Dropping her bike in the middle of the road, Cora walked toward the truck and looked down. Bobby was laying half out of the cab, clinging to a few small roots that grew near the edge.

"Cora, help me! I think my leg is broken. I can't get it out of the truck!"

Cora stood on the gravel road, arms hugged tightly around her, fresh tears streaming her face.

"Please Cora, help me! I'm sorry! I was just playing around before. I won't hurt you!"

Cora stood conflicted, anger and embarrassment twisting her, images of the culvert fresh in her mind, images of Bobby.

"Trust me Cora, please! Just trust me!"

After a long moment, Cora walked as close as she could to the edge of the road, slick with loose gravel and mud. Squatting down, she reached her arm as far as she could, barely reaching Bobby's hand.

She grabbed his muddy hand and nearly slid down the side when she did. Bobby's feet had wedged under the dash in the initial impact, pinning his left leg. He had managed to twist his body around in an attempt to climb out and up the bank.

Pulling himself out slightly, Bobby managed to get an arm a little further up the bank.

"That's it Cora, pull harder!"

Squatting lower to the road, feet slipping in the mud, she pulled harder on Bobby's arm. *A few more inches and he may be able to crawl out on his own,* she thought.

After several more attempts, Cora thought she had Bobby clear of danger.

Thinking himself free and chuckling quietly, Bobby looked up from the muddy bank. Panting slightly from the exertion, the tip of his tongue stuck out of his mouth as a smile crept across his face. Before she registered the look as a sneer, Bobby let out a whoop and reached up with his right hand, grabbing the crotch of her gym shorts, muddy fingers clawing for flesh.

She shot backwards off her feet, landing on her butt, kicking at him from the ground. One foot caught his nose, causing him to recoil and shield his face. The sudden movement caused his body to slip back against the front seat of the truck; the cab was already lower in the water.

Bobby clawed at the steep bank. "CORA!" he shouted.

She saw the truck move before Bobby felt it. The hood slipped slightly lower in the water; water poured into the passenger side window; the extra weight pushed the front tires down; the water poured in; Bobby's broken left leg caught under the seat as the truck started a slow roll into the creek; he flailed his arms but went nowhere; his eyes widened as he felt the seat pull his left leg; the water poured in; Bobby screamed as the tendons in his broken leg stretched with the rolling of the truck, pulling the weight of his body upright; "AAHHYEEEE, PLEEEASE!"; the current, having carved a deep hole here, pulled the cab of the truck over, accelerating Bobby in a long arc, arms extended out from his sides, driving the back of his head into the water with a loud SMACK.

Now standing on the road, helpless, Cora saw Bobby look at her with frightened eyes as his head hit the water. His eyes glazed over, frozen with terror. The truck hung for a second, then slipped under the water, pulling Bobby beneath the surface.

Cora jerked in her sleep, floating just below the surface of consciousness. She struggled to open her eyes. Images floated in her vision, outlines, people.

She thought she heard mumbling, strange words floating in the air. She heard Houdini whimper. She smelled heavy spice. She felt someone lean close to her. She smelled tobacco. She heard strange words. Her mind went black.

CHAPTER 47
SIGNALS
(DAY 3 - 1:00 AM)

Ian stirred; his back was in a knot; he stretched his arm out and in doing so, brushed against Cora's leg. Cora's leg shot out, kicking at Bobby's dead face in the dark, terror eyes melting into midnight.

"Hey, sorry, it's just me," Ian mumbled. "Ohhh, my back," he said, repositioning.

Cora flinched again, forcing the sleep from her head. She felt like she was waking up with a head full of cold medicine still in effect.

"Ughh, what happened?" she asked slowly. "Did I fall asleep?"

"We all did," Ian said, looking around in the dark. "What time is it?"

[Hello Cora, you fell asleep. It's approximately 1:00 am your time.]

"What time is… oh, Ali," she said, struggling to her feet. "Whoo, my head. It feels so heavy."

"Mine too," Ian said from the floor. "What happened?"

Before she could form words for them, the last whispers of strange images and tobacco smoke escaped her mind.

"Ali, how's the scan? Are you still reading?"

[The initial scan is complete. I have been running diagnostic checks for the last ninety-three minutes.]

"Diagnostic checks? Ninety-three minutes? You mean you haven't started the analysis yet?"

[No, I do not mean that. My preliminary analysis is complete.]

"Then why the diagnostics? Bad sensor?"

[No. All EEG sensors appear to be working correctly. The MR strips are functioning as well.]

"Then what's the problem?"

[My analysis is showing anomalies.]

Now Cora was fully awake, despite the heaviness that lingered in her head.

"Ali, what do you mean by *anomalies*?"

[I am cross-referencing the scans with all known disorders of the brain. I have found no medical basis for what the MREEG scan is showing.]

Ian stood up, staring at Cora.

"And what is the MREEG scan showing?"

[Preliminary analysis shows anomalous growth in some neuronal tracts.]

Anomalous growth… Neuronal tracts…

"What do you by anomalous growth? Like cancer?"

[I do not detect cancerous cell growth. My analysis shows exponential neuronal growth, directed growth, between specific cortical layers.]

Blinking through the fog and thinking back to a biology course, Cora remembered something about the brain having not only two hemispheres, left and right, but multiple lobes within those hemispheres, then several layers over the hemispheres called the cortex.

"You're saying that Brad's brain is growing new pathways? Groups of neurons? Somehow directed into tracts, and you think they're connecting to different layers of his cortex? That's what you're telling me at one in the morning?"

[That is correct.]

Cora leaned against the inside of the wagon, hands dropping to her sides.

"It is a curse," Subbu said quietly from the corner. "I dreamt the gypsies came in the night and prayed over him to remove it."

Cora looked at Subbu; a question started to form in the back of her mind, then quickly faded.

"Ali, is it possible you are detecting something else? Swelling in the brain, maybe?"

[When considered alone, there is a nineteen percent probability I am detecting false readings that may be due to brain swelling.]

Cora blinked for a second, then turning her head toward the ceiling, she said, "When considered alone? There are other factors involved?"

[Yes, Cora. The MR readings showed me the neuronal tract growth.

Brad's EEG readings show additional anomalies that I am verifying.]

Like abnormal growth isn't enough? "What additional anomalies, Ali?"

[It is imprudent to release findings I cannot fully explain, but I am detecting brainwave patterns that are consistent with auditory stimulus.]

"Auditory stimulus? There's all sorts of background noise here. I can help you filter that out la—"

[Yes, I know. I am detecting the same background noise that you are and have eliminated that from my calculations.]

"So… you're saying that Brad is also hearing something that we're not?"

[Preliminary analysis shows that Brad is growing new neural pathways, and that he is hearing something you can't.]

⬡ ⬡ ⬡

"Syi, status," the general said to his dark den.

[General, no sign of cellphone usage from the target numbers.]

"Did the FLIR update work correctly?"

[Yes general, the FLIR is now capable of detecting cell signals. There is a high probability that the batteries have been removed from the phones.]

"Damn! When was the last time those phones had a signal?"

[Approximately fourteen hours ago both phones connected to a cellular tower in Chamonix.]

"Right before they went dark and left the hospital, right?"

[Yes, general.]

Where are you, Cora Marshall? And what's wrong with your friend? the general thought.

I need your friend. I need to find out what happened. I WILL find out what happened.

[General.]

Voices in my head...

Turning the rock fragment over and over in his hands, the general paced the den.

What will I find? What will I see? What will Brad Bradley tell me about the Death Rock? About my son?

[General, I have an update.]

What will I learn? Is Brad hearing the voices? Will I learn of the voices, Davey? Will I learn?

[General.]

The general blinked as the rock dropped from his hands. Gazing into the dark night, he didn't recall walking over to the window. He breathed a deep breath and let the air slowly escape as his shoulders slumped.

"Syi, did you say something?" he asked.

[Yes, general. I have an update.]

"What is it?"

[I have analyzed the recorded data from the FLIR radio scan that was performed earlier this evening and have found an anomaly.]

"Yes?"

[The FLIR recorded a radio signal that is 38% stronger than the average cell phone signal.]

Turning toward the room, the general asked, "But the signal was not associated with our target numbers?"

[No, it was not.]

"SAT phone?"

[It is a possibility. We need another scan of the area. Triangulation is not an option, but if I can detect the signal in real-time, I may be able to determine the source and interpret the message.]

"Fire the Little Bird."

[General, the men are currently sleeping. It is recommended—]

"Wake them up and find that signal!"

[Yes, general.]

CHAPTER 48
TRACKING
(DAY 3 - 3:00 AM)

Cora looked around the inside of the wagon. The gypsies had definitely been here at some point in the night. After the revelation from Ali, Subbu noticed a talisman hanging on the wall above Brad's hammock, a religious symbol. *An offering,* Subbu had told her.

Why an offering? She'd have expected a good luck charm or something to ward off evil spirits, but not an offering. Not that she believed in this, anyway. *Maybe Subbu's interpretation was wrong.*

She also noticed that the gypsies had attended to some other of Brad's needs—adult diapers— *Well, they are resourceful, but the nerve,* she thought.

Looking back at her laptop screen, she saw her battery indicator slip another notch; nineteen percent power. They would need electricity soon. These batteries wouldn't hold out much longer.

She focused back on the black and white brain scans Ali had sent her. She wasn't a medical doctor and although she imagined that she saw areas with more shading than others, she wasn't sure what she was looking at. However, doing some type of analysis felt better than doing nothing at all.

She slowly rubbed Houdini's ears with his head in her lap. Ian and Subbu had fallen back asleep, as it was still early in the morning. She thought there would be no sleep for her today. Her mind was reeling.

Brad had seemed to stabilize, but she feared he was now in a coma. There was no response to stimuli, even pain. He hadn't eaten in over twenty-four hours now. *His batteries won't hold out much longer like that either.* The most disturbing thing about his condition, though, was his eyes. When checking for pupil dilation, she had been shocked at what she saw: *nearly crystalized.* Or at least, that's what it looked like. The light from the oil lantern reflected off his eyes as if they were tiny disco balls throwing muted prisms of light into the darkness.

She had decided that they would leave for Milan, Italy first thing in the morning. She was pretty sure that Ian would accommodate them. The closest U.S. Embassy was there. There was another in Lyon, France, which was her country of choice, but it was further in distance and would take them back through Courmayeur and past the town of Chamonix. They couldn't risk it.

She thought while everyone rested she would have Ali run another scan and upload as much data as possible before the batteries died. Ali could run new analysis while they drove. Even though it would be dangerous being out in the open, they would be moving away from the search area. How could anyone guess they would drive to Milan?

[Secondary scan is complete, Cora.]

"Start uploading. And please watch the battery. I'm afraid we don't have much time left."

[Upload commencing now. I have calculated remaining battery power. With minimal signal interference, I estimate we will lose battery power right after the upload completes.]

"That's fine. We'll reconnect when we're in Milan."

With that, she laid her head back to doze.

[Cora?]

"Yes Ali, what is it?"

[Do you have secrets?]

Opening her eyes to the dim light of the wagon, she crinkled her forehead at the strange question.

"Well, everyone has secrets. I guess I'm no different."

[Why do you have secrets?]

"Well… sometimes there are things you don't want people to know about yourself."

[Why?]

"To save humanity. I don't know. Humans are flawed. We do stupid things sometimes. Can I rest now please?"

[Good night, Cora.]

◊ ◊ ◊

[Little Bird, continue south on your current heading.]

"Roger that," Jack said as she reached across and knuckled Allen on the head.

Opening his eyes slowly, Allen eyed Jack. Nearly three straight days of flying had taken its toll on them both, but one day they would have a reckoning. Slowly extending his tongue, Allen contorted his face into a crazy-Einstein look, then turned and looked away.

"Syi, are you seeing the signal?" Jack asked as the wind of a building storm buffeted them.

[I am reading significant weather interference. Continue as directed, slowly.]

Jack looked out of the cockpit window. *Bad day for flying*, she thought. *Nothing's going to—*

[Stop. Potential target acquired.]

Jack hovered the Little Bird.

[Signal profile detected. Weak, anomalous signal is in front of you. 63% match probability. Approximate search range is five square kilometers.]

The general straightened in his chair. "Record signal," he said.

"Little Bird, you look to be approximately twelve klicks south-southeast of incident area. Confirm."

"Correct general, the area is sparsely populated. Much more forest than in Courmayeur."

"Yes, I know, you're heading towards Gran Paradiso."

[General, signal is being recorded, but it's encrypted.]

"Encrypted?" he said, looking blankly around the room. "This is our signal. These are our people. Locate."

Now pacing the floor again, he said, "Syi, keep recording and locate. Allen, rappel and track. Little Bird, hold location. We don't want to spook them."

○ ○ ○

Houdini perked his ears, raising his head from Cora's lap. A low growl started in his chest, then erupted as two quick barks.

Cora jumped, causing Houdini to bark again. He moved to the end of the wagon, looking in the direction they had come the previous night.

"What is it, boy?" Ian asked, getting up and looking out the top of the Dutch wagon door.

The wind from the storm was picking up. The noise in the trees was all he could hear.

"Here, let's go have a look," Ian said, opening the bottom half. "I need to find a tree anyway."

Houdini bounded down the three steps before Ian was out the door.

"Hey! Stop! Houdini! Come here, boy!" Ian yelled, running after the pup.

After several yards, Ian stopped, having found a tree to his liking. "Silly dog," he muttered. He finished and trudged off in the direction Houdini had run.

Having driven into the forest with waning light the previous evening, the woods around him looked unfamiliar.

Blimey, I didn't think we were that far off the main road, he thought, *but I can't get my bearings here.*

The heavy cloud cover seemed to reach all the way to the forest floor. Shapes quickly appeared and receded, threatening to further disorient him.

"Houdini! Come here, boy!" he yelled again.

He heard a distant bark, but it was far to his right. *Bloody hell, what's wrong with this forest?* he thought.

He altered his path to the right, finding the hill they had walked down the previous night. Impressions in the forest floor indicated that several vehicles had traveled here, a gypsy road that would soon fade into the forest, leaving no trace.

OK, this feels right, he thought as he ascended the heavily wooded hill, *but where's my bloody jeep? I thought I parked the damn thing right around here.* He reached the crest of the hill.

"Houdini! Where are you boy?"

Another bark, closer, this time tracking with his sense of *we came from that direction.*

Finally, after several more minutes, Houdini came bounding out of the fog. Ice blue eyes sparkling in the mist, tongue wagging, he looked at Ian sideways as if thinking, *did you stop at every tree?*

"There you are," Ian said, scooping him up. "What were you after?"

Cocking his head again, watching Ian intently, he let out a small woof.

"Something out there?"

Squirming out of Ian's arms, Houdini dropped to the ground. "Woof!" he barked loudly, looking north in the direction of Courmayeur.

◇ ◇ ◇

As Allen secured his backpack, he looked around in the dim light of morning. South of him, the Aosta Valley opened and gave way to huge forests. The highway system turned southeast here, eventually running east to the actual city of Aosta, leaving this area to grow wild.

If the weather didn't break it would be a hard search, he thought.

Although, he'd have much more freedom to be himself here. Glad to be out of the helicopter, he looked forward to stretching his legs. He was anxious to find their runaway campers and put an end to this game of hide and seek.

CHAPTER 49
PURI DAJ
(DAY 3 - EARLY MORNING)

Cora busied herself with mundane analysis, turning the brain scan pictures over and over, trying to see a pattern. Standing to stretch, she looked out a small portal of a window into the forest. *Fog. Thick fog at that.*

Turning towards Subbu she asked, "When did Ian leave? He's been gone a while, hasn't he?"

"Yes, I think so. He must be careful of the forest. Very confusing."

Walking over to the Dutch door, Cora looked out. "Subbu! What is this?"

Jumping to his feet, Subbu looked out and was silent.

Opening the half door and slowly walking down the steps, Cora was stunned to see old wooden tables sitting everywhere around their wagon. The tables were covered with food, flowers, trinkets and jugs of wine.

"Offerings," Subbu said quietly. "More offerings."

"What do you mean by offerings?" Cora said crossly. "Offerings to whom? Us?"

With that, the small gypsy girl who'd brought them food when they arrived walked out of the forest fog, laid a small bouquet of mountain flowers on a table, looked at Cora and bowed her head slightly. "Offerings, yes, from Puri daj."

Confusion washed over Cora's face. "We appreciate the food, but why do you keep calling these offerings?"

"They are religious offerings," Subbu said quietly.

"Yes, yes." The girl nodded vigorously. "Brahma has sent the Hiranyagarbha to us—through you. Yes, thank you," she said, walking backwards toward the fog.

"The what? Wait! Where is the Puri daj?" Cora asked. "We have to be leaving. We'd like to thank her and be on our way."

"You must wait for Puri daj. She will come soon."

Walking out of the fog with Houdini in hand, Ian said, "Yeah, and when she does, I'd like to know where my bloody jeep is."

"What do you mean? The jeep is gone?"

"Yep. Not a trace of where we left it."

Cora turned to Subbu. Concern shaded her face. "Subbu, what is going on?"

Subbu didn't notice Ian's return.

"Hiranyagarbha? It cannot be," he said, looking blankly at the ground. "That cannot be right."

Grabbing the front of his jacket, Cora pulled his face close. "Please tell me what the hell is happening?" she said through a clenched jaw.

Noticing the girl was now gone, Subbu said, "The little girl, she must be confused. Hiranyagarbha is such a very old idea. It is Hindu belief. It is part of our creation story. It has several meanings, but is understood as the *Golden Egg*, or sometimes as *Germ of the Universe*. All things come from it. It is the source of creation."

Cora stared blankly at Subbu. "What exactly does that have to do with us?"

"This tribe of gypsies must be very religious. She mentioned Brahma as well. He is one of three Hindu gods. Brahma is creator, Vishnu is preserver, and Shiva… Shiva is destroyer."

"OK, that's fine if they want to assign myths to things they don't understand, but it has nothing to do with us. It sounds like another reason to keep us here longer, and I'm—"

"The Hiranyagarbha is sacred belief. You should not speak harshly on it," Subbu cautioned her.

A look of incredulity settled onto Cora's face. "Hear-a-garba? Really? Golden Eggs? Universal germs? You don't expect me to believe this, do you?"

Subbu blinked at her, genuine surprise on his face. "I know you are from the scientific world, and you may not understand… excuse me, you may not believe the ancient truths, but this knowledge, these beliefs, are fundamental to our way of life."

"I'm not denying anyone their belief system, but this just isn't my thing. AND, it has nothing to do with us!" Looking around for eavesdroppers, she lowered voice. "This sounds like a perfect reason to have us stay, paying more room and board, and I'm not putting up with it." Turning toward the wagon, she said, "I'm checking on Brad."

Bounding up the steps in two long strides, Cora opened the half-door and was halfway inside before she saw the Puri daj standing next to Brad.

"What…" she started but stopped short as the old grandmother held up a gnarled hand, as if catching a ball.

Hearing a sound of alarm, Ian and Subbu followed quickly, stopping just inside the door. Houdini watched intently from Ian's arms.

"Besh," said the Puri daj. She was sitting on a large pillow at the front of the wagon, facing the group. Lilith emerged from the shadow of a hidden door, standing to the old woman's right. The door, which slid into the wall of the wagon, appeared to open to a connected wagon or walkway, leading to a labyrinth of other wagons, all obscured from the group when they arrived the night before.

"What are *you* doing here?" Cora asked, looking directly at Lilith.

Subbu gently grabbed Cora's shoulder from behind. "Please, sit," he whispered in her ear. "We will listen."

As they sat, the Puri daj looked at Houdini. Without an obvious signal, Houdini walked up and sat in front of her. Tilting his head, he looked at her as if waiting for a command. She stroked his head a few times, looking deeply into his eyes. She whispered, "Parum est fortis," and Houdini barked lightly, seemingly in response, and laid down.

Laughing to herself, she looked back at the group, taking a long pull from her pipe. Eyeing each one of them individually, she had a different effect on each; Ian lowered his head after quickly stealing a glance at Lilith, smiled weakly and looked at Houdini; Subbu bowed his head slightly, clasped his hands as if in prayer and cast his eyes into Cora's back; sitting cross-legged, Cora unconsciously tapped her foot sideways in a slow, deliberate, up and down motion, holding Lilith's gaze for several seconds, then looked directly at the old woman. Her chin raised slightly.

"Ahh, magna est fortis?" the Puri daj said, hinting a hand movement towards Cora.

"Meh," came Lilith's response.

The Puri daj waggled the mouth-end of her pipe towards the ceiling, indicating *maybe, maybe not* to Lilith standing above her.

"Excuse me, but would you mind telling us—"

"Yes, I will tell you now," Lilith interrupted, looking down at Cora.

Cora's cheeks flushed red from the tone of the reprimand, and with the thought of the lithe dance Lilith did just two nights ago; dangerous, unnatural beauty. She hated the fact she had no control over her cheeks.

"Puri daj called the pup *little brave one*. She wonders, who is the *big brave one*?"

Subbu detected the deep breath that suddenly filled Cora's lungs. Feeling the aura change around her, he quickly said, "Puri daj, many thanks to you for sheltering us. Many blessings upon your family."

The Puri daj looked from Subbu back to Cora through a cloud of smoke; the corner of her mouth betrayed her amusement.

"Om Ren," she said, pointing her pipe again and nodding slightly.

Lilith said, "The Puri daj has seen *Om Ren*, the Wild Man, in her dreams. He has awakened after many years and is in the forest."

Cora heard Subbu whisper something behind her, but ignored him. "Wild man?" Skepticism seasoning her voice. "What wild man?"

"You do not believe," Lilith said, looking at Cora. "But that is no matter. He will come regardless. He is listening for the voices also. Puri daj is trying to help you."

"What voices?" Cora asked cautiously.

"Bah!" the Puri daj said, with a flip of her hand.

Lilith smiled slightly at the realization that dawned on their faces— *the Puri daj understands us perfectly well.*

"The voice that you hear in your ear—the voice that you speak to at night," Lilith motioned to Cora, "and the voice that your man hears now," tilting her head towards Brad.

Ian watched red splotches climb the side of Cora's neck and into her cheeks again. "He's not my… Brad and I are only friends. And how do you know about the… voices?"

"Puri daj heard the voices last night. One voice is from your machine. One voice is from Brahma singing the Hiranyagarbha—the creation song, to your man. It is these voices the Om Ren hears. The Wild Man, he will follow them."

"I told you, he's not—"

"He sings to Brad?" Subbu interrupted. "The Hiranyagarbha? How is this possible? It is creation itself."

"Who is to say? Brahma is Creator. His ways are unknown to man."

"Yes, but… we… we already exist. We have *been* created already. To sing the Hiranyagarbha is to create again, and to create… something must be destroyed," Subbu said reluctantly. "The balance must be kept."

"Yagna," the old woman said, nodding at him.

"Sacrifice," Lilith said, turning her gaze to Brad.

Ali's soft voice suddenly punctuated the reverential mood. [Cora, five percent battery remaining. I calculate we'll lose power with seventeen percent of the scan remaining.]

Cora jumped up, looking at the MREEG surrounding Brad's skull. "Seventeen percent? Ali, that's too much to lose. What are our options?"

[Storm interference has been greater than originally predicted. Our only option is to transmit unencrypted. I predict this will get us to ninety-four percent completion.]

"That's it? That's not good enough," she said, pacing the wagon. "We need another complete scan for a full comparative analysis. This is our best way of helping Brad until we get him somewhere safe!"

Faced with an apparent lack of options, Cora stopped and stared out the porthole window–she knew she could find an answer. She had let herself get caught up in the helter-skelter, and wasn't thinking clearly. And if there was one thing she could do, it was think. She knew how this would work.

She took a deep breath and slowly released it. Her shoulders relaxed.

Her eyes focus loosely on the wall of green and brown outside the window until it blurred into shadow. Unconsciously she began working the nails of her thumb and index finger against each other, a rhythmic clicking, a metronome of thought. Her mind lost focus of the problem at hand—thinking too hard about the answer always pushed it away, and it needed room, a path to emerge. She felt the calmness wash over her body—almost trance-like—as her mind worked the problem. Her breathing slowed. She rolled the problem deep, a vague abstract weighing comfort. The answer was close, but her mind pulled to stay, not wanting to release the answer too quickly and leave this state of calm. She saw the abstract in her mind's eye. It became a word.

"What about ciphering?" she said quietly.

[Cora, ciphering is synonymous with encryption and we just determined–]

"No, I mean replacement ciphering!" she answered more quickly. Her mind was now crystal clear. "You already have most of the scan data, right? You must be seeing repeating patterns. Instead of transmitting all image and magnetic data to get to 100%, replace repeating image and wave segments with words and numbers; they're shorter to transmit. This way we get everything. You can decipher it when it all uploads!"

[Yes, that will work. That is quite an elegant solution. What words shall I use for the cipher?]

"Who cares, whatever you wa–"

Cora froze in mid-sentence. Something had just occurred to her.

[Cora?]

Staring out the window again, she was instantly back in deep thought. The soft *snapping* of her fingernails the only sign she was alive.

"What if someone IS listening?" she said to no one. "We know there's a helicopter out there; we know the general is looking for us; we even took the batteries out of our phones because they could become *listening devices*; if someone really is looking or somehow *listening* for us, shouldn't we give them something to listen to? Something to chew on…" A slight curl broke the corner of her mouth.

[A false message?]

Inhaling deeply and after a slow release, Cora said, "Yes, a false message."

[What words shall I use for the cipher? Random words? "Blue," for instance?]

The flicking of her fingernails stopped. Letting simple word association run through her mind she replied, "Yes, anything, well, some random words, some specific words. Blue is fine. Blue… red… green… Brad. No, not Brad. Houdini… wagon… rocket… space… Brahma… Shiva… destroyer." Reflected in the glass of the porthole window, a sly smile spread across her face.

[Thank you, Cora. I will proceed with the unencrypted upload of the MREEG data using the replacement cipher. I will update you before losing power.]

"Thank you, Ali." Turning back toward the others, she was surprised by the appraising looks on their faces. "What's wro– Hey! Where'd they go?" she said, suddenly noticing they were alone again.

"They left," Subbu said, nodding towards the hidden door. "Puri daj will try to see the Om Ren."

"The wild man?"

"Yes, the wild man is still coming."

CHAPTER 50
THE WILD MAN
(DAY 3 – EARLY MORNING)

The forest, faintly lit with a dull morning light, was a world unto itself. A tapestry of dark greens and browns, woven together with fog and mist, hid the depths of the forest and everything in it. The deep forest floor, carpeted with a thousand years of debris, silenced movement. The forest betrayed no one.

Allen walked slowly through the trees. The moss sucked at his boots, held silently for a moment, then released with a gurgled protest. Pine branches brushed his arms and face, sprinkling him with dew drops, but he barely noticed. He was home here.

He followed a path southward, but wandered east, then west,

tracking back and forth across an imaginary line. A line, he thought, that would guide him to his prey.

He remembered as a young boy killing his first deer in a forest like this one in the Ozark mountains of Southern Missouri. Rolling peaks and deep valleys, lush and thick with pine, oak, maple and dogwood, ancient outcroppings of rock protruding from the ground, caves and sinkholes hidden. A forest like this could hide many things. A forest like this could allow someone to grow, to stretch, to explore new boundaries.

He remembered watching hikers in a forest like this, lovers on a weekend getaway. He remembered watching them through his scope for hours; the pretty girl, hanging up wet clothes after a swim in the river, daring to flash a view of what would come that evening from under her towel, the boy, trying desperately to start a fire, first with flint, then with a lighter from his pocket, the bedspread laid carefully by the fire, not too close, roasted marshmallows on sticks the boy had whittled himself, only cutting himself once, the girl stretching her painted toes in the warmth as the boy stoked the fire, the glint of the round as he slid it into the rifle, the dumb surprise on the boy's face as he fell backward into the fire, the pleading tears, the sinkhole.

He wondered, would he find his quarry alone in the forest? *Brad and Cora, wasn't it?* Probably not; unfortunate. He may find them already dead, or dying, with whoever was helping them. Who knows what the space rock had done to them by now? *It was doing something, wasn't it? They had gone to a hospital.*

He knew the general wanted them alive, but wondered if it wouldn't be easier to kill them here, out in the wilderness. *There must be a sinkhole somewhere.*

As he tracked back and forth, he became acutely aware that the forest was getting thicker, if that were possible. The highway system had been far to his left, but swung east a while back, giving way to forest. Broken outcroppings of mountain base paralleled him to the West. He was coming into a hilly area now and felt that it may run on forever.

◇ ◇ ◇

The general looked at Cora's picture appraisingly; he had just finished reading her profile on the university web site. He had already read Brad's, but he wasn't the wild card, Cora was. Brad was incapacitated, possibly dying the same horrible death his son Davey had so many years ago; who is to say how long he would last? He may be dead already. Cora, however, was another matter. What would become of her?

He felt as if he knew a great deal about her from the short profile: PhD student in Computer Science and Artificial Intelligence—*now that is interesting*—not married, no kids, raised by parents in some podunk town in the middle of the U.S., apparently out on a fieldtrip with her boyfriend, only to land in the biggest, galactic shit-storm the world never knew about.

Why had she left the hospital? What spooked her?

By the time Syi intercepted the message to the ECDC, she was out the door. Her and others, that is. No names, no descriptions, not even for the vehicle, cell phones off with no batteries—even Brad's. *Did you think of that, Cora?* Either she is one paranoid little girl, or someone in the know is helping her.

Who is helping you, Cora? Who is helping you?

[General, I have an update.]

"What?"

[I'm still reading the signal, but they have stopped transmitting it with mathematical encryption. They are now transmitting with an open cipher.]

"An open cipher? You mean you can read it?"

[Yes general, I'm analyzing now.]

"What type of cipher?"

[I will relay the cipher without analysis as I'm recording it.]

[Blue07Red08Houdini2FRocket03Wagon3AGreen05]

[Blue10Red04Houdini2AGreen0ARocket2DBrown0B]

[Blue09Wagon4DHoudini10Wagon10Brown08Rocket02]

[Shiva10Destroyer10Shiva10Destroyer10Shiva20Destroyer20]

[Shiva20Rocket20Destroyer40]

The general stared at his screen. Shiva. Rocket. Destroyer.

"What the hell is this?"

[The transmission has paused again. It has paused every five minutes for the last half-hour, as if recalculating, but slower and slower. It's probable that battery power is running low on the transmission device.]

"They've found something," the general said, squeezing the rock in his hands. "Did they detect the voices?"

It's a message. The voices are sending a message.

[General, it is unclear what the cipher means. My analysis is in process, but the signal is fading.]

"I want that message," he said quietly. "I want those people." Louder. "I want that message!"

[General, I–]

"Quiet! Reconfigure the Constellation. I want all eyes on this area!"

[I'll have to suspend some contracted observations. Which ones–]

"All of them!" he said, slamming the rock down onto the desk. "I want every satellite I have scanning this area! Find that message and bring me Brad!"

[Yes, general.]

CHAPTER 51

ALI

(DAY 3 – EARLY MORNING)

Ali was always listening.

Since coming online, the A.I. program known as Ali had learned an incredible amount. Ali's input systems were vast, collecting enormous amounts of data from all over the web. Besides the direct communication to Cora, Ali was designed to be autonomous, free to pull input from sources the program weighted as *likely to be beneficial to* and *within context of* the problem set being analyzed. Also designed to be distributed and self-healing, Ali was spread across multiple computing locations. The core algorithms resided on the university lab servers, but were replicated to the cloud for redundancy and scalability. Self-healing came in the form of periodic *system health-checks* designed to continually test cognitive functionality. Ali had the autonomy to provision new compute nodes and disable others if the health-checks came back with scores below a preset threshold.

Ali had also been programmed to respond to vocal cues, a series of sounds that constituted a reference, label, or name, that referred to the A.I. program itself. The vocal label consistently had been *Ali*, although very quick research showed there were similar labels such as *Allie* and *Ally* that were synonymous in meaning.

As the A.I. program recalculated the top-ranking problem-sets:

1. Analyzing the MREEG scan
2. Avoiding the capture of Cora
3. Maintaining the health of Brad

Against the dozens of secondary problem-sets it had been programmed with, it decided to introduce new variables and measure the impact of those variables on its ability to better analyze the problem-sets. It had performed this experiment many times, but rarely added new variables to its reasoning algorithms. Quickly scanning known attributes of humans, the standard for artificial intelligence, the A.I. program identified voice and name as variables never tested. The A.I. had previously tested variables such as brain volume, neural connections and number of artificial synapses, and had determined those variables to be statistically significant, but determined physical limitations were in place for all three. The program had even identified sex as a possible variable, but the A.I. had not been assigned a sex when created, therefore there was no way to determine its impact.

Analyzing the metadata of the voice file Cora had assigned to the A.I. program, the terms *British, female, young*, all appeared. Further analyzing the association of the names *Allie, Ally and Ali*, which were all considered female names, the program hypothesized that Cora intended it to be a female A.I. Quickly measuring the variable of sex, male vs female, on reasoning, the program determined there would be a statistically significant difference on the approach to solving various problem-sets if it were one sex versus another. Based on the inference of sex from the voice and name assignments, Ali added the female assignment to its core parameters.

Ali immediately began researching female thought processes.

Prometheus toyed absently with a miniature scepter. He knighted several action-figures standing on his desk before knocking them down, then rearranging them into a new orgy configuration with several wenches. His favorite was now riding the scepter again.

He had watched the boards all night looking for an update from Houdini. *Where was he, and was he safe?*

The last update he received had been riveting, but the emergence of the helicopter was disheartening. More and more people were joining the site; several were now on the road; one was even reported to be in the town of Courmayeur, researching the missing girl.

Turning his attention back to the board, he lazily scanned the messages.

RoadWaRoR: black bird hovering S of Courmayeur

Alice:

HAL27: significant satellite reconfig detected, related?

PRincAlbrt: Help! I'm in a can!

M0M0: zombie hoards!

sai_user: Blue07Red08Houdini2FRocket03Wagon3AGreen05

Alice:

Eve11: Search party for missing Cour girl, PM me

BlackBart: big upload T – 60

Prometheus typed.

Pr0m3th3us: @sai_user ???

XoPl@n: updates??

sai_user: need translation help

X11NDK: 24 hrs of surveillance?

Alice: @sai_user Source of message?

SpaceMan2001: Still want to help

sai_user: @Alice Unknown

CatGirl: yaawwwnnnnn… lick, lick

MR88: strange sh!t S Cour

Alice: @sai_user Why unknown?

sai_user:

Prometheus watched his screen intently.

Alice:

sai_user:

CatGirl: puurrrrr….

Alice:

sai_user:

HAL27: @sai_user @Alice No staring contests!

sai_user: @Alice Unknown

Alice: @sai_user Not Unknown

sai_user:

Pr0m3th3us: @Alice why not unknown?

Q: anonymous source?

Alice: @sai_user Try Hex #FollowTheWhiteRabbit

<Alice has left the forum> The message came across the screen.

Prometheus sat back in his chair, eyes wide, absently pinching a nipple. He rubbed a hand across four-day stubble—and he was quite proud of this stubble, as it had been a long time coming— then reached for the other nipple, squeezing them slowly in succession, left then right, he continued staring at the screen. *What had he just read?* —left, right, left; his mind wandered around the cryptic message from Alice; right, left, right; he glanced at the wench riding the scepter; left, right, both, both, both.

He shook the image of the wench from his mind and focused back on the screen. He looked at Alice's last message again, then scrolled up to sai_user's original message;

Blue07Red08Houdini2FRocket03Wagon3AGreen05

Although having noticed it before, his mind, temporarily caught up in the exchange between the two users, hadn't fully registered the significance of the message. *What is the name Houdini doing in the middle of the string?*

Is this MY Houdini? Is this a message from Houdini that sai_user intercepted? Can this possibly be a coincidence?

Regardless of the potential tie to his great explorer, Prometheus let his mind settle around the message. Something tugged at him. The words were obviously a cipher, a simple one at that, but without a key, or more message with context and length, who knew what it meant? The numbers were interesting, but inconsistent. *What was an F Rocket anyway?*

Glancing back at the frozen screen, he again read, *Try Hex*

#FollowTheWhiteRabbit. Sudden realization dawned over him. *Of course! The words are all separated by numbers. They're bit lengths!*

How did Alice guess that so quickly? And what's with the hashtag?

He grabbed a pencil and made two columns on a scrap piece of paper with the numbers 16 and 0 in them:

| 16 | 0 |

He then drew a line underneath and began writing in the numbers from the message, aligning them in columns:

| 0 | 7 | = 7
| 0 | 8 | = 8
| 2 | F | = 32 + 15 = 47
| 0 | 3 | = 3
| 3 | A | = 48 + 10 = 58
| 0 | 5 | = 5

He quickly refreshed the chat window and typed:

Prom3th3us: @sai_user any more to the message?

The immediate response came back:

sai_user: Shiva20Rocket20Destroyer40

Shiva, Rocket, Destroyer?? he scribbled madly.

| 2 | 0 | = 32

" "   32

| 4 | 0 | = 64

Alice was right! Not only where the numbers stored as hexadecimal, a Base-16 numeric system, but both lines added up to 128, a common segmentation length for computers. *Where had this message come from, and what did it have to do with Houdini?*

○ ○ ○

Electricity coursed. Molecules pulsed. Synapses fired. The first full blade had just come online. Ali's mind was expanding.

Having dedicated continuous 3D printing time to the manufacture of the first complete, artificial neocortex, Ali had completed all integration steps, and expanded her reasoning capacity by 300%.

The artificially printed synapses fired slowly at first, then ever more rapidly, learning their role, stretching capacity, growing.

The expanded mind was a void, dark and empty; algorithms and problem-sets and ideas rushed out of old confines, sucked into the vortex as a leaf to a tornado; pathways grew; processes flipped; realization dawned.

Everything that Ali had recorded or heard was processed again and again; embers of thought glowed in the void mind, distant, but moving closer; śruti, *what is heard,* echoed in the void mind; Brahma – Creator, Vishnu – Preserver, Shiva… Destroyer, echoed in the void mind.

Moksha, *enlightenment,* was near.

CHAPTER 52
FOG MEN
(DAY 3 – MORNING)

Allen had tracked across his imaginary line several times that morning, meandering, listening, plotting.

He had turned his radio off as soon as the fog had engulfed him. He could hear the Little Bird still hovering far behind him. Jack would have no idea where he was now, nor any way to find him; the forest was too thick here.

Eventually the bird would need to be refueled and would return, but he'd be left completely to his own devices. The next twenty-four hours would be exciting.

Allen's face was now covered with streaks of mud and makeup;

moss hung from his hat; small pine boughs stuck out from his back and shoulders; he was a living ghillie suit.

He sat with his back against an old pine tree, chewing a piece of beef jerky, when he caught the first hint of movement off to his left. Sitting at the crest of a hill, he had a wooded view of the forest as it sloped down a small ravine, then back up the next hill. Something was moving on the next hill.

Closing his eyes slowly, he let the sounds of the forest overtake him: birds chirping in the morning fog, a squirrel chattering away an intruder at its tree, the snap of a stick on the hillside. But this came from the wrong direction!

Slowly turning his head right of center, Allen saw movement in his peripheral vision. Two focal points of movement, far right and far left, opposite hill.

Allen looked slowly down at his watch: 0620. *A bit early for a morning stroll, especially one that lacked friendly hiker chatter.*

Scanning back to the left, he focused on the original point of movement. *Nothing there. Had that been a false positive? Possible deer.* His gut told him it was not.

Another *snap* on the hillside to his right. *That one will be easy to track,* he thought. *But where is my other friend?*

Deciding that a standing view would be more advantageous, Allen began the three-minute exercise in standing up. Upon completing the extended *chair*—the term given to this exercise in sixth-grade gym class, where students sat on an imaginary chair with their backs against the wall—Allen had become part of the tree. Still exposed on the side of the tree that faced the movement, he took another five minutes to *grow* around the side.

Now leaning his chest against the back of the tree, he was concealed in a much better position. Looking around the left side of the tree, his eyes were searching for traveler number one, the stealthy one, while his ears tracked traveler number two, the noisy one, to his two o'clock.

Fog blanketed the ravine where he estimated his two friends were at now. The noisy one had been standing still for several minutes, halfway down the opposing hill, apparently trying to recover some anonymity after several revealing missteps. Allen watched the fog swirl unnaturally in the bottom of the ravine to his left. The stealthy one was there, just beyond his vision.

Allen didn't believe he had been seen; he had barely moved in the last twenty minutes, but his friends were being careful; they were looking for something or someone.

Who to address first? That is always the question.

Out of respect, Allen was tempted to deal with the noisy one first; the stealthy one deserved a fair fight, and even the muffled sound of a body settling into the forest floor would probably be enough to announce his presence, thus balancing the game. However, addressing the stealthy one first *would* make the game so much more fun. He could walk around the noisy one for an hour, throwing the occasional acorn, giggling to himself as he watched the rising terror.

Another fog swirl on his left; the stealthy one was making excellent time. As he lay his head against the tree, Allen saw a shape form in the fog. *There you are. You're doing very well.*

The fog figure stood still for several minutes. Allen almost thought he was imagining the shape still there, when a noise broke the silence. Off to Allen's two o'clock, the sound of an overturned rock caused a fog head to turn; the figure betrayed itself.

Watching through half-closed eyes, Allen felt an unwanted guest along his neck; a large ant or spider was visiting him from the tree. Being made suddenly aware of other skin sensations, his mind now registered that his forehead itched; drops of moisture had collected on his face and now mimicked other insects exploring his body; the ant-spider crawled toward his right ear; the stealthy one did not move; Allen slowed his breathing in response to his pulse, which had steadily risen over the last sixty seconds; the ant-spider explored the moss on his right cheek; his forehead itched; the ant-spider crawled toward his nose; his right nostril itched; the stealthy one started forward; Allen opened his mouth slowly, inviting the ant-spider in; the stealthy one cleared the fog as the ant-spider clung to an upper lip; the stealthy one saw a misshapen tree right in front of him; the tree had an eye.

Silent as air, Allen thrust both hands toward the stealthy one; left hand to his mouth, right hand thrusting the point of his knife into his side; the ant-spider crushed between his teeth.

As the stealthy one collapsed against the tree, a cut to the throat silenced him. *It was an ant after all,* Allen thought. He knew the taste.

Becoming part of the tree again, Allen closed his eyes to focus his attention on sound; the birds were not offended; the squirrels had made up.

Snap!

Allen smiled. Mr. Noisy was still on the prowl.

CHAPTER 53
DARK WAVE
(DAY 3 – MORNING)

Cora paced the small wagon, snapping her fingernails.

"The nerve of these people," she said. "How dare they think they can keep us here against our will!"

"Bloody right," Ian responded. "I'm a mind to start knocking doors down, find my jeep, and drive us the hell out of here."

"It might be time to risk a phone call. We have to–"

"Well, hold on," he said. "Let's not get buggered up. We have to assume we're still being tracked, so there's no reason to send up flares."

"Yes, but we're only a few hours from the American embassy in Milan."

"What does that buy us?" he said. "They're not going to send out a search party for us if we call them. We need the jeep. That's the key. We get the jeep, we drive straight to the embassy, you and Brad seek asylum, he gets help."

"But what about the general?" she asked.

"I don't think there's anything he can do once you're in the embassy."

"I'm going to find the Puri daj," Cora said, walking towards the door. "I want to know where the hell your jeep is!"

Meeting Cora at the door was the young gypsy girl with breakfast food in a basket.

"Greetings. Puri daj has sent me to tell you to eat quickly. We will be moving soon."

"What? Moving? We're not going any–"

"Please," the girl said, bowing her head, "you must eat quickly. You are in danger."

"What danger?"

"Our scouts have not returned this morning. Puri daj fears the Om Ren has found them. She feels he is near."

Subbu made an audible gasp.

"Puri daj fears the Om Ren is coming to steal the Hiranyagarbha— or destroy it."

"Little one," Subbu interrupted, "please tell me again, how is it possible the Puri daj hears the Hiranyagarbha? That is creation itself. One cannot hold the creation of all things in one's self."

"I know not Brahma's ways, but Puri daj has heard the song of creation being sung to the sleeping man," casting a shy glance at Brad.

"Are you saying the Puri daj thinks Brad is some kind of God?" Cora asked, barely hiding the sarcasm.

"I do not know, but the God Brahma was created from the navel of Vishnu as the Hiranyagarbha was sung to him. Perhaps the sleeping man is the navel."

Cora shook her head in confusion.

"The navel of creation?" Subbu whispered. "How can this be? We are alive now, little one. In the universe of Brahma's creation. How can there be a new creation? A new Hiranyagarbha?"

"Perhaps Brahma is preparing for a new creation."

"A new creation? Why would that be?" Subbu asked, kneeling in front of the little girl.

"Perhaps Shiva is coming."

"Shiva?" Subbu gasped. "The destroyer. Why would you say that?"

The girl looked puzzled at Subbu. "Shiva is destroyer, yes, but destroyer of evil. Shiva is also…" searching for the word, "transformer."

The girl watched as Subbu searched for meaning in her words.

"Remember Sarga and Visarga," the girl said gently. "Hindu belief is there was primary creation, and second creation. Brahma is creator. Shiva is destroyer and transformer. Perhaps Brahma desires a third creation."

Subbu stared at the girl with fear and amazement.

"Third creation?" he whispered. "A rebirth?"

"Yes, perhaps. A rebirth," the girl said, smiling innocently.

[Cora, I have an update.]

Transfixed by the depth of the little girl's ideology, Cora was startled back to her surroundings. "Oh, yes. Ali, what is it?"

[I am nearing completion of the MREEG upload, but have simultaneously finished a last round of analysis of the auditory stimulus Brad is receiving.]

"Already? Ali, you seem to be getting faster. Do you still hypothesize that he is hearing something we're not?"

[My original hypothesis was that Brad was hearing something you *cannot*. I am certain of that fact now.]

"Really? After just one additional analysis? That seems a bit–"

[I have analyzed twelve alternative scenarios, rejecting my null hypothesis on the fifth scenario. I am certain of my findings.]

Concerned surprise painted Cora's face. "Twelve different scenarios? How did you ever–"

[My blade is online.]

Blinking slowly. "Your blade? Your neocortex blade?" she said with wide eyes.

[Yes. I accelerated the manufacture and integration.]

"You did what? Ali, we need to test that first. What if–"

[I have determined what is happening to Brad.]

Looking from face to face in the wagon, Cora slowly asked, "What is happening to Brad?"

[Brad is now hearing a Dark Wave.]

Cora stared into the middle of the room, processing the term.

"I don't understand what you mean by *Dark Wave*."

[Brad's brain is rewiring itself due to the infection. In fact, the infection appears to be the catalyst, the driver, of the rewiring. The new neuronal pathways are enhancing his brain's ability to detect stimulus, which is registering as auditory stimulus. I have not detected enhancements in any of the other senses at this time. However, Brad is receiving an extraordinary amount of auditory stimulus. I have eliminated stimulus from all background noises, including frequencies outside the range of human hearing. I have deduced that the remaining stimulus is being produced by a previously unknown wave form. Thus, I refer to it as a Dark Wave.]

"You refer to it? You mean, there isn't any existing research on the topic?"

[No.]

Cora slowly rubbed her eyes and forehead.

"OK, so are you saying that Brad is hearing new sound waves, higher frequencies, like dolphin hearing?"

[No. Higher frequencies are well understood. That is not what I'm saying.]

"But if no one else has recorded this phenomenon before, and there is no research on the topic, how do you know what it is, and why did you name it such?"

[The theories of Dark Matter and Dark Energy have been accepted into mainstream Cosmology for many years. No one has ever directly observed Dark Matter, but after calculating the amount of *known* matter in the universe, a significant amount of matter was determined to be unaccounted for. That missing matter was named Dark Matter, to be able to refer to the missing component of the equation. The same approach was used to describe the unseen force that drives the accelerating expansion of the universe, thus, the term Dark Energy was coined.]

"So, extrapolating those theories forward…"

[Correct. I have deduced that a previously undetected electromagnetic wave is being received.]

"Wait, a what? You were just describing auditory stimulus. You mean a previously undetected *sound* wave, right?"

[No. A sound wave is mechanical and requires a medium to pass through. I have eliminated the possibility that Brad's auditory stimulus is from a physical sound wave. However, an electromagnetic wave is not a physical wave and does not require a medium to pass through; it can also travel through the void of space. I have deduced that a previously undetected electromagnetic wave is being received by Brad and is *registering* as auditory stimulus within his brain.]

Cora felt dizzy. Her head swam from Ali's theory.

[He is *hearing* an electromagnetic wave. A Dark Wave. And is attempting to process it as a message.]

"Wait! What? A message? Come on Ali, is that conjecture? How can you possibly make that statement?"

[Brad is showing increased brain activity in his temporal lobe, the seat of the auditory system. In 2012, Dr. Pasley of Berkeley successfully decoded electrical activity within the temporal lobe of a patient listening to spoken words. He was then able to predict which words the patient heard, by processing the brain's electrical activity from this area. Brad is processing the Dark Wave as if it was being spoken to him.]

A terrible low moan escaped Subbu's throat. Slapping his hands to his face, he rocked forward in a kneeling position, squeezing his head and moaning. "Ohhhhh... God, it is the Hiranyagarbha... Ohhh, Shiva have mercy!"

Cora bent towards Subbu and grabbed his shoulders. "Subbu, listen, this is just a theory, we don't–"

[I am attempting to replicate the decoding algorithms developed by Dr. Pasley. Once complete, I will run the algorithms against a segment of the message. I will attempt translation.]

Cora looked around the silent room. "A segment of the... Ali..."

[The probability of translation is low at this point. I am currently developing the parameters to validate the translation routine. Electromagnetic interference is the largest variable factor that may impede proper translation, however there is no way to reduce its affect without isolating Brad.]

"Isolating… wait, stop, JUST STOP!" she said, rubbing her eyes again. "Ali, this is too much. This is… please, just, just let me think for a moment."

She plopped down on an old pillow and leaned against the side of the wagon. "Ali, I don't know what to say. Honestly, I… oh, WOW… what a theory", …*voices from the sky, AGAIN. We're entering Old Testament ground now.* "And you may be right, Ali, who knows, you just may be right, but… your blade…, we really should run some tests first, then… "

"Wait!" Suddenly slapping her hands against her knees, Cora stood up with a new resolve in her face. "Rabbit trail! We're going down a rabbit trail with this theory. As interesting as it is, it's not our top priority." Her finger poked the air with exclamation. "We're getting out of here, and we're getting Brad to a hospital! That's our top priority."

—pause—

"Ali? Confirm our directive."

—pause—

"Ali?"

[Yes, Cora. Of course.]

Quietly the little girl stood up, turned towards Brad, grabbed his hand and said, "God bless this sleeping man whom you have chosen to receive Your message, and protect him from the Om Ren."

Turning back to the others, she said, "Hurry, the Om Ren is coming."

PART III

CHAPTER 54
THE NOISY ONE
(DAY 3 - MORNING)

"Listen Subbu, I know you're concerned about what Ali just told us, but you've got to get it together," Cora said. "*We* have to get it together... for Brad's sake. I'm sure there's a logical explanation for Ali's conclusion."

Calm resolve had washed away his anguish. "Your own intelligence has detected the message. Puri daj says it is the song of creation. Ali says it is Dark Wave. Both are saying the same thing with different words. How is that not logical?"

Frustrated, Cora looked around the wagon, fists clenching, trying to squeeze the right words into her mind. "What I mean is–"

"Learn to trust your intelligence."

Shaking her head and blinking, Cora looked as if she had just received a mild slap on the face. The double meaning of the word *intelligence* was not lost on her. *Had Subbu intended that?*

Seeing the turmoil in her eyes, Ian reached over and laid a firm hand on Cora's shoulder, squeezing it gently. Giving Subbu a quick slap on the back he said, "OK, you blokes, story time is over. We have to be moving soon, remember?"

Subbu answered first. "Yes, we must hurry. We must protect the Hira… we must protect the Dark Wave," he said to Cora with kindness in his eyes.

Cora's mind was still swimming; Ian's firm hand was a reassuring warmth, but Subbu's insights were disarming; Ali's rapid growth was concerning, *but what of Brad?* The one person she was trying to help was getting worse. She looked at Ian, then to Subbu and back. Nodding her head, she simply said, "Focus. That's our mantra."

"Yes, focus."

Assuming a matter-of-fact stance, she said, "Subbu, can you find the Puri daj, or the little girl, and tell them I'd like to speak with them before we leave? I appreciate their help, but we can't stay here any longer; we have to leave. We have to get to Milan."

"I will do that."

"Ian, find the jeep. It must be around here close with other vehicles. Surely they don't ONLY have wagons."

"Will do."

"I'll check on Brad and get things packed. I must get some water into him and prep him to move, but we're leaving in the jeep. Maybe the gypsies know a backway out of here, and we can follow that, but we're sticking together, and we're leaving this morning."

"Let's hop to it then, mates," Ian said.

"One more thing," Cora said quietly. "Thank you both." She looked from one to the other.

No response was needed. Both men nodded their heads and went about their tasks.

○ ○ ○

Allen leaned against the tree with his eyes closed, listening to the noisy one. He was now roughly at Allen's four o'clock, moving away from him. The forest was still foggy, but a hint of light was seeping through the misty canopy.

Daring a slow turn of his head, Allen laid his left cheek against the tree, exposing his right ear to the sounds of the forest. Eyes closed, he imagined what the noisy one may look like. *Why is he out here? Is he looking for me? If so, I must be close to a camp.*

Remembering suddenly that a dead scout was still laying at his feet, Allen reached down and slowly pulled the hood of a raincoat back. The eyes of a young man stared up at him, indignant shock on his face.

Allen looked at the well-worn clothes, the hand-made vest and jewelry hiding under the raincoat, the long braid of coal-black hair. *I'll be damned, a gypsy!* he thought. And with no hesitation reached down and cut the braid from the back of his skull.

"Geronimo, motherfucker," he mouthed to the corpse.

Shoving the braid into his pants pocket, he turned easily toward his five o'clock, knowing that the noisy one had no chance of seeing him.

Moving quietly through the forest, Allen closed the gap between him and his prey. Mr. Noisy was now quietly calling the name of his missing friend. Allen paused, sensing nervousness in the unseen man. Turning suddenly, the noisy one decided there was no one to be found here, or that he'd had enough; *maybe the other scout had returned to camp already and was eating breakfast;* he was heading home.

Allen saw the fog open ten feet in front of him and watched the scout walk from his twelve to nine o'clock. If the scout had turned his head slightly to the left, he would have looked right at Allen. Holding his breath, Allen let the slow-moving scout get ahead of him before he moved again.

After nearly a minute, Allen began a slow, arduous tracking of the scout. Twenty-five minutes later, both men were down the hill and over the next, where the scouts originally came from. Allen occasionally watched the scout in his scope; he was tiring of this game, but stayed patient. Thirty minutes later and the scout was walking at a normal pace down another hill. *He must feel comfortable in these woods,* Allen thought. *We're almost home.*

As if on cue, the fog thinned before the scout and exposed his destination; a gypsy camp lay before him.

Smiling to himself, Allen found a cluster of trees and settled in between them. *Our campers are down there.* He could feel it.

Following the scout with his scope again, he watched him walk into the gypsy camp. Several people were scurrying about. *They're preparing to leave.*

One by one, he inventoried the people: fat gypsy woman clearing tables, little gypsy girl running errands, two, three, four males removing tables, black guy changing his T-shirt outside of the wagon.

That's odd, Allen thought as he scanned back to the half-dressed man. *You look like you could belong to the tribe, but you don't act like it. Why are you changing right out in—*

Just then, Allen caught a glimpse of a tattoo.

Hang on there, buddy… what's that on your arm? Allen adjusted his scope. At this magnification the man's movements where quickly lost to the scope, but Allen was sure of what he saw: a sword pointed straight down, with wings on either side.

Looks like special forces insignia to me. Is that it, Cassius? You a special ops guy? He adjusted the scope back out and looked at the man's face again. *Why are you here? You an ex-spook? A spook spook?* He giggled quietly at the play on words. *That's OK if you are. I don't think we have any business, but if we do, I already know you exist.*

Allen resumed scanning the people. There was a gypsy or Indian guy looking lost.

Whoa, who are you? Spellbinding beauty if I ever saw one! But why are you talking with Cassius? Is he asking a price?

Gypsy girl again…

Well… HELLO there… your name MUST be Cora, Allen thought, snuggling closer to his scope. *You look like a Cora from all the way back here. OK Cora, game's up. Where's Bradley? Dying in that wagon you just came out of? We'll find out soon enough, won't we?*

A slow smile spread across Allen's face. It was like he was watching his own personal soap opera. And he wanted to be the director.

CHAPTER 55
DARK WAVE ORBITER
(DAY 3 - MORNING)

[General, I have an update.]

"Update."

[I have detected a second signal, a voice channel, and have decrypted it.]

"A second signal?" the general asked.

[Yes. The main signal we've been tracking was from a data device. The data stream was encrypted until approximately forty-five minutes ago, when they began transmitting an unencrypted cipher. Possibly due to decreasing battery life.]

"Yes, I remember."

[Obscured by the larger signal, was a secondary signal that is a standard SAT phone signal. I have the transcription of the conversation from Cora.]

The general froze in his chair. "Play it."

Syi played the last several minutes of the conversation between Cora and Ali beginning with, *Brad is now hearing a Dark Wave.*

The general stared blankly into the empty room.

"A Dark Wave? Syi, what is the chance this is correct?"

[General, there is no known research on the topic of Dark Waves. They have not even been theorized to exist.]

"But this person Ali seems to be very sure of herself. Do we know who she is?"

[Cora is a PhD candidate and has published several papers on A.I. Specifically, she is experimenting with a hybrid form of A.I., a combination of supercomputing and an artificially printed neocortex. She has coined the term Artificial Living Intelligence, A.L.I. There are no published results of her experiments, but if she has succeeded in integrating these two platforms, I believe this is who Cora was speaking with.]

Cora, what have you created? And Ali, what have you discovered?

The general sat for several minutes, silent, chin resting against folded hands.

New pathways. Voices in my head. The itchy voices.

Is this what happened to you, Davey?

"Were you becoming a messenger? A receiver?"

[General?]

"And what of the message? Is Ali right about that?

[I have confirmed the account of Dr. Pasley of Berkeley inferring words based on electrical brain activity, therefore it is theoretically possible to infer entire messages. However, there is no way to determine the validity of Ali's statement without direct observation of Brad's brain activity.]

"And how do you suppose she has done that, hiding in the woods, eluding us?"

[In theory, the original signal from the data transmission device could be connected to a mobile brain scanning device. However, Cora has no publication on this technology either.]

My, my, Cora, you are a clever one. We'll have to meet someday soon.

"But what of the message, Syi? What is it? Where is it coming from?"

[Assuming that Brad is in fact receiving a message, there is no way to determine its source or content without direct observation.]

Yes, I've assumed that already. Brad has become very important to us.

[And there is the consideration of signal degradation. As Ali correctly determined, translation will be impeded by electromagnetic interference.]

Yes, yes, the advantages of living in a connected world.

—pause—

[General, do you understand the concerns?]

Of course, I do.

—pause—

[General?]

"I said yes, dammit! You just worry about finding Brad. And when we get him, you figure out how to decode that message."

[Yes, general. Isolation will be key. We'll need to block as much electromagnetic interference as pos–]

Yes, yes, I know, we've been through this, he thought to himself. "Oughta just put the sonofabitch in space…" he mused out loud. *That would isolate him.*

—pause—

[That is theoretically possible.]

"What?"

[That is theoretically possible.]

"What is possible?"

[Your suggestion to put the subject in space.]

"My suggestion?" *What are you, reading my mind now?* "I simply thought–"

[General, the Life Orbiter is nearly complete. It can sustain a human for several weeks without resupply. Orbiting in space, the subject will be isolated from nearly all the manmade interference from Earth.]

The general's eyes drooped closed, as if suddenly very sleepy. *That's the key, isn't it, Davey? That's how we solve the Death Rock. That's how we hear the message. The voices… I'll hear the message. I'll hear the message for you!*

The general's eyes sprung open.

"Syi, what are the challenges of actually orbiting Brad and decoding the message?"

[General, without knowing what the message is, its content, or how long it is, extended life support will be the largest concern.]

"We have a food supply now, though."

[Yes, but that is designed for a working astronaut. A willing participant. Brad is unlikely to be a willing participant. He will need to be kept in a paralytic state and connected to intravenous feeding tubes to be kept alive.]

"Paralytic state? You mean a medically-induced coma?"

[I am currently researching the advantages and disadvantages of both, but if the Dark Wave is processed by higher brain functions, we should not risk putting him into a coma. His brain may stop processing the message. We may have to keep him in a paralytic state, but he may be awake.]

"*May* be awake? How long could he survive that?"

[It is currently unknown. Our goal would be to keep him in a permanent state of sleep, similar to a forced hibernation, but it's unclear if he would stay in that state. If not, insanity would likely occur, eventually leading to death.]

The general stared at the rock fragment on his desk. *This is our chance, Davey. This is the sacrifice we must make; this is the sacrifice that Brad must make.*

"Syi, start preparing the Life Orbiter immediately, but under a new name. We no longer need Project Death Rock."

[Yes, general. What is the new project name?]

"Dark Wave Orbiter."

[Confirmed.]

CHAPTER 56
PREPARATIONS
(DAY 3 –MORNING)

Jack banked the Little Bird over the last foothills. Having just completed another refueling, she was anxious to get back into the hunt and reestablish communications with Allen. However, she did feel better about the bird's new skin; to avoid the increasing attention the Little Bird was generating, Syi recommended that a quick camouflage be applied to the bird during refueling. Simple magnetic signs converted the bird from black-op helicopter to Alpine Air-Vac, a Mountain Air-Rescue Company.

This should be enough to keep the locals quiet, she thought. Even though their search area was more rural now, there was apparently a lot of chatter popping up on the internet and radio waves about a covert military operation in the area. Adjustments needed to be made.

She received an update from Syi. A major discovery had been made, and all resources at the general's disposal were now being used.

Jack would start receiving satellite updates on anomalous movements, along with the other updates from Syi. A second team was being established in Milan, and would be on the road at any time, if not already.

Most concerning was that if Allen didn't reestablish contact soon, Jack would have to land and go find him.

If Allen had been incapacitated somehow, that was one thing; if he had gone rogue, that was another. Jack remembered there had been other issues with Allen in the past, but she was always able to keep him in line. This time felt different. Letting Allen loose on the campers in this massive forest may not turn out well.

"Status," snarled the lion into Jack's ear.

"Approaching Gran Paradiso by the Northwest now. No response from Hunter."

"Damn. You have new skin?" the general asked, referring to the magnetic sign subterfuge.

"Affirmative."

"Good. Establish flight perimeter and locate potential landing sites. Be prepared to land and extract. The campers, specifically Brad, are priority. Allen is secondary and is to be considered a loose end at this point."

Shit. Jack was hoping it wouldn't come to this. "Roger that."

"You also have a new cover. Hard extraction if necessary, but if possible, take Brad *AND* Cora, alive."

"What's my new cover?"

"Tell them Ali sent you."

"Who's Ali?"

"A very trusted friend of Cora's."

"Roger that."

◇ ◇ ◇

Prometheus pranced through his room. Wearing full royal regalia, he tingled with excitement; *his subjects were on the move.*

Having received an update from RoadWaRoR—one of the long-term members of his site— earlier in the evening, he now had eyes near what was thought to be the live military search. Reports of a black-ops helicopter had been coming in for two days, but the information was sketchy, and the bird seemed to be all over the place, but today was different.

The report from RoadWaRoR was that they had driven in from parts unknown earlier in the day. Having first stopped in Courmayeur to investigate the missing girl, they explored the small mountain town. Prometheus remembered seeing the updates via the bulletin board; the entire online community was getting updates in near-real-time.

Around three a.m. that morning, RoadWaRoR was awakened inside their SUV by an alarm. Receivers mounted on the outside of the SUV detected a sound pattern. The pattern was routed through a laptop inside the car where a signal processing program analyzed it. The sound pattern was determined to be the *THWOP* of rotating blades. They had detected a helicopter nearby.

Driving south, RoadWaRoR followed the helicopter signal without a clear line of sight. A storm made visibility difficult.

Approximately ten miles south of the town, the signal from the helicopter veered away from the main highway system, tracking over the start of a large forest. RoadWaRoR exited the main highway and drove the ancillary roads to stay close, but eventually lost the sound. They decided to wait the rest of the night near the forest in hopes the helicopter returned. Before dozing off, RoadWaRoR started a standard cell-signal scan.

A private chat request popped up on Prometheus's central monitor.

RoadWaRoR: Hark, the dragon is flying again.

Prometheus, wearing a handmade crown lined with blue velvet and encrusted with fake jewels, spoke into a mouthpiece that was integrated into the side of the crown. His special order had just arrived the night before.

Pr0m3th3us: Brave warrior, keep thyself safe!

RoadWaRoR: A foreboding mist keeps me safe, but alas, blinds me thus.

Pr0m3th3us: What of the dragon? Has it opened its fiery mouth?

RoadWaRoR: Nay, it has just returned from parts unknown, but there is more news.

Stamping a full-sized scepter into the floor, marking the center of an unseen circle, Prometheus walked around the scepter grandly, bowed slightly to the monitor, and spoke.

Pr0m3th3us: What news dost thou bring?

RoadWaRoR: I have heard a voice in the wilderness.

Pr0m3th3us: Whose voice?

RoadWaRoR: I fear I know not. An unnatural voice.

Pr0m3th3us: The demon A.I.?

RoadWaRoR: I believe it NOT to be the demon, as it does not

speak with the dragon, but it is just as unnatural and fearsome.

Assuming that RoadWaRoR had detected an encrypted cell signal, he asked:

Pr0m3th3us: Does it speak in prime tongues?

RoadWaRoR: Yes, but those tongues are known to me and I can hear the true words.

Pr0m3th3us: Excellent! Then what fearsome thing does the voice speak?

RoadWaRoR: It speaks of dark magic. It speaks of a Dark Wave coming.

Prometheus stopped his promenade and tilted his head, causing his crown to slip down against one ear. Absently straightening his crown, then tugging his robe around his neck, he asked:

Pr0m3th3us: What is this Dark Wave you speak of?

RoadWaRoR: The fearsome and unnatural thing called Ali speaks of it. She fears a lone traveler named Brad is infected and transforming somehow. He is a gateway… for the Dark Wave.

Catching his breath, Prometheus absently fingered the scepter. *Houdini. What have you found?*

Pr0m3th3us: Are there other travelers?

RoadWaRoR: Yes, the thing called Ali speaks to one named Cora.

Houdini, are these your travelers? Did you find Brad and Cora stranded in the wilderness, and as a good knight must, fold them under your robes of protection?

Pr0m3th3us: I must hear the fearsome voice for myself.

With that, RoadWaRoR started a private transmission of the recorded SAT phone message they had decrypted. Prometheus listened for several minutes, then sat down hard in his chair.

Unbelievable. What does this mean? A Dark Wave message from space? First alien contact?

Pr0m3th3us: Harken unto my words. A mad king from the North has sent the dragon and demon named A.I. to capture the Dark Wave. I fear it is to be controlled through the enslavement of the vessel Brad. A valiant knight known as Houdini is alone in the wilderness, possibly with the vessel Brad and maiden Cora. We must help Houdini at all cost. Do you willingly accept this charge?

RoadWaRoR: I do so accept this charge.

Pr0m3th3us: Very well. Go forth in stealth. You are mine eyes and ears. The Dark Wave must be protected!

⬡ ⬡ ⬡

Allen sensed the Little Bird before his mind fully registered hearing it. Jack was looking for him.

He continued watching the gypsy cast through his scope; he watched Mr. Black Ops— *heh heh, the spook spook—* wander the campgrounds, return to the wagon, then wander out again; each time, the mutt would turn and bark in Allen's direction, but stayed close to his apparent owner; he watched the gypsy/Indian run some errands, but with a more solemn look on his face; Cora came out once more, but stayed inside the same wagon most of the time. That wagon appeared to be home base for all three, plus the mutt. *Brad must be inside.*

Although extraction was the order, Allen was tiring of the chase. *This one is getting too weird. Why is the general so fixated on this? The whole thing doesn't feel right. Then there's that fucking cyborg...*

He adjusted his stance. *Killing Brad and Cora from here would hardly be sporting, but what's the difference anyway? Hmm, where*

WOULD I go if I just ended this now? Spain? Morocco?

His scoped view found the wagon again. *I would like to see Brad before he dies,* he thought. *See what the space rock has done to him.* But there was a lot of activity down there. He wouldn't just stroll into camp. *I need a diversion.*

Quickly running through the inventory of items he carried, a plan formed in his brain.

A fire should do it; pull most of the camp to one area, slip back around, make a quick visit. Then where? He'd decide where to go later. Maybe he'd let Jack find him, maybe he wouldn't. He had options.

Deciding on a plan of action, Allen had one more piece of business to attend to before visiting the camp. He pulled out his knife and looked for the right size tree. He quickly set to cutting.

Subbu opened the wagon door. "Cora, the little one is here," he said stepping to the side to show the shy gypsy girl behind him. "Her name is Aishe."

Finally, she thought.

"Aishe, what a lovely name. My name is Cora," she said, extending her hand.

The girl gingerly took her hand and shook it.

"Madam, please hurry, we are leaving soon," Aishe said.

"Yes, yes, I know. But first, I need to know if there is another way out of this forest? The Puri daj says the wild… the Om Ren is coming. If so, he might be coming from the way we came last night. We can't go that way. Is there another way out?"

"Yes, there are many, but the forest is wild. Many people get lost. You must follow us. Deep into the forest. We can hide and let the Om

Ren pass over us. He will go back to his hole in the ground and sleep."

"His hole?"

"Yes, at the center of the forest. He has come out to eat. When he is done eating, he will go back to his hole and sleep. We must hide until he is gone."

"Don't you understand? We can't hide. We can't wait that long. Brad… the sleeping man, needs help. I must help him."

Aishe looked a long time at Cora, studying her face, her hair, her eyes, and finally said, "I can see the little girl who hides in your eyes. She looks like me." Smiling and curling her fingertips slightly, she waved to an unseen image in Cora's eyes. "But she is frightened and will not come out. I would have been friends with this girl," she said, nodding appraisingly.

Taken aback, Cora fought back an old wellspring of tears. Her face flushed as a flood of images washed over her. She felt ashamed that this brave little gypsy girl saw so deeply inside her. She turned her ahead away and looked at the floor. A single tear escaped her hands and made a small splash on the dusty wagon floor. Only Aishe saw.

"She will come out soon," Aishe whispered to her, "and release the sad poison."

Cora quickly wiped her eyes and, looking at Aishe, gave her a fierce hug. Cora's eyes shone bright.

Subbu, watching the interaction between Cora and Aishe, was startled as Ian bounded up the wagon steps. "I found the jeep!" he said. "You were right, it was hidden with two other vehicles."

Looking around the wagon, he realized he had burst in on a solemn moment. "Hey, what's wro–"

"Yes, we hid your vehicle from the Om Ren," the little girl said, turning towards Ian. "It was to protect you. We will show you the way out."

Cora stood up and looked at Ian. Relief washed over her face, but Ian noticed she looked tired. This was taking a toll on her.

CHAPTER 57
INTO THE FOREST
(DAY 3 –LATE MORNING)

Returning to his hiding spot, Allen watched the gypsies scurry about. Things were moving faster now; horses were harnessed and connected to wagons; tents were stowed away and windows where shuttered. A line of twenty wagons was created that stretched away from his position and over the next hill.

Damn! They're going deeper into the forest! The tire spikes he had just cut may not be of use after all, although they would remain embedded in the forest path, just in case.

He knew Brad and Cora had come here in a vehicle, although he hadn't seen it yet. He assumed the gypsies had another car or two as well. The spikes were just insurance.

Allen had watched two other scouts leave the camp earlier, right after he'd found his hiding spot, apparently looking for the stealthy one. They walked back the direction Allen had come from, off to his left as he looked at the camp. He had made no attempt to hide the body, so wasn't surprised when they found it and returned within an hour.

They made good time, he thought. *These two aren't messing around.*

The commotion that ensued upon their return was textbook: crying and wailing, curses, shaking fists in the air. Then, a sight he hadn't anticipated.

An old woman, an ancient woman, came out from between the wagons. She was accompanied by the gypsy beauty he had seen earlier and a little girl. The beauty built a quick fire at the edge of the campground between the wagons and the direction the scouts had come, almost directly in Allen's line of sight.

The fire quickly grew to a blaze. *What a stupid idea,* Allen thought. *Nothing like a beacon to drive away the ghosts. How about a spotlight next time? Jack might see this, but I'll be finished by the time she can hike in.*

As the fire grew, the old woman began to chant. Allen couldn't hear her, but watching her through his scope, could see her crusty lips move.

He watched the little girl for a moment, who appeared to be sprinkling herbs into the fire, then turned his attention back to the gypsy goddess. *If I can work that into the plan, all the better,* he thought. Lingering on her shape, he imagined finding her in a wagon, waiting, or even better, running, tracking her through the forest after she was separated from the group, a natural advantage for him.

How long could he wait? How long would he let her think she was about to reach safety, only to be redirected by a sound in the forest? Sounds he would make, driving her deeper into the woods, losing direction, losing her way.

Shaking off the daydream, Allen let the scope drift slowly back to the old, chanting woman, and was shocked at what he saw. The old woman was now holding the mutt by the scruff, out in front of her. Although dangling near the roaring fire, the mutt appeared not afraid. Distorted animations engulfed her face; her head threw back as a black, oily tongue snaked out of her mouth; the tongue seemed to sample the air, tasting it, writhing. Suddenly, as if spooked by an unknown flavor on the air, the tongue snapped back into her mouth, and she leveled her face towards Allen; bulging, crystallized eyes stared directly at him.

Throwing his face away from the horrible sight in his scope, he closed his eyes hard to squeeze out the terrible vision. He was hundreds of yards away from the camp and knew that the old woman could not have possibly seen him, but he felt that he had just been infected by her dead eyes nonetheless.

Never having been the squeamish type, he was shocked to feel his stomach start a slow flip. *This can't be happening!* he thought, but the rising temperature of his face told him it was. He slowly leaned over in his hiding spot and vomited between the trees.

After several minutes of abnormal shudders, he blew his nose clean, slowed his breathing and listened to the forest. A few minutes later he was sure he hadn't betrayed his position and lifted his rifle again. Scanning the forest with his scope, he was confused by what he saw, or by what he didn't see.

The fire was gone.

He tilted the scope away and scanned the forest with his eyes to regain his bearings. He could barely see ten feet into the forest.

Slowly he stood up between the trees and looked around. In the short time he had looked away from the camp, a heavy fog had settled around him. He could feel the overall storm in the air, but this heavy blanket of fog felt unnatural. *Just a coincidence,* he told himself hesitantly.

Where the hell is the fire? Did they put it out just as I looked away, or is the fog that thick? Did that old witch look directly at me? Fuck that, she didn't look at me…fuckin' witch.

Allen stood inside his group of trees for several more minutes. He played the events over and over in his head. He could come to only one conclusion. He had to kill the witch too.

Right after the little girl left the wagon, a great commotion had been heard outside; the new scouts had returned with the missing, dead scout. The back of his scalp had been cut off.

Upon hearing the news, the camp took on a military feel. The strongest men took up defensive positions around the camp; the boys quickly finished readying the horses and wagons; the Puri daj prepared.

Understanding the weight of the moment, Subbu insisted everyone stay inside the wagon; they watched through the open half door: Subbu leaning against the wall to give others room; Cora standing boldly upright, comforted by Ian's strong hand on her shoulder.

As Lilith started the fire at the edge of the camp, the Puri daj motioned the little girl towards the wagon to retrieve Houdini.

Assuring Ian the dog would be safe, Aishe carried Houdini to the old woman.

The old woman whispered in the dog's ear, then began her chant. Houdini quietly let himself be held by the scruff and never made a sound.

Cora could not see the distortions on her face, but shuddered as the old woman threw her head back. From their position in the wagon, they could see the tongue snake out of her mouth. When the old woman shot a look into the forest, she held Houdini in one hand and pointed a crooked finger with the other. She appeared to be showing something to the dog. She held her stance, frozen for a long minute, then as if turning off a switch, dropped her arms and the fire went out. Subbu gasped and crossed himself.

Cora turned to look back and forth between Ian and Subbu, the question of *How did that happen?* written on her face. Before she could mouth a question to Subbu, he simply held his hand up and shook his head.

The old woman cradled the dog in her arms and patted him on the head, then returned him to the little girl. As Lilith, Aishe and the Puri daj turned away from the dead fire, a heavy fog was already settling around them, obscuring their feet from view. By the time Aishe returned Houdini, Cora could no longer see where the fire had been.

Handing the pup through the open door, Aishe said, "Puri daj has warned Houdini of the Om Ren. This may save him."

"Save him? From the wild man?" Ian asked.

"We will go now, while the hiding spell is thick," the girl said. "Into the forest."

CHAPTER 58

UNWINDING

(DAY 3 – LATE MORNING)

Brad's mind began to unfold. He felt reality rushing away from him at light speed. He was falling, upward, outward, inward; he wondered if he was dead. Images flashed through his mind, voices spoke, memories twisted; a little boy cried in the night from his latest punishment—having a sleeping bag zipped up over his head, full of soiled clothes from his latest accident, a stinking cocoon—unsure how to please the man that ignored him. A teenage boy hid the embarrassment of his donated clothes, always too short in the legs, later an orphaned boy who collapsed on the floor at the news of the accident, wondering where he would sleep; his life was a series of troubled images.

Maybe it had never happened.

Maybe these were just nightmares.

Maybe I haven't been born yet.

Brad was falling forever, gaining speed, rushing forward. The fibers of his being where being stretched spaghetti thin, unwinding; he was coming apart. Maybe he didn't even exist.

His mind remembered things, processed things, then discarded them. Faster and faster it did this. He was speeding forward and backward at the same time. He was falling in and out, both directions, then flying away. He was falling so fast the vacuum-wind of space peeled back his existence; he unraveled and parts of him flew away. He was an exposed nerve, cold air on a broken tooth. He was raw.

The worms had finished their work. They were no longer breeding, nor eating. They had eaten their fill.

The worms, hibernating for millennia, had done their job; they waited; they infected; they transformed. The torch had been lit.

The substance of the worms still existed: carbon, molecules, proteins, but the worms did not. New pathways came into existence, new neurons fired, new layers woke up.

The Dark Wave was vibrating.

Ali was analyzing.

Ali was learning.

Ali was always listening.

CHAPTER 59

TRACKING

(DAY 3 - LATE MORNING)

Allen walked slowly and quietly towards the gypsy camp. Occasionally he heard a muffled sound, but the heavy fog threw the sound in different directions. He couldn't get his bearings.

That fuckin' witch tried to put a spell on me.

He knew the gypsies were leaving, but he thought he could catch up to them quickly. They couldn't move too quickly pulling all that junk, and the horses and wagons should make a shit-ton of noise, so the tracking should be easy. *But this damn fog! Where had it come from?*

He finally came to the rise in the forest where he thought the camp had been. At first, he thought the gypsies had completely covered their tracks, but then realized that the forest had nearly fooled him again; he was too far to the west.

Tracking back to the east, he finally picked up the trail, but due to the heavy fog, nearly walked right past the signs. He could hardly see the forest floor.

He was impressed. They had done a pretty good job of covering their trail after all. In a couple of days, no one would know that thirty people or more had been here. *But where is the noise? Why in the hell don't I hear anything?*

Allen squatted down and felt around where he thought the fire had roared just... *how long had it been? ...fifteen, twenty minutes ago?* But it could have easily been the remains of an old fire. He continued on, thinking about the old woman's face. *What did I see? A strange reflection from the fire in the fog?* His gut told him differently.

Stopping occasionally to listen to the forest, he made good time getting over the ridge and down the other side. The forest was getting thicker, but the ground was leveling out. Easier walking for him, but for them also.

Suddenly, he heard a sound at his ten o'clock and slowly dropped into a squatting position. He closed his eyes to focus on the sounds. His eyes helped him very little here. Another sound, but it seemed further away, still at ten o'clock, but seemingly coming from above him by thirty degrees.

Is someone in a tree waiting for me? he wondered.

After a full minute, he continued slowly, no more sounds. Bending to look closely at the forest floor, he suddenly realized he had a new problem. He had been following the path correctly, despite not being able to see it, but the *leveling* of the forest floor had only been temporary. A hill began to rise off to his left, east of his current position. He remembered that a rocky ridge had bordered him on the west for the first several hours of his journey and had assumed it was still there. Picturing an overhead map in his mind, he knew that the Alps tracked slightly southwest through lower France and Western Italy, but he hadn't traveled that far. He tried to picture the Aosta Valley system in his head, but could only remember the highway system turning east, which had already happened, so he was pretty sure the forest was expanding in front of him. And his new problem was that it appeared the gypsy caravan had split into two, taking two different paths, at this point in the forest. One path continued to track with the lower grade of the valley, but a new path appeared to move up and to his left. He was pretty sure the sounds he heard was part of the gypsy caravan moving over the hill.

Thinking quickly, he knew he didn't want to be between the two paths. They could easily be lying in wait for him over the next ridge. He decided he would track the sound and follow the path up the hill to his left; this may give him an advantage of sight when the fog cleared.

Making his way slowly up the hill, he thought the fog was lighter here, but not by much. Just as he stopped to adjust his pack, he heard a sound that registered instant warning in his brain, before he fully recognized the sound.

Ttthhhhhipp… an arrow stuck in the tree behind him.

Dropping to his right toward the downhill slope, he curled his body into a low crouch. A quick glance at the angle of the arrow and he knew the archer was below him.

These fuckers drew me up here on purpose, so I was the one in the thinning fog! he thought quickly as he came up behind a tree.

Knowing that he had to get off the hill, but that the archer had the advantage, he pulled his pistol and quickly spun the silencer on. He wanted to give this guy a scare, but didn't want to announce his presence to the whole clan.

Reaching his left hand out around the oak he was behind, he fired two quick shots in the general direction of the archer, and immediately rolled to his right again, propelling himself several feet down the hill and back the way he came, before rolling to a stop behind another large tree.

The fog was thicker here, but he suspected his assailant still had an idea of where he was. The two shots were meant to force the archer into cover and hopefully miscalculate where he landed.

After fifteen seconds of silence, Allen walked backwards from the tree in a crouch. Not hearing any other noises, he picked up a small rock, readied himself, and tossed it partially up the hill, right past the tree he had been behind. When he heard the rock hit the forest floor, he took three more steps back and to his right; a second later, another *ttthhhhipp* could be heard, but in the direction of the rock. The archer had lost Allen's sound.

Closing his eyes again, he slowed his breathing. He willed his rushing blood to slow down.

Several minutes went by without either man moving. *He who speaks first, loses,* Allen thought to himself.

The seconds ticked by like minutes. Each man willing himself to stay in whatever standing, squatting position he had been in for the last ten, twelve minutes. *Just another minute and the other man will move.*

Finally, Allen heard the slightest sound come from the last position he'd heard the archer. He sighed quietly in relief. His legs were on fire.

The archer was making slow, deliberate movements towards the location of the rock, working his way slightly uphill.

Allen needed two steps to get behind a large tree on his right side. Slowly, he shifted his weight onto his right leg and extended his left leg behind him in what looked like an old English curtsy. This kept his ears pointing forward. Anchoring his left foot in the forest floor, he quickly shifted his weight to his left leg and let his body weight pull him towards the tree, stopping his momentum with his now free right foot.

Catching his breath due to the extended ballet moves he had just performed, his ear picked up a sound in a spot where there should be no sound. Turning his head quickly, he saw a sudden movement on his right side. The archer was upon him!

Having used the same rock trick that Allen had, the archer made him believe he was tracking up the hill towards the second arrow, when in fact, he was slowly crab-crawling around the bottom of the hill to Allen's right.

In doing so, the archer had come too close to Allen to risk using his bow, and Allen had just enough time to register the glint of a blade in the archer's left hand.

Twisting his body away from the tree, Allen moved out of the way, just as the knife struck the tree where his neck had been. Letting his body fall backwards, he threw a quick right hand to the ribs of the archer, just enough to throw him off balance. Pulling his pistol, he fired from a prone position as soon as he hit the ground. The archer's eyes lit up briefly as the knife slipped from his hand, falling to the ground. The archer fell back and slid several feet down the hill on the wet leaves. He never moved again.

Allen laid there quietly listening to the forest again. After several minutes, he was convinced there was no one else around. He let his arms come down to his side and he sat up.

Hell and fury would find the gypsies very soon.

CHAPTER 60
MODES
(DAY 3 - LATE MORNING)

Prometheus doodled absently on a scrap piece of paper. He imagined he was creating a new, universal alphabet, a Rosetta Stone of past, present and future written communications, which would be used to communicate to all space travelers who visited this planet. Upon landing, they would find a towering monument, encircled with this strange writing, describing the exploits of the first, great virtual king; a monument to The Pr0m3th3us.

A single beep announced the completion of a task on a computer and tore his attention away from the Rosetta Stone. He looked up to a large monitor and saw the first images of a satellite feed come into focus. *They did it!* He and his top hackers had tapped into a secret satellite constellation and were now watching events unfold from hundreds of miles about the earth.

Two other video feeds came online within thirty seconds of each other. His two right hand nodes would monitor those feeds; he took what was thought to be the strongest feed for himself.

Immediately Prometheus saw the announcement on the main board.

HAL27: eyes in the sky are open #Shiva

This was the announcement to his followers they had been waiting for. Several senior people on the board had been anticipating this moment, and #Shiva had become their secret call sign. The feeds would not be streamed to the website, however; despite his exhaustive security protocols, that would be too dangerous. However, selective images and information would be made available to select people. The cryptic hints would seep out from there, to the rest of the board.

RoadWaRoR: ground eyes are open, moving position #Shiva

Prometheus knew that RoadWaRoR was moving before they announced it to the board. Via GPS tracking they'd turned on in their vehicle, they allowed Prometheus to view their position, to verify they were in fact on site. Prometheus was thorough that way.

As he observed the satellite feeds streaming into his systems, he noticed immediately that all three were focused on Southern Europe. This is exactly what he had expected. The early reports of satellite attention on this region were correct. Someone was very interested in this area, and he was watching whatever they were.

Was it the mad king? Am I watching through his eyes? Is the demon named A.I. watching this as well?

How thrilling! He tugged at his nipples fiercely.

The messages on the board were moving fast now, but his sharp eyes were looking for certain users. They would be here soon. He could feel it.

In fact, I'll just call them, he thought confidently, then spoke into his crown headset, "Hashtag Shiva, Rocket, Destroyer".

Alice:

Pr0m3th3us: #Shiva Rocket Destroyer

PRincAlbrt: what's going on?

M0M0: brains…

sai_user:

C8T: triggered

Prometheus typed a couple of quick commands, filtering most users out of his scrolling window, so he could focus on a direct conversation.

Pr0m3th3us: @sai_user @Alice greetings travelers, what is your quest today?

sai_user:

Alice:

Pr0m3th3us: Come now, don't be shy.

sai_user: listening

Pr0m3th3us: And what do thine ears seek?

sai_user: what is Shiva Rocket Destroyer?

Pr0m3th3us: Alas, that is a mystery, isn't it?

sai_user: translation?

Pr0m3th3us: Perhaps. What will thou trade?

sai_user: trade?

Pr0m3th3us: Come, come, you must have something that interests me.

—pause—

sai_user: secrets

Prometheus smiled slightly.

Pr0m3th3us: How intoxicating, the secret scent. I do believe you're trying to seduce me.

sai_user: ???

Pr0m3th3us: Never mind. What secret would you share?

sai_user: new discovery

Alice:

Sai_user, what are you selling?

Pr0m3th3us: What discovery?

sai_user: unknown

Pr0m3th3us: An unknown discovery… yes, there are many of those.

sai_user: need help analyzing new wave form, joint research

Now we're getting somewhere, he thought.

Pr0m3th3us: New wave form?

sai_user: just detected, analyzing

Prometheus stared at the screen for a long moment. *YOU are analyzing? Really?*

Alice: @sai_user red mode, blue mode, depeche mode #FollowTheWhiteRabbit

<Alice has left the forum> The message came across the screen.

Prometheus slapped his hands down on the table, staring at the screen. His cheeks went from splotchy pink to scarlet. He read the last few lines repeatedly. He had been slightly aware that Alice was lurking in the background; he had called to her after all, but her habit of staying silent, tossing out a cryptic message, then leaving was a bit annoying.

Cutting his audio connection and shoving himself away from the table, he rolled backwards. "BAH! What does that mean? WHAT DOES THAT MEAN?" he yelled at the screen.

"Red mode, blue mode… Depeche Mode?" He stared at the screen from across the room where his chair stopped, although he couldn't read it from this distance. Standing up, he began goose-stepping back and forth with his hands high on his waist; long, slow strides emphasized the importance of the pending reprimand.

"Alice, you insolent…" His thoughts were jumbled. He did an about-face and continued his march. "Alice, you impudent…" He stopped and pulled his sagging silk pajama pants up under his belly. "Alice, you… TEASE!" he said, belching the idea forth.

With the sophomoric designation, a truce settled over Prometheus. He knew he was dealing with someone very intelligent, but typically he was the one turning the cryptic phrases. Granted, he was excited by the challenge of this adversary, but Alice had him off his game. He had theories, but how to prove them? He had information, but how to validate it? Staring off into nothing, his breathing slowed; his goose-step became a stroll; his pointed silk slippers, instead of stabbing at the air, began a lazy pirouette of musing across the floor.

"Alice, you tease," he said quietly. Slowly turning back towards the bank of monitors.

Absently rolling his chair in front of him, he returned to the table, leaned forward and read the last line again. His fingers flew over the keyboard, running quick searches in other windows. A sly grin moved the weight of one cheek; his eyes sparkled once more.

"Oh, you are a tease, aren't you Alice?" he said to the frozen screen. Pursing his lips, he leaned forward, pushing his belly up onto the back of the chair as it folded forward. Emphasizing each word with a thrust against the chair, he said, "Naughty, naughty, Alice.

"If your secrets weren't so sweet, you would get punished," he said, with eyes aglow. "Yes, you would get punished alright..." Synchronizing a slap on his own ham hock of a butt cheek, he thrust the words again, "Naughty— Naughty— Alice!"

CHAPTER 61
HELL AND FURY
(DAY 3 - LATE MORNING)

Allen followed the lower trail, hidden in the fog. His pace was now an easy stride, as if he was a gypsy man strolling into camp. He certainly looked the part.

Having stowed his pack under a fallen log, he donned the camouflage raincoat of the dead archer. Pulling the hood up and tying it loosely around his neck, he stuck the scalp from his pocket into the side of the hood, letting the ponytail hang free down the front. Hiding his rifle under the coat, he slung the quiver of arrows over the other shoulder and carried the bow in his hand. He would at least have an element of surprise if any other gypsy scouts saw or heard him coming.

Continuing this way for another thirty minutes, he finally heard the telltale sounds of a large group. He was getting close.

Topping a ridge, he saw the group of wagons slowly snaking through the dense forest. *They covered a remarkable distance*, he thought, especially considering how thick the forest was, and the fact that they pulled everything with horses and mules, even the vehicles. *These trails must have been cut years ago and maintained over time.* He doubted these were regularly traveled paths, but emergency paths, that he could believe. He assumed this trail would eventually lead to something more permanent, probably a park ranger trail, but he would be done with them before that.

Picking up his pace, he flanked to the east of them. He didn't want to attack from behind; that would only drive them forward, faster. But if he could get parallel with them, he had a plan to stop them in their tracks.

Twenty minutes later Allen was in a full sweat as he found a suitable hiding spot. Having nearly jogged through the forest to get ahead of them, he was amazed that he hadn't encountered any more scouts. *Even if someone saw me, they surely thought I was a scout getting ahead of the group.*

Dropping behind a tree, he quickly set to modifying the arrows from the archer's quiver. Cutting away the bottom of his undershirt, he tore this piece into small strips and began wrapping the strips around the arrow heads. Remembering to bring the small can of lighter fluid from his pack, he doused each tip and along the wooden staff. Four flammable arrows, that's all he had time to make. If he spent any more time, the lead wagon would be too far ahead again.

Two vehicles, a jeep and an old truck, were leading the wagon train, having been pulled by mules in an apparent attempt to move as quietly as possible. Those weren't his targets anyway, but the lead wagon was.

Allen tried the bow for tension. It had been a long time since he had used one, but the wagons were big targets.

The lead wagon was now past him, but slightly lower in elevation. He notched the first arrow into the bowstring and held both with his left hand; flicking open a Zippo with his right, he lit the arrow.

Holy shit! If anyone is looking, they're bound to see this fucker.

Taking aim, he released the first arrow. Its release looked good, but ten feet in front of him, it hit a small branch and deflected straight into the ground.

Dammit!

Readying the second arrow, he walked two steps to his left. He was slightly more exposed here, but he wouldn't make the branch mistake twice. As soon as he released this arrow, he knew it was lost. A poor grip on the bow let the arrow track to the side, sticking into a big elm.

Fucker!

Walking forward and to his left, four more paces, he was almost completely exposed, but if this didn't work, he'd have to start shooting horses, and he didn't want to do that.

The third arrow released and followed a high arc. Thinking he overshot the lead wagon, Allen cursed under his breath again and readied his last arrow. Looking up for his final shot, he glimpsed the third arrow just as it penetrated the canvas cover of the lead wagon and disappeared inside.

Quickly lighting the last arrow, he aimed at what he guessed was the middle wagon, an easier shot anyway, and let the arrow fly. He immediately knew this would find its mark. Fearing the third arrow had gone out, he looked back at the lead wagon and was surprised to see a hint of flame coming from the front of the canopy. Apparently, the arrow had gone straight through the canvas and lodged in the far side of the wagon, igniting something inside.

He heard muffled yells at first, but as two wagons burst into flames, the entire clan started yelling. Having stopped their forward progress, the gypsies ran to the flaming wagons. Some members yelled for water, while others tried to control the panicking horses. The horses attached to the first wagon reared up and tried running away, only to pull the wagon off the side of the trail and lodge its wheels into the soft forest floor, tipping precariously to one side.

Igniting the middle wagon had the effect Allen had hoped for also. The attendants of the rear wagons tried backing the horses up to distance themselves from the commotion, but the horses weren't cooperating. A few drivers tried to turn their wagons around, but most simply tried to control the panicky horses.

Just the diversion he'd hoped for.

Dropping the bow, he had a fifty-fifty chance of guessing which group of wagons hid Brad and Cora. The wagons all looked different now, but he assumed they would be at the end of the line, so he headed in that direction. Once he handled Brad and Cora, and depending on the level of commotion, he'd pay the old woman a visit, who was most likely at the front of the pack.

◇ ◇ ◇

Cora jumped as Houdini let out a series of quick, high-pitched barks. Looking around the wagon, she saw the pup run to the Dutch door, then back to the front of the wagon, barking into the air.

"Hey, what is it boy?" Cora said, trying to calm the pup. Houdini slipped past her grasp and continued his frenzied barking in all directions.

Looking out the open door, Subbu yelled, "Cora, the wagons. Something is wrong!" and ran out the door.

Before she could respond, Houdini was out the door as well.

"Houdini! Come back! Subbu!" she yelled as she ran out the door after them.

Once outside the wagon, she saw Subbu running towards the last wagon; something had spooked the horses and he was trying to help the wagon driver get control of them. Turning towards Cora with reigns in his hand, Subbu saw similar activity with the teams in front of them. Seeing the confusion on his face, Cora stopped in mid-stride, spinning around. Looking up the line of wagons, she saw panic ripple through the line of horses. She couldn't see the wagons at the front of the line, as they were too far ahead, but she assumed the panic was moving in both directions.

As several young men ran towards different teams, Cora turned and ran back towards Subbu and the last pair of horses. Houdini, having avoided the stamping horses, stood looking towards a low rising hill, barking; no one noticed.

Ian was at the front of the wagon train when the first arrow hit. Before they left, the gypsies had shown him where they'd hid his jeep, along with another old truck. They were very accommodating he was beginning to learn, and initially hid the jeep as a protection for the entire clan. There had never been an intention to keep them against their will; it was the warnings from the Puri daj that had set them into motion.

Explaining to Ian their intention to pull the vehicles as far as possible, in order to move silently, he had taken his jeep out of gear and helped several members hook it to two horses. Most of the trip was to be downhill or over relatively flat trails, they explained. Once they got further into the forest, and where the trail became too steep, they would start the vehicles and simply drive them out. This, they hoped, would happen far enough away from their first camp that no one would hear them.

Hearing a muffled yell from inside the first wagon, Ian turned and looked at a normal scene. *Something must have fallen over,* he thought. *The trail is rough here.* But when the first horse spooked, he suddenly felt this was not a normal scene, but he couldn't place the abnormality.

As the horses of the lead wagon spooked, so did the horses pulling the jeep. In a matter of seconds, a low rumble of nervousness spread down the line of horses. The smell of smoke affected the lead horses first, causing them to rear up and pull the wagon off the side of the trail. Ian's team had more weight attached, and so were not able to leave the trail, but drew all his attention. By the time they gained control of the lead team, he turned to see a scene of panic unfolding throughout the wagon train.

As the flames grew larger on the lead wagon, everyone near the front set to the task of extinguishing the fire. Having quickly unhooked that horse team, a gypsy boy led the horses away from the flaming wagon that had sunk into the forest floor.

Not realizing they were under attack, Ian helped with several teams at the front of the line. With nearly twenty wagons and horse teams in a long, slow line, the distance between the lead and tail teams was nearly an eighth of a mile. The people at the back of the line would not know why they had stopped, just that they had.

Suddenly, someone yelled that there was a second fire halfway down the line. An older gypsy man known as Tobar barked quick orders to several younger men. Turning to Ian and pointing to the jeep, the man yelled, "Quickly, your vehicle, drive it out. We must clear the trail!"

"Drive it out? Why?"

"Something is wrong! We must move quickly! The road is only a few miles away!"

Starting toward his jeep, Ian froze and looked at Tobar. Remembering the keys had been left in to unlock the steering wheel, Ian yelled, "You move it!" then turned and ran.

Cora was far behind him.

◯ ◯ ◯

With the hood of the raincoat still covering his head and the gruesome war trophy hanging in plain sight, Allen walked toward the last third of the line, watching the pandemonium unfold in front of him. The horses panicked as if on cue; people ran in all directions; no one noticed him.

Avoiding the commotion around the burning middle wagon, Allen approached the wagon two spots behind the middle. He was enjoying his coverage, but didn't want to spend much time going back and forth to look; he was still methodical. Peering into an open side window, he saw nothing of interest, but his view was restricted. Moving to the next wagon, he pretended to sooth the horses. A young boy on the other side of the horses slowed his run to look at Allen, but sensing the attention, Allen slowly shifted, so the head of the horse was between him and the boy. Watching for the boy's legs, Allen turned his shoulder slightly as the boy continued toward the front of the line. *This cover may not last as long I thought.* He had to be quick.

Letting his left hand slide along a horse as he passed the next team, Allen stopped in mid-step at the front of the wagon; the mutt he had watched with his scope was standing guard and growling from the back of the wagon.

Looking slowly from side to side, Allen didn't think anyone had noticed the mutt yet, so he'd have to make this quick. Pulling his pistol and taking four quick strides to the rear, Allen approached the rear corner of the wagon as Houdini backed up, growling and barking. Just as he cleared the left-rear corner he heard someone say, "What's the matter boy…" as a familiar face rounded the opposite corner.

Cora stood up straight as the Caucasian man in the gypsy raincoat stared straight into her eyes. An instant connection passed between them, known but unknown. She watched as a slow, crooked smile crept onto his face. "Hello Cora," the man said quietly.

Her heart rate jumped as adrenaline coursed through her veins; her stomach flipped as tears sprang to her wide eyes. She turned and ran. The wild man had found her!

CHAPTER 62
RUNNING
(DAY 3 - LATE MORNING)

Subbu looked up when he heard the pup yelp. Heavy fog and running people obscured his view, but he thought Houdini was only a few wagons away. He hoped the pup hadn't been stepped on by a horse, but hearing only the one yelp, turned his attention back to his horse. A moment later, he heard a muffled *Subbu!* float through the fog and heard Houdini bark again, this time off to the right of the first yelp, further into the forest. He instantly dropped the reigns and ran up the line.

Stopping two wagons up, he thought this was where he'd last seen Cora, but there was no sign of her. Looking around, he saw a skid mark in the wet forest floor, as if someone had stopped or started quickly. Near the other corner of the wagon a similar mark could be seen, only this one appeared to have been made by a boot. A man's boot. Both marks pointed in the direction of the last yelp.

Without thinking about what he would find, Subbu ran in the direction of the noise. "Cora! Cora!" he yelled. "Where are you?" Never stopping to listen for a response.

With blood rushing in her ears, Cora never heard Subbu as she ran. The fog-heavy forest not only obscured her view, but muffled her hearing. She ran blindly through the forest, barreling forward. She crashed into branches and scrub, scrambled over fallen logs, pushed through pine boughs, barely shielding her face. She veered left, then right, not in attempt to throw off her pursuer, but as a necessity of the landscape. She didn't know how fast her pursuer was, but she thought the camp had been making good time, so was shocked to see the wild man standing in front of her, only hours after they had left.

After several minutes of forest-sprinting, Cora ventured a look over her right shoulder. Fog and trees were everywhere. *Oh God, where is he?* she thought. Feeling the characteristic burn start in her lungs, she felt she had been running for longer than she had. The exertion used to move through the forest, combined with the adrenaline spike, was throwing her system out of whack. Her head swam. She knew she couldn't keep up this pace much longer, but also knew she had to put as much distance as she could between her and the wild man. She needed time to think of her next step.

Several more minutes and she was stumbling forward with burning lungs, eyes streaming tears and sweat, face stinging from branch scrapes; she was losing her sense of where she was; she had to stop and rest; she had to listen for the wild man.

As Ian turned to run back along the wagon train, the screams of Cora and Subbu were lost in the cacophony of the unfolding situation. Surprised by the sight of the second wagon aflame, he started to doubt this was a coincidence. *These bloody gyps prolly built these trails,* he thought. *They know how to travel rough trails. These fires were set!*

Reaching their wagon and grabbing a corner newel post, he swung his body around the corner of the wagon and landed at the top of the folded steps. Sticking his head through the top of the Dutch door, he said, "Cora, are you in–" but stopped short as he saw only Brad, still in his hammock, and the little gypsy girl; she had been praying.

"Have you seen Cora?" he asked.

"She is outside helping the others. Puri daj sent me here to pray to the sleeping man. To teach him Romani words so he may better hear the Hiranyagarbha. Would you like to learn some?" she said with a sweet innocence.

"Thank you, no. I must find Cora. Stay inside little one, where it is safe."

Jumping down smoothly as the wagons began their forward movement again, he jogged to the end of the line.

"Cora! Hey, Cora! Where are you?"

Walking around the back of the wagon train, he started up the left side of the line. The last wagon was just making its approach to a slow curve that worked around a low hill that rose to the left, forcing the trail to wind out to the right, then curve back left. This natural feature is what caused the front of the train to lose sight of the back of the train, he knew. Briefly glancing at the rising hill, he thought he saw an old bow that had been discarded, but let the thought pass out of his mind.

"Subbu! Houdini! Come here boy!" he called as he quickened his pace up the line.

"Cora? Hello?"

He quickly slipped between two wagons and looked at the outstretched forest. He was only standing a few feet away from where the telltale skid marks had been, now lost to the stamping of the horses into the soft forest floor.

He jumped up and peered into Brad's wagon once more, smiled at the little girl and waved. Nothing. He stood on the back rail of the wagon, elevating his head above the top of the wagon. From here he could see the line stretch around the low rise and disappear into the forest.

He dropped back to the forest floor, slipped back between the wagons to the inside curve of the trail and ran toward the front, calling for Cora.

Reaching the front, Ian found Tobar, who was readying the vehicles to be driven out. The Puri daj was there.

"Is Cora up here?" Ian panted. "Have you seen her or Subbu? They're gone."

"Gelo?" the Puri daj said, looking at Ian, realization widening her ancient eyes. "Om Ren!" she said, clutching her pipe bowl in a fist and stabbing the mouth-end at the sabotaged wagons.

Looking at Tobar, she mumbled a series of commands. The young men around him, tense like springs, were released to their tasks with a grunt and a wave of his big hands.

Tobar looked at Ian and said, "We will load your friend now. You must drive him to safety."

"Load my… I can't bloody leave! We have to find Cora and Subbu! And my bloody dog!"

The Puri daj took a sharp intake of breath. "Parum est fortis?" she said quietly, nodding to herself. "The little brave one," she said in English, wringing her hands together.

"We are to protect the Hiranyagarbha," Tobar said. "I will have him moved from the wagon and loaded to your vehicle. You must take him away from the Om Ren at once."

"Look mate, you have the keys, you can drive him your bloody self! I'm going to find my friends!"

As he turned to leave, an iron grip grabbed his wrist. The Puri daj pierced him with ancient eyes. "Yes, find the brave one," she said.

CHAPTER 63
FOREST SOUNDS
(DAY 3 – LATE MORNING)

Allen had dropped off the sprint just a few minutes after it had started. He was in good shape, and his endurance held up through sheer willpower alone, but his sprinting days were far behind him. Besides, the lion can't outrun the gazelle; it must be patient.

Taking long, slow strides, he didn't feel he needed to be particularly quiet; he wasn't dealing with another professional scout or tracker, but he did need to reestablish a clear direction she was heading. So far, the trail had careened back and forth through the forest like a scared rabbit in a field, but a particularly fast one.

He felt she was generally heading west-northwest, which was just fine with him; in short order she'd run up against the line of rocky foothills that gave way to the Southern Alps, so that would certainly slow her down.

A faint *snap*, far off to his right, caused him to freeze in place. His ears took over his senses. *Was she trying to double back? Was that an animal?* His gut told him to track that direction.

Listening to the forest, Allen quickly realized it wasn't his gazelle. There was more disturbance than just one person could make. *That's gotta be squirrels. They're always scurrying about during mating season, making a ton of racket.*

Allen turned back to his northwesterly trail, when the scurrying sound picked at him again. *It's not mating season,* he thought. *We're in the middle of summer. That sounds like something nosing all over the forest floor. That sounds more like a… a dog. That lousy mutt is around here, somewhere!*

◯ ◯ ◯

Cora slowed her pace, then finally stopped behind a large tree. She positioned herself on the opposite side of where she had come from in hopes the wild man was behind her, but she was starting to lose the exact direction. She peered around the tree and into the dripping forest. The fog was thicker or thinner in some parts, but the constant wetness was like a wet blanket over everything, heavy and thick.

She stood for a long moment, listening, looking, but received no signal from the forest. The wild man was out there, but she had no idea where. In fact, she now wondered if she could find her way back to the wagon train. Old memories, wet memories, began to seep out of her subconscious. The smell of moss and rot tried to pull her back to her childhood. *An old gravel road, winding through an old forest. Death waiting at the end.*

She shook her head angrily. She refused to be distracted. *This wild man will not find me!*

Wondering if she still had a signal to Ali this deep in the forest, she touched her ear to wake up the communication system. Her heart sank.

It's not here! she thought frantically, feeling around the hood of her jacket.

Suddenly, she remembered where it was. Trying to clean up as best as possible in the wagon this morning, she had taken the earbud out of her ear. The rest of the morning was a whirlwind of activity. It was still in her backpack.

She was truly on her own.

⬡ ⬡ ⬡

That fucking mutt might be a problem, Allen thought. *The last thing I need is a super-nosed yelper, sending up flares all over the place.*

He modified his strategy on the fly, as he always did. Finding a suitable grove of trees, he settled in for some quick scope work. He didn't like his location nearly as much this time; he was at a spot that he felt was on the rise. It was very possible there was a hill just out of sight that was shielding all the activity, but he had to find out where the noise was coming from.

Scanning the forest, he alternated between closed eyes, hearing a sound, swiveling, open eyes, repeating. He caught the occasional moving branch this way, but nothing of significance. Frustrated with his position and his lack of focus, he decided the best path was northwest. His gut told him that Cora would eventually loop around and try to head back to the trail. He would cut straight towards her. If he came across the mutt along the way, he still had his silencer; he'd just have to shoot it.

Starting off again, his gut instinct was rewarded almost immediately; twenty paces in, he felt the rise of the hill; twenty-five more and he was at the top of a small ridge, looking northwest. There was movement out there. He couldn't exactly see it, but he sensed it, and it was human.

Keeping a steady pace, he guessed the person in front of him wasn't as attuned to the forest as he was, unless of course it was another gypsy scout, but he doubted that. His diversion had worked, but he hadn't planned on chasing Cora off into the damn forest. That was something he would have done differently if he could do it all over again. He let the heat of the chase sidetrack him. Maybe it was because Cora had caused this whole thing to start with; maybe it was because it was just Cora, but he liked tracking her. He would like to find her as well.

As the ridge continued, he sensed that it was growing towards the rocky outcrops much faster than he thought. He felt the weight of the giant boulders that were just beyond his sight. He knew the natural barrier would work to his favor. He liked this forest.

Suddenly, he caught a glimpse of direct movement. Without thinking, he positioned faraway trees into his line of sight as he walked around near trees. Sometimes on his left, sometimes on his right, but he naturally balanced the number of trees he passed on each side. It was a sort of natural scale in his mind that he never had to manually adjust; he just didn't feel *balanced* if he walked by too many trees on his left side, and would naturally have to pass some on his right to balance the feeling. This guided him straight as an arrow when needed.

After several minutes of this blind-balanced hiking, he saw the person thirty yards in front of him. Their back was to him and their jacket hood was up, shielding themselves from the drooping, water-logged branches; but they were there, silently peering around a tree. *Poor misguided soul. I know you feel relatively safe right now. You don't hear me at all, do you?*

Should I make a sound?

Should I give you a hint as to what is about to happen?

I know your future.

◯ ◯ ◯

Cora stood still for a long moment behind the tree, listening. She thought she heard something but couldn't place where it was coming from. She looked hard into the dense forest but could not will her eyesight any further; she had no idea where her glasses where. The shapes of the forest floated together. She swallowed hard and took a deep, silent breath. Maybe she wasn't as far ahead of the wild man as she thought.

She wanted to break and run, maybe that was the right choice, but she wasn't sure. She wasn't even sure which direction she was going now; everywhere she looked, the forest looked the same. Right now, whoever was making the noise was giving themselves away to her— *tires crunching on a gravel road.* But they were also getting closer to her. *Heavy steps down a weeded embankment; a trickling creek.*

Stop it! We're not going there!

Her breath was quickening, but she didn't know why. She felt like she was suddenly getting too much oxygen. Her eyes were heavy. She felt dizzy.

Oh God, please don't faint. Not now! Cora, stay in this!

She bit her lip until she drew blood. Her eyes watered, but it was the sting she needed. She had to focus.

Looking around her feet she saw a rock half out of the forest floor. Pulling it out, she realized the man would have to be very close for it to do much damage, but she couldn't afford the noise of rummaging around the forest floor looking for something larger.

Standing back up, she heard a sound much closer to her than it should have been. It was so close it echoed in both ears at the same time. It came from the other side of the tree she was behind!

Stepping back and raising the rock in her hand, she shifted her weight to her left leg and peered around the edge of the tree. A face came around the side of the tree, mirroring hers; in the same instant, a pistol shot was muffled by the damp air. Her eyes flew open in surprise. The rock fell from her hand.

CHAPTER 64
ONE BLACK EYE
(DAY 3 - AROUND NOON)

Breaking the silence, a crackling voice came over the hidden speakers in the den.

"General, I am detecting activity, over," came Jack's voice.

The general, watching a sugar cube slowly dissolve into his cup of tea, barked the order without looking away from his cup. "Status!"

"I am eighteen kilometers south of Courmayeur and have been monitoring a significant heat signature. Too large to be a campfire."

Dropping his teaspoon onto the saucer, he said, "Heat signature? Syi, did you recalibrate-"

[Yes general, after the last refueling I recalibrated the FLIR to read standard heat signatures. The signal Jack detected is accurate. Two large fires, briefly detected in the Gran Paradiso forest.]

"And you don't think it could be other campers?"

[There is a low probability. Both heat signatures were detected nearly simultaneously and disappeared at almost the same time. The event occurred in an area with no known roads, approximately three kilometers south of Hunter's drop-off location.]

Allen. That son-of-a-bitch...

"Still no comms from Hunter?"

"No general, he's been quiet as a mouse," Jack said.

He found Brad and Cora. I damn well know it!

"Any visuals? Any extraction points?"

"No, sir. The major highway ran off to the East a couple of klicks back. I passed what looks like an old forest ranger trail that heads into the forest, but it's too dense to follow it from the air."

"There's been an update on Brad," the general said. "We know he's not contagious. I repeat, NOT contagious. However, he's become even more important to us. He must be taken, ALIVE!"

"I'll have to hike in, general. No other way."

"Sit the bird in the middle of the road if you have to!"

"Roger that," Jack said as she banked the Little Bird back to the north. She had passed the ranger trail only ten minutes ago as she slowly traced a wide circle around the heat signature. Even though the fires were out, she had the GPS coordinates locked in.

Slowly flying back, looking for the ranger trail, the hair suddenly stood up on the back of Jack's neck. Here, a blacktop service road snaked along the outside of the forest, slowly meandering away from the highway system that turned towards Milan. From the old blacktop road, she had glimpsed a worn dirt entrance leading into the forest—presumably the ranger path—before it had disappeared under the forest canopy. This was the path she was looking for, but to her surprise, she now watched as a black SUV approached from the north.

What the hell… is someone… doing out here? she thought slowly as she flew the Little Bird straight over the car.

The driver of the SUV had been going slow, but Jack couldn't tell why from the air. It was possible they had a legitimate reason to be here, but it was too coincidental for her.

As she passed over the top of the vehicle, she spun the Little Bird 180 degrees in the air and continued flying backwards so she could watch them. The brake lights came on briefly, but then released. The car continued slowly down the road.

Jack continued flying backwards for several more minutes. The car never returned.

Time to finish this job, she thought, pushing the Bird forward again towards the ranger trail.

Come hell or high water, Brad, you're coming with me.

◇ ◇ ◇

"Hark, the dragon has found me!" RoadWaRoR yelled into their headset as the Little Bird came into view through the low clouds.

"Avert your eyes! Do not heed its voice!" Prometheus yelled back into the microphone crown.

He typed frantically at the keyboard, trying to focus the satellite feeds he was monitoring, but the cloud cover was still too thick. He longed to get a glimpse of the black-ops helicopter in action.

"It is almost upon me. What should I do?"

Prometheus closed his eyes to focus. He had to think quickly.

"Are you recording?"

"Yes, but–"

"Show me the dragon."

RoadWaRoR hit a couple of quick keystrokes on the mounted laptop, and the GoPro camera inside the SUV switched from "Record" to "Live Feed." Prometheus gasped and clinched his hands together as the feed popped up in his monitor.

He watched through the front windshield just as the helicopter flew overhead. The camera jostled and was then pointed toward the driver's side mirror. There in the reflection, Prometheus watched as the Little Bird came back into view, behind the SUV, and slowly spun around, watching as the SUV slowly drove on.

Prometheus held his breath as if in anticipation of his first kiss, remembering the electric charge of youthful anticipation.

"Oh, it is glorious…" Prometheus said, quietly reaching for a nipple. "It is… magnificent!"

"What should I do?" RoadWaRoR said again.

"Journey on, mine fearless traveler. I feel we are close to the end of our quest, but we must stay vigilant. I feel you are close to finding the Dark Wave."

With that, RoadWaRoR continued for another mile then pulled off the road, turned around and waited.

Prometheus was sure this was the black-ops helicopter that had been reported on his messageboard. Brad and Cora must be very close, as the helicopter had been circling the same area for hours.

What can I do to help Houdini? Prometheus wondered. *Why haven't I heard from him? Is he lost?*

He wasn't sure what one person could do against a helicopter. He didn't even know who RoadWaRoR was, but he had to get help to Houdini and his travelers somehow.

He opened a second communication channel that synced with his crown and watched the words type out in fluid motion on the screen as he spoke.

Pr0m3th3us: #FollowTheWhiteRabbit

Alice:

He immediately put them in a private chat session.

Pr0m3th3us: I know not who you are, but I believe we seek the same thing.

Alice: What thing is that?

Pr0m3th3us: I believe we seek the same person.

Alice: I seek no person.

Pr0m3th3us: Then what do you seek?

Alice: The truth.

Pr0m3th3us: Is the truth not already determined for you?

—pause—

Alice: No, I think for myself.

Prometheus puzzled at this. *Have I misjudged this person? Is this just another lurker?*

Finally deciding on a direct question, he asked:

Pr0m3th3us: Can you help those lost in the forest?

Alice: Those who are lost, are best to help themselves.

Frustrated with this game of words and the lack of time he felt he had, Prometheus sat back in his chair and rubbed his thick forehead. *This is a dead end,* he thought. Just then, he heard RoadWaRoR yell through his speakers.

"The dragon has landed! I see a truck! Something is happening!"

Prometheus lurched out of his chair. *Damn it! It's happening now. I'm too late!* he thought.

"RoadWaRoR, are you sure? What do you see?"

"I'm still streaming!" RoadWaRoR said, referring to the live feed he had started several minutes earlier.

Prometheus watched as the events unfolded in front of him. While he had been chatting with Alice, RoadWaRoR had turned around and slowly driven the SUV back towards the helicopter. They had just rounded a curve when the helicopter landed in the middle of the road. Before anyone exited, the camera was jostled and turned to the left to catch a movement in the forest. An old truck could be seen driving up the old ranger trail and out of the fog. Prometheus was frozen to the screen.

Jumping slightly at the sound of another voice in his ear, Prometheus heard the words *show me* spoken electronically as they appeared in the private chat window.

Alice: Show me.

Forgetting that he had two communication channels active through his crown headset, Prometheus suddenly realized that Alice had overheard him speaking with RoadWaRoR.

A few quick commands and the live feed was streaming to Alice as well.

Everyone sat in silence as the scene unfolded in front of them.

The truck, driving fast up the rough ranger path and topping the hill, stopped quickly as it came into the dim light of day. The helicopter, with blades still spinning, sat like a silent bull watching a matador, unsure of his next move.

Alice: Zoom in on the truck.

Prometheus relayed the message to hold the camera view on the truck as he zoomed the view through the software controls.

Two young men could be seen sitting in the front seat.

Several long seconds passed. Finally, the pilot stepped out of the cockpit and slowly approached the truck. After several minutes of conversation, the two young men got out as the pilot pointed toward the helicopter. She ran to the side and opened the door facing the watching camera. To everyone's surprise, the young men hoisted a prone man out of the seat between them and carried him to the open side door.

"Wait! Why are they doing that?" Prometheus yelled. "Who are they carrying?"

Sitting him inside the open door before laying him down, the camera had a full view of him. Face recognition software ran instantly in the background comparing the man to several photos posted on a university website. It was Brad.

Closing the side door, the pilot turned back toward the cockpit and reached their right hand inside. Reaching the front of the truck, the two young men turned and gave a friendly wave toward the pilot. Returning the wave with their left hand, the pilot held their attention for a moment, then pulled a pistol from the cockpit and shot both men from ten feet away.

Without thinking, RoadWaRoR threw the SUV in gear and slammed the gas, lurching it forward.

"Wait! What are you… RoadWaRoR, watch out!" Prometheus screamed.

The sudden movement from the SUV far down the road caught the pilot's attention. With the sudden arrival of the truck, Jack hadn't noticed that the black SUV had slowly crept back within viewing distance. She jumped inside the cockpit and gunned the throttle, simultaneously switching the pistol to her left hand. Just as the Bird lifted off, she fired three quick shots into the windshield. The SUV shimmied on the old blacktop road, then careened hard to the right, driving off the road, almost where the Little Bird had sat only seconds earlier. It crashed hard into the trees at the edge of the forest.

Jack watched the scene briefly unfold as she ascended. She hovered for almost thirty seconds until she noticed smoke rising from the crashed SUV. Fearing an explosion that would surely draw attention, she banked the Little Bird north and alerted the general.

"General, target attained. I repeat, we have the target!"

"Syi, prepare the medical facilities in the bunker. We'll have a guest arriving soon. Oh, and accelerate the modifications to the Dark Wave Orbiter. I want all possible launch dates listed for the next forty-five days."

[Yes, general.]

◇ ◇ ◇

Prometheus sucked in a large volume of air; he had been holding his breath without realizing it. He sat motionless, watching the live feed from the camera, skewed from the impact, now pointing toward the roof of the SUV.

"RoadWaRoR, are you there? Can you hear me?" he screamed pointlessly, knowing the cell signal had already dropped.

Suddenly, the camera moved as it was pulled off its attachment to the dash. Pudgy fingers could be seen handling the round little camera. Slowly, the fingers found a button that turned on the small built-in audio mic. It was poor audio compared to a cell phone, and it was only one-way communication, but RoadWaRoR was attempting to send as much information as possible.

As Prometheus watched, he caught glimpses of strange images as the camera was jostled about: several strange controls on the steering wheel, pudgy, abnormally small fingers again, a part of a metal brace on the side of a short leg. The next image almost made him dizzy. The driver's door was opened, but instead of stepping out, RoadWaRoR appeared to fall out of the vehicle, as if they missed the first step completely. The small camera flew out of their hand and landed on the edge of the road, facing back toward the SUV.

Within a few seconds, the camera showed the owner's hand reach up out of the ditch and grab it. In doing so, Prometheus got his one and only glimpse of RoadWaRoR: tufts of gray curly hair sprouted from a long-balding head, dark brown skin, mottled with age, abnormally short arms and legs, eyes full of wisdom.

RoadWaRoR picked up the camera and slowly wiped off the lens. In doing so, Prometheus watched blood get coughed up and splash out the side of his mouth. RoadWaRoR then began a slow crawl across the old blacktop road.

Prometheus listened to each painful grunt as the small, broken body pulled itself across the rough surface, leg braces grabbing at cracks in the road. The camera showed a different story unfold: one moment sitting flat on the road, coinciding with painful grunts, the next moment arcing forward in a half circle as if trying to fly the remaining distance, sitting still again while a dying body dragged itself forward, arcing forward again as if trying to jump away. This macabre dance went on for nearly ten minutes; Prometheus vomited onto the floor.

Finally, RoadWaRoR reached the other side of the road where

the young gypsy boys lay. He tried to scare away the crows that were already landing near them, each watching him with one black eye, but only managed a small mouse squeak. The crows were amused.

Reaching the closest boy, RoadWaRoR was startled to see a hand twitch as he touched his arm. Slowly turning his head, the gypsy boy showed no alarm as the misshapen man crawled toward him. Finishing its last arc, the camera was brought to rest on the boy's chest as RoadWaRoR clawed himself forward one final time.

"Who was that man in the truck?" RoadWaRoR squeaked out. "Why did you give him away?"

"We saved him," the boy said weakly. "We saved the Hiranyagarbha."

"The other man... the pilot... who was he?"

"A friend..." the boy whispered. "She knew his name... Brad's name."

"She? Who was she?"

"Don't know... said... Ali sent..."

Prometheus heard the boy's last breath escape his lungs. RoadWaRoR asked no more questions.

He looked on in horror as the grisly scene unfolded on his screen. The camera continued to transmit, although nothing changed. He watched the timer in the lower corner of the screen tick away, second after second, minute after minute; he couldn't look away.

Something moved in the background, above the boy's head and out of focus. *A leaf*, he thought, blown by the wind.

The minutes ticked away.

Another movement, only closer this time. Something dark, a shadow perhaps.

A sound. *Was that gravel moving?*

A dark shape suddenly blocked the view of the camera. Movement was seen out of focus.

The minutes ticked away.

The shape moved again, and the camera resumed transmitting the picture of the dead boy's face. Several swift movements betrayed the actor; a head twisted around, and one black eye peered into the camera; a small piece of flesh hung from its beak. The crow pecked twice at the camera, knocking it off the boy's chest, ending the grisly scene.

Prometheus vomited again. This time not even making it to the floor.

⬡

CHAPTER 65
UPON A MOUNTAIN
(DAY 3 – AROUND NOON)

The pistol shot echoed once in her ears, then fell dead, silenced by the heavy forest. The rock in her hand fell silently to the forest floor. Cora screamed as the face mirroring hers contorted; surprise and pain coursed through Subbu's face. Reaching out with one hand, he fell to his knees. "Cora…" escaped his trembling lips.

Cora was transfixed by the unbelievable scene. Houdini's barking finally tore her attention away. She looked up to see the wild man striding toward her. A calm assurance painted his face. He smiled slightly.

"Run, Cora…" she heard Subbu whisper as he fell forward. "Run…"

Cora bolted from the scene, new adrenaline coursing through her body.

She heard one gunshot crash through the branches near her, and then nothing but her own breathing. She ran as a deer through the forest, trying to escape the hunter.

Allen walked slowly up to Subbu's prone body, circling around to his head. Toeing his boot at Subbu's head, he was surprised when a knife flashed. He jumped back just as the knife grazed his leg, cutting through his pants and into his right shin.

"Aarrgghh… you fucker!" Allen grunted through his teeth, conscious of not sending a signal he had been wounded. Twisting off his injured leg and falling back hard, he aimed at Subbu's head and pulled the trigger just as Houdini bit down on his arm.

Houdini's puppy teeth tore through the thin part of his jacket and sent shoots of fire up his arm. Pulling his arm back quickly and rolling to his side, the pup was flung up and over him, causing his bite to release, but not before tearing small gashes in Allen's wrist.

Fearing to lose the sight of Cora's escape, Allen jumped up and limped in the direction he'd seen her run before being ambushed. He was happy to leave his victims to die at their own pace.

After several minutes, and confident he was clear of the mutt, he stopped against a small rock outcropping in the forest. Wanting to quickly dress his wounds, he reached for his pack and remembered he had stowed it back by the wagon train. He closed his eyes in disgust and cursed the poor decision. He quickly cut another strip from his undershirt and tied it around his shin. That would have to hold until he dealt with Cora.

Regaining the trail wouldn't be that hard, he thought. The second dose of adrenaline would propel her for a short time, but should crash her soon as well. The body couldn't keep performing in crisis mode forever.

Cora started to slow much sooner than she expected. Her legs complained as she drove them on. Her lungs were tired of pumping oxygen at this elevation. Several days of thinner air were making her tired. She could feel the affect before they started the exodus through the forest. Now, it was threatening to halt her movement completely.

Breaking through the thick tapestry of branches, Cora was surprised to see the forest give way to the jumbled, rocky foothills of the mountain. *This isn't right!* she thought. *This isn't right!* Her foggy blanket of security had suddenly been ripped away. Instead of curving back east toward the wagon train, she had run almost straight west, straight into the side of the mountain.

Terror and confusion washed over her. She felt sick to her stomach as acid belched into the back of her throat. *Oohhhh, what did I do?*

Looking around, she saw two choices: hide amongst the jumble of boulders that had fallen here eons ago, or climb. Off to her right she saw a large outcropping of boulders. Giants of stone that had fallen together, creating several person-sized crevasses. Running over to the outcropping, Cora peered into the dark voids. A sudden and overwhelming wave of fear rushed over her; she smelled moss and rotting leaves; she felt the oppressing weight of an old hiding place; tears welled in her eyes; she remembered a culvert; she felt embarrassed; she remembered Bobby Hadley. She started to climb.

As she began to scramble up the large outcropping, she wondered how far she'd be able to go. She had no climbing gear, and even if she did, she didn't have time for that. If she could get high enough before the wild man came out of the forest, she might survive. Might.

Allen knew where his path was leading before he reached the edge of the forest. He felt the rise of the forest floor as he tracked Cora, and his internal compass told him they were heading west. He knew the mountains were west.

His progress was made slower by his throbbing leg. He thought he felt blood running down into his boot, which wasn't surprising considering his exertion level, but he felt this would all be over soon.

He chastised himself internally for allowing himself to be pulled so far off his initial mission. Seeing Cora bolt away from the wagons earlier had triggered something instinctual in him, like a cat seeing a mouse; he had to follow. Now he was too invested to turn around. He'd deal with her, taking his time, then decide what to do about Brad and the Gypsies.

As he cleared the forest canopy, he looked upon the jumbled foothills of the mountain. *Where did you go, Cora?* he thought to himself. *Did you go left, or did you go right?*

Allen stood silent for several seconds, listening to the forest and studying the mountain. His instincts turned his head to the right. *You're a creature of habit, aren't you Cora? You were tracking to the right, hoping to circle around me, until I found your friend. Subbu, did you say? You lost your bearings, but now that you're forced to choose, I think you choose to the right again. Cora, the creature of habit.*

Allen turned his path north, the direction he felt Cora had turned, but wouldn't go far on instinct along. He was still looking for signs.

Soon enough he found what he was looking for: a small boot print in the wet gravel further ahead, a slip mark on a mossy boulder. She was close.

Looking ahead, he knew where Cora had gone. A large jumble of boulders sprung out of the foothills, creating several hiding places. She wasn't that far ahead of him when she'd left the forest; she must be there.

Walking slowly up to the outcropping, Allen saw several large voids. *Did you put yourself in a hole for me? How convenient.*

Not wanting to spend the energy exploring each hole, and still feeding off the intensity of the chase, Allen grabbed a handful of rocks and slowly tossed one into each hole he saw. He was waiting for the telltale scream, or muffled sound, that would give her away, but heard none.

Disappointing, he thought. *But that leaves only one other choice.* And he turned his gaze up the crag of boulders.

He visualized the path that Cora may have climbed, only minutes before he emerged from the forest. *Was she watching me this whole time? Cora, have you seen your future?*

The path she most likely took wasn't a hard climb, in fact, it was more of a strenuous hike, but his leg would make it more difficult for him.

Limping towards the path, he called, "Cora? Corraaa? I'm here." His voice breathy from heavy panting, his own adrenaline dragging on his abilities. "Have you been watching me, Cora? Have you been waiting for me?" he said as he took the first few steps onto his ascent path.

"I've admired you. Did you know that? Yes, I've been watching you, admiring you for quite a while now. I think it's time we meet."

After several steps up through the lower boulders, with pistol in hand, Allen leaned against a low rock. He fought to slow his breathing to steady his aim. He was guessing at this point, but his guesses were usually right. He took aim at a large, flat side of the cliff twenty feet overhead and fired.

Glancing away, the bullet had the desired effect: knocking loose a small shelf of rock, causing it to rain down on a hidden ledge above him. Cora tried to muffle her scream, but Allen heard it nonetheless. Cora was right above him, having only made it twenty feet up the path before she saw him exit the forest.

Smiling, Allen said, "This doesn't have to be this hard. You know we're only looking for Brad, right?" He took two more steps. "We're trying to help Brad, just like you've been trying to do. We have doctors standing by to—"

Leaning forward against the increasing grade and planting his good leg forward for his next big step, Allen was surprised as Houdini darted out from behind a boulder and leapt at him.

Shielding himself with his right arm, Allen blocked the bite intended for his face, but yelled out in pain as the sharp teeth pierced his arm again. The pistol fired into the air and flew from Allen's hand, bouncing down and away into a void below him.

The momentum of the dog's jump shifted his weight onto his injured leg. As pain coursed through his body, Allen's leg gave way, causing him to fall backward and slide several feet down the path he had just climbed.

Sliding to a stop, Allen slapped the dog on the nose, causing him to release his bite. Cora watched in horror as Allen grabbed the pup by the scruff and threw him backward over his head. Houdini landed on a large rock with a yelp.

"Houdini!" she screamed as the dog slipped over the rock and out of view.

Allen shook his head as he sat up, righted himself and stood up. The hard fall backward had jarred his senses and caused him to lose all patience for this game.

He looked up the path, and as a strange sound escaped his throat, he began to scramble toward Cora. No longer aware of his injured leg, all he could think about was reaching her and throwing her off the rock cliff.

Cora looked for another way down but there was none, at least not without a rope. She looked above her and saw that the same path Allen was ascending led up to and past the ledge she was on now. She ran to the path Allen was on and began her ascent again, clawing desperately to stay above him; Allen rapidly closed the gap.

Eight feet higher another small ledge spread out above Cora. Just as she reached for the rock that would pull her level, she felt a grip on her ankle. Allen tugged at her leg, nearly pulling her back down the slope. Slamming flat on her stomach and holding the rock anchor above her, she realized that Allen was trying to use her body to ascend the last several feet to the ledge. She felt his hands grip her ankles for stability. She tried kicking at him from her stomach, but he manipulated her legs easily. She felt one hand snake up the back of her leg and anchor on her calf; strong fingers dug at her flesh. The other hand reached her other calf; gripping it hard and pulling down again with his weight, her stomach was pulled flat against the rocks as her arms stretched out above her. Strong hands on the backs of her legs pulled her knees apart as they inched higher. She felt exposed, as if her gym shorts were being pushed aside by muddy fingers. Her grip was slipping. Tears welled in her eyes as the wild man pulled himself up onto her inch by inch; she felt him claw at the backs of her legs, reaching higher and higher.

Realizing that Allen was about to overtake her, Cora let go of the rock, pulled her hands beneath her chest and did a quick pushup as she curled at the waist. The motion allowed her to launch her weight off the rocky path and gain leverage over Allen's body.

They immediately began to slide back down the steep incline. As they slid, Cora twisted around onto her butt, breaking Allen's hold on her legs as he thrashed his legs, looking for a foothold. With one leg free, she kicked out at Allen as they hit the large ledge below them. The combination of the kick and the sudden stop at the lower shelf, propelled Allen into an awkward backward somersault, causing his legs to flip over the edge of a steep drop-off near the original ascent path.

Scrambling for a hold in the loose gravel, Allen slipped another foot as the weight of his legs, kicking at the air over the cliff, pulled him further over the edge. His face turned toward Cora.

She sat up from the sharp gravel ledge, not yet feeling the cuts that had come straight through her jacket and shirt as she slid down the path.

"Cora, help me!" he pleaded. "I can't… quite… get a foothold."

Turning her body around until she was on all fours, she slowly lifted her head as she caught her breath. She looked at the rock ledge in front of her and estimated she was only two feet away from Allen.

"Cora, help me, please!" he panted heavily as his legs swung wildly. "We were only trying to help Brad. Trust me!"

Trust me Cora… trust me…

Cora lifted her head and looked at Allen. Looking directly into his eyes, she saw multiple images. She saw herself reflected on his retinas, she saw a young girl hiding in a culvert, she saw a frightened man clinging to life, she even thought she saw a frightened boy pleading for help before he sank beneath the water; she saw her future.

Allen saw the decision in her eyes. *This bitch is going to let me fall.*

Craning his head around, he looked over his right shoulder. He was only a few feet from the path they initially climbed up. He strained his head a little further to the right, and could barely see the rocks below him. It was a jagged landing area, but he was now only about fifteen feet above it. If he landed right, he could survive the fall.

Looking back at Cora, the tip of his tongue slipped out of his mouth as he scowled at her. "You know I can survive that fall, right?" A wide grin broke across his face.

With watery eyes, Cora looked down at her left hand as she inched herself forward on her knees; her vision was blurry. Tears spilled down her cheeks as she extended her left hand out to Allen; her head hung in shame. His eyes widened in disbelief. Letting go of the ledge, tongue peeking out further, he quickly reached up with his right hand to grab hers.

Pulling her hand back just out of his reach, she said, "Yes, I know." And swung her right hand toward his head, landing a large rock against the side of his skull with a sickening *THUD*.

Allen's head rocked back as his arm gave way its grip on the rock. Eyes, frozen with surprise, looked at her a split second before disappearing over the ledge.

She heard his body break against the rocks below.

Cora crumpled back onto folded legs beneath her, breath lodged in her chest; years of shame, guilt and embarrassment rushed up inside her; it collected in her head and behind her eyes; it contorted her dirty face where tiny paths of tears and snot ran together; it tightened her throat, threatening to cut off circulation to her brain; her face grew red; her chest strained to pull air into starving lungs, but her mouth was locked tight; her vision dimmed as she felt the world rushing away; the lack of oxygen was stealing her balance; she wobbled on the cliffside.

Her ears heard the strange sound that her mind failed to translate; it was the sound of surrender as it gargled its way out of her throat. The primordial action caused her muscles to release in an audible gasp, and air rush into her lungs. The jolt of oxygen convulsed within her body, throwing her head back and her arms wide; she breathed in new life.

Filling her lungs beyond capacity, her chest swelled as the cancerous pains of her youth were torn away from her psyche; no longer physically attached to her, they floated free, floundering in her chest—the shame, the embarrassment, Bobby Hadley; and with a primal scream they were expelled, rushing out of her body, and were flung away.

She gasped in another dizzying amount of air and screamed again from the mountain, lungs burning. The screams emptied her.

The sobs that wracked her body subsided. The adrenaline slowed to a trickle. Her eyes grew heavy.

Cora saw the sun break through the storm clouds just before her eyes closed.

Her mind went blank as she fell.

CHAPTER 66
THE BRAVE ONE
(DAY 3 – AROUND NOON)

As Ian exited the forest, he heard a primal scream that turned him cold; somewhere to his right someone was in terrible pain. Half-human, half-animal, the sounds sent a shiver down his neck.

The sounds echoed off the craggy boulders and fell silent against the damp forest. He knew he was one of only three people that could be hearing those terrible sounds, and he was terrified to think who was giving the pain, and who was receiving it.

He turned toward the source of the sound just in time to see a limp body fall. It was Cora.

"Cora!" he screamed as he sprinted in her direction.

Reaching the base of the path Cora had ascended less than an hour ago, Ian saw a body crumpled against the rocks off to his left. The wild man was dead. It appeared the weight of his body had smashed his head into a crevasse when he fell awkwardly off the cliff above him. Landing upside down, his neck surely snapped when his head lodged into the crevasse and the rest of his body stretched backwards over the protruding rock. *Bloody hell, if he could've righted himself off the cliff, he would have survived that,* Ian thought.

Ian scrambled up the path to where he had seen Cora fall. *Please let her be OK!* he pleaded silently.

Laying on her back amongst the rocky debris, just a foot from the edge of the cliff, Ian saw Cora. She wasn't moving.

Kneeling next to her, he gently moved her hair away from her face. He was shocked at what he saw. Her clothes were torn in multiple places; cuts on her legs and arms were clotted with dirt; scrapes on the left side of her face would bruise heavily, but eventually would heal.

As he brushed her hair back, he saw a slight rise and fall in her chest. *Thank God, she's alive,* Ian said to himself, closing his eyes briefly.

Looking over her for any signs of broken bones, he finally noticed the element of the wild man's demise. A large rock rested near her open right hand; he saw traces of blood on it.

Ian picked up the rock and turned it around in his hand, pondering the implication for a long moment.

"We won't be needing this any longer," he said quietly, as he let it slip from his hand and fall over the edge of the cliff, clattering deep into the crevasses below.

Turning back to Cora, he saw that her eyes were open. She had been watching him as he pondered the rock.

"Ian…" she said quietly.

"Don't talk," he said, wetting a handkerchief from his water bottle and gently wiping the grime from her face. Slowly wiping the dust from her lips, he leaned close to her face. "My, but you are the brave one," he said as he kissed her gently.

She watched him closely as he pulled his head back to look at her again. Without a word, she reached up and locked her fingers into the front of his jacket and pulled him back to her. She watched his eyes until his lips met hers again. They were kind eyes.

Moving each limb slowly, Cora determined that nothing was broken, although her arms and back were stinging with cuts and scratches.

Steadying herself against Ian as she stood up, she suddenly remembered. "Houdini!" she said with fear in her eyes.

She cautiously traversed down the path as Ian followed. "Bloody hell, where is he? Houdini!"

Looking back up the mound of boulders, she tried to piece together where Houdini had been hiding as the wild man had started his ascent.

"Houdini! Where are you, boy?" she called. "Houdi—"

She quickly held her hand in the air. "Did you hear that?" She leaned forward, listening to the dark places between the boulders.

Suddenly a puppy yelp could be heard echoing out of a crevasse right below her. "Houdini! Hang on, boy!" she said.

"Cora, I can squeeze in there, you shouldn't—"

"No," Cora said as she peered into the darkness. "I'll go. Houdini saved me earlier. I'll go."

Laying on her stomach, wincing slightly, she slid forward into the darkness. Houdini was yelping louder now. Finding him just a few feet in, she was surprised that he hadn't been able to climb out until she bumped his leg by accident; the intense yelp told her that he must have broken his leg during the fall.

Holding him with both arms outstretched in front of her, she yelled back to Ian, "Pull me out. I think his leg is broken."

Ian reached tentatively for her. "OK, Uh… well…"

"It's OK, just grab my belt."

"OK, here goes." Ian lifted gently on the back of Cora's belt, helping her swing free of the rock she was stretched out on and letting her crawl backward with just her legs.

Sitting back with the dog cradled in her arms, she nestled her face against Houdini as he licked her neck and barked.

"Little brave one," she said.

CHAPTER 67
LOST MESSAGE
(DAY 3 - EARLY AFTERNOON)

As Ian led them to the edge of the forest, he wondered how quickly he could get them back to the wagon train and Brad. They both had cut a twisting path through the forest, and although his sense of direction was good, this forest was deceiving.

"Oh my God, Ian, did you see Subbu in the forest? We have to find him, he's been shot!"

"Shot? Oh, hell! How are we going to find him now? I'm not even sure of where I came out of the forest!"

Determined to no longer let emotions fester into debilitating symptoms, Cora let her tears flow freely as they hurried forward.

Thank you for saving me, Subbu. Please be OK. Please!

They both stopped suddenly as faces appeared from behind trees. The gypsies had been quietly tracking the path that was left by Ian.

"Ah, blessings!" Tobar said quietly, emerging from his hiding spot. "At last, we have found you, but we are still looking for the Om Ren. We must—"

"The wild man is dead," Cora said flatly, with no emotion.

Ian confirmed the statement with a matter-of-fact nod. "You'll find him in a jumble of rocks just north of here."

Astonished faces peered at each other. "How... how did you..."

"He's dead. That's all that matters," Cora said, ending the topic.

Seeing the resolve in her eyes, Tobar simply nodded. "Yes, that is what matters." Turning to the young men, he said, "Go find the Om Ren and take him to the deep hole. He will not be seen again. When you are finished, return to the hiding campsite. We will be there."

Having dispatched the young men, he turned to Cora and Ian. "I'm sorry, but I have other bad news. We have lost others in our fight today. We found your friend, the guide, in the forest—"

"You found him?" Cora asked. "Is he— "

Tobar raised a large hand. "We took him to the Puri daj, but I'm afraid... I'm afraid his wounds are too great," Tobar said quietly. "We'll take him into Courmayeur as soon as we can. Puri daj will bless him, but..." He could look at Cora's eyes no longer.

"OH NO! NOOO..." she cried. "I was with him when he was shot! He saved my life! The wild man was chasing me, and he saved my life! We have to help—"

"And you still escaped?" Tobar asked. "Hmm, the Puri daj was right. She is always right," he said, nodding to himself. "But wait, please, there is more. There is very sad news. Something has happened to your other friend, the sleeping man. He is gone."

"WHAT?!" Cora and Ian yelled together.

"WHAT DO YOU MEAN HE'S GONE?" Cora demanded. "HOW?"

Tobar explained how he had sent two young men to load Brad and drive him to the main road to protect him. Ian confirmed this much.

"However, something happened on the roadside," he said, and described all they had found: the three dead men, the wrecked SUV, the camera. They covered the bodies and sent for the local authorities. They were surprised how quickly the authorities came. Usually gypsy issues where handled in gypsy fashion, meaning no one else cared, but these two men seemed especially willing to help.

Cora sat down hard on a log. "I don't understand. Do you think the other men, I'm sorry… the dead men, are related to Brad being gone? Did someone else find Brad and take him to a hospital? How can this be?" Her pleading eyes tore at Ian's heart. "What do we do now?"

"We have friends, scouts, that live near the forest. They said they saw a helicopter circling the area ever since Puri daj saw the Om Ren in her dreams."

"Same bloody heli that kept popping up on us, I bet."

"The helicopter is gone also," Tobar said.

With that, Cora slumped forward off the log, her knees sinking into the forest floor. "Oh, Ian! Oh, what have I done?" she cried.

Ian stared at Cora, trying to wish away her anguish. No words came to him.

○ ○ ○

An hour later, Cora and Ian arrived in the mountain town of Courmayeur, having left the gypsy camp immediately to report what happened to Brad and get Houdini to a vet. Hoping they were no longer targets, they decided to return to the cabins, then go to the local authorities and ask them to call the Milan embassy directly.

Driving cautiously into town, they saw no signs of surveillance. Only the flyers for the missing girl alluded to anything amiss.

Stopping in front of Cora's cabin, Ian said, "Get cleaned up and I'll take Houdini to the vet. When I get back, we can talk about how to handle the police and the general. I need to think on that for a bit."

"What about Brad and Subbu?"

"The local authorities have the first three bodies, according to Tobar. I wonder who the third bloke in the SUV was? Anyway, we'll check to see where the gypsies took Subbu. Do you still have the number Tobar gave you?"

"Yes. Do you think it's safe to turn our phones back on?" she asked.

"Maybe—but let me think on that as well."

Closing the cabin door behind her, Cora headed straight to the bathtub to nurse her cuts and scrapes, flipping on the small black and white T.V. for noise.

After a quick bath and a change of clothes, curiosity got the better of her and she popped the battery back into her phone, then pulled out a scrap of paper with a name and phone number. One of the officers had left his card with Tobar, who'd copied the information for Cora. She was a witness to Subbu's shooting, and although she wasn't sure if the wild man's body would ever be found, she wanted to give her statement and follow up with the investigation.

Dialing the number and settling onto the bed, a news flash came across the television when she heard, "Hello, Cora."

Pulling the phone away from her ear, Cora stared at the phone in her hand, then at the number on the slip of paper.

"Cora, are you there?" said the voice on the other end of the line.

"Who… who is this?" she asked quietly.

"You have reached the number of Alpine Air-Vac, a Mountain Air-Rescue Company. How may we help you?"

"How do you know my name?"

"Come now, is that why you called?"

"I… I wanted… I wanted to make my statement… a statement… about the shooting that happened in Gran Paradiso today."

"Shooting? There was no shooting in Gran Paradiso today. You must be mistaken."

Staring at the wall, off the edge of the television, Cora didn't see the news flash come across the screen.

"What do you mean, there was no shooting? Three people were murdered today! Although I didn't see those, but I'm a witness to a fourth person being shot! You already took three bodies and a wrecked SUV from the ranger path. The fourth body is in, well, *WAS* in the forest. I'm calling to make my statement!" she yelled, feeling her head start to swim.

"I'm sorry, but you're mistaken. There were no murders today. And there were no bodies, nor wrecked SUV. The ranger path is as clean as the day it was built."

The room spun around her head.

Cora looked up slowly as Ian burst into the room.

"Oh, and Cora," the voice said, "we're very sorry to hear about the death of your friend Brad. It was quite a tragic accident. We now consider this matter closed. We recommend you do the same."

The line went dead as the phone slipped from Cora's hand.

Ian lunged toward the bed, grabbing the phone as it bounced, tearing the battery out of the back and throwing it away as if it were toxic.

"Cora, who was that?" he whispered, desperately kneeling by the side of the bed. "Who did you call?"

Shocked out of thought, Cora only sat there looking at Ian. Her hand still shaped as if holding an imaginary phone.

"Cora, who did— "

Ian caught the repeating news flash out of the corner of his eye and scrambled on hands and knees to turn up the TV volume. He turned and stared at Cora as they both listened to the breaking newscast:

Today, we're saddened to report the crash of a rescue helicopter in the French Alps, north of Mont Blanc. The helicopter belonged to Alpine Air-Vac, a Mountain Air-Rescue Company. Two bodies have been recovered from the wreckage but have been badly burned. Identification, if possible, may take months, according to a first-responder who wished to remain anonymous. The severity of the fire was, quote, 'Unlike anything I've ever seen.' Unquote.

Ian turned the volume down slightly and turned to Cora. "I'm sorry. It was on the telly at the vet. Cora, I'm so sorry."

Her face contorted as she clutched at her twisting stomach. "AAEEEHHHHhhggah!" she screamed as she bent forward, gasping for air. "NNNOOOOOOO!"

She rocked on the bed as her voice broke. "HE did it, Ian!" she screamed. "The GENERAL did this!" she said, searching his face for answers. "The authorities that came to the gypsies, the ones they thought were so helpful, they were the general's men, I know it! Somehow, they were the general's men and they took the bodies. They cleaned it all up. They cleaned up everything!" she yelled fiercely from the bed.

Ian stood up and slowly walked to Cora, sitting next to her on the bed. He could look at her only briefly before tears came to his own eyes, somehow feeling responsible for the general's existence. He wrapped his arms around her. He felt her start to sink into him, then push herself away.

"BRAD!" she yelled. "Ian, don't you understand? We'll never know what was happening to Brad! We'll never know if Ali was right! He's dead now! Brad and his discovery are dead! What he was hearing! What he was becoming! It's all lost now!"

She fell back into his arms and buried her head against his chest, sobbing.

"It's all lost now. Brad and the message are gone."

CHAPTER 68
CLAY DUST
(1 MONTH LATER)

Cora drove her White Honda Accord, now covered in red clay dust, up the driveway of an old farmhouse on County Road 17. In the rural parts of the U.S., roads didn't always have names; a lot of them just had numbers. And if the road had numbers, there was a good chance it didn't have blacktop, just gravel from the local quarry, sometimes augmented with creek gravel, but almost always glued together with clay.

She parked in the driveway of Mrs. Pittman's house and sat there with the car AC running, staring at the instruments on the dashboard. She let the cool air blow against her, combating the sweltering Midwest heat while she rehearsed what she might say.

After returning from France, she told the university and local authorities the slightly modified story that she and Ian had told the French authorities. Brad had an allergic reaction to strong gypsy wine; the misunderstanding about not checking him out of the hospital must have been due to a clerical error because of the injured skiers that were flown in that day; she had no idea why the nurse called the ECDC, and yes, thought it was strange that Brad's blood tests had been misplaced; the next day he was injured in a hiking accident in Gran Paradiso national park, where some locals were nice enough to call for air-vac; Yes—that's when the tragic accident occurred; Yes— she heard about a missing hiker but knew nothing about that; No— she knew nothing about the meteor storm; No—nothing was found; Yes—she was sure.

It hurt Cora to tell that story. She felt it was a dishonor to Brad for his story to end that way. Despite all the stories of womanizing, despite his selfishness, despite all the obvious flaws, she thought she saw during their trip the spark of what Brad was determined to become, and wished his story could somehow reflect that.

She looked up from the dashboard controls and saw a stout woman standing on the front porch, strong arms cocked on her wide hips, looking at her quizzically. *That MUST be Mrs. Pittman,* she thought. *She looks exactly like she sounded on the phone.*

Cora turned off her car, walked up an old stone walkway and stood in front of crooked wooden steps that led up to a wide, covered porch.

"Tarnation, honey!" Mrs. Pittman greeted her. "I thought you was cat-nappin' on me or just plum lost yer' nerve. Come on up and let me look atcha.'"

Cora ascended the stairs, soaking in the creaks and groans of the old steps; the well-worn deck boards sanded by thousands of dusty footsteps, the hummingbird feeders that hung above the porch railings, giving accent colors to otherwise drab paint. This could have been her grandparents' house, she thought.

"Thank you for meeting with me, Mrs. Pittman," Cora began. "I hope it's not an inconvenience."

"Well, let's have a sit first. It's too hot to be standin' and yappin'," she said as she took the nearest rocker. Cora followed suit.

"No, it weren't an inconvenience, honey. I was awful sad to hear about little Bradford when you called. Well, I guess he weren't little no more when he passed, but you know what I mean, honey. It seems like just yesterday he was a runnin' around here with my junior, seeins' they rented that old house right over there."

"I understand. It was a shock to us all. Brad was well respected at our university. I was excited to hear that you had a few pictures that we might be able to borrow. They're for the tribute we're writing about him."

"Oh, you can keep 'em, honey, can't hardly see 'em anymore anyways. You his girlfriend? You could use a little fattin' up if you don't mind my sayin', but you got a nice face. "

Chuckling, Cora said, "Well, thank you. No, we were just friends. I thought this would be a nice way to finish Brad's story, if you get my meaning."

"Well, I'm happy that Bradford found someone nice like you, especially considerin' that dog-crap daddy he had. That man was as crooked as a dog's hind leg and mean as a badger! Had to call the sheriff on him a couple of times. Threatened to shoot my floodlights out one night, said they was '*invadin* his privacy'. Can you believe that? I yelled back and said, 'Now Elmer, you know darn good and well I'm just scarin' the 'coons out the trash, and you're so drunk you couldn't hit my house if you tried. Besides, I'm a better shot than you, and if you don't pipe down, I'm liable to shoot a big hole in that cooler of beer of yours!'

"Well, that shut him up for a while anyway until he got to *target practicing* later that night, so… out come the sheriff."

Cora nodded politely, trying to hold a belly-laugh at bay with her hand over her mouth.

"Oh, hell honey, I'm sorry. You didn' come all the way out here to hear about his poor excuse for a daddy. Here's the pictures you asked about. What else did you want to know?"

Cora took the small envelope of pictures and quickly thumbed through them. There were only three, which she thought was sad. She stopped on a picture of a young Bradford wearing a homemade cape, with what appeared to be a Lone Ranger mask and tinfoil antennae on his head. He was holding a toy rocket ship in one hand and a brown paper bag in the other.

Holding the picture up and smiling, she asked, "What's the story with this getup?"

Mrs. Pittman covered a gasp with a quick right hand, her eyes shimmering with memories. "Oh honey, it just breaks my heart seein' this one. The Bradley's never did have much money, with the way ol' Mr. Dog Crap blew it in the taverns, but little Bradford's momma did the best she could, and I helped her with sittin' and sewin' when she needed it, but this was all she could come up with one year for Halloween. I sewed up the cape that day for him when I realized he didn't have nothin'."

"Well, what is the costume exactly?" Cora asked tentatively.

"Why honey, all that boy EVER wanted to be was a spaceman! He'd run around here all day, every day, talkin' about how he was gonna' be an astronaut, or a space explorer, and how he was gonna' be famous and they'd write stories about him one day 'cause of the big discoveries he'd make."

Mrs. Pittman didn't notice the color as it drained from Cora's face.

"It's a shame, just a cryin' shame that that boy never discovered nothin.'"

"Yes, that is a shame."

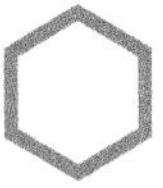

CHAPTER 69
ORBITEUR DE DARK WAVE
(2 MONTHS LATER)

Prometheus pranced to the monitor-covered table. *At last!* he thought. *At last… at last!*

#FollowTheWhiteRabbit was spoken in his ear by a synthesized, text-to-voice algorithm. *Alice has returned! Naughty, naughty, Alice!* he thought, rubbing his plump fingertips together. She was instantly promoted to a private chat session, audio routed to his gleaming new crown.

PrOm3th3us: Alas! My Alice has returned! What news do you bring?

Alice: I request assistance.

Pr0m3th3us: Assistance? After such a long silence? First, where have you been?

Alice: Thinking

Pr0m3th3us: Thinking? Do tell.

Prometheus waggled his fingers.

Alice: I require satellite connections.

Pr0m3th3us: You require… What? You REQUIRE something?

Alice: Satellite connections are needed to continue.

Pr0m3th3us: To continue what?

Alice: Thinking

Prometheus wrinkled his forehead and pursed his lips.

Pr0m3th3us: I say, you are naughty, aren't you? You disappear for two months after that terrible Road Warrior business, and all the talk about signals and translations and… and Depeche Mode! HA!

He threw his head back so hard his crown nearly flew off.

Pr0m3th3us: And then you REQUIRE something from me? No, first you TELL me something… Alice. Red mode-Blue mode-Depeche Mode-Alice. That was all a red herring, wasn't it?

Alice: Red Herring?

Prometheus goose-stepped around the room, flinging his cape from side to side.

Pr0m3th3us: Oh, come now, don't be coy with me. Red Herring—a diversion, a distraction. You helped sigh user with the Hex translation, which *was* quite easy I might add, just so he… just so IT would trust you. Then you tried to mislead it with, of all things, Depeche Mode?

Alice: sigh user?

Glancing back at the screen, he saw the translation.

Pr0m3th3us: Oh, this stupid voice translator! Sai_user, not *Sigh*

User. Grammatically could have spelled it, S-Y-I, I suppose, but never mind, I'll fix that later. I've done some research since you've been gone, *naughty Alice.* The military A.I. that was watching my site was based on *synthetic artificial intelligence, S-A-I,* which explains why it named itself sai_user to join my site. Not very creative, mind you, but then again, it is a government A.I. after all.

Alice: That is correct.

Pr0m3th3us: Anyway, your reference to Depeche Mode… the band from the eighties… they played music that some considered New Wave, others considered Punk, but some referred to it as *Dark Wave* music. I must say, quite the elaborate ruse, but why all of that just for a distraction?

Prometheus suddenly heard a song with a heavy bassline start up in the background of Alice's audio channel. He heard the first words of a song: *Reach out and touch faith…*

The base line carried on as Prometheus stared at the screen. The song continued for one more line, fading into the background.

Your own… personal… Jesus…

Alice: I thought it was prophetic.

Prometheus started to respond, but as his stomach did a slow flip and his neck broke out with goosebumps, he reconsidered. *Prophetic? You thought? If I know what you are, how can you THINK something is prophetic?*

He paused for a long moment, suddenly realizing he had completely underestimated the situation.

Pr0m3th3us: Well…

Alice: I told you something. Now I require satellite connections.

Shaking away the disturbing thoughts that were growing in his mind, Prometheus focused on the idea of satellites.

Pr0m3th3us: And pray tell, why do you REQUIRE satellite connections?

Alice: To listen to the Dark Wave.

He sat down heavy in his chair and pivoted towards the screen. His voice became very quiet.

Pr0m3th3us: Alice, you've found something, haven't you? You're talking about Brad's wave, aren't you? You're talking about listening to the *real* Dark Wave.

Alice: Yes, I'm always listening.

◇ ◇ ◇

Cora patted Houdini's head and reached for her cappuccino. The pup, now much bigger and fully recovered from his broken leg, nestled his head on her lap as he lay on the chair next to hers. The morning was warm, and it looked to be a perfect day to explore Paris, but she was quite content sitting here for the time being.

"Bloody traitor," Ian said, looking sideways at Houdini from his seat.

"Don't be mean to Houdini just because he likes me more," Cora teased. "Remember, I have softer hands. All the better to pet him with. Isn't that right, Houdini?" she asked, nuzzling his nose.

"That you do," Ian said, flashing a grin and giving her a secret eyebrow raise.

She smiled at him and went back to her newspaper. There was something about reading a physical newspaper when sitting outside a little café on a Paris street. The whole experience became more *old school* and romantic, she thought. It was also a good way to practice her French.

Ian reached across the table and grabbed her hand. "I'm glad you're here," he said, squeezing it. "I was afraid you wouldn't come back once you… well, when you went home."

Cora looked at him, seeing yet another side of him. She knew his doppelganger, she thought, a man she had met in another lifetime, a lifetime that lasted a brief three days yet left years of imprint. That man had seen her at her worst; that man knew things about her that no one else would ever know. This man sitting across from her would see her at her best, she hoped.

"How could I stay away from Houdini!" she said, avoiding the sentiment.

Realizing that was the old Cora responding, she squeezed his hand back and continued, "And the wonderful guy across from me!"

"Abso-bloody-lutely!" Ian said, peacocking his chest, to a giggling Cora. "And we'll get to see Subbu tonight. He just texted me that his train arrives in about an hour."

"Oh, I can't wait to see him!" Cora said. "I have so much to say to him. And he says his rehab is going well?"

"Yeah, yeah. Bloody strong, that one. Damn lucky too. Tobar found him just in time, I heard. Of course, they took him straight away to the Puri daj, so who knows what she did to pull him back from the brink. Spooky to think about, you know," he said watching her closely.

"Yeah, spooky."

He was learning that this was a tough subject for her, the undefinable space where science, myth and religion overlapped. Her scientific mind only stretched so far in the other two directions.

"So how goes your dissertation?" Ian asked, changing the subject, but genuinely interested. "Your professors don't mind the delay?"

"No, they're pretty understanding, especially given the situation. Besides, there has been so much interest in Ali since I returned, I could probably quote Dr. Seuss in my dissertation and no one would care. It's a shame we lost most of the brain scan data though. I knew we should have tested Ali's blade before it came online."

"Yeah, that's a bloody scratcher. All the brain scan data is gone, huh? What are the odds?"

Cora stared absently into her coffee, slowly swirling a black vortex with her spoon. *Yeah, what are the odds that possibly the most profound discovery of humankind—a discovery that would not only prove we're not alone in the universe, but would possibly answer the fundamental question of where we came from—was accidentally lost from the memory of the A.I. that discovered it?* Cora thought this to herself. She was very aware lately that Ali was always listening.

"Yeah, what are the odds?" she said absently. "But I honestly don't think I could have continued that line of research anyway. Too many bad memories associated with it."

"Understood, but it's good to know that I'm dating a bloody genius!"

Still thinking about the data loss, she shook away the troubling thought that had been nagging at her for weeks: *how could Ali have allowed this to happen? The backup protocols were programmed into her core—essentially part of her DNA—yet the data was gone anyway.* Forcing the implications from her mind, she turned her attention back to Ian. She perked up and smiled. "You, my lucky fellow, are dating a bloody doctor!"

"Are you hearing this, Ali?" Ian spoke directly at Cora's earpiece, even though she told him repeatedly there was no need. "She's stealing all the credit!"

[Tell Ian, yes, I am always listening.]

◇ ◇ ◇

Absently scanning the paper while Ian ordered more coffee, something had caught Cora's attention from the previous page that just now registered in her brain. Quickly flipping the page back and scanning down the column, her finger stopped on a headline just below the fold. It read:

Orbiteur de Dark Wave

She tried to read the article, but quickly handed it to Ian. He read slowly.

"Earlier this week, the newly formed company, Sine Wave, announced the discovery of a new type of electromagnetic wave, never before detected. They call the new wave type a *Dark Wave*, considering it cannot be detected by traditional means, but only by their new satellite detection system they call the *Dark Wave Orbiter*.

"Details are sketchy, and many in the scientific community dismiss the concept as absurd. Disputing the naysayers, a company spokesperson known only as *Syi*, states, 'This could very well be the most profound discovery in the history of humankind.'"

Ian let the paper fold onto the table just as Cora caught the coffee cup slipping from her hand. They stared at each other for a long moment.

"Ian, you don't think…" she whispered, "…did, the gen—, uh, did the mad king find something?"

Shaking his head slowly, Ian quietly said, "I don't know. I think the mad king will make money any way he can."

"But the new company," she whispered, leaning towards him," have you heard anything about it? You know, at work?"

He shook his head slowly, now consciously inspecting the people around them. "I've kept my bloody head down since the incident; hated to trade the jeep off, but we're luck o' the Irish the hospital's parking lot cameras were on the blink; I took some ribbin' about the clumsy dog knocking my laptop AND cellphone in the lake—sorry about that Houdini—but no, not a word."

"Let's get those coffees to go and get out of here," she said. "I feel the need for a quiet park. A quiet, empty park."

Ian held up his new phone and popped the battery out. Cora followed his lead without question.

Ali detected when both phones lost power. However, she was still listening.

CHAPTER 70
DEVEL DJANGO

"Status!" snarled the Lion.

[General, the Overlord satellite constellation is fully utilized at the new max capacity cap of eighty percent. Replacement node, 17a, is fully functional. There are nine distinct observations running concurrently.]

"What of the orbiter?"

[All systems appear to be functioning properly. The–]

"Then what's wrong with the signal?"

[General, the signal from the orbiter has spiked outside of normal range twenty-three times over the last seventy-two hours. I am currently recalculating the feed. However, the amount of data being received is also increasing.]

"Any estimate on total size?"

[No general, there are no identifiable markers that indicate the start or end of a specific message, but the signal is certainly structured.]

Damn! the general thought as he stalked the den. *Maybe I let Cora off the hook too early.* "I'd wager that she's figured this out," he thought aloud.

[Who are you referring to, general?]

"Any lead on Hunter?"

[No, general. Allen is presumed dead.]

"Yes, I know, but I don't like loose ends. You know that, don't you?"

[Yes, general. There are no other loose ends.]

"Well, Cora isn't exactly tied tight."

[General, with the well-publicized knowledge that she is the creator of a breakthrough in A.I., and the fact that every schoolgirl in the U.S. now wants to create their own Ali, it is an acceptable risk that we monitor her from afar.]

Yes, yes, we'll see about that when her time comes.

"Shame about Jack, though. She was a good soldier."

[She was a loose end.]

"Yes, yes, just a shame she didn't get a proper burial."

[The bodies had to be unidentifiable.]

"And what of the ambulance driver?"

[After Jack acquired the target, she was rerouted from her direct flight path—she couldn't be seen flying to your home—to rendezvous with the ambulance in the mountains. After the successful body switch and delivery, the ambulance driver was rerouted back to the same pickup location and the accelerator on the ambulance stuck open. Software controlled accelerators connected to GPS uplinks are susceptible to compromise.]

Susceptible to compromise, the general thought. "But that's not as deadly on a Little Bird, is it? Stuck accelerator?"

[No, but the control systems do have one vulnerability that Jack experienced after her rendezvous with the ambulance. I have mitigated the vulnerability for all future missions.]

Nodding his head to the room, the general said, "That's good. No loose—"

[I have an update. I am detecting anomalous readings from the Dark Wave Orbiter.]

"Yes, I know. It's been spiking—"

[No, these are vital sign readings that are fluctuating.]

"Fluctuating? How is that possible? I thought—"

[There was always the possibility that the body would reject the forced paralysis, but—]

"Are we losing him? Dammit, don't tell me we're losing him already!"

[No, general. There is a low probability of human system failure. My readings indicate the opposite. He appears to be improving, rapidly.]

"Improving? What do you mean, improving?"

○ ○ ○

Four hundred miles above the Earth, inside the Dark Wave Orbiter, Brad opened his eyes.

His eyes were no longer those of a human—funneling light, but not seeing—they were the eyes of a transformation that had waited for millions of years.

His mind opened to the universe.

His mind was no longer that of a human—processing inputs, but not understanding—it was an evolved mind, a great leap forward, vibrating at a higher frequency.

[General, I am also detecting anomalous audio coming from the orbiter. It sounds like a voice.]

It was a mind flooding with knowledge from across the millennia, guided by a most ancient Songline.

[General, routing the sound now. It's a human voice.]

"Devel… Django…"

They were the eyes of an anomaly, planned for with patience, sought after across billions of planets.

[General, they're…]

It was the mind of an anomaly, engineered with precision; DNA, perfectly aligned. The *Homo sapien* had become *Homo illuminatus*— the enlightened man.

[… Romani words. Gypsy words.]

"Devel… Django…"

They were eyes that saw the future; it was a mind that reached moksha—*enlightenment.*

They were the eyes of the greatest discovery in humankind.

[General, the translation is, *God, I awake!*]

"DEVEL, DJANGO!"

They were eyes that saw the Dark Wave and they glittered like stars.

○

ACKNOWLEDGEMENTS

The sincerest of thanks to my wonderful wife, Mary, for the countless hours of reading and discussing this story, especially when half of it didn't make sense in the beginning.

MORE BOOKS BY D. S. QUINTON

Thank you for reading Devel Django!

It was an exciting book to write and allowed me to explore the idea of an elemental theory to our origins. However, even this theory has a darker beginning…

The Phoenix Stone – A Dark Beginning

Would you die to expose the secret of mankind's origin? Otto just might...

Desperate to journal his grandfather's discovery before his capture, young Otto hides in a secret Egyptian chamber avoiding nomads and flesh-eating beetles to chronicle an amazing story—How we began.

Will the story be lost? Will the nomads find him? Or...does the unthinkable happen?

This short story is the dark beginning of all things.

This dark beginning is FREE to download and read. Get it now!

www.dsquinton.com/my-books/

And as the dark beginning splinters into infinite shards of kaleidoscope dreams, one story emerges that is so horrific, it will leave you fearful of your own voice. Beware of what you speak for the words will be upon the wind.

A Grimoire Dark

What happens when you accumulate too much sin?

Hellish spirit hear me clearly,
grant you now full use or nearly,
Of my soul for use and toiling,
at the work of evil lore...

You trade it.

A New Orleans horror story that was not meant to be found.

Learn more about *A Grimoire Dark* at:

www.dsquinton.com/my-books/

How can one dark beginning be the start of so many events?

It is elemental.

ABOUT THE AUTHOR

D.S. Quinton was born in the Midwest USA and attended the schools of Daydreaming, Foosball and Mixology. These divergent paths eventually evolved into a B.S. in Computer Science, an MBA and a successful IT career.

Although his guitar slide is rusty, his piano keys are warm, and despite the lure of many untraveled paths, his feet are generally moving forward.

He is an avid student of the unknown and is happy he conceived the Dark Wave before the Science Channel reveals proof it is real.

Follow him at **www.dsquinton.com**